JEREMY BATES

World's Scariest Places: Volume 2

Helltown & Island of the Dolls

First published by Ghillinnein Books 2016

First edition

ISBN: 9781988091099

This book was professionally typeset on Reedsy.
Find out more at reedsy.com

Preface

The novels in the *World's Scariest Places* series are based on real places.

And for a limited time, visit the author's website at www.jeremybates-books.com to receive a free copy of the critically acclaimed novella *Black Canyon*, winner of Crime Writers of Canada The Lou Allin Memorial Award.

CONTENTS

I

HELLTOWN

Chapter 1

"Abby doesn't need a man anymore.
The Devil is her lover now!"
Abby (1974)

Inside the mold-infested abandoned house a brass Chinese gong reverberated dully, followed by liturgical music minced with electronically produced effects. The door at the far end of the room opened and a large woman emerged clothed in the customary habit and wimple of a nun. She held a cased ceremonial sword in one hand, a black candle in the other. The deacon and sub-deacon, both clad in floor-length robes, black and hooded, appeared next. The high priest came last. Unlike the others, his face was visible, the top of his head covered with a skin-tight cowl sprouting horns made of animal bones. He wore a black cassock and matching gabardine cape with scarlet lining. His eyes were dark, shimmering, though his long bushy beard was far from Mephistophelean.

The procession congregated a few feet in front of the altar, the high priest in the middle, the mock-nun and deacon to his left, the sub-deacon to his right. They all bowed deeply, then looked down at the naked woman who lay atop the holy table. Her body was at right angles to its length, her arms outstretched crucifix-style, her legs spread wide, each limb secured in place with ropes anchored to iron eyelets in the floor. Her pale white skin contrasted sharply with her brightly made-up face and ebony hair. The number of the beast, 666, was scrawled in blood across her bare breasts. On the wall above her, painted in red, was the Sigil of Baphomet: a goat's

3

head in an inverted pentagram within a circle. A large upside down cross hung directly before the face so that an eye peered ahead from either side of it.

The organist switched to *The Hymn to Satan*, a perversion of Bach's *Jesu Meine Freude*. The deacon rang a deeply toned bell nine times. Then the high priest raised his hands, palms downward, and said: "*In nomine Magni Dei Nostri Satanas, introibo ad altare Domini Inferi.*"

The black mass had begun.

The car in the driveway was the first in a string of bad omens for Darla Evans. It wasn't a pickup truck or even the rusted Ford Thunderbird that Mark's friend Henry Roberts drove. It was a little red Volkswagen Beetle. It occupied most of the small driveway, so Darla pulled up to the curb, bumper to bumper with Mark's aging Camaro. She got out and retrieved her suitcase from the Golf's trunk, breathing in the crisp autumn air.

Seeing her recently purchased home, Darla felt a burst of nostalgia, even though she'd only been away in Akron at the career fair for two days. The house was a quaint turn of the century, three bedrooms, two baths, with a large backyard—a perfect place to start a family.

As Darla wheeled her suitcase up the front walk, her hand absently touching her barely noticeable baby bump, she glanced at the Bug. She wondered who it belonged to. Not the construction guys. They wouldn't be caught dead in anything so dainty. Someone to do with the wedding? Darla and Mark's mother Jennifer were taking care of most of the preparations, but Mark had been tasked with organizing the photographer.

Darla didn't bother fishing her keys from her handbag. Mark never locked up when he was home. Sure enough, the front door eased open, and she stepped into the small foyer. Stairs on the left climbed to the second floor; the living room opened to the right. The entranceway to the latter was sealed with transparent plastic. Through it she could see a jumble of masonry, a few scattered tools, and a gray coating of dust on the floor, marred with a zigzag of booted footprints. She and Mark were refinishing the original redbrick fireplace mantelpiece, which dated back to the 1920s.

Mark's loafers rested at the base of the cast-iron radiator, next to a pair of black pointed-toe sling-backs with high heels. A work associate? Darla wondered. She tilted her head, expecting to hear conversation. She heard nothing. She thought about calling out, announcing that she'd returned from the career fair early, but given the silence she decided Mark and his guest were likely out on the back patio.

She left her suitcase standing upright and followed the hallway to the kitchen. She frowned at the two empty fishbowl wine glasses on the counter, next to an empty bottle of Merlot. Confusion stirred within her and, hovering beneath that, like a dark shadow, alarm. She told herself a perfectly innocent explanation existed as to why Mark would be sharing wine with someone who wore pumps and drove a red Bug. Of course there was. She and Mark had the ideal relationship. Everyone said so. They'd just bought the house, were expecting a baby. There was no room in that scenario for what the whisperings in her head suggested. She felt ashamed to be considering such a thing.

She continued to the rear of the kitchen and looked through the sliding glass doors. Plastic patio set, old barbeque, sagging shed—nobody anywhere in the yard. Darla thought about calling out again, but this time she kept quiet for a different reason. *Because you might disturb them? Because they might have time to—to what? Get themselves decent?* She returned the way she'd came, her head suddenly airy, her stomach nauseous.

Back in the foyer Darla stood at the bottom of the stairs, hesitating. She thought she heard a faint something, maybe someone speaking at a low volume. She started up the steps. Ten to the landing, right turn, six more. Carpeted, they didn't creak. The plan was to toss the carpet and restore the original hardwood hidden beneath.

When she reached the second floor, she confirmed what she'd thought she'd heard. Voices, murmurings, coming from the master bedroom. She started in that direction, floating now, disconnected from herself. It was as though her body had flooded itself with a cocktail of potent chemicals to numb her from the inevitable pain lurking very close. She knew that men and women cheated on each other. It was a fact of life in a monogamous society. She just never imagined Mark doing it to *her*.

It can't be him in there, she thought irrationally. *It has to be someone else.*

Halfway through the third segment of the black mass, the Canon, the sub-deacon fetched a chamber pot from the shadows and presented it to the nun, who urinated into it, smiling beatifically, while the organist played a low-pitched, rumbling hymn. The high priest said, "In the name of Mary she maketh the font resound with the waters of mercy. She giveth the showers of blessing and poureth forth the tears of her shame. She suffereth long, and her humiliation is great, and she doth pour upon the earth with the joy of her mortification. Her cup runneth over, and her water is sublime. *Ave Maria ad micturiendum festinant.*"

When the nun finished urinating, the sub-deacon retrieved the font and held it before the high priest, who dipped a phallus-shaped aspergillum into the fluid. He turned to the four cardinal compass points, shaking the aspergillum three times at each. "In the name of Satan, we bless thee with this, the symbol of the seed of life. In the name of Lucifer, we bless thee with this, the symbol of the seed of life. In the name of Belial, we bless thee with this, the symbol of the seed of life. In the name of Leviathan, we bless thee with this, the symbol of the seed of life." He raised the phallic aspergillum breast-high in an attitude of offering to the Baphomet, kissed it, and placed it back on the altar. Then he uttered the purported last words of Jesus Christ upon the cross: "*Shemhamforash!*"

"Hail Satan!" the assemblage replied.

Darla stopped on the other side of the bedroom door. She could hear a woman's voice purring, the words punctuated with throaty laughter. She wanted to turn around, leave, pretend this wasn't happening, but she couldn't do that. Steeling herself, she opened the door—and everything inside her collapsed at once. Her lungs, so it was hard to breathe. Her nervous system, so she became numb. Her heart, slit in half, emptied, hollow.

Mark lay on his back on the queen bed, his well-toned body naked except for a pair of blue briefs. A tanned peroxide blonde straddled him, groin on groin. She wore nothing but a black frilly thong. In one hand she held a pink feather duster, in the other, a red candle, which she was using to drip scalding wax onto Mark's chest.

Mark turned his head toward Darla, as if sensing her presence. Seeing her, he threw the woman off him and sat bolt upright. "Jesus!" he said, and for a moment he appeared furious, as if outraged that Darla would have the gall to walk in on him while he was getting it on. Very quickly, however, he adopted a suitably ashamed and worried countenance.

"Wha...?" The woman turned and saw Darla. Her eyes widened in surprise.

"Get out," Darla told her evenly, venomously.

"Hey, sorry, we should have gone somewhere else—"

"Get out!" she screamed.

"Okay, okay, like chill out." Her casual tone was infuriating. She would walk away today and likely gossip about what happened with her friends. It wasn't her life abruptly in shambles.

Darla marched over and grabbed the slut by the blow-dried hair and yanked her off the bed. The woman yelped.

"Hey, Dar, hold on," Mark said. "Take it easy. Let's talk."

Ignoring him, Darla dragged the woman—bent over, shrieking, bare breasts flopping—across the room, shoved her into the hallway, slammed the door shut.

Then she whirled on Mark. She wanted to hurl every curse word she knew at him. But she could articulate nothing. She bit her bottom lip to keep it from trembling.

"Listen, Dar," he said, scratching the back of his head, "it's not what you—"

"Don't give me that! Don't you *dare* give me that!"

He closed his mouth and seemed at a loss for what to say next.

"How long?" she said.

He got off the bed, pulled on his acid-wash jeans.

"How long?" she demanded.

Banging at the door. "Mark! I need my clothes."

Mark started toward Darla, thought better of it, kept his distance. "A few weeks," he said.

"Who is she?"

"It doesn't matter."

"Who is she?"

He shrugged. "Someone from the ski resort."

"Hey!" the woman persisted. "I'll go. I just need my clothes."

"Let me send her off," he said, "and we'll talk."

"Get out."

"What?"

"Get out of this house."

"Dar, you're not thinking straight. Let me get rid of her—"

"Get the hell out of this house, Mark, or I swear to God I'm going to hit you."

"Dar—"

"Go!"

He frowned, angry again, undecided. Then he scooped up his yellow Polo shirt with the embroidered logo of his auto repair business, a black bra, and a red tartan dress. He left his socks, inside out, on the floor. On his way to the door he stopped in front of Darla and tried to touch her on the shoulder. She slapped him across the cheek. He recoiled in shock. More anger, then weary resignation. He left the bedroom.

"Hey, thanks," the blonde said, taking her dress. "And sorry about this—"

"Not now," Mark snapped.

Darla remained where she was, arms folded across her chest, beginning to shake. The front door opened and closed. A car started. Then another. Moments later the sound of the engines faded, and she was alone.

The high priest removed the black veil that covered the chalice and paten.

He lifted the latter in both hands, on which rested a wafer of turnip, and said, "Blessed be the bread and wine of death. Blessed a thousand times more than the flesh and blood of life, for you have not been harvested by human hands nor did any human creature mill and grind you. It was our Lord Satan who took you to the mill of the grave, so that you should thus become the bread and blood of revelation and revulsion." His voice became harsher, more guttural. "I spit upon you, I cast you down, because you preach punishment and shame to those who would emancipate themselves and repudiate the slavery of the church!" He inserted the host into the woman's labia, removed it, and raised it to the Baphomet. "Vanish into nothingness, thou fool of fools, thou vile and abhorred pretender to the majesty of Satan, the true god of gods! Vanish into the void of thy empty Heaven, for thou wert never, nor shalt thou ever be!" He dropped the host into a small bowl and pulverized it with a pestle. He mixed what remained with charcoal and incense and set it aflame with a white candle. While it burned he picked up the Chalice of Ecstasy, which was filled not with blood or semen but his drink of choice, Kentucky bourbon. He raised it to the Baphomet and drank deeply. He replaced the chalice on the altar, covered it and the paten with the veil, then bowed and gave the blessing of Satan, extending his left hand in the Sign of the Horns: the two outermost fingers, representing the goat, pointing upward in defiance of Heaven, the two innermost pointing down in denial of the Holy Trinity. "*Shemhamforash!*"

"Hail, Satan!"

Darla returned to the Golf with her unpacked suitcase and drove. She couldn't stand to be in the house any longer. Every room reminded her of Mark. The kitchen where they'd spent so many mornings in their housecoats making each other breakfast, the den where they'd snuggled up on the sofa together in the evenings to watch TV. Certainly not the bedroom. God, the tramp had been in her *bed*. How could Mark have allowed that? How could he violate the sanctity of the place where they'd conceived the baby that was growing inside her?

With this acid in her head, Darla tooled aimlessly around Boston Mills.

She felt lost, confused, as if half her identity had been torn away from her—and in a sense she supposed it had. She'd been with Mark for ten years, ever since he'd asked her to their high school prom. He'd been the only stable fixture in her adult life.

Despair filled her. The house was Mark's. He'd paid the down-deposit with his savings, and the bank loan was in his name. So she couldn't stay there. She was homeless. Not only that, she had less than a hundred dollars in her bank account, no job, and a baby on the way. There had been a couple of jobs at the career fair she'd thought she might do okay at, but even if she was hired for one tomorrow, she likely wouldn't start for a few weeks, and she wouldn't be paid for another few weeks after that.

Family, she thought. She still had family. Her parents had moved to Florida several years before, and her older brother was teaching English in Japan or South Korea or China—somewhere too distant to think about. But her sister, Leanne, was only forty minutes away in Cleveland. Darla could crash there for a bit, maybe even look for work in Cleveland.

Then again, that meant Darla would have to deal with Leanne's husband, Ray. He was a smug white-collar bank manager who'd always thought of Darla and Mark as uneducated country bumpkins. No, she couldn't show up on his doorstep pregnant and single and broke. It would be humiliating.

Darla began running through a mental list of her friends—and realized she didn't even know who her friends were anymore. They would have to take sides, wouldn't they? How many would choose her over Mark? Likely not many. It didn't matter that Mark was a cheating slime ball. He'd been the extrovert in their relationship, she the introvert. He had an easy way with people she didn't. He'd come out of this scandal unscathed, while she would end up ostracized, an outcast in the very town where she had grown up.

Suzy, she thought. Yes, Suzy. She was single, had just been through a brutal divorce herself. She would sympathize with Darla's predicament. She'd make some strong coffee, they'd sit down, she'd listen to Darla bawl, she wouldn't judge or take sides.

Suzy lived ten minutes away in Sagamore Hills. It would be fastest to travel north on Riverview Road, then east along West Highland. But Darla decided to detour through Cuyahoga Valley National Park. It would give her a bit more time to get herself together.

She crossed over the Cuyahoga River, then turned left onto Stanford Road. Soon the trees of the national park closed around her—oak, ash, maple, walnut, hickory—and she began to feel calmer. Nature had a way of doing that to her, as she supposed it did for most people. Also, she enjoyed the isolation the park offered, the idea of being on her own. She felt free. *And now I am free*, she thought defiantly. *Mark's gone, out of my life. And maybe that's for the best. Better to find out about his cheating ways now than later on. I'm still young, only twenty-six. I'll meet someone new, start over again...*

Darla had been so preoccupied with her new-life fantasy she didn't realize it was nearly dark. That was the thing with October in Ohio: you had day, and you had night, and you had about ten minutes of dusk in between.

She clicked on her headlights—and in the rearview mirror noticed a car behind her do the same. She'd had no idea anyone had even been there.

The car seemed to be accelerating toward her. Darla watched it approach, waiting for it to overtake her. It didn't. Instead it came right up behind her and sat on her tail.

What was the idiot thinking?

Darla was about to pull over to the shoulder, to give the car more room to pass her on the narrow two-lane road, when it rammed her back bumper. She cried out in surprise. The car rammed her again, harder. The steering wheel jerked dangerously in her hands.

The lunatic was trying to run her off the road!

Was he drunk? On drugs?

Heart racing, Darla stomped on the gas, pushing the speedometer needle past fifty, past sixty. The car stuck behind her as the road angled upward steeply. Then the car rammed her once more. This time it remained glued to her ass, *pushing* her. She had to fight the steering wheel to keep it straight, and just as she thought she was going to lose control, the vehicle fell back.

Darla cried out in triumph a moment before the road disappeared in front of her—and she realized her mistake. This stretch of Stanford Road was nicknamed The End of the World because the hill culminated in a brief summit that dropped off sharply on the other side, creating the temporary illusion that you were driving off a cliff—or the end of the world.

Darla had breasted the summit at eighty miles an hour and shot clear into the air.

When the Golf crashed violently back to earth, the front bumper tore free in a fiery display of sparks. The vehicle wrenched to the left, plowed through the smaller shrubbery lining the verge, into the forest, and struck the trunk of a large tree, coming to an abrupt, bone-crushing halt.

With the human sacrifice now at hand, the organist began to play deep, furious chords, while the gong-ringer struck the instrument with the heavy mallet rhythmically, continually. The nun handed the high priest the ceremonial sword. He held it aloft with both hands and recited Lovecraft in a loud, commanding voice, "Oh, friend and companion of the night, thou who rejoiceth in the baying of dogs and spilt blood, who wanderest in the midst of shades among the tombs, who longest for blood and bringest terror to mortals—Gorgo, Mormo, thousand-faced moon—look favorably on our sacrifice and win forgiveness for me and for all those for whom I have offered it. *Tuere nos, Domine Satanus!*"

"Shield us, Lord Satan!" the assemblage cried.

"*Protege nos, Domine Satanus!*" he shouted.

"Protect us, Lord Satan!"

"*Shemhamforash!*"

"Hail Satan! Hail Satan! Hail Satan!"

The high priest sank the sword into the woman's belly.

Mark's infidelity, detouring through Cuyahoga Valley National Park, the maniac in the car behind her—these were the first thoughts Darla had entertained, or at least the first ones she could recall, since the crash. But with each passing second she felt herself becoming more lucid, more self-aware. It was as if she'd been in a black abyss deep underwater, and now she was floating upward toward the surface, to the world of the senses.

Indeed, she could hear voices, she could smell some kind of incense, she could feel...oh God, the pain! Her body throbbed, nowhere and everywhere at once. Still, she held onto the pain, she wouldn't let it go, because where there was pain there was consciousness.

The surface drifted closer. She could almost reach out and touch it.

Darla's eyes cracked open. She made out several men hovering over her, their faces lost in the shadows of their cowls.

A fireball exploded in her abdomen, far worse than the pain that had lured her from the void, and with wide, glassy eyes she saw that the blade of a sword protruded from her navel, blood pooling around the wound, coloring the surrounding flesh a blackish red.

She screamed.

Chapter 2

"Groovy!"
Evil Dead II (1987)

The headlights punched ghostly tunnels through the shifting fog. Birch stripped bare of their fiery Autumn colors and towering evergreens lined the margins of the two-lane rural road. A cold rind of moon hung high in the starless sky, glowing bluish-white behind a raft of eastward-drifting clouds.

Steve slipped on his reading glasses, which he kept on a cord around his neck, and squinted at the roadmap he'd taken from the BMW's glove compartment. "We're on Stanford Road, right?" he said.

"Yup," Jeff said, one hand gripping the leather steering wheel casually. He was eyeing the rearview mirror, either making sure their friends were still following behind them in the other car, or admiring his reflection.

Steve wouldn't be surprised if it were the latter. Jeff was about as vain as you could get. And Steve supposed he had the right to be. Not only was he tall, bronzed, and blond, he was also athletic, successful, and charismatic—the proverbial stud every guy wanted to be, and every girl wanted to date.

Steve himself wasn't bad looking. He kept in shape, had neat brown hair, intelligent brown eyes, and a friendly manner that girls found attractive. However, whenever he was hanging out with Jeff he couldn't help but feel more unremarkable than remarkable, intimidated even.

"I don't see this End of World road anywhere," Steve said, pushing the glasses up the bridge of his nose.

"No duh, genius," Jeff said. "The End of the World's a nickname."

"For Stanford Road?"

"Yup," Jeff said.

"Why's it called The End of the World?" Mandy asked from the backseat. "Does it just end?"

"I'm not walking anywhere," Jenny said. She was seated next to Mandy.

"Will you two give it a rest?" Jeff said, annoyed. "I have everything planned, all right?"

Mandy stuck her head up between the seats to study the map herself. Her wavy red hair smelled of strawberries and brushed Steve's forearm. "Hey, the road *does* just end," she said. "What gives, Jeff? Can you tell us what we're doing out here already?"

"Sit your ass down, Mandy," he told her. "I can't see out the back."

"Noah's still behind you, don't worry."

"Sit down!"

"Jeez," she said, and flopped back down. She mumbled something to Jenny, and they giggled. They'd been doing that all car trip: mumbling and giggling with each other, like they were schoolgirls. Steve found it hard to comprehend how they could be so comfortable with one another, considering they had met for the first time only a few hours before.

Jeff glared at them in the rearview mirror, but said conversationally to Steve: "You know, legend has it that cutthroats and thieves hang out along this road and rob anyone driving through."

"That's bull," Mandy said. "How do you rob someone in a car?"

"With a giant magnet," Jenny said, pulling her blonde hair into a ponytail, which she secured with an elastic band. "It drags the car right off the road, like in the cartoons. Pow!"

"Right, just like that," Jeff said. "And you're in med school?"

"So how?" Mandy asked.

"Because the road doesn't just end," Jeff told them. "Part of it was closed down, yeah. But you can still go around the barricade and drive on the closed-down part. You have to go super slow though because it's really narrow and twisting. That's how the cutthroats get you. They just slip out of the woods and—" He hit the brakes. Inertia slammed everyone forward against their seatbelts. Mandy and Jenny yelped.

Laughing, Jeff accelerated. Behind them, Noah blared his horn.

"God, Jeff!" Mandy said. "You're such a dick!"

"A small dick I've heard," Jenny added, and the two of them broke into more giggles.

Jeff scowled. "A small dick, huh?" he said. "You've never had any complaints, have you, babe?"

Mandy rolled her eyes.

"Well?" he demanded.

"No, hon," she said. "No complaints."

Mandy turned her attention to the haunting black forest whisking past outside her window. It really did look like the type of woods that would be home to a ruthless band of cutthroats. The shadowed maple and oak and elm had already shed all of their foliage, leaving their spindly branches denuded and shivering in the soughing wind. They stood interwoven with the larger pine, spruce, and cedar, the great needle-covered boughs sprouting from the trunks like dark wings, masking whatever may lay behind.

What if Jeff was telling the truth? she wondered. What if when they eventually got to this closed-off road and had to slow down a deranged man—worse, a *pack* of deranged men—swarmed the car, dragged her out by the hair, and slit her throat?

What if—

No. Mandy banished the "what ifs" from her mind. There were no cutthroats living in the forest. She was safe. They were all safe. Jeff was full of it. Not only that, he was full of *himself* too. *You've never had any complaints, have you, babe?* Who said stuff like that? The answer, of course, was Jeff. His ego was so big it couldn't see its shoes on a cloudy day.

Mandy and Jeff had been at a party a short time back, a "model party," or at least that's what everybody called it. It had been hosted by Smirnoff vodka. The models had been hired for the glam factor. There were no Christy Brinkleys or Brook Shields in attendance. The models all hailed from the no-name talent agencies that dotted the backstreets of New York City. They were the D-list hired out for photo shoots in obscure magazines or low-budget cable TV commercials. Not that you'd know this by talking to them. Everyone Mandy had mingled with had a tale about brushing shoulders with Burt Reynolds or Christian Slater—and missing out on their big break by inches because of some unfortunate reason or another.

Anyway, they did have their looks going for them. Mandy knew she was attractive. She'd been told this her entire life. People often said she resembled a red-haired Michelle Pfeiffer, even though Mandy thought her eyes were a little too close together, her nose a bit too pointy. Yet the no-name models made her feel positively average. They were all taller than her, had the flawless, thin bodies of fourteen-year-old boys, although with breasts, and most importantly, they knew how to flaunt their sex appeal.

At the end of the evening, while waiting for a cab, Jeff, tipsy, had said, "Did you see that guy? The one with the long hair?"

"They all had long hair," Mandy told him.

"White shirt unbuttoned halfway down his chest."

Mandy had seen him. He'd been gorgeous. "What about him?"

"You think he was good looking?"

"Ha! You're jealous," she said.

"Hardly. But I'll tell you this much. He's probably the first guy I've ever seen who's better looking than me."

Mandy stared at Jeff, thinking he must be kidding. He wasn't. Up until that point in his twenty-six years of existence, Jeff had seriously considered himself to be the best looking man on the planet.

Mandy blinked now, and instead of the trees and the blackness beyond the car window, she saw her glass-caught reflection. It was vaguely visible, transparent, ghostlike. It gave her a case of the creeps.

Shivering, she faced forward again. No one had spoken since Jeff had challenged her to find fault with his love-making.

Mandy didn't like prolonged silences, they made her uneasy, and she said, "Complaints, huh?" She wrapped a lock of her hair around a finger. "Do we have time? This could take a while."

"Name one," Jeff said.

She leaned close to Jenny—who she'd been happy to discover shortly after they met shared a similar goofy sense of humor—and whispered: "He has a hairy butt."

"Grody!" Jenny whispered back.

"And he likes to be spanked—it's like spanking a monkey!"

They broke up in laughter, and when Mandy's eyes met Jeff's in the rearview mirror, she stuck out her tongue at him.

"Real mature, Amanda," he muttered.

"Whatever," she said, and continued laughing.

Jeff clenched the steering wheel tighter. Mandy could be a real pain in the ass sometimes. He wondered why he put up with her. He was a securities trader clearing a hundred grand a year, for Christ's sake. He could have any woman he wanted. Didn't she realize that?

He needed someone smarter, someone more on his level, someone, well, like Jenny. She wasn't only a long-legged blonde bombshell; she was a medical school student to boot. He visualized the two of them on paper: Wall Street Trader and Cardiovascular Surgeon. It was certainly more impressive than Wall Street Trader and Makeup Artist. And was that all Mandy was going to aspire to in life? Really, how much difference was there between a makeup artist and a carny face painter? He chuckled to himself, considered mentioning this comparison out loud, but decided not to sink to her childish level.

Jeff focused on the road ahead. The occluding fog was as thick as pea soup, as his grandmother had been fond of saying, and he needed to pay attention. Last thing he wanted was to run into a deer or a bear. The 1987 BMW M5 was less than a month old, in pristine condition, and he would like to keep it that way. Did he need the car? No. He took cabs to work every day and rarely left the city. Same went for the prewar Tribeca co-op he'd been renting since last July. It was far too big for just him, he rarely set foot in the two spare bedrooms, but they were good to have to show off when people came over. Success, he had learned, was more than earning a six-figure salary. It was cultivating an image that people envied and respected.

And Mandy wasn't jiving with that image, was she? They'd been together for four years now, and she was still as clueless to business and politics and world events as when he'd met her. What was it she'd said to Congressman Franzen the other week while he'd been discussing with Jeff the recent armistice reached in the Iran-Iraq war? Why don't they call it the Middle *West*? Good God, she was becoming an embarrassment.

Jeff's thoughts turned to Jenny again. He visualized her wearing a white doctor's coat, a stethoscope around her neck, and nothing else. What a fantasy that would be! Of course, that's all it was: a fantasy. Steve was his good friend. He wasn't about to hijack his girlfriend, even though he was sure he could if he wanted to. No, there were plenty of other smart, successful women out there.

Through the mist, a bridge appeared ahead of them.

"Hell yeah!" Jeff cried out. "There she is!" He crunched onto the gravel shoulder just before the bridge and killed the engine.

"What's going on?" Steve asked, looking up from the map and removing his glasses.

"Crybaby bridge!" Jeff announced.

"Are you for real?" Steve said.

"Crybaby bridge?" Mandy said, poking her head up between the seats once more. "Why have I heard of that?"

"It's an urban legend," Steve told her. "A baby gets thrown off a bridge, it dies, you can hear its ghost crying in the middle of the night. Crybaby bridges are all over the country."

"Yeah, but this one's different," Jeff said.

Steve looked at him. "How so?"

He grinned wickedly. "'Cause this crybaby's genuinely haunted."

Steve undid his seatbelt, stuffed the map back into the glove compartment, and got out of the car. The night air was cool and fresh and damp, the way it is after a storm. It accentuated the raw scent of pine and hemlock. Fog swirled around his legs, sinuous, amorphous, reminding him of the dry ice used in horror movies to turn a mundane graveyard into a hellish nightmare crammed full of the shuffling dead. He tilted his head, looking up. Directly above the bridge the canopy had receded to reveal a patch of black sky framing a full moon.

Steve howled. It was a mournful, lupine sound, the effect of which turned out to be surprisingly eerie and realistic.

"Nice one, Wolfman!" Jeff said, tossing his head back and joining in gleefully.

"Boys will be boys," Jenny said, sighing with put-upon melodrama.

Mandy said, "You know they're going to be trying to scare us all night?"

"Let them," Jenny said. "I can handle a werewolf, or vampire. I have a black belt in judo."

Steve's lungs faltered. His howl cracked. He looked at Jenny and said, "You have a black belt in judo?"

"I trained with Chinese Buddhist monks."

"Nice try. Judo's Japanese."

"What do Chinese monks practice?" Mandy asked.

"Kung fu," Steve said.

"Well, maybe the Chinese monks Jenny trained with also practiced judo too."

Jeff's wolf howl sputtered into chuckles. He began shaking his head.

"What?" Mandy said, planting her fists on her hips.

"No comment," he said, shooting Steve a this-is-what-I-deal-with-everyday look.

"Hey," Mandy said. "Shouldn't we put our Halloween costumes on?"

Everyone agreed and went to the BMW's trunk. Steve scrounged through his backpack for the white navy cap he'd brought, found it at the bottom of the bag, and tugged it on over his head.

He heard a zipper unzip behind him. He started to turn around only to be told by Mandy to stop peeking.

"Peeking at what?" he said.

"I'm changing," Mandy said.

"Right there?"

"Hey, bro, stop perving on my girl," Jeff said, eyeing Steve up and down: the white navy cap, the red pullover, the pale trousers. "Who the hell are you supposed to be?"

"Gilligan," Steve said.

Jeff guffawed and turned his attention to Jenny, who was slipping on a pair of cat ears to go with her black eye mask and bowtie. "Come on, help me out," he said to her. "A dog? Wait, a mouse? Hold on—someone who is completely fucking unoriginal?"

"What are you?" Steve asked him.

Jeff shrugged out of his pastel blue blazer and yellow necktie—he had come straight from work to pick Steve and Jenny up out front NYU's Greenberg Hall—and exchanged them for a black leather jacket. He held his arms out in a ta-da type of way.

"No idea," Steve said.

"Michael Knight! You know, from that *Knight Rider* show." He whistled. "Sexy mama!"

Steve turned to find Mandy adjusting her boobs inside a skintight orange bodysuit with a plunging neckline. Accentuating this were shiny orange boots, yellow tights, and a feisty yellow wig with black highlights. In the center of her chest was the ThunderCats logo: a black silhouette of a cat's head on a red background.

"Cheetara," she said, smiling hopefully.

Noah, Austin, and Cherry were approaching from Noah's green Jeep Wrangler, appearing and disappearing in the swiftly morphing clouds of mist. Austin, carrying an open bottle of beer, was in the lead. He'd shaved the sides of his head and styled the middle strip of hair into a Mohawk a year or so ago. With his satellite ears and angular face, however, he looked more like Stripe from *Gremlins* rather than a punk rocker. A flock of crows, tattooed in black ink, encircled his torso, originating at his navel and ending on the left side of his neck, below his ear. Now only a couple of the birds were visible, seeming to fly up out of the head hole cut into the cardboard box he wore. Condoms were taped all over the box, some taken out of the packages and filled with a gluey substance that surely couldn't be semen.

"You get one guess each," Austin told them, tipping the beer to his lips.

"A homeless bum," Steve said.

"A total jackass," Jeff said.

"Homework," Mandy said.

Austin frowned at her. "Homework?"

"That box is a desk, right?"

"Right—I dressed up as homework."

"Don't keep us in suspense," Jeff said.

"A one-night stand, mate!"

Steve and Jeff broke into fits. After a moment Mandy laughed hesitantly. Then she said "Oh!" and laughed harder.

"Gnarly, hey?" Austin said, smiling proudly. "So, how the fuck is everyone?"

"Not as good as you apparently," Jeff said.

"This is my first beer. Right, Cher?"

"I've lost count," Cherry said. She was perhaps five feet on tip toes, though her teased hair gave her a couple more inches. Jeff called her Mighty Mouse, which always ticked her off. She'd grown up in the Philippines, but moved to the States to work as a registered nurse a few years ago. She had nutmeg skin, sleepy sloe Asian eyes, a cute freckled nose, and the kind of sultry lips that would look good sucking a lollipop on the cover of *Vogue* magazine, or blowing an air-kiss to a sailor shipping off.

Noah joined Steve and took a swig from a bottle of red wine. He was the polar opposite of Austin: wavy dark hair, unassuming good looks, mellow, disciplined. Even more, he was an up-and-coming sculptor. His first exhibit a couple months back had been well-received by critics, and he'd even sold a few pieces.

"You a boxer?" Steve said to him, referring to the black shoe polish he'd smeared around his left eye. He'd also drawn a large P in black marker on the chest of his white long-sleeved shirt.

"A black-eyed pea, dude." Noah nodded at Austin and Cherry, who had gravitated toward Jeff and the others, and said, "Those two are a nightmare together." He was speaking quietly so only Steve could hear.

"Fun drive?" Steve said.

"How about I drive you and Jenny back. Jeff can deal with them in his car. We almost crashed into an eighteen-wheeler when Austin was getting into that stupid box." He took another swig of wine, glanced about at the trees and vegetation deadened by the mist, and said, "So what's the deal? Why'd we pull over here?"

Steve shrugged. "First stop on the haunted Ohio tour."

"Can't believe we agreed to this."

"Hey, you never know—we might actually see a ghost."

"Yeah, and Austin will get through the night without spewing."

"I'd put my money on seeing a ghost."

"He's already had four or five beers in the car."

"Maybe he'll puke *on* a ghost. That'd be something."

Jeff released Austin from a headlock, kicked him in the ass, and hooted with laughter when Austin whimpered. Then Jeff clapped his hands loudly, to get everyone's attention. "Okay, listen up, ladies and dicks," he said, immediately commanding attention the way he could. "This bridge—it's called Crybaby Bridge, and it's the real deal."

"Why do I feel like I'm being sold blue chip stock?" Jenny said.

"Snake oil," Mandy said.

"I'm being one hundred percent legit," Jeff said. "Hundreds of people have verified that this bridge is haunted. *Verified*, pussies. And if you want to—"

"How'd they verify it?" Steve asked.

"With those spectrometers the Ghostbusters use," Noah said.

Jeff darkened. "Will you two twits listen up?" He dangled his car keys in the air. "This is my spare set. I left the other set in the ignition."

"Why would you do that?" Mandy asked.

"'Cause the legend goes, you leave your keys in the ignition, lock the car,

23

and take off for a bit—"

"How long?" Mandy asked.

"I don't know. Ten minutes."

"And go where?"

"Down the bank to the river, I guess. Fuck, Mandy, who gives a shit? We just have to be out of sight of the car. Then we wait ten minutes. When we come back, the car should be running."

"You're serious?" Steve said.

"As a snake." Jeff stuffed the spare keys in his pocket and started down the bank to the river.

Steve glanced at Noah, who shrugged.

"As a snake," Noah said, and followed.

Chapter 2

*"It's Halloween, everyone's entitled
to one good scare."*
Halloween (1978)

Thick colonies of blood-red chokecherries and bracken fern and other shrubbery overran the bank, so Steve couldn't see where he stepped. He lost his footing twice on the uncertain terrain, but didn't fall. He called back to the others to be careful. A second later Austin stampeded past him, his arms pin-wheeling. Steve was certain his momentum was going to propel him onto his face. However, he crashed into Jeff's back—on purpose, it seemed—which brought him to an abrupt halt, his beer sloshing everywhere.

"Thanks, mate," Austin said jocularly, slapping Jeff on the shoulder and sucking on the foaming mouth of the bottle. Lately he'd been adopting a British accent when he was drunk because he got off on saying words like "lad" and "mate" and "geezer."

Jeff scowled. "I'm giving you the bill for the dry cleaning."

"Fancy rich chap like you can pony up a couple bucks."

Steve stumbled down the last few feet and stopped beside Jeff, who had produced a mickey of vodka from the inside pocket of his now beer-stained jacket. Jenny appeared next, emerging from the fog like a wraith. She was moving slowly, cautious of where she stepped. Her leather pants clung to her long legs, the black elastic top to her small breasts, outlining the triangular cups of her bra. She frowned at the vegetation as she passed

25

through it and said, "I hope there wasn't any poison ivy in there. I got it once as a kid. It bubbles between your fingers."

Steve said, "That'll make gross anatomy interesting."

"I know, right? No one will want us on their dissection team if we can't hold a scalpel."

"Yo, nerds," Jeff told them, "check it out." He pointed to the bridge's piers and abutments. "That's the foundation from the original bridge."

"The original one?" Mandy said, pushing through the last of the ferns. Then, higher pitched: "Oh shoot! My tights!" A good three-inch tear had appeared in the yellow Spandex high on her upper right thigh, revealing white flesh beneath. "Stupid branch!"

"Are you wearing underwear?" Jeff asked.

"Jeff!"

"I can't see any."

"Stop it!"

"Anywho," Jeff said, "the original bridge was an old wooden thing that washed away a while back during a flood. This one replaced it."

"Isn't that bad news for your ghost?" Steve said, trying to ignore Mandy, who was fussing over the tear and inadvertently making it bigger.

"What do you mean?" Jeff said.

"Ghosts haunt old places. Once something's gone, they're gone."

"You're an expert on hauntings now?"

"When was the last time you heard of a ghost haunting something new? You don't go out and buy a new Ford and find it comes with a poltergeist in the trunk."

"You're blind wrong there, my dear castaway. Ghosts haunt the places where they died. The baby died here, so it haunts here. It doesn't matter if this bridge is rebuilt a dozen times, it's still going to haunt here."

"What's so scary about a baby haunting anyway?" Austin opined. "I'm telling you, I see any baby ghost waving its spectral rattler at me, I'm gonna punt it so far downriver it'll shit its diapers before it touches down again."

Steve ducked beneath the bridge and was surprised to find almost no fog there at all, as if the area was somehow off limits. And was it cooler? Or was that his imagination? He took a box of matches from his pocket and ignited a match off his thumb, illuminating the sandy loam before him.

"One, two, Freddy's coming for you..." Austin sang.

Ignoring him, Steve troll-walked forward. The dried riverbed was littered with dead leaves that had blown beneath the bridge. He heard someone following him and turned to find Jenny there.

"Where are you going, mister?" she said, tucking her blonde hair behind her ears.

"Seeing what's under here," he said.

"I imagine we would have heard the baby by now if there was one."

"I'm expecting a Garbage Pail-ish thing."

"Cindy Lopper."

"Bony Joanie." She paused. "Hey, where's the fog?"

"Strange, I know."

The bridge was less than twenty feet in diameter, and Steve could make out the other side where the inky shadows gave to the mist-shrouded night once more.

He didn't see the baby shoes until he was nearly on top of them.

They were newish, white, and so small they would only fit a newborn.

"What is it?" Jenny asked, moving up beside him. "Hey!" she exclaimed. "Baby shoes!"

"Some kids probably left them there to propagate the legend."

Jenny studied the ground ahead of them, then turned and studied the ground behind them. "There aren't any other footprints except for ours."

She was right, he realized. "Guess they raked them away."

"It doesn't look like the sand's been raked."

"Well, a baby ghost didn't leave its shoes here, Jen."

"Doesn't this bother you, Steve? Seriously—look at them! They're just here, in the middle of perfectly undisturbed sand."

"Ow!" The flame had winnowed its way down the matchstick to Steve's fingertips. He tossed the match away. He lit another and said, "Do you believe in ghosts?"

"I've seen one before," Jenny stated.

"Where?"

"In my bedroom."

"When?"

"A long time ago. I was just a kid. I woke up in the middle of the night, and a face was staring in my window."

"Maybe it was a neighborhood perv?"

"My bedroom was on the second floor."

"Did your bedroom face the street?"

"It did, as a matter of fact."

"Maybe it was the reflection of a streetlamp?"

"I don't think there were streetlamps on my street."

"It could have been anything, Jen. That's the thing with ghosts and UFOs and stuff like that—just because you can't immediately explain them doesn't mean they're real."

"It doesn't mean they're not real either. I'm simply keeping an open mind."

"I've spent the last year cutting open dead people and sorting through their insides. I've yet to find any evidence of a lurking spirit. Have you?"

"We share different metaphysical beliefs. Let's leave it at that."

"Not so fast," Steve said. "I'm having a hard time believing an intelligent person such as yourself, a future doctor no less, believes in the boogie monster."

"I don't believe in the boogie monster, Steve."

"You said you saw something peeking in your window. That's what boogie monsters do, isn't it?"

"I said a ghost. They're two very different things."

He shrugged. "Okay, a ghost, whatever. But can you tell me why a ghost would want to peek in your window? I mean, you'd have to be a borderline megalomaniac to think something made the effort to cross dimensions just to spy on you when you were sleeping."

"There are more things in heaven and earth, Horatio."

"Shakespeare's not going to bail you out of this one, babe."

Jenny cocked an eyebrow. "Babe?"

Steve frowned. "What?"

"I'm not a 'babe,' thank you very much."

"Jeff calls Mandy babe."

"Maybe Mandy likes being a babe, but I haven't spent the last year of my life, studying eighty hours a week, to become someone's possession."

"Possession?"

"Calling a woman a babe diminishes her to a younger and therefore more controllable state—so, yes, a possession."

"So what am I supposed to call you?"

"There are plenty of other terms of affection that don't have the same degrading connotations, but I can't help you there. It's your job as my partner to choose one. You have to think of something that represents the complexities of my personality."

"I'll give it a hard think, princess."

"And it shouldn't be condescending."

Steve and Jenny continued to the far side of the bridge. When Steve emerged from beneath it and was standing erect again, he stretched his back, popping a joint in the process.

Jenny, still crouching next to him, cupped her hands to her mouth, and shouted: "People! There're some rad baby shoes under the bridge, if you're interested!"

"We're shaking!" Jeff called back.

"For real!" Jenny replied.

Austin said something, though Steve couldn't hear what he said.

"Nice friend you have," Jenny said.

"What did he say?" Steve asked.

"Not something I'd care to repeat," she said, and started up the bank.

Steve followed, grasping shrubs and saplings for purchase, his glasses bumping against his chest on their cord. At the top, parked on the shoulder of the road, Jeff's BMW was exactly how they'd left it: dark, empty, clearly not idling.

"So much for the legend," he said.

The night was cold and getting colder, and Noah wished he'd brought a jacket, considering all he wore on his upper body was the shirt with the hand-drawn P. To make matters worse, an icy wind had begun to blow. It came and went in unpredictable gusts and was strong enough to tousle everyone's hair and to rattle the skeletal branches of the nearby trees.

Shivering, Noah unfolded his arms from across his chest and produced from his pocket a joint he'd rolled earlier. He was not only cold but restless from the eight-hour drive from New York City and wanted to unwind. Moreover, he had a feeling they were going to be in for one long slog of a night. Getting high would be the only way to make it remotely interesting. He wondered again why he had agreed to come. He wasn't superstitious. In fact, ghosts and ghouls and all that jive didn't interest him in the least. He didn't watch horror movies, didn't read Stephen King. Growing up, he hadn't even liked Halloween. He'd appreciated the candy, sure, but the idea of witches on broomsticks and skeletons lurking in closets and Frankenstein monsters eating brains never did anything for him. He guessed he simply didn't have a scary bone, the way some uptight people didn't have a funny bone.

Noah sparked the joint, took a couple tokes, and passed it to Mandy, who was standing to his right. She took a mini puff and blew the smoke out of her mouth quickly, probably not inhaling. Noah had to make a conscious effort not to stare at her tits, which were practically bursting out of her top. He thought Jeff was crazy for not appreciating her the way he should. She was drop-dead gorgeous, a real sweetheart too, a rare combination. And she put up with Jeff's bullshit. Someone "more on his level"—a phrase he'd been using a lot lately to describe his ideal woman—likely wouldn't. They'd be clashing nonstop. In fact, they'd be just like Austin and Cherry, a recipe for disaster, each with one eye constantly on the big red nuke button.

Noah suspected Steve and Jenny had the best chance of sticking it out together. Even so, this was no guarantee either. They both had another two or three years of med school ahead of them, then equally long and brutal residencies. How much quality time could they possibly spend together? Then again, maybe their workloads would be an advantage. Absence makes the heart grow fonder, right?

The joint did the rounds and returned to Noah, almost finished. He took a drag, then ground the roach out under his shoe just as another blast of wind swooped through the trees, whipping everyone's hair and clothes into a frenzy. Noah turned his face out of the worst of it and found himself looking at Mandy's breasts. Her nipples poked against the thin Spandex of her costume.

Abruptly Jenny called to them from the far side of the bridge: "People! There're some rad baby shoes under the bridge, if you're interested!"

Noah could just make out Jenny and Steve's silhouettes.

"We're shaking!" Jeff called back.

"For real!"

"Blow me!" Austin said.

Jeff slapped him on the back of the head. "Don't be so crass."

Austin frowned. "What's your damage?"

"You barely know her. None of us do. Show a bit more class."

"Why do you care?"

"It's called respect, dickweed." Jeff turned to the others. "So, what do you guys think? Wanna take a look under the bridge for these shoes?"

"It's pitch black," Cherry said.

"You'll be fine," Jeff told her. "You won't even have to crouch."

She glared at him.

Austin said, "Respect, huh?"

"Hey," Jeff said to Cherry, "where's your costume?"

Cherry was wearing an everyday fluorescent green blouse, denim miniskirt, and pink leg warmers.

Austin scowled. "She wouldn't do it."

"Do what?" Jeff asked.

"She didn't bring a costume, so on the ride down here—"

"He told me to take off my clothes and wear my underwear around," Cherry finished.

"Right," Austin said. "A lingerie model."

"Hey, that's not a bad idea," Jeff said, looking at Cherry with X-ray eyes.

31

Mandy harrumphed and Jeff pulled his eyes away and said, "Well, whatever, Mighty Mouse, if you're too scared to come, stay here. No skin off my back. Noah, Mandy, Austin, let's roll." Without waiting for a response, he turned and ducked-walked into the darkness beneath the bridge.

While waiting at the BMW for the others to return from the riverbed, Steve and Jenny were playing a tongue-in-cheek game which involved one-upping the experiences they'd had thus far at med school.

"Pathology is snooze-worthy," Steve said. He was leaning against the hood of the car, his arms folded across his chest to ward off the chill, studying the trees and thinking about those cutthroats Jeff had mentioned. Although he knew Jeff was only trying to scare them, he couldn't help being on edge, his eyes trying to pick out anything moving in the dark that shouldn't be moving.

"You used that last time," Jenny said.

"Fine...don't ask others about their grades."

"I know! I hate gunners," she said. "Okay. Umm...you'll at some point walk down the street still wearing your stethoscope and people will look at you like you're crazy."

"Or like you're a pompous asshole." He thought for a moment. "You'll learn that for almost any set of symptoms the answer could be diabetes, pregnancy, SLE, or thyroid problems."

Jenny nodded. "Good one. Okay. At least once a week a professor will think fifty minutes is long enough to get through one hundred slides."

"And fail."

"Miserably."

Just then movement in the vegetation caused Steve to start. He pushed himself off the car, wired. A moment later Jeff appeared, tall and lean, clawing through the shrubbery lining the bank.

Steve relaxed.

"Thanks for the wild goose chase, you two!" Jeff called, crossing the road toward them.

Noah and Austin and the girls appeared behind him, one after the other, single file.

"You didn't see the shoes?" Steve said.

"We checked everywhere, mate," Austin said, tossing his empty beer bottle over his shoulder into the trees. Glass shattered. "But I did smell something foul down there."

"Something dead," Mandy said.

"A chipmunk," Cherry said.

Steve looked from Jeff to Austin to the others. "Are you guys having me on?"

"You don't know when to give up, do you?" Jeff said. "But I gotta say, I appreciate the effort."

Steve chuffed to himself, shaking his head. Then he started away from the car.

"What are you doing?" Jenny asked him.

"Getting the shoes to convert the unbelievers."

Steve made his way down the bank, keeping to the path they'd already forged through the chokecherries and bracken fern. At the bottom he stopped in the center of the riverbed and faced the vacuous blackness that had gathered beneath the bridge. It seemed somehow blacker than it had earlier, threatening even.

It's all in your head, Steve. Now get on with it.

He lit a match off his thumb, picked out his and Jenny's original footprints among all the others, and followed them beneath the bridge to the baby shoes—or where the baby shoes had been.

Because now they were gone.

Frowning, he turned in a circle, searching the sand—and heard a noise behind him. He jerked around and squinted into the darkness. Nothing there. He wondered if it had been the wind. Only right then there was no wind. The night was tomb-still. Besides, since when did wind sound like chattering teeth?

Chattering teeth...or a baby's rattle?

This thought raised the hackles on the back of his neck.

"Hello?" he said, though he didn't wait for a reply. He scurried out from beneath the bridge and up the bank, irrationally convinced a rotting baby corpse was going to latch onto his legs and drag him back down to the riverbed, where the sand and the silt and the clay would swallow him whole just as it had swallowed the baby shoes.

This didn't happen, of course, and when he was on the road again, the night sky above him, he chided himself for spooking so easily.

Everybody was back inside the two vehicles. Headlights pierced the omnipresent fog, turning it iridescent so that it seemed to glow with a radiance of its own. Jeff honked the BMW's horn impatiently.

"Yeah, yeah," Steve mumbled, swallowing the lump in his throat. "I'm coming."

Chapter 4

"You know that part in scary movies when somebody does something really stupid and *everyone hates them for it? This is it.*"
Jeepers Creepers (2001)

As soon as Steve climbed into the front passenger seat, the cool leather crackling beneath his weight, Jeff said, "Well?"

Steve looked at him. "Well what?"

"Show me the shoes."

"Did you take them?"

"Take them?" Jeff said. He was chewing a shoot of beard grass, which dangled from his mouth like a long, limp cigarette.

"Are you really going to play dumb?"

"I have no idea what you're talking about."

"The baby shoes," Steve said patiently. "You took them."

"They weren't there?" Jenny said.

Steve shook his head. "They took them."

"Whatever you say, li'l buddy." Jeff tossed the beard grass in the foot well, swallowed a belt of vodka from the bottle in his hand, then tucked the bottle neatly into his jacket's inner pocket. He turned the key in the ignition slot. The engine vroomed to life. Hot air roared from the vents. "Need You Tonight" by INXS blasted from the speakers.

"I like these guys!" Mandy said. "They're from the UK or Scotland, I think."

Jeff snorted laughter.

"Australia," Steve told her, deciding not to point out that the UK included Scotland. He turned down the volume. "Anyway, I'm serious. Let me see them."

Jeff seemed pleasantly exasperated. "There were no fucking baby shoes, bro," he said. "Mandy—tell him."

"We didn't see them," she said.

Steve shook his head; he didn't care. He knew they were having him on. In fact, now that he thought about it, he wouldn't be surprised if one of them had leaned over the side of the bridge and made that noise he'd heard.

He was about to mention this when a black car thundered past them so fast it left a wake of air that rattled the BMW.

"Fucking hell!" Jeff said, the curse drowned out by Mandy and Jenny's exclamations of surprise.

"Asshole!" Mandy said.

"That was a hearse," Steve said, noting the vehicle's distinctive quarter panels.

"Bloody kids!" Jeff said.

"It was a hearse!" Steve repeated.

In the distance the red taillights flashed, angry red eyes in the eddying fog.

"Look, it's stopping," Mandy said.

The brake lights disappeared, replaced by the sweep of the headlights as the vehicle turned to face them. Two small, bright orbs glowed malevolently.

"Are they coming back?" Jenny said, a tremble in her voice.

"Maybe we should turn around?" Mandy said.

The hearse high beamed them.

"Oh the little pricks!" Jeff said, grinning. "They've got balls!" He flashed his high beams back.

"What are you doing?" Mandy demanded. "Jeff? Answer me!"

Jeff buzzed down his window, stuck his fist out, and effed them off with his middle finger. It was a pointless gesture, considering there was no way they could see his finger through the mist.

The hearse's engine revved, building into a chainsaw-like screech. Then the vehicle shot toward them.

Jeff released the parking brake, shoved the transmission into first, popped the clutch, and goosed the gas. The tires squealed as the car lurched forward.

"Jeff!" Mandy wailed. "Don't you dare!"

"Stop!" Jenny cried. "Please! I want to get out!"

Jeff smashed through the gears, reaching third and sixty miles an hour in a few seconds.

The g-forces flattened Steve to his seat. He fumbled for his seatbelt, tugged it across his chest, buckled it. He wanted to tell Jeff to stop, but the girls were already shouting at him to do exactly that, and he wasn't listening.

As soon as they shot past the end of the bridge the canopy knitted together and blotted out the sky once more, creating the sensation that they were bulleting down the bore of a pistol.

Jeff stared intensely ahead at the road, his mouth twisted into a bitter grimace, his hands gripping the steering wheel in the ten and two positions tight enough to squeeze the blood from his knuckles.

He was a man who'd just gone all in on the pot of a lifetime, and right then Steve knew that he wasn't going to yield the road.

Steve was suddenly furious. He couldn't believe Jeff was risking a potentially fatal head-on collision, risking all of their futures, to prove he wasn't a chicken.

Mandy and Jenny gave up yelling and buckled their belts. A fear-soaked silence followed, magnifying the purr of the engine and the hum of the tires.

Only a handful of seconds had passed since Jeff gunned the gas, but it felt like much longer. Steve's fear had warped his perception of time, slowed it down, and for a crazy moment some mordant part of his brain contemplated jumping out of the speeding vehicle. But it was traveling too fast. He would break his back or neck—and likely get run over by the oncoming hearse. Besides, he was frozen stiff. All he could move were his

37

eyeballs, which he strained to the left so he could read the speedometer. The needle wavered just below seventy miles per hour.

He looked back at the road. The hearse was sixty yards away, the headlights bleeding together to form a blinding wall of shimmering white.

Fifty yards.

We're going to die, Steve thought.

Forty.

He braced his hands against the dash.

Thirty.

"Jeff!" Mandy shrieked.

Twenty.

"Jeff!"

Jeff swerved to the left. The hearse screamed past. Jeff yanked the wheel to the right but overcompensated. The car knifed across the dotted line toward the opposite shoulder. He yanked the wheel left again. Right, left, right, left, trying to regain control of the now fishtailing vehicle.

They careened off the road and plowed through a small tree, shattering bark and branches. They hit something that launched the BMW into an airborne somersault. For a moment Steve floated in zero gravity, and he was thinking this was it, this was how he was going to die, and there was nothing he could do to prevent it—

The car struck the ground nose first. The impact accordioned the engine block and slammed Steve with the force of a sledgehammer to the chest. The seatbelt strap bit into his flesh and held him suspended above the dash, which was no longer in front of him but below him. The handstanding vehicle crunched forward onto the roof, where it rocked back and forth before coming to rest in the still, silent forest.

Noah had been seconds away from getting out of the Jeep and going to talk to Jeff about the assholes in the hearse when the BMW's rear tires squealed and literally burned rubber. Through wafts of smoke, he watched the car shoot away down the road.

"He's playing chicken!" Austin exclaimed from beside him.

Noah didn't know what to do, but he knew he couldn't sit there doing nothing. He shoved the Jeep into gear and accelerated.

"He's not going to give!" Austin said. "Jeff's not going to give. The motherfucker's going to get them all killed."

"The hearse will give," Noah said automatically.

"Don't get too close," Cherry said from the backseat in a borderline terrified voice. "Stay to the shoulder. Do you hear me? *Stay to the shoulder.*"

"I'm straddling the goddamn shoulder!" Noah said. In fact, he could hear loose gravel spraying the Jeep's undercarriage.

Then, ahead, Jeff arced sharply to the left. For a moment it appeared as though the hearse had plowed straight *through* the BMW, but Noah knew that had to be a trick of the fog and the glare of the headlights. He eased fully onto the shoulder and slowed.

Two seconds later the hearse thundered past, hogging the center of the road, bovine horn moaning. Noah tried to glimpse the driver, but the hearse's headlights had blinded him. No one turned to watch the morbid vehicle depart. No one said anything. They were all staring in horror at the slewing BMW ahead of them. In the next instant it bucketed off the left side of the road into the mix of evergreen and deciduous trees.

Cherry sobbed and screamed in the same breath.

Austin shouted: "Go!"

Noah was already accelerating again.

When Steve realized he wasn't dead, and when his shock subsided, he heard moaning from behind him. "Jen?" he said. "Mandy?" He tried to crane his neck around to check on them, and that's when he saw Jeff in the darkened cabin, crawling through a hole in the windshield. Then he realized Jeff wasn't crawling; his lower body was ragdoll limp.

Steve couldn't see the upper half of his friend, the half that had been launched through the windshield, because the glass had gone gummy and opaque with cracks.

"Fuck Jeff," Steve mumbled. "You stupid fucking fuck..."

"Steve?" Mandy said shrilly. "What's wrong? What happened to Jeff? Is he dead? *Is he dead?*"

Steve unclasped his seatbelt and collapsed onto the car's ceiling. He twisted himself around so he could see Mandy and Jenny. They were both layered in shadows, hanging upside down like bats. Mandy was sobbing into her hands. Jenny was either unconscious or dead.

In the distance came the unmistakable drone of an approaching vehicle. The hearse coming back for them?

Steve maneuvered his body in the awkward space so he could grasp the door handle. He tugged it. The door was stuck.

Tires screeched to a halt.

Steve drove his heels into the window. The glass spider webbed. He kicked it again, harder, and again, harder still, until his feet stamped through it. He rolled onto his hands and knees and scrambled through the shattered window. He heard branches snapping, vegetation crackling, and he was suddenly filled with an exquisite terror, sure the driver of the hearse was going to be something with a hole for a face and leathery wings and—

Austin shouted Jeff's name; Noah, Steve's.

"Here!" Steve managed, standing and swooning into the upturned car. Austin and Noah and Cherry burst through the thicket. They came to an abrupt standstill.

"Oh no," Austin said, those two words barely audible but powerful enough to halt a marching band. "No, no, no..."

Steve pushed himself away from the car on splintered pegs for legs and faced the wreckage. In the frosty light he could see it clearly enough. Jeff's head and shoulders protruded from the windshield like a half-eaten meal. He lay on his back. Given that the vehicle rested upside down on top of him, his nose kissed the hood.

Noah brushed past Steve, dropped to his knees, and pried open the back door. He climbed in and spoke calmly to Mandy while attempting to extract her.

Steve wobbled around the front of the car—the BMW's distinctive headlights and kidney-shaped grille were an unrecognizable mash of metal—and all but collapsed next to Jenny's door. Blood smeared the window. He gripped the handle and pulled, expecting the door to be stuck. It swung open with ease. He felt one of Jenny's dangling wrists for a pulse, but his hands were shaking too badly to perform this action correctly. He unbuckled her seatbelt, lowered her body into his arms, then dragged her out onto the leaf litter. The fog billowed around her, caressed her. He noticed her chest moving up and down and said a silent prayer of thanks.

Meanwhile, Austin had crawled into the gap beneath the hood and now he shouted, "Jeff's alive! He's breathing!"

While Noah and Austin discussed what to do next in urgent tones, Steve patted Jenny on the cheek, urging her to wake up. All the while his heart was filled with guilt. He had invited her on this trip. She had wanted to spend the weekend studying, but he'd insisted they needed a break from school, he'd wanted her to finally meet his friends, and now here she was, lying on the damp earth, bloody and broken.

Her eyes fluttered open.

"Jenny!" he said. "Thank God! Are you okay?"

"Okay..."

"You hit your head."

"Hurts..."

"It's just a little—"

The rest of the sentence died on his lips.

He could smell gasoline.

Gas? Jenny thought slowly. What was Steve talking about? Were people camping nearby?

"We have to move away from the car," Steve was telling her now, though it remained difficult to hear him through the ringing in her ears. "I'm going to carry you."

"I can...okay..."

Steve helped her to her feet. Pain flared in the left side of her head. She almost toppled over, but Steve caught her in his arms.

"Let me carry you," he insisted.

"No, I..." She couldn't find the right word. "Just...dizzy."

Jenny allowed him to lead her away from the wreckage. Without warning her trembling legs gave out beneath her. She dropped to her knees. Steve was saying something to her, though the words seemed suddenly far away. Her vision blurred, darkened—and then she was floating above her body, which was lying on the operation table in the cadaver lab, nude and lifeless. Nine fellow students were gathered around the table, everyone wearing brown lab coats and dishwashing gloves to protect against formaldehyde. Nobody seemed shocked or saddened that Jenny was the cadaver today. Professor Booth was giving some sort of eulogy in Latin that she couldn't understand. She wanted to tell them she wasn't dead, but she couldn't speak, only hover, insubstantial, like a ghost.

Belinda Collins stepped to the table. She was one of the gunners in the class, ambitious to a fault. Ever since Jenny scored higher than her on their first assignment, Belinda had done her best to make life miserable for Jenny, and Jenny knew she would be thrilled to be performing the dissection.

Belinda raised her scalpel to make the first incision. Jenny squeezed her eyes shut against the anticipated pain. She felt nothing. Surprised, she opened her eyes again. The cadaver lab had disappeared, replaced by a cold night filled with nacreous fog and towering trees.

"Jen? Jen!" Steve said. "Can you hear me?" He was cradling her head in his lap.

"Where...?" she said, disorientated. Then she remembered with a punch of dread: the hearse, the accident. "Jeff? Mandy?"

"Mandy's fine. Jeff's...okay. I have to go help get him out of the car. Are you going to be all right for a couple minutes?"

She tried to sit up. It took all her strength, but she managed. She saw the upside down BMW for the first time. Mandy and Cherry stood on one side of it, Noah and Austin on the other. Everyone was speaking and gesturing wildly.

"Where's Jeff?" she asked.

"He's still inside the car," Steve said. "I'll be right back—" He frowned.

"What?" she said.

"How do you feel?"

"Pummeled."

"How many fingers am I holding up?"

"Two. Steve, what's wrong?"

"Nothing. You hit your head though. I just want to make sure you're okay."

Yet the concern that had appeared on his face a few moments ago was still there. She suddenly wondered whether she'd been disfigured somehow. She touched her lips, her nose. "What's wrong with me, Steve?"

"Nothing."

"Steve!"

"Nothing—it's just your eyes. One's dilated a bit more than the other. Probably nothing more than a mild TBI. It's not a big deal."

Jenny went cold. A traumatic brain injury. If it was indeed mild, she had nothing to worry about. But Steve had no way of knowing whether it was mild or not. It could very easily be moderate or severe. She could have intracranial hemorrhage or brain herniation, both of which could lead to disability or even death. She'd need a CT scan to determine the true extent of her injury.

Noah and Austin, she noticed, had started working to get Jeff out of the BMW. Jenny said, "Go help them."

Steve glanced at the car, then back to her. "You're not going to pass out again, are you?"

"No."

"Because you can't pass out—"

"I know! Now go. I'm fine."

He hesitated, nodded, and hurried off.

Steve reached Noah and Austin just as they were easing Jeff out of the mangled cab and onto the ground. Bloody lacerations raked Jeff's face in a dozen places. Several of them appeared deep enough to require stitches. A chunk of glass was embedded in his left cheek like a grisly jewel.

"We have to move him farther away from the car," Steve said.

Noah shook his head. "I don't think we should move him anywhere."

"Can't you smell the gas?"

Noah and Austin raised their noses and sniffed, like prairie dogs trying to catch wind of prey.

"Shit, you're right!" Austin said. He eyed the car apprehensively. "You think it might explode?"

"No," Steve said simply. He didn't know much about cars, but he was pretty sure you'd have to shove a torch into the gas tank for something as dramatic as an explosion to happen. But the fact they could smell gas meant the seam between the fuel tank and the rest of the fuel system had been broken, or the fuel lines had been sheared. Either way, gas was leaking from somewhere, and an electrical spark could turn it into a full-out blaze.

He faced Mandy, who had come around the vehicle. She was knuckling her mouth and staring at Jeff, her complexion bloodless. "Mandy, give us a hand moving him," he told her.

She didn't respond.

"Mandy!"

She blinked, pulled her eyes away from Jeff. "What?"

"We need help moving Jeff."

Abruptly flames whooshed to life in the BMW's engine.

"It's gonna blow!" Austin cried hysterically. "Grab him!"

Steve took Jeff's arms, Noah and Austin his legs, and they dragged Jeff twenty feet from the burning wreckage to where Steve had brought Jenny—only now she was on her side, eyes closed, limbs askew.

"Jen!" Steve dropped Jeff's arms and dashed over to her. "Jen? Jen!" He turned to the others. "We have to get her and Jeff to the hospital. Now!"

"Do you know where it is?" Noah asked.

"Someone in town can tell us." He scooped Jenny into his arms and stood. "You guys carry Jeff."

Noah and Cherry grasped Jeff's legs, Austin and Mandy, his arms. On the count of three they lifted him off the ground. However, they only made it a few steps this time when Jeff's eyes flailed open and he screamed.

"Set him down!" Steve ordered.

They rested Jeff on his back. He continued to scream with tremendous force. When he expelled the last of the air from his lungs, he began to hyperventilate. His eyes, glossy and as wide as silver dollars, stared at the black sky overhead.

"Jeff?" Steve said. He'd set Jenny down on the ground and was bending over his friend. "Jeff? Can you hear me?"

"It hurts!" Jeff bleated through clenched teeth. "It hurts it hurts it hurts!"

"Where does it hurt?" Steve asked him. The calmness in his voice didn't match the panic chilling his blood.

"Back...my back..." Jeff's face had flushed liver pink. It was sheathed in perspiration. The tendons in his neck were bunched into ropey cords.

Steve took Jeff's hand, as if they were shaking, and instructed him to squeeze it.

Jeff let loose another choked scream and crushed Steve's hand in his. He squeezed tighter and screamed louder before falling abruptly silent. His eyes slid closed. His grip slackened.

Steve snatched his hand back and clenched and unclenched it against his chest.

"What the hell was that?" Austin said, running his hands through his Mohawk. The wildness in his eyes made him appear ten years older.

"He said his back," Mandy mumbled. Tears streaked her cheeks, while her hands were clamped over her ears, as if in anticipation of more screams. "Did he break it?"

Steve shook his head. "I don't know."

"But he squeezed your hand," Austin said. "So he's not paralyzed, right? At least he's not paralyzed?"

"He could be from the waist down," Steve said.

"Don't say that," Mandy whispered.

"It's not going to change the fact if he is."

She sobbed and turned away.

"Maybe we did it," Austin blurted. "We moved him. You're not supposed to move someone with a broken back. Maybe we made it worse."

"If we left him in the car," Steve said, "he would be dead right now."

They all glanced at the burning BMW. Stout yellow and orange flames now engulfed the entire vehicle, feeding off the foam and leather seats and other combustible items. Grayish smoke streamed upward into the black night.

Noah broke the silence. "How are we going to move him now?" he said quietly.

"We're not," Steve said. "Austin, Mandy, Cherry—you guys stay here with Jeff. Noah and I will take Jenny to the hospital and bring help back."

"What do we do if Jeff comes to again?" Mandy asked. She'd finally removed her hands from her ears.

"Just talk to him. Tell him an ambulance is coming. But don't move him."

"That's all?" she said.

"That's all," he said. "We'll be back soon."

Chapter 5

"Goddamn foreign TV. I told ya we
should've got a Zenith."
Gremlins (1984)

Cleavon sat in his recliner with one eye squeezed shut, the other open, because this seemed to help keep the headache thumping against the inside of his skull at bay. The Sony color television glowed softly in the dark room, though it didn't produce any sound because the volume knob was busted. On the fourteen-inch screen, a customized '86 Toyota Xtra Cab sporting a lifted suspension and oversized tires idled at the track's starting line some five hundred miles away in Mississippi. Then the flag dropped. The truck leapt forward. A dozen cameras flashed.

The truck shot toward the bog, windshield wipers waving back and forth. When it hit the water it sprayed curtains of mud down both flanks, turning the bright red and blue paint job—BAD TO THE BONE airbrushed across the hood—a shitty brown. A few seconds later it got caught up and stopped, shimmying back and forth, dipping and rising, smoke billowing from the raised wheel wells. It made Cleavon think of an antelope or zebra losing their battle to cross a muddy river on one of those nature shows.

"It's them big fat tires," Earl said from his own recliner a few feet away. "They just slow you down, am I right?" He reached for a fresh beer from the six-pack in the cooler resting between the two of them. The recliner squealed in protest at the sudden shift in his six-foot-seven, four-hundred-pound body. It was no wonder the fucking thing hadn't collapsed under his

47

weight yet. It wasn't made for someone so big. Clothes weren't either. Earl always had trouble finding clothes that fit him, not that he bought clothes much, a pair of jeans, a few wife beaters every few years, if that. The white, stained tank top he had on now stopped halfway over his gut, above his bellybutton. The jeans stopped a few inches shy of his ankles. He looked like a fucking retard, Cleavon always told him, but Earl didn't care. Cleavon didn't either. He just liked telling him he looked like a fucking retard.

"The skinnier the better, ain't that right Cleave?" Earl went on. "That's what you always say. Leave them fat meats to the pretty boys who can pay someone to change the bearings and seals every year. That's what you always say, Cleave." He burped, a loud, maggoty one smelling of food left in the sun for a few days. "And he don't got no sense using a stick shift. Not for a big old slophole like that. Am I right, Cleave? Am I right?"

Cleavon grunted but said nothing to his brother. On the screen a young fella began wading into the waist-deep muck to attach a tow strap to the truck's front hook. Suddenly the picture hiccupped, then went haywire, flickering all over the place.

"For fuck's sake!" Cleavon said.

"It's all right, Cleave," Earl said. "You just gotta leave it for a bit, is what you gotta do."

Cleavon eased himself to his feet and crossed the room, delicately, like he was walking on egg shells, one hand pressed to his forehead. He smacked the top of the TV, the headache making him hit it harder than he'd intended.

"Hey!" Earl said. "That ain't helping—"

"Shut it," Cleavon growled. He began fiddling with the rabbit-ear antennae. "Get the light, Earl, I can't see shit in the dark."

Earl set his beer on the floor, which his gorilla arms reached sitting like he was. Then he heaved his monstrous bulk out of the recliner, which sprang back and forth with what might have been joy. He lumbered across the room, burping once again, and hit the light switch. The sixty-watt bulb dangling from the socket where their parents' chandelier used to hang blinked on.

Cleavon fiddled with the antennae for a full minute, but all he managed to do was wake his fucking headache. Grimacing, he tore the rabbit ears loose and tossed them across the room.

"Hey, Cleave, why'd you do that?" Earl said, going to pick them up. "That's not helping, throwing them like that. How's that helping? You gonna break them. And you break them, and that's it, they just won't work."

"Shut the fuck up, Earl," Cleavon snapped. "I'm in no mind for your bullshitting right now. I been in the garage all day, I'm beat to shit, and also, I got a headache like a motherfucker. So shut the fuck up with your bullshitting." He went to the cooler, rubbing his forehead. There were no beers left. Four empties sat in a line next to Earl's recliner. "You drank all the beer, Earl?"

"I did not, Cleave," Earl said. "We shared them. They were sitting there, we were sharing them."

"I had two, you had four. That don't sound like sharing to me. That sounds like you having twice as much as me, you fat shit."

"I wasn't counting." Earl shrugged his big shoulders. "Besides, I got them, didn't I? I went to the shed, I told you, I said, the TV got a signal, some monster truck racing, you wanna watch it, have some beers. Then I filled up the cooler with ice and a six pack. You didn't do nothing but come in here and sit down—"

"Aw, shut up, Earl," Cleavon said. He left the den and went down the hallway to the kitchen. The headache felt like a drill behind his eyes. While he'd been sitting in the recliner, it had almost faded to nothing. But all that fussing around with the TV had pissed it off, and it was drilling like a sonofabitch now.

He stepped into the kitchen and stopped at the sight of the Corn Flakes scattered on the floor, the soured milk puddled on the countertop. "Floyd!" he shouted, then cringed as the headache drilled deeper. "Floyd!"

There was no answer. Cleavon didn't expect one either. Floyd was deaf as a fencepost and had been that way for a good ten years now. You wouldn't believe what happened to the stupid fuck. Cleavon didn't at first. He could still see Floyd as clearly as if it were yesterday, come stumbling back to the

49

farm, clothes torn, blood pouring down his face, looking like he'd gone insane. But he and Earl had never changed their story, not once, so Cleavon believed it happened the way they'd said it happened.

Floyd and Earl had been hunting rabbits. What they'd do, they'd catch one of the rabbits in a trap, tie a stick of dynamite around it, light the wick, and let it go. Nine times out of ten it'd head straight underground. When the dynamite blew, Thumper might turn a couple of his pals inside out, but the rest would leave the warren and hop around in loopy circles. You could stroll right over and pluck them up by their ears, just as easy as picking daisies. Floyd and Earl caught as many as two dozen a day this way. They sold them to Pete Scoble in town, who in turn butchered them and sold them as meat in Akron. It didn't make anybody rich, but it paid the bills and put food on the table.

On the day Floyd lost his hearing he'd been sitting in the pickup while Earl strapped a stick of dynamite to the rabbit they'd caught in the trap. When he let it go, however, it didn't go underground; it made like the devil to the pickup, TNT strapped to its back, fuse burning. Earl had his rifle and tried to shoot it, but he didn't have the best of aim, and a moving rabbit was a tough target. The critter took cover under the truck. Earl yelled at Floyd to haul ass, but Floyd had never been quick upstairs, not even back then.

According to Earl, the truck did a big cartwheel, flipping ass over tits before landing on its wheels again. Floyd received a dozen deep gashes to his face and complained of ringing in his ears for a good week. None of the cuts healed properly because he kept picking away the scars, and his ears didn't heal either, because he kept digging his fingers into them all the way to the knuckles.

Nevertheless, Cleavon thought now, being ugly and deaf didn't give him the right to be a pissing slob. Who couldn't make a bowl of cereal without spilling shit all over the place? Cleavon scowled. He would get the lazy oaf to clean up the mess later; he didn't want to deal with any more idiocy right then. He just wanted a beer and a cigarette and some peace and quiet.

Stepping on the cereal, crunching it beneath his boots, he opened a counter drawer and rifled through Scotch tape and screwdrivers and a bunch of other junk until he found a bottle of Aspirin. He popped the cap and upended the container to his mouth. He chewed the five or six pills that flopped onto his tongue, thinking they'd get to work faster ground up. Then he opened the old Kelvinator refrigerator and snagged a cold Bud. As an afterthought he bent back down and scanned the near empty shelves. There were another six beers, a bag of carrots, a carton of milk, a couple loaves of bread, a bowl of eggs, a jar with two pickles floating in it, and not much else.

He closed the door, twisted off the beer cap, and was about to head outside to have his smoke in the cool night air when the telephone jangled.

He picked up the handset. "Yeah?"

"That was fast you quick sumbitch," Jesse Gordon said.

"I was standing next to the phone," Cleavon said.

"What you doing standing next to the phone? You some mind reader now, know I was gonna call?"

"I was getting a beer from the fridge. On account of the fridge being in the kitchen, and on account of the phone also being in the kitchen, I was standing next to the phone." He paused. "Listen, Jess, what'd'you say about coming over tomorrow for a coupla beers, throw some steaks on the grill?"

"And I'm guessing you want me to bring the steaks?"

"Now there's an idea."

"As much as I'd like to sit around and listen to you bitch about your dumb ass brothers, Cleave, I got other plans."

"Other plans, huh?"

"Plans with the missus."

"Connie? Since when you start having plans with Connie, that fat cow?"

"Since she told me she's making her famous roast pork tomorrow night. She stuffs it, you know? Only cooks it on special occasions. You wanna guess what this special occasion is? I'll tell you—she's starting a diet."

"She gonna cook a roast pork to kick off a diet? Shit, Jess, that's why she's so fat all the time, all she does is cook and eat what she cooks. No way this diet's gonna work. She ain't gonna last two days on no diet."

"I don't care she lasts until her midnight snack. I'm still getting her roast pork tomorrow night."

"Maybe I'll come by and try some of that famous roast pork?"

"Don't think so, Cleave. It don't work like that. You can't, you don't just invite yourself over 'cause you don't got no good food of your own. You got a coupla pigs. Go stick one on a spit and you got your own roast pork, bacon, ham, whatever, as much as you want."

"So why you calling me? To tell me your fat cow of a wife is cooking a roast pork dinner that I can't have none of? I tell you, Jess, Connie can't cook for shit, so go on and have your fuckin' roast pork—" He cut himself off. "Shhht—you hear that?"

"Hear what?" Jesse said.

"Someone just picked up." Cleavon and his brothers shared a party line with Jesse and Connie Gordon, and four other households who'd refused to sell their properties to the National Park Service when it started buying up land fourteen years ago. "Who's there?" Cleavon said. "Speak up."

"Cleavon?" a voice said.

"Higgins?" Cleavon said.

"Yeah, it's me Weasel. Who you talking to?"

"Me," Jesse said.

"Jess? Good, that's easy—I was just about to call y'both." He was speaking fast, excitedly. "Boys, we caught us some new does!"

"Lick my leg!" Cleavon exclaimed, unconsciously using a saying his pa had often favored before he blew his brains out with a double-barrel shotgun. "Doe" was code for the out-of-town women they used in the black masses. "How many?"

"Three."

"Three!" Jesse crowed happily. "Good work, Weasel, you sumbitch! They not too, they not like the last one, too cut up, are they?"

"I don't know, Jess."

"The hell don't you know?" Cleavon said, frowning. "You didn't just leave them there, for Christ's sake, did you?"

"You don't understand, Cleave," Weasel said. "They were with four bucks. I couldn't, there were too many, for me to go back. That's why I'm calling. I need help rounding them up."

Cleavon blinked. "Seven in all? The fuck they driving, Weasel—a goddamn limousine?"

"Driving?" Weasel said, playing dumb.

"Hell, Weasel," Cleavon said. "It's just us, nobody else is on the line listening in, now start talking some sense."

"It's just that, Mr. Pratt told us, he said—"

"Fuck Spencer! Now spill it. What were they driving?"

"Cars, Cleave. Normal cars. One was, one was a Jeep, green, if I remember right. Everything happened so fast, you know? The other, blue, I think. That's the one I ran off, that crashed. Ballsy driver. Came right at me straight as a bullet. Never seen anything like it. He kept coming, he held it together a second longer, I might've been the one in the woods."

A silence followed.

Cleavon said finally: "You pulling our legs, Weasel?"

"No, Cleave. Why?"

"Why? *Why?* You better be messing with us, Weasel."

"I'm not messing, Cleave. What's wrong?"

Cleavon's headache, which he'd temporarily forgotten about, was back and worse than ever. He kneaded his eye sockets and tried to keep from throwing the phone across the room like he'd done to the rabbit ears. He had to deal with two retards in Earl and Floyd all day long, every day of the year, he didn't need it from Weasel too. But he got it, didn't he? He sure did. "I'll tell you what's wrong, Weasel," he said. "Those people you ran down—"

"Does, Cleave, does and bucks—"

"Those fuckin' *people*," he snapped, "you think, what, they're just gonna sit there where they crashed and have a barbeque? Shit no, Weasel, they gonna get in the second car and go for help. They gonna go to town. They gonna raise hell, that's what they gonna do! Now where the fuck are they?"

"Damn, Cleave, I didn't think, I thought, you know, I thought they'd..."

Damn, Cleave—they're right near your place, not a hundred yards north of the bridge."

"Listen up, Jess, and listen good," Cleavon said. "Me and the boys're gonna cut through the woods, get this under control. You and dipshit here, you two drive up and meet us quick as you can. I'm gonna call Lonnie now."

"Get him to stop anyone coming his way?" Jesse said.

Cleavon nodded, then realized nobody could see him. "They'll probably stop at his place looking for help. Probably. But who knows for sure. They might drive right on past, so, yeah, get him to stop them whether they want to stop or not."

"Hey, Cleave," Weasel said. "I wasn't thinking, I'm sorry—"

Cleavon slammed the handset down. He waited a few seconds, picked it up again, and began dialing Lonnie's number.

"Cleave?" It was Weasel.

"Get off the fuckin' phone Weasel!"

"Sure, Cleave, okay, see you soon."

Cleavon depressed the switch hook, counted to five before releasing it, then dialed Lonnie's number. After two rings Lonnie's boy picked up. "Hello?"

"That you, Scottie? It's Cleavon McGrady. Your pa there?"

"Naw, he's gone to Randy's for the meat draw."

Cleavon swore to himself, then said, "Scottie, listen up, okay? I have something important you gotta do. You listening?"

"Yeah?"

"Some people might be coming by, on the way to town. They might stop by your place, looking to use the phone. You can't let them do that. You tell them you don't have no phone. You got that?"

"Why they wanna use my phone? Who they calling?"

"It don't matter. You just tell them you don't got no phone. Can you do that?"

"I guess."

"I'm gonna call your daddy now. You remember what I told you."

"I ain't got no phone."

"Good boy. Your daddy will be home soon."

Cleavon hung up and dialed Randy's Bar-B-Q. He knew the number by memory; Randy's was one of only two bars in Boston Mills, the main watering hole so to speak, and he often called there when looking for Jesse or Lonnie or whoever else he wanted to find for whatever reason.

"Randy's," a man drawled in a Southern accent. Randy had lived in Louisiana his entire life, a small claims court lawyer. Then he got in some kind of financial trouble and moved out here—fleeing the law you might say—and opened up the bar. The running joke between Cleavon and the guys was that he was going to need a damn good *criminal* lawyer whenever the IRS or FBI or whoever tracked him down and came knocking on his door.

"Listen, Randy, it's Cleavon, I need to speak to Lonnie. He there?"

"Does shit stink? Hold on a sec."

Cleavon waited. He could hear a cacophony of sound in the background: laughter, talking, someone speaking on a mike, reading out numbers. A long thirty seconds later: "Cleave?"

"Lonnie," he said harshly. "You gotta get back to your place, now."

"My place?" It came out "My plash?"

"Listen to me, you drunk shit," Cleavon said, "and listen good. Weasel got us some new does. But he fucked up, he fucked up good, 'cause there were two cars and one still works just fine. Me and the boys are gonna go round them up now. But if some took off in that second car, they're gonna be heading to town. That means past your place. They might even knock on your door, looking for help. I've already spoken with your boy. He's gonna tell them you don't got no phone. If they're still there when you return, you keep them there until me and Jess arrive. If you see them on the road, you don't let them pass—"

"How many does we got, Cleave? Are they lookers—?"

"Pay attention, Lonnie, for Christ's sake! This is important. You do whatever it takes to make sure they don't get to town. Now get going. We've wasted enough time talking."

"Hold up, Cleave, hold up," Lonnie said, sounding more alert, no longer slurring his words. "How'm I supposed to stop them if they're on the road?"

"You got your rifle in your truck, don't you?"

"'Course."

"So you see them coming, you block the road with your truck. When they stop, shoot their tires. Fuck, shoot the driver, you have to. Just make sure they don't go nowhere 'till me and Jess arrive."

"Yeah, right, okay, don't you worry, Cleave, you can count on me. But you didn't tell me, Cleave, these does, they lookers or not—?"

Cleavon hung up the phone, then returned to the den. The TV picture was still on the fritz. Earl was snoozing in his recliner, snoring and drooling a river. Cleavon clapped his hands loudly, startling Earl awake, and said, "Get up, shithead. And go find your deaf-ass brother. We got business to take care of."

Chapter 5

"Ding dong. You're dead."
House (1986)

The road angled upward. Noah slowed the Jeep to forty miles an hour. Anything faster would be reckless in the fog, which seemed to have become denser and more opaque during the last half hour. As soon as he breasted the summit he started down the other side, which dipped sharply. The slope was so great the bottom dropped out of his stomach. He leaned back against the seat, his arms at right angles to the steering wheel, the way you hold the safety rail while zipping down the big hill of a roller coaster.

The road finally flattened out and came to an abrupt end—at least, to a crude wooden barricade with a grime-covered, reflective "Road Closed" sign.

"A dead end!" Noah said, braking.

"No, it's okay," Steve said. "You can go around it. The road still leads out of the park."

Noah peered into the gloom. Visibility was nearly zero. "How do you know that?"

"Jeff told me. He did the research for this trip, so I assume he knows what he's talking about."

Noah contemplated that. "And if we get lost?"

"We can't if we stay on the same road. And if worse comes to worse, we'll backtrack. We passed a few houses before the bridge. We'll knock on a door, tell whoever answers there's been an accident, get them to call an ambulance. But going straight ahead is by far the fastest option right now."

Accepting that logic, Noah circumnavigated the barricade. The road immediately deteriorated, a victim of the elements and neglect. Weeds overran the shoulders and sprouted up here and there through the blacktop. Low branches bounced off the Jeep's windshield and slapped the roof, as if to shoo the intruders away. Noah thought briefly of the vehicle's paintjob, then told himself this was a trivial, selfish concern, given Jeff and Jenny's conditions.

And exactly what were their conditions? he wondered with a hollow feeling in the pit of his gut. Was Jeff going to lose his ability to walk? Was Jenny going to live out the rest of her life in a vegetable state until her family decided to pull the plug? Or was his overactive imagination blowing things out of proportion? "They'll be fine," he mumbled to himself.

"What?" Steve said. He had been examining his shattered reading glasses.

"Nothing," Noah said, embarrassed he'd spoken his thoughts out loud. "Have you ever had a bad accident before?" he added, to say something.

"I broke my collarbone skiing in Aspen, if you can call that a bad accident."

"Aspen, huh?"

"My parents were both into skiing. As a kid I probably saw every major ski resort west of the Rockies."

"You still ski?"

"Not for years."

Steve tossed the useless eyeglasses onto the Jeep's dashboard, and a silence fell between them. The trivial talk was awkward given the circumstances.

Finally Noah said, "How long does it take to recover from a broken back?"

Steve shrugged. "It depends on the type of fracture."

"How bad do you think Jeff's fracture is?"

"We don't know he has a fracture. There's no way to tell the extent of his injury without an X-ray."

"But if it is fractured?"

"A single fracture, and no associated neurological injury..." He shrugged. "Most tend to heal within a few months."

Noah frowned. "Neurological injury? You mean, spinal cord injury?"

"Yeah."

"Back at the crash, you mentioned he could be paralyzed from the waist down."

"I shouldn't have said anything. I was caught up in the moment. Again, it totally depends on the extent of the injury."

"But there's a possibility he could be paralyzed?"

"I'm not a spinal surgeon, Noah. I haven't examined him. I don't know."

"Be straight with me, Steve. I'm not his mother."

Steve hesitated. "Yeah, there's a possibility. Even so, there's always rehab, physio..."

"Which could last years."

"Better than never walking again."

"Yeah," Noah said sourly. "Better than that."

Noah saw the gravel driveway and white mailbox at the last moment. He slammed on the brakes. The Jeep squealed to a stop.

"What the hell?" Steve said, alarmed.

"A house!" Noah said, already swinging the Jeep onto the driveway.

The house was set a hundred feet back from the road, barely visible in the spectral haze. It had projecting eaves, tall windows, and a wrap-around porch. Yellow light glowed from behind a window in a square belvedere, which protruded vertically from the eastern corner of the low-pitched roof.

"Thank God," Steve said. He twisted in his seat and checked Jenny's breathing and circulation.

"How is she?" Noah asked.

"Her pulse is weak."

"That's not good, is it?"

"Could be due to shock, or internal hemorrhage."

Noah banged over a pothole.

"Hey!" Steve cried out. "Careful!"

"Sorry, dude," Noah said. "I'm trying. This driveway's in shit condition."

Steve sat forward again.

Noah avoided a few more potholes and stopped next to a waterless stone birdbath. He killed the engine but left the high beams on.

Steve hopped out. "Wait with Jenny. This shouldn't take long."

Noah nodded and watched Steve hurry up the veranda steps. Several spindles in the veranda railing, he noted, were snapped in half or missing altogether. In fact, the entire house seemed to be falling apart. Broken slate shingles littered the scorched-grass lawn, while the paint on the weatherboards and ornate pediments above the windows was blistered and peeling.

Steve knocked on the front door, waited, knocked again, waited longer. He turned and shrugged.

Swearing, Noah joined him on the veranda. The knocker Steve had used was big and brass and couldn't have gone unheard.

"Someone's gotta be home," Steve said.

Noah rapped the knocker three times, hard, angry.

Silence.

Steve cupped his hands against the small window in the door's upper carved panel and peered inside. Then he reached for the door handle.

"Whoa," Noah said. "What are you doing?"

"Seeing if it's unlocked."

The handle twisted in his grip. The door swung inward.

"This is trespassing," Noah said.

"It's an emergency," Steve said.

Steve stepped into the atrium and flicked on an overhead light. After a moment's hesitation, Noah joined him. A vase of dead flowers sat on a small deal table. A mirror hung on the opposite wall. Noah caught his reflection—and barely recognized the wide, frightened eyes staring back at him.

Directly ahead of them a staircase led to the second floor, and beside that a long hallway, which ended at a closed door. To their left was a small dining room. The table appeared not to be used for eating, as it was covered with newspapers and magazines. Six Chippendale chairs were tucked beneath it, the decorative backings broken in several of them. To their right was the living room. Stuffy antique furniture and moody oil paintings in ornately carved gilded frames shared the space with discarded socks, dirty dishes, ashtrays overflowing with cigarette butts, and boxes stocked with an assortment of junk. A wood-paneled television sat on a small table next to the fireplace. A brown wire snaked from it across the floor to an upholstered Lay-Z-Boy recliner, on which sat a controller box the size of a large book.

Noah thought of his grandparents' big old place in upstate New York—if they died and his lazy Uncle Phil moved in.

Steve said, "Don't see a phone anywhere."

"Me neither," Noah said.

"Hello?" Steve called.

No one replied.

"Hello?" Noah said. "We've had an accident! We need to use your phone to call the police."

Silence.

"Fuck it," Steve said. He started down the hallway.

Noah followed close behind him.

Although the hardwood floor was covered with a turkey-colored rug-runner, their footfalls nevertheless caused the boards beneath to groan and squawk. It was stealthy, ominous—the sound a thief made.

The door at the end of the hall gave to the kitchen. It was the most unkempt room yet with gunk-hardened dishes piled in the sink, opened cans of tuna fish and baked beans and other preserved food left on the counters, and dried spills on the linoleum floor tiles. On a small drop-leaf table sat close to twenty empty brown bottles of Bud Light.

Noah wrinkled his nose against the stench of stale beer and cigarettes, and beneath that something sweet and greasy. "This place is a dump," he said. "Maybe whoever lives here doesn't have a phone after all?"

"Living way out here, isolated?" Steve shook his head. "They have to have one." He crossed the kitchen to a narrow butler's stairwell that led upstairs.

"Forget it," Noah said quietly. "If there's some drunk up there—"

"If there is, he's passed out."

"We don't know that."

"Then why hasn't he answered us?"

"You think there's going to be a phone in the bedroom?"

"Maybe there's a study, or a library."

"Let's just go. We could have been at the hospital by now."

Steve placed a foot on the first tread. "You coming or not?"

"I think I'll keep looking down here. Yell if someone stabs you."

"Thanks."

Steve disappeared up the steps. Noah returned to the living room. He searched beneath the scattered newspapers, behind pillows, under furniture, but came up empty handed. He went to the dining room next. He was opening the doors to a large cabinet—more out of curiosity as to what it held than any expectation of finding a phone—when he sensed movement behind him. He turned just as a kid whacked a hockey stick across his back. Noah cried out in surprise and pain. The kid swung the stick again. Noah absorbed the blow with his left side, then grabbed the stick's shaft. The kid was half his size. A few good shakes caused him to release his grip and tumble to his ass.

Noah cocked the Titan hockey stick like a baseball bat but didn't swing it. "It's okay!" he said. "Calm down. I'm not going to hurt you."

The kid glared at him from behind a piece of oval cardboard with slots cut out for eyeholes and a dozen stitches drawn on it in black felt marker. The flimsy Jason Voorhees goaltender mask was strapped to his head with pieces of shoelace.

Steve appeared a moment later and stared at the kid. "Jesus!"

"He came from nowhere," Noah said. "Started whacking me with this fucking hockey stick."

"Who are you?" Steve asked the kid.

"I live here," the boy replied in a high, petulant voice. He couldn't have been any older than nine or ten. "Who're *you*?"

"Why didn't you answer the door?"

"I ain't gotta. This is my house."

"Why'd you attack me?" Noah asked.

"You broke in!"

"The door was unlocked."

"So what. It's my house. You can't just come in."

"We didn't mean to scare you," Steve said, "but we've had an accident, a car accident. We need to use your phone to call the police."

"Don't got no phone," the boy said smugly.

"You don't have one?" Steve said suspiciously.

"Nope."

"Where are your parents?"

"Pa's coming back right now, and you're gonna be in deep shit."

Steve glanced at Noah, who shrugged.

"Keep an eye on him," Steve said. "I'll keep looking upstairs."

"Get outta my house!" The kid leapt at Steve, grabbing his red pullover and tugging, as if trying to tear it.

Noah tossed aside the hockey stick and wrapped the boy in a bear hug, pinning his arms to his side and lifting him free. "I got him!" he grunted. "But hurry up, I can't hold him forever."

Steve dashed back up the stairs.

The kid kicked and squirmed and shook his head so violently his mask flew off.

"Stop it, you little shit!" Noah said. "What's your problem? We'll be out of here in a minute."

"Get out now!"

"Give it a rest."

Sharp teeth sunk into Noah's right hand, in the fleshy valley between thumb and index finger. He cried out and released the kid, who quickly seized the hockey stick and swung it. Noah absorbed the blow again with his left side and grabbed the blade end of the stick with his good hand. They tugged the stick back and forth before Noah lost his grip and let go.

The kid, off-balance, stumbled backward and collided with an old cast iron radiator that was leaning against the wall, the plumbing disconnecting from the floor pipes. He fell to his back. The radiator rocked precariously forward.

Noah shouted, "Watch out!"

The boy's angry eyes bulged and he raised his arms in a futile effort moments before the radiator toppled over and crushed his skull. The sound was brittle and wet at the same time, like bones snapping underwater. Then thick crimson blood seeped out from beneath the radiator's finned columns in a rapidly spreading pool.

Steve was just exiting the kid's barebones bedroom, about to move on to the next room along the hallway, when Noah began shouting.

Swearing in frustration—how hard was it to restrain a ten year old?—he returned downstairs to the dining room.

He froze in shock at the scene awaiting him.

Noah stood in front of a cast iron radiator, which lay on its side. The kid's pelvis and legs stuck out from beneath it, making Steve think of a bug that had been squashed beneath a fly swatter: plump middle part flattened to a gooey pulp, legs spreading out from the remains all akimbo. Noah turned his head toward Steve, slowly, almost as if he were in a trance. His eyes were dark and unfocused. He opened his mouth but didn't say anything.

Steve rushed to the radiator and hooked his hands beneath it.

"Help me!" he said.

"He's dead," Noah rasped softly.

"Help me!"

"I heard him die. I *heard* him."

With a loud bellow Steve lifted the radiator. The thing must have weighed a good two hundred pounds. It strained his shoulders and back. He got it to knee level and feared he was going to drop it back on the boy when Noah moved next to him and helped lift.

They got it upright. Steve steadied it with his hands until it stopped rocking on its scrolled feet. Then he looked down at the boy—or what remained of the boy.

He swallowed back a jet of bile. He thought he'd seen it all in gross anatomy, but this took the cake. The kid's jaw and mouth were strangely undamaged, but his forehead was split open like a broken eggshell, revealing a flattened mess of loose blood, brain tissue, and cerebrospinal fluid. The left eyeball lay in a lumpy red bed a few inches from where it should have been. Tuffs of dark hair protruded from flaps of skin that were no longer attached to the skull.

Steve turned away without checking for signs of life. Noah had been right.

The kid was about as dead as you could get.

Chapter 7

"No tears please, it's a waste of good suffering."
Hellraiser (1987)

Mandy stared at the glowing fireball that had once been the BMW, trying to think of anything except Jeff—Jeff lying two feet away from her, silent and unmoving and maybe paralyzed. Seeing him so helpless made her think about her mother on her deathbed, frail, feverish, a breathing tube taped to her nose. This had been eight months after she was diagnosed with inoperable ovarian cancer. Initially doctors gave her one year to live without chemotherapy, five with the treatment. She chose the latter option, but the cancer spread faster than anticipated and metastasized through her body. Each time Mandy visited her at the hospital the prognosis became worse and worse. One week her mother's doctor said she had six months, the next week he said three. During the final days Mandy, sitting by her mother's side, broke down and cried hysterically. Her mother, momentarily lucid, asked, "What's the matter, honey?" and Mandy said, "Don't leave me." Her mother took her hands and promised she'd always be with her. She died later that night.

After the funeral Mandy's world seemed darker, grittier. She became angry at everybody and everything and began hanging out with other angry kids. She dropped out of high school in grade eleven, became a compulsive shoplifter, and was in and out of juvie until she was eighteen. That's when her parole officer sat her down and painted a grim picture of her future if she didn't clean up her act. At the same time her father told her she was an adult now and kicked her out of the house. She got a job at Burger King and worked forty-hour weeks just to pay her rent and bills and feed herself. The job sucked, but on the plus side it kept her busy and out of trouble. It was also a wake-up call. Realizing she was going to be working behind a cash register for the rest of her life if she didn't learn an employable skill, she saved enough money to enroll in a three-month fashion makeup artistry program. Once degreed, she found work with a bridal company where she remained until moving on to the Broadway theater scene. By twenty-two she had become the go-to stylist for a number of top stage performers and had a healthy list of private clients.

One evening in late summer of 1984 she and her roommate Lisa Archer were in the small upstairs area of a Midtown bar when the waitress—a tall brunette with a Russian or Polish accent—brought a bottle of Dom Pérignon to their table and told them it was from the two gentlemen at the bar. Jeff and another young trader, both wearing Miami Vice suits, waved and smiled at them.

"Invite them over," Lisa whispered.

"Seriously?" Mandy said.

"They're hot!"

"They're sleazy!"

"You know how much that champagne costs?"

Mandy pushed out a spare chair with her foot. Jeff and his pal came over. She took an immediate disliking to Jeff. He was too smooth, too confident, too good-looking. But the longer they spoke, the more he grew on her, and she realized he wasn't putting on airs; he really was the complete package. She ended up going back to his place that night, and soon they were spending all their free time together. Although he'd just been starting out at the investment management firm then, he was already a big deal, attracting the notice of important people. Consequently, he was constantly being invited to fashionable dinners and events. Mandy felt like Cinderella, living the rags to riches dream.

At the same time, however, she was uneasily aware that the clock was going to strike midnight at some point. She was just some messed up kid from Queens, the daughter of an accountant, pretty, successful in her own right, but nobody special. She had no business mingling with the Establishment. She knew Jeff was disappointed she had not become the socialite he wanted, knew he was losing interest in her, but what could she do about that? He had successful, intelligent women of high breeding fawning over him whenever he went out. How could she compete with them? The knowledge that she would inevitably lose him gutted her, but she was too proud to let it show. Instead she became snarky, poking fun at him when she could, as she had done in the car earlier. This wasn't winning her any points, but she couldn't help it. She wanted to hurt him as much as she could before he hurt her.

Mandy forced herself to look at Jeff now, and she was flooded with guilt at her petty behavior. His face, yellow in the light from the fire and slick with blood, looked like someone had taken a box cutter to it. He would be left disfigured with a half-dozen scars.

Poor Jeff, my baby, she thought. *My arrogant, narcissistic, beautiful baby...*

She gritted her teeth. If only she had stood her ground, they wouldn't be in this hellish predicament. Two weeks ago a makeup artist named Cindy had invited Mandy and Jeff to her white-trash-themed Halloween party. Mandy had initially accepted, but when she mentioned it to Jeff, he scoffed, telling her he wouldn't be seen dead at such a party. A couple days later he sprung the idea for the current trip.

"It's called Helltown, babe," he told her while they were getting dressed to go out for dinner with friends. "It's supposedly one the most haunted spots in all of the country."

"It's in Ohio!"

"It'll be a road trip."

"A boy's trip."

"Austin will bring Cherry."

"Whoopee." Mandy had never shared much in common with the Filipina.

"And Steve said he'll ask that chick he's seeing."

"The med student?"

"Whoever. So what do you say? There's a spooky bridge to check out and a couple haunted cemeteries and other neat stuff."

"If you're twelve years old."

"Sure as hell beats a party mocking the white working class. Don't you realize how crass that is? Would you go to a party mocking underprivileged blacks or Asians?"

"White trash isn't an ethnic group, Jeff," she said, thinking of the teenage deadbeats who'd almost ruined her life. "It's a description of lazy people who make poor life choices."

"I think it'd be a poor life choice to attend such a party."

"It'll be fun."

"Helltown will be fun, babe. I've found us a great little hotel to stay in."

"You've already booked it, haven't you?"

"You'll love it."

"Forget it."

"So that's a yes?"

"It's a no, Jeff!"

But of course it was a yes. It was always a yes. She would have a better chance giving birth to identical quadruplets than persuading Jeff to do something he didn't want to do.

Austin was pacing back and forth, chain smoking Marlboros, when Mandy said something. He turned to face her. She was bent close to Jeff, as if examining him.

He tossed away his cigarette and hurried over. "What is it?"

"He moved," she said.

"He moved?" Austin repeated, filled with sudden hope. "His legs?"

"No, his cheek. It twitched. At least I thought it did. Jeff?"

He didn't reply.

"Jeff?"

Nothing.

Austin said, "You must have imagined it."

"I don't think I did."

Austin patted Jeff's cheek. "Hey, buddy? You hear me? You wanna open your eyes for us?"

"Stop that!" Mandy said. "You're going to wake him up."

Austin frowned. "So?"

"What if he starts screaming again?"

"So he screams. He'll stop eventually, and we can find out..."

"Find out what?"

"If he can move his fucking legs!" He patted Jeff's cheek again, harder. "Jeff? Wake up, buddy. Jeff!"

"Stop it!" Mandy cried.

Austin ignored her and continued hitting Jeff's cheek. "Wake up, Jeff. Wake up—"

Mandy grabbed his wrist. "Stop it!"

He shoved her backward. She fell on her butt. Tears welled in her eyes. "Fine!" she blurted. "Wake him up! Listen to him scream!"

Austin hadn't meant to push her so hard. "Mandy, I'm sorry."

"Jesus, Austin," Cherry said. She'd been sitting off by herself but joined them now. "Apologize to her."

"I just did!" he said as Mandy covered her face with her hands. He looked at Cherry helplessly. "Can you talk to her or something?"

Cherry crouched next to Mandy and offered words of comfort.

"I'm not hurt!" Mandy said. "I just want to leave this place!"

Austin returned his attention to Jeff. He ran his hands through his Mohawk in frustration. God, he couldn't take this. He really couldn't. He had to know. He slapped Jeff's cheek, hard.

"Don't touch him!" Mandy screamed.

"Just scrape the bottom of his stupid foot!" Cherry said.

Austin frowned. "Huh?"

"If he has feeling below the waist, his toes will curl down. It's instinctual, like when the doctor checks you reflexes by hitting your knee with a hammer."

"Bloody right!" Austin exclaimed. "Why didn't you mention that before?" He tugged off one of Jeff's reddish-brown dress shoes, then a diamond-patterned sock. He dug his key ring from his pocket, chose the largest of the three attached keys, and scraped the tip along Jeff's sole.

His toes didn't curl. They didn't even flinch.

Austin scraped Jeff's sole a second time.

Nothing.

"Try again," Mandy said, staring at him with pleading eyes.

"He can't feel it," he said numbly.

"Do it harder."

"It won't make a difference."

"Do it harder!"

"I did it twice!" he shouted. "He can't feel a fucking thing!"

Austin stumbled away from Jeff's inert body, his collar damp with sweat despite the cold, the air suddenly greasy, unpleasant to breathe. Through a part in the fog he spotted the road and wished he'd taken the case of beer from Noah's Jeep before he and Steve had left for the hospital, because if he'd ever needed to get shitfaced, it was right then.

Jeff, he thought. A paraplegic.

Austin blamed himself and the others for this sad fact. Steve had said they had to move Jeff or he would have been barbequed alive. Fine. Austin agreed with that. However, it was *how* they moved him, half dragging him like he was a heavy side of beef—*that* he couldn't get out of his mind. They should have kept their cool, made a litter, carried him properly.

Austin lit a cigarette and inhaled greedily.

Jeff. A paraplegic.

The words were like oil and water, chalk and cheese. They had no business being grouped together. Maybe if Jeff had been some poor slob the idea of him wheeling around in a chair for the rest of his life wouldn't have been so hard to accept. But Jeff was the poster boy for success and vitality. Austin had met him on the first day of grade nine at Monsignor Farrell High School. Austin had been sitting in the back row of third-period math when Jeff had strolled through the door seconds before the bell rang. He had been tall even then and could easily have been mistaken as a senior. His blond hair had been brushed back from his forehead, his maroon school golf shirt perfectly fitted, his gray slacks pressed and creased, a preppy sweater draped over one shoulder. He swept his eyes across the room, then started down the aisle to the empty desk next to Austin, poking students with his pencil along the way, eliciting nervous chuckles from the victims. Ten minutes into the lesson he made a *pssst* noise and passed Austin a note. Austin opened it and read the three words: "Suck my dick!" He was so surprised he laughed out loud. Mr. Smith, the bespeckled teacher with a bushy brown mustache and yellow sweat stains under his arms, paused in his explanation of the course outline and asked him what was so funny.

"Nothing, sir," Austin replied.

"Stand up, Mr...." He checked the roll call. "Mr. Stanley."

Austin stood up.

"Now tell the class what is so amusing."

"Nothing, sir."

Mr. Smith crossed the classroom and collected the note from Austin's desk. He read it, his face impassive. "Who gave this to you?" he said.

"No one, sir."

"You wrote yourself a note?"

"Yes, sir."

"And you laughed at your own note?"

"Yes, sir."

"I'd like to see you back here during the lunch break. Do you understand, Mr. Stanley?"

"Yes, sir."

After class, in the hallway bustling with students, Jeff found Austin and hooked his arm around his shoulder. "Thanks for not ratting me out to Armpits," he said.

"No problem."

"What's your name?"

"Austin."

"I'm Jeff. I'll see ya round."

After that day Austin and Jeff started hanging out more and more. Their personalities complimented each other in so much as they were both smart-mouths and troublemakers. Yet this was as far as their similarities went, because while Austin despised sports and could barely keep his grades above water, Jeff made the varsity golf and baseball teams, graduated with a 4.0 GPA, and was one of three students named valedictorian. And while Austin dropped out of community college and ended up buying a crummy bar with his grandmother's inheritance and battling alcohol addiction, Jeff went the Ivy School route and was now trading securities at a top tier investment management firm, living the dream.

Was living the dream, Austin amended.

A paraplegic.

Fuck.

Cherry had moved away from the burning BMW and sat beneath a large tree with a thick trunk, wanting to be alone. The fragile calm that had existed since Steve and Noah left with Jenny had deteriorated quickly. Mandy was a total mess, while Austin seemed ready to explode. She didn't blame either of them. Mandy had dated Jeff for four years; Austin had known him since high school. This was the reason she hadn't mentioned the plantar reflex stimulation earlier. She knew there was a chance Jeff could be paralyzed from the waist down, and she didn't want to verify this was the case, for it would only demoralize the others further. But Austin had totally wigged out. He had been slapping Jeff, inadvertently moving Jeff's neck, which could compound his spinal cord injury. So she told him to scrape Jeff's foot, and the diagnosis turned out to be as bad as she'd feared.

Cherry herself remained clinically detached to Jeff's predicament. She wasn't close to him like Austin and Mandy were. In fact, she didn't particularly like him. Not only had he been making fun of her height from the moment they'd met, he was an asshole in general. Moreover, as a registered nurse, she had become used to seeing sickness, disease, and injury.

Just last week there had been a mentally disabled man in the ER with an infected stasis ulcer in the back of his calf. The necrotic tissue around the black eschar had been gnawed away by maggots that were still in residence in large numbers. During debridement surgery the man decided he had to urinate and could only do this standing up, so he got off the operating table, bleeding and dropping maggots everywhere, and peed in the middle of the floor.

And then there was old Ray Zanetti who had cancer to the mandible. Cherry had been his primary caregiver, and pretty much every time she checked in on him he would be looking in the mirror and peeling away pieces of his flaking skin. By the time of his death his face had all but fallen off.

Situations like these were grotesque and sad certainly, but they didn't faze her anymore. They were simply part of her job, what she experienced on a daily basis. All in a day's work, so they say.

Nevertheless, Cherry had never questioned her career choice; it had provided her a new life, literally. She had been born in Davao, in the Philippines. Her family had been dirt poor. Her father didn't work, while her mother was a housecleaner, mostly for Western expatriates. She earned two hundred pesos, or approximately four dollars, a day. This went to support her husband, Cherry, and Cherry's two siblings. They lived in a cinderblock house with a corrugated iron roof and no running water. They battled lice and rats on a constant basis, and they wasted nothing. Her mother often told her how disappointed she was with her Western employers, whose refrigerators were always full of expired food and spoiled vegetables.

Most of Cherry's friends dropped out of high school to work at McDonald's or one of the big malls. These positions didn't pay any more than her mother made cleaning houses and apartment units, but you got to hang out with your friends and spend the day in an air conditioned environment out of the stifling tropical heat. Cherry, however, had greater ambitions. She wanted to get a university degree and work in a call center. She would have to work night shifts to compensate for the different time zones in the UK or US or Canada, but the money was decent and, in the eyes of other pinoys, it was a highly respected profession.

However, when Cherry heard about a friend of a friend who had become unimaginably wealthy as a registered nurse in the US, she promptly changed her degree to nursing. Her mother, starry-eyed at the prospect of having a daughter who could lift her family out of poverty, offered to sell the *carabao*—water buffalo—to help pay for Cherry's schooling, but Cherry refused. She began working at a massage parlor servicing Western expats because the hours were flexible and could accommodate her classes. The company exploited her shamefully, paying her twenty-five cents each massage she gave, regardless of whether it was one hour long or two. Even so, they turned a blind eye to "extra" service. Cherry was raised Roman Catholic, went to church every Sunday, and was conservative by nature, but money was money. For her, a hand job was a service, nothing more, and depending on how cheap (not poor—Westerners were never poor) or generous her client was, she could make anywhere from ten to fifty dollars for a few minutes of work. She could have made even more by offering sex, for which she was often propositioned, but she would not cross that line. She was not a prostitute.

Once she completed her BS in Nursing four years later, she passed the US licensure exam, applied successfully for a green card, and was offered an entry position with New York Methodist Hospital in Brooklyn. She'd been there for three years now, had a mortgage, a car, and enough money in the bank to send hefty sums to her family in Davao on a regular basis, making them the envy of all their friends.

Cherry pulled her eyes from the ground and glanced at the others, relieved to see they had settled down somewhat. Austin was pacing again, but he no longer seemed like a ticking time bomb. Mandy had stopped crying and was staring inward.

Cherry checked her Coca-Cola Swatch and saw that only ten minutes had passed since Steve and Noah had left with Jenny. How long would it take them to find a hospital, explain what was going on, and bring back help? Half an hour? Longer?

A nippy breeze ruffled the nearby reeds and saplings and stirred the mist into searching, serpentine tendrils. Cherry folded her knees to her chest for warmth, wrapped her arms around them—and spotted three flashlight beams bobbing between the trees some fifty yards away.

Chapter 8

"They're here!"
Poltergeist (1982)

Mandy hurried over to Austin and Cherry to watch the crisscrossing flashlight beams approach. She frowned as an uneasy feeling built in her gut. She told herself there was no reason to be concerned, whoever was out here had come to help. But there was something about random people in a dark, unfamiliar forest that scared her silly.

"Do you think they're campers?" Mandy said anxiously.

"Out here?" Austin said.

"Maybe they live nearby?" she said. "They heard the crash and are coming to help?"

"Maybe," Austin said, though he didn't sound convinced.

"Why else would they be out here?"

"I don't like this," Cherry said. "I don't like this at all."

Mandy frowned, momentarily despising the Filipina. She wanted to hear that they were safe, that they were fine; she didn't want to hear fear and paranoia.

Soon the strangers were close enough Mandy could make out the snapping of branches, the crunch of footsteps on dead leaves, the general rustle of disturbed foliage.

"'Lo there?" one of them called.

"Hello," Austin said.

A few seconds later three men dressed in checkered lumberjack jackets emerged from the gloom of the night into the firelight produced by the burning BMW. Mandy gasped silently in surprise and horror. The slim one in the middle sported stringy black hair, bushy muttonchops, and a handlebar mustache. Despite skin the color and texture of old vellum, and a hooked beak for a nose, he appeared normal enough. The other two, however, might have just escaped from a carny sideshow. The freak on the left had a round moon face, piggish eyes, stood close to seven feet tall, and must have weighed somewhere in the neighborhood of four hundred pounds. The freak on the right had misshapen features covered by a jigsaw of wormy white scars and a vacant expression, as though his brains were nothing but mush.

Mandy forced herself not to stare and focused on the middle one, who was visoring his eyes with his hand while he studied the flaming vehicle.

"Good Lord almighty, will ya look at that," he crowed.

"We had an accident," Austin said.

"No fooling," he said. "Anyone hurt?" His eyes fell on Jeff. "Aw, shit. He ain't dead, is he?"

"No!" Mandy said, shocked by the man's blunt manner.

He looked at her. His eyes were dark, unreadable. They appraised her from head to toe and lingered on her breasts. "Well, now," he drawled, "that's quite an outfit you got on, ma'am."

"It's a Halloween costume."

"I reckoned as much. And a good choice at that." He turned his attention to Austin. "How about you, Cueball? No costume?"

Austin twitched at the insult. "I took it off."

"And you, little lady?"

"I didn't bring one," Cherry said quietly.

"All Hallows' Eve, my favorite night of the year, when all the ghoulies come out to play, ain't that right?" He grinned, revealing a missing front tooth. "Anywho, the name's Cleavon. What can I do to help y'all?"

"Our friends have already left to get help," Mandy said. "They'll be back any minute," she added purposefully.

"Any minute you say?" Cleavon said to her. "When did they leave?"

"Forty minutes ago," Mandy lied.

"Forty minutes, huh?"

She nodded.

"And they ain't back already? Shit, maybe they got lost?"

"Do you live out here?" Austin asked him.

"Over yonder, in fact." He hooked his thumb over his shoulder.

"And you wander the woods at night?"

Ignoring the question, Clevon took a few steps toward the BMW and said, "Well knock me down and steal my teeth. It's a genuine Bimmer, boys! Or *was*, I should say. So you some uppity rich kids, that right? Where you from?"

"New York," Austin said.

"The Big Apple! Never been there myself. Always wanted to go, but don't reckon I'd fit in too good. I'm 'bout as country as a baked bean sandwich. Ain't that right, boys?"

The four-hundred-pound freak nodded. "Right-o, Cleave."

"My apologies," Cleavon said. "That there's me brother Earl. And that's me other brother, Floyd. Floyd don't say much. He only got two speeds: slow and stop. And he don't hear too good neither unless you shout." He raised his voice. "Ain't that right, Floyd?"

Floyd nodded.

"Well?" Cleavon said, smiling expectantly at them.

"Well what?" Austin said.

"Ain't you gonna introduce yourselves?"

Mandy glanced at Austin and Cherry. She saw her fear reflected in their eyes. Cleavon and his brothers were not just assholes; they were dangerous. But there didn't seem to be any choice other than to keep Cleavon talking until Steve and Noah returned with help.

"I'm Mandy," she said.

"Mandy," Cleavon repeated. "That's short for Amanda, ain't it?"

She nodded.

"I like it. Mandy. Suits you." His eyes floated to her breasts.

"I'm Austin," Austin said. "And this is Cherry."

"Austin and Cherry—now those are a coupla fine names as well. Had an uncle named Austin. Sat on the porch all day drinking hooch, his own concoction, from a big ol' jug. By suppertime he would be drunker than Cooter Brown on the fourth of July." He smiled his gap-tooth smile at Cherry. "Never knew a Cherry though. The pleasure's mine, darlin'."

Cherry looked away from him. Her lips were pressed together in a thin line.

"Well," Cleavon went on, "now that we're all fine friends, why don't y'all tell me what happened? What caused this unfortunate accident?"

"Our friend lost control of the car," Austin said simply.

Cleavon eyed Jeff. "That the friend, huh? And just lost control, you say?"

"Another car ran him off the road. It was a hearse."

"A hearse? You sure you don't need to get your eyes checked, boy?"

"We all saw it," Mandy said sharply.

Cleavon held up his hands. "Hey, no need to get worked up, darlin'. You say ya'll saw a meat wagon, ya'll saw a meat wagon. Now, enough talk. How 'bout we give you a hand bringing your friend there back to the house. We got medicine and enough food to feed the lot of you to your heart's content."

"Like I mentioned," Mandy said, "our friends went for help. They'll be back here any minute. But thank you for the offer."

"And if they got lost? Could be hours 'till they get back. We got a telephone. We'll call the sheriff. He knows exactly where the ol' McGrady house is. He'll be there with an am'blance in fifteen minutes."

"We're going to wait here," Austin said tersely.

"Hey! I ain't liking your tone, *boy*," Cleavon growled. "Didn't your mama teach you no manners? When someone offers you help, you be gracious."

"Listen, mister...Cleavon," Cherry said pleasantly. "We appreciate your offer. We really do. But we can't move our friend. He has a broken back. Moving him will make his injury worse."

"Don't worry, darlin'. We'll be careful with him."

"We're not going anywhere," Austin said, stepping forward.

"I'm 'fraid I have to insist," Cleavon said. "Boys, get the cripple."

Floyd and Earl started toward Jeff.

"Don't you touch him!" Mandy shouted. "His back is broken!"

Austin made to intercept them.

"Hold it right there, Cueball," Cleavon said, and to Mandy's horror he produced a monstrous machete which had been hidden beneath his jacket. "I wouldn't do nothing stupid if I was you."

Chapter 9

"They will say that I have shed innocent blood. What's blood for, if not for shedding?"
Candyman (1992)

Austin acted without thinking. He charged Cleavon and jump kicked him in the gut. Caught by surprise, Cleavon didn't have time to swing the machete. However, the jump kick was uncoordinated and did little more than knock Cleavon backward a few steps while Austin crashed awkwardly to the ground. Before Austin could regain his feet, Cleavon was on him, raising the machete. Austin kicked the psycho in the shins, dropping him to his knees. Austin lunged, driving his shoulder into Cleavon's chest, knocking him onto his back. He grappled for the machete, but the man wouldn't let go. Then Cherry appeared beside him, also grappling for the weapon.

Austin landed a fist in Cleavon's face, then another. Still, Cleavon wouldn't relinquish his grip on the blade.

Abruptly Cherry disappeared, lifted free from the skirmish. A moment later the left side of Austin's head went numb. Cleavon had walloped him with his free hand. The world canted, his vision blackened, but he didn't release Cleavon's other hand, which was still holding the machete. Cleavon struck him again, this time catching his chin. Austin tried to head butt Cleavon, but his forehead deflected off the asshole's temple. White-hot pain tore through his face. Cleavon was biting him! He shoved himself free, his hand going to his bloody cheek.

82

The chaotic scene around him registered in a heartbeat. Earl holding Cherry off the ground, arms around her chest, her feet kicking wildly. Mandy on her butt, as if she'd been pushed over, her hands held protectively in front of her face. Cleavon shoving himself onto his knees, glaring at him. He didn't see Floyd anywhere, and knew the man must be behind him—

Something heavy slammed into the back of his head.

Mandy was still dazed from Floyd's open-handed slap across her face. Her eyes watered, her cheek smarted, and when she blinked away the stars she saw Floyd looming up behind Austin, swinging a tree branch. It struck the back of Austin's head with a snappish crack. His eyes rolled up in their sockets and he fell limply onto his chest.

This happened so quickly Mandy had no time to react. Now she leapt to her feet and ran at Floyd, screaming at him to leave Austin alone. Floyd kicked Austin in the side of the head twice before she reached him. She grabbed his arm, trying to pry him away. He shoved her aside and kicked Austin again. The impact of his foot striking the side of Austin's skull made a heavy, dead thunk. Mandy felt ill, and all she could think was: *This can't be happening! This isn't happening! He's going to kill him!*

Shouting hysterically—she hadn't quit shouting the entire time—she flung her weight into Floyd, knocking him off balance and away from Austin. While she drummed her fists against his chest, he clutched her around the throat with his hand. She gripped his wrist but could do little else except make rusty, rasping noises. He squeezed tighter, crushing her windpipe. His eyes were shining like a rabid animal—intense yet emotionless.

"...stop..." she gasped.

Her body was going weak. Blackness seeped into her vision.

She tried to rake the freak's face with her fingers, but his arm was outstretched at full length, and his arm was longer than hers. She swiped at air.

He's killing me. He's going to kill me right here.

The realization was like a shot of adrenaline to her heart. She kicked with all her strength and connected with his groin. He bellowed, sagged, and released her.

She ran.

Encouraged by Mandy's escape, Cherry raised both her legs and drove her four-inch heels into Earl's shins as hard as she could. He grunted and dropped her to the ground. She fled in the opposite direction Mandy had gone. The forest was a blur of darkness and fog, shadows layered upon more shadows. Still, she didn't slow. She knew her life had boiled down to two scenarios: escape and live, or get captured and die.

Mandy thrashed through the scrub, out of control, like a drowning swimmer. Her throat, already raw from being strangled, was now on fire. Her breathing came in gasping sobs. The scent of rot and evergreen seared her nostrils. She dodged vegetation left and right, leaping and ducking obstacles she saw at the last second, praying she didn't poke out an eye. She raised her arms for protection against the brittle branches clawing at her face, but she could do little to prevent them from piercing the thin Spandex of her costume, scouring her stomach and legs, drawing warm blood from a half-dozen different cuts.

Cherry thought she had lost Earl when a hand suddenly seized her shoulder. She felt resistance, felt herself slowing. Then a loud tear. Her top. She was free, picking up speed. But she only made it a few more steps before Earl seized her shoulder again, this time dragging her to the ground.

She scrambled forward on all fours, the giant clawing her back, her rear, searching for purchase. He snagged her leg, his fingers pinching her flesh. She kicked her foot, once, twice, and connected with his face or shoulder. Yet he wouldn't let go. She rolled onto her back, gasping for breath, struggling to free herself. He raised a fist. She brought up her arms in front of her face to block the blow. His swing came from the side, plowing into her left ear, knocking her senseless. He raised his fist again. She yelled and squirmed. He smashed her jaw.

Holding onto consciousness by a thread, Cherry shoved her hands into his face, pushing him away. One of her thumbs found an eye socket and she dug deep.

Earl reared up with a startled cry. She wormed out from beneath him, flipped onto her front, and crawled away. She didn't get far. A moment later he appeared next to her and mumbled something that might have been, "Nice try, little girl." He kicked her in the stomach, lifting her clear off the ground, turning her turtle onto her back. He kicked her in her side again and again, relentless. She heard her ribs snapping with twiggy, gristly sounds, and the certain realization that she was going to die filled her with an incomprehensible terror the likes of which she had never experienced.

Mandy blundered blindly into a glade of waist-high grass and cattails. She tripped on a root, pin-wheeled forward, and fell, slamming her chin against the ground so hard her upper teeth punctured her lower lip. Blood gushed into her mouth. She attempted to push herself to her knees, but didn't have the strength. Instead, she was reduced to pulling herself forward, like something primordial that had just slithered out of the ocean for the first time.

When a shrill cry shattered the night, Mandy knew it belonged to Cherry. Still, she didn't contemplate turning back. What could she do? She'd tried to fight them, and she'd failed. She was too small, too weak, outnumbered. Cleavon and his freak brothers were animals, crazy, sick. They would surely do to her...whatever they were doing to Cherry.

Cherry wailed again in abject pain and misery.

Somehow Mandy regained her feet.

She ran.

Chapter 10

"Here we are, I guess," the driver of the white Pontiac Firebird Trans-Am said. "Boston Mills." He had only spoken a few words since he'd picked up Beetle fifty miles back on Interstate 77, mostly to tell him he could take him as far as the Ohio Turnpike. "Sorry it's not someplace bigger," he added. "But I'll be heading east now to Warren. You'll be fine here for the night?"

Beetle nodded. His real name was Frederick Walker, but in the army you got nicknames, and they stuck—enough at least Freddy still thought of himself as Beetle, which he'd received because of his thick eyebrows and square face. "I'll be fine," Beetle said, "and thanks for the ride." He got out and watched the Firebird drive off, vanishing into the fog, there one moment, gone the next, like a ghost ship glimpsed momentarily at sea.

The street was deserted. The only light came from a nearby sodium arc streetlamp that cleaved an inverted copper cone through the mist.

Beetle glanced at his wristwatch. 8:40 p.m. Not so late that there shouldn't be a coffee shop open, or a couple out for a walk. Then again, it being Halloween night, he supposed everyone had closed up to take their kids out trick-or-treating in the residential neighborhoods.

He started walking in the direction the Firebird had gone and passed the typical businesses you found along the main drag in most small towns: a barbershop, a bookstore, a diner, a druggist, a real estate office, a shoe store. The exteriors were weatherworn, most in need of a coat of paint, the display windows as frost-blank as cataracted eyes. Graffiti covered the boarded-up entrance of an out-of-business tavern.

At the end of the block the street signs told him he was at the intersection of Main Street and Stanford Road.

While deciding which way to go he made out voices and laughter from somewhere ahead of him. Some ten seconds later two silhouettes materialized in the gray gloom before resolving into teenage boys. They were sixteen or seventeen, both dressed in torn jeans and wool football jackets with leather sleeves. The one on left had a buzz cut, the one on the right a mushroom cut with bangs that went to his chin. They were each gripping open wine bottles by the necks. They stopped when they saw Beetle. Their bantering ceased. Then, realizing he was too young to be a parent, they continued toward him with the awkwardness of kids who knew they were doing something wrong and were hoping you didn't say anything about it.

"Excuse me," Beetle said when they were a few feet away.

They slowed but kept walking. Buzzcut eyed him warily. "Yeah?"

"Can you tell me where the nearest motel is?"

Buzzcut stopped. Angry red splotches of acne marred his face. His mouth hung open slightly, and he could have done with a pair of braces, maybe one of those full headset deals. Mushroomcut slouched against a newspaper box and cleared the bangs from his face with a quick, neat jerk of his neck.

"You a soldier or something?" Buzzcut said, eyeing Beetle's woodland camouflage shirt.

"The motel?" Beetle said.

The kid shrugged. "Only two in town. The Pines has an indoor pool, but it's way over on the south side. The Hilltop's closer, down that ways a bit, but no pool." He pointed north along the cross street. "Keep going for a couple blocks to the edge of town. Then keep going maybe five more minutes. You'll see it right up on a hill like the name says. Can't miss it. Oh, and so you know, the church with the upside down crosses is another five minutes farther on, right on the edge of the national park."

"Upside down crosses?" Beetle said.

Buzzcut nodded. "That's why you're here, isn't it?"

"To see the church?" Beetle asked.

"The church, the graveyard, the slaughterhouse." His face lit up with an idea. "Hey, you want a guide tomorrow? I can meet you at Hilltop. Five bucks and I'll show you everything."

"I don't have any idea what you're talking about."

"You don't know about the legends?"

"What legends?"

"You know you're in Helltown, right?"

Beetle shook his head.

"So what you doing out here?" Mushroomcut said. "Passing through or something?"

"Or something."

"Huh," Buzzcut said. "Don't get many passer-throughers. Most visitors come to check out the legends." He frowned. "So you don't want a guide?"

"No, but thanks for the directions." Beetle started away, then hesitated. He took his wallet from his pocket, turned back around, and handed Buzzcut a fifty-dollar note. "Split it," he said.

"Holy Christ! A fifty! Thanks, mister!"

Buzzcut took off down the street, hollering like an ape, dollops of wine jumping from the mouth of his bottle. Mushroomcut followed on his heels, grasping for the bill, telling Buzzcut they had to share it.

Beetle continued down Stanford Road, in the direction of the motel.

The houses he passed reminded him of those you might find at a military base that had long since shuttered its doors and had been frozen in time, forgotten by the world. Most were dilapidated things with weed-infested front yards littered with rusted bicycles and neglected toys and garden equipment. From inside a bungalow bunkered behind a corrugated iron fence, a woman cried out in a bitter, hysterical voice, something about the dog and dinner and "getting off your ass and helping out!" The husband shouted back, punctuating every few words with expletives.

The arguing made Beetle think of Sarah—or, more precisely, his relationship with Sarah, how it had been at the end. It was funny, he thought, how something so good between two people could go so bad. But that's how it worked, wasn't it? If he and Sarah hadn't loved each other the way they had, they wouldn't have bothered hating each other the way they had.

Beetle had met Sarah shortly after he'd finished Ranger School. He'd already completed Basic Training, Advanced Individual Training, Airborne School, and the Ranger Indoctrination Program. And he'd already been assigned to the 1st Ranger Battalion for the previous eleven months. Ranger School was more of an old tradition than anything else, but it was a requirement for leadership positions within the 75th Regiment.

To celebrate graduating the two-month course, during which he'd managed on less than three hours sleep a night and one and a half meals a day, Beetle and a few other soldiers secured thirty-six hour passes for the weekend. They rented rooms in a Sheraton in downtown Savannah, Georgia, went for dinner at a steakhouse recommended to them by their commanding officer, then moved on to the bevy of Irish pubs the city was famous for. By midnight only Beetle and a guy named Tony Gebhardt remained from the original group of six; the others had either gone off with girls they'd met, or hookers. Beetle and Tony were contemplating calling it a night when Beetle spotted Sarah at the bar. With her dark hair tied into pig tails, and a splattering of freckles across her nose, she was cute rather than sexy, though still quite attractive.

Tony wiggled his eyebrows at Beetle, and Beetle decided what the hell. He went to the bar, waved to get the bartender's attention, and said to Sarah, "Hi, I'm Beetle."

"Hi," she said, giving him a quick up and down. Drinking and smoking were prohibited while on pass, so he was dressed in civilian clothes to avoid drawing attention to himself.

"I know how this sounds," he said, "but you remind me of someone."

"Punky Brewster, right? I get it all the time."

Beetle laughed. Because she was right. She did look like Punky Brewster, albeit a grownup version. "Maybe that's it," he said.

"So—did you come over to buy me my drink?"

"Sure," he said as the bartender arrived. "Coors for me, and put, uh—"

"Sarah."

"—Sarah's drink on my tab."

Sarah smiled at him, raised her blue cocktail, then started walking away.

"Hey," he called after her. "Where're you going?"

"My table—join if you'd like."

And so he did. Tony did too, given Sarah was with a girlfriend. The four of them drank and smoked, played billiards and darts, and danced to the occasional song. At last call Tony and Beetle invited them back to the Sheraton. The friend was game, but Sarah wouldn't budge on her "I don't go home on the first night" policy, and Beetle settled for a telephone number and a brief kiss.

In the weeks that followed garrison life at Hunter Army Airfield went on as usual. Physical training, paperwork, squad and platoon evaluations, parachute jumps. Beetle never called Sarah. The army was his life. He could be deployed anytime. A relationship would be messy. Nevertheless, the next time he was in Savannah on pass he found himself thinking about her, the fun they'd had, and he discovered he still had her number in his wallet. He called her from a payphone. He expected a snub, but she said she was getting ready to go out with friends and, whatever, if he wanted to come to Congress Street, maybe they could meet up. He got the name of the place she would be at and convinced the guys he was with to change venues. They were all keen except for Tony Gebhardt, who didn't want to see the friend again. But Tony was outnumbered, and they went.

While searching the Congress Street club, Beetle realized he couldn't remember exactly what Sarah looked like, and when he found her on the patio out back, he was surprised by how beautiful she was. They were both more sober than they had been at the Irish pub, and they spent the rest of the night at a secluded table, talking, touching, making out. This time it was her suggestion to return to the hotel.

After that they saw each other as often as possible, and they fell madly in love the way only the young and naïve could. Beetle proposed on the anniversary of the day they'd met. They married a short time later on a beach on Tybee Island. He moved out of the barracks, and they rented a house off post together on a cul de sac in a quiet Savannah suburb. Sarah chose it because of the mature vegetable garden in the backyard. The idea of being able to step outside and pick basil or tomatoes or chili peppers delighted her to no end. Also, they had been talking about having children, and the house had a spare bedroom, which they could convert into a nursery.

Sarah found employment as a receptionist at a small law office, while Beetle was promoted to Specialist, then Sergeant, given a team leader position, and eventually his own squad.

Their lives had been near perfect.

Then, in October of 1983, President Regan issued orders to overturn a Marxist coup. Beetle kissed Sarah goodbye in the middle of the night, and within hours he was on an Air Force C-130 Hercules four-engine transport, configured to carry paratroopers, heading for the tiny Caribbean island of Grenada.

Beetle arrived at the motel before he'd realized it. Directly to his left a stand of pines had been cleared to make room for a parking lot, which was currently empty. A sign perched atop a twenty-foot metal pole announced in red and yellow neon: "Hilltop Lodge - Vacancy." A tacky, flashing arrow pointed to a cement staircase that carved a path through the trees to the top of the hill.

An icy wind blew in from the west, sneaking down the throat of Beetle's shirt and causing his skin to break out in gooseflesh. Rubbing his arms to generate warmth, he climbed the steps, seventy or eighty in total.

The motel rose two stories behind a grove of twenty-foot fir, which, given their calculated spacing, had been planted some years back. The shiplap siding was rotting in places, though someone had attempted to give it a facelift recently with a rich brown coat of stain. A thick hedge of privet lined the perimeter of the plateau and substituted for a fence to prevent visitors from plunging down the steep slopes. On a clear day those same visitors would have been afforded a sprawling panorama of Boston Mills and the national forest those kids had mentioned, though tonight little was visible behind the drab gray curtains of mist.

Beetle followed a stone path between two towering fir to the reception. A placard in the window read: "Great Rates, Free Movie Channel, Imaginary Friends Stay Free." He opened the glass door, stepped inside, and wrinkled his nose against a spoiled cheese smell. He crossed the thick-pile, hunter-green carpet to the front desk. It was currently unmanned. He rang the small brass bell on the counter. A moment later a wizened old man emerged from the back room. He wore pastel slacks and a heavy wool cardigan buttoned to the neck. Gray hair curled out from beneath a beat-up Baltimore Orioles baseball cap. A rosy blush colored his cheeks, nose, and ears. He fixed Beetle with bright blue rheumy eyes and said, "Help ya?"

"A room for the night, please," he said.

"Ranger, huh?" the man said, reading the bars on Beetle's right sleeve. "Was in 'Nam myself. Spent most my time in a resettlement village, twenty miles southwest of Da Nang, three miles from the 5th Marines Combat Base. Supposed to be hell on earth, target practice for the commies, but I didn't see no combat my entire tour. Never met no Rangers neither. They weren't officially incorporated until a few years ago, that right?"

"A room, please," Beetle said.

The man studied him for a moment, then nodded. "You're in luck." He produced a key attached to a piece of red plastic from beneath the counter and dangled it between his thumb and index finger. "Got one room left."

Beetle thought of the empty parking lot but didn't say anything.

"It's a superior suite so a little pricier than the others," the man went on. "But it got a private balcony and views of the Chaguago National Park you won't soon forget. Guests say they like to sit out there with their coffee in the morning. If you're lucky, you might spot a whitetail or elk. Had a few moose about too. You haven't seen nothing until you've seen a buck with a full set of antlers. They shed them each season, you know. The lot simply drop off. Found a set myself few years back. Was going to put them on the wall over there, but couldn't find nobody to mount them without charging an arm and leg. How many nights you say?"

"One," Beetle said, taking out his wallet.

"Suit yourself." The man glanced at the wad of bills in the wallet sleeve. It was a discrete glance, no more than a flick of the eyes, easy to miss. But Beetle didn't miss much. "That'll be forty-nine ninety-nine," the man said reasonably. "Say, I'll make it an even forty nine, give you change for the soda machine."

"Forty nine bucks for one night, huh?" Beetle said just as reasonably.

The man nodded. "That's right."

"That the going rate, or the sucker rate?"

The man blinked. "Huh?"

"I asked you if that was the going rate, or the sucker rate?"

"The sucker rate?"

"Do I look like a sucker?"

"No, sir."

"Then why are you treating me like one?"

"No, sir, I'm not—"

Beetle grabbed the old man around the throat, moving fluidly and quickly. He pulled the shylock's face close to his own. "Let's do this again," he said quietly. "I'd like a room for the night."

"Nineteen...ninety-five..."

"You didn't ask me what type of room I'd like."

"They're all...same..."

Beetle stared into the shylock's terrified eyes. They had popped wide, blood vessels webbing the whites. Why he wanted to live so much, Beetle didn't know, didn't care. He didn't care about anything anymore—not even, he realized, getting ripped off in some shitty backwater motel.

Beetle released the old cheat, who stumbled away, wheezing, cowering. Then he slapped a twenty-dollar bill on the counter and scooped up the key.

Without looking back, Beetle crossed the reception to the staircase that led to the second floor. At the top of the stairs a bronze placard on the wall indicated that rooms 200-206 were to the left, 207-210 to the right. The key was labeled 209, so he went right. Pink carpet and floral wallpaper had replaced the hunter-green carpet and paneled wood of the reception. The spoiled cheese smell remained.

At his room Beetle inserted the key into the lock, opened the door, and flicked on the light. The interior was larger than he'd expected and included a kitchenette with wood-trimmed white cabinets. The lavender bedspread matched the upholstery on the armchair in the corner. A TV was bolted to a Formica table, next to a fake flower arrangement. White satin curtains that looked like they came from the inside of a coffin were drawn across the pair of doors that gave to the balcony.

Beetle upended his rucksack on the bed and messed through his clothes until he found the one-liter bottle of Stolichnaya vodka he'd bought at a Piggly Wiggly in Columbia that morning. He twisted off the cap, took a drink, and set the bottle next to the television set. Next he unzipped a toiletry bag and withdrew a matte black M9 Beretta and a fifteen-round magazine, which he set next to the booze.

Tonight, he decided in a vague, almost blasé way, not wanting to acknowledge what he was thinking. If he did, if he contemplated, reflected, felt, he would become too emotional, and he wouldn't do it. And it had to be done. Sooner or later, it had to be done.

Tonight.

Shrugging out of his fatigue shirt—WALKER written above the right breast pocket, US ARMY above the left—Beetle went to the bathroom and drew water for a hot shower.

Chapter 11

"We don't need a stretcher in there.
We need a mop!"
A Nightmare on Elm Street (1984)

"I just let go," Noah said monotonously, almost to himself. "I didn't push him. He was trying to take the hockey stick from me. I just let it go."

He and Steve were standing a few feet from the dead boy. Both had turned their backs to the body.

"That radiator shouldn't have been leaning there against the wall like that," Steve told him. "It was a hazard."

"Fuck!" Noah ran his hands up and down his face. "*Fuck!* I'm in deep shit, aren't I?"

"It was an accident."

"Yeah, an accident...an accident." He shook his head. "What the hell was he doing, Steve? Attacking us like that? We knocked on the door, didn't we? We called out, said we needed to use the phone. Robbers don't do that, do they? So what the fuck was his problem?" He shook his head again. "This is fucked. This is so totally fucked."

"Listen," Steve said, "I'm going to go give one last look upstairs for that phone. There were a couple rooms I didn't get to. If I can't find it, though, we need to get moving. We can explain what happened here to the cops after we get help for Jeff and Jenny."

Noah stiffened, his disposition instantly flipping from tempestuous to calculated. "Whoa, hold up a sec, Steve. Slow down. We haven't discussed this yet. I mean, what are we going to tell them?"

"The cops?" Steve said. "What do you mean? We're going to tell them the truth—the kid attacked you. He fell and knocked the radiator on his head."

Noah snorted. "You think they'll believe that?"

"That's what happened, man. What do you want to tell them?"

"I don't know. Maybe, I don't know...but why do we even need to mention the kid?"

Steve stared at him. "Because he's dead, Noah."

"I know that! But, look, nobody knows we've been here, right? Nobody knows we stopped. We can hide the body in the woods or something."

"Hide the body?" Steve said.

"He's already dead."

"Are you kidding me? Jesus Christ, Noah! We're not hiding his body in the woods. *This wasn't your fault.*"

"No one's going to believe—"

"It was an accident—"

"His teeth marks are in my fucking hand! Look!" Noah thrust his hand out so Steve could see the bloody wound. Several deep teeth punctures formed a half moon in his flesh. "How's that going to look, huh?"

"He attacked you. You were restraining him. It was self-defense."

"We broke into his house!"

"We were getting help for Jeff and Jenny. It was an emergency. The cops will understand that—"

"Dude!" Noah exclaimed. "We're a bunch of boozed-up out-of-towners. Jeff smashes his car while he's half soused and jumping from coke. Yeah, he was, did a couple lines when you and Jenny were under the bridge. You think the cops are going to have much sympathy for him? Much sympathy for *us* getting *him* help? Then another boozed-up out-of-towner—this one testing positive for pot—breaks into a house and kills a kid who's trying to protect his home from what he believes are burglars. Shit, Steve, the cops aren't going to be on our side in this. They're going to be gunning for us. What I did might not be premeditated murder, but it sure as hell is manslaughter. I'll go to prison."

Steve frowned. He hadn't thought about the full ramifications of their collective actions. But Noah was right, wasn't he? They'd been drinking. Not only that but Jeff was high on coke and Noah thoroughly stoned. "Fuck, Noah..." He cleared his throat. "Okay, let's say you're right. Okay? Maybe you're right. But hiding his body... It won't work. They'll find it. They'll have dogs."

Noah's eyes brightened, became intense. "Then we drive it somewhere, somewhere far away."

"There's blood all over the floor."

"We can clean it up," he said urgently, almost manically. "I'll clean it up right now." He jerked his head about, as if searching for a mop.

"No," Steve said, aware his dithering was encouraging his friend. "No," he added more firmly. "Forget it, Noah. Forget it."

"Dude!" Noah grabbed his arm. "We can do this!"

Steve tugged free. "We have to report this."

"We can't—"

"We're reporting this!"

"Jesus! Don't you—"

"Yeah, I do! I understand!" Steve said, stepping away, putting space between them. "And I'm sorry, Noah, but we're doing this right. We start lying, it's only going to get worse—a lot worse."

Noah shook his head disgustedly.

"It'll be okay," Steve told him. "It will." He softened his voice. "Don't worry, man. We'll sort this all out."

Then he was gone around the corner, back upstairs.

Noah remained where he was, thinking.

Lonnie Carlsbaugh shoved through the front doors of Randy's Bar-B-Q and tottered out into the cold, starless night to his car, trying his best to keep in a straight line. He had driven home from Randy's beer-eyed too many times to count, and he had no reservations about doing so this evening, even after polishing off what must have been seven or eight pints of Coors Extra Gold. Given that it was that time of month again—that time being the end of the month—he had no cash on hand and put the beers on his tab. Randy knew he was good for it. One thing Lonnie did, and did well, was pay his debts. Every two weeks, after receiving his workers' compensation check from the government, he would stop by Randy's for a beer and to clear his tab. Keith and Buck and Daryl and his other pals would show up throughout the course of the evening to get away from their wives, and he'd square up with them whatever he owed them from their Tuesday night Texas Hold 'Em games. This would usually leave him with just enough money to pay any outstanding utility bills and pick up a few groceries. He didn't eat much himself, but his son Scottie could eat a man out of house and home. Last week Scottie's cunt of a schoolteacher had the nerve to call up Lonnie in the middle of the day, like he had nothing better to do than waste his time talking to her, and ask if Scottie was eating breakfast because he had been caught stealing his classmates' snacks at recess time. She also blamed what she called "hunger pains" for his rowdy behavior and poor attention span. Lonnie told the stupid cunt Scottie was eating just fine, had eggs every morning. And that was mostly true. He ate whatever the hen laid. That was usually one egg, but sometimes it might be two. And on the days the hen laid a zero—well, how was that Lonnie's fault? He couldn't control the biology of a chicken. He wasn't fucking God, was he?

It really pissed Lonnie off, Scottie's teachers calling him up like they did. Didn't they understand he was a single father doing the best he could for the boy? Georgina, his wife and the boy's ma, had died in childbirth from something the doctors had a big fancy word for. That had been shitty luck. Georgina might not have been a looker, but her family had money coming out of their collective gazoo. Her parents bought him and Georgie the house for their wedding gift, and furnished it with stock from one of their furniture stores. Lonnie had been in the crosshairs to manage one of those stores. But when Georgie died the family didn't want anything to do with him or Scottie. So he was stuck raising the boy by himself. And it hadn't been easy either. No sir. But he'd done it, hadn't he? He'd raised

Scottie fine and well. So what if the boy had a few behavioral problems. Hell, all kids did. What was a parent to do about that? Let them live and learn and fend for themselves, was Lonnie's mantra. That's how you built character. That's how Lonnie's father raised Lonnie, and he'd turned out all right.

Lonnie made it to his rusted puke-green Buick Skylark without falling on his ass and spent a good ten seconds finding the right key to unlock the door. He dropped in behind the steering wheel with a great sigh of satisfaction. His eyes drifted closed, and when he realized this, they snapped back open. He slapped himself across the face to wake himself up, got the car going, and reversed, bumping off a particularly high part of curb. The Skylark's back bumper kissed the road loudly.

Lonnie mumbled something incomprehensible, shoved the column shifter into drive, and accelerated. He didn't drive too fast because clouds of fog hung low over the streets, turning the largely residential neighborhood into something out of a monster movie. At the corner he turned left onto Westside Lane. Some of the houses he passed had jack-o-lanterns sitting in their front windows or out on their front stoops, though only two were lit from within with candles.

Halfway down the block Lonnie spotted his first trick-or-treaters: a little girl dressed as a princess with fairy wings sprouting from her back and a little boy dressed in a full-body tiger suit with a limp tail that dragged on the sidewalk. The mother walked a few feet behind them. She was on the chubby side, but not a bad looker. Lonnie had seen her around town before. You saw everyone around town now and then in a township of nine hundred souls. He thought she might work at the art gallery on Edgeview Street, but he couldn't be sure because he'd never gone in, only glanced through the window when walking past on random occasions.

Seeing the woman and her kids made Lonnie think about Scottie again. He'd promised to take the boy trick-or-treating tonight. Scottie had even made a mask to wear. Lonnie frowned. How had he forgotten? Well, he hadn't, had he? Not really. It was more a case of time getting away from him. He went to Randy's for a couple beers, and those couple beers turned into eight. What was he supposed to do about that? He couldn't control time, let alone turn back the clock. He wasn't fucking God, was he?

Maybe he'd buy Scottie a chocolate bar tomorrow, surprise him with it at dinner? Sure, that was a good idea. He'd get him one of those Twix bars he liked, because there were two cookies in the package, which made him think he was getting more bang for his buck.

Lonnie made a right onto Mayapple Drive, then a left on Colony Drive, passing six more trick-or-treaters. Then he was on Stanford Road, leaving Boston Hills behind him.

Trees closed in around him, their canopy blotting out the silvered light from the full moon. He flicked on the high beams and kept the speedometer needle at sixty miles an hour. The fog was just as bad as it had been in town, and although there might no longer be kids to worry about, there were plenty of deer in these parts, and some of them were plain suicidal. Last summer he'd been driving back from Randy's in the early hours of the morning, nicely licked and minding nobody's business but his own, when a whitetail bounded right in front of him, like it got its wires crossed or something. It took out the car's left headlight, crunched the bumper, but at least had the courtesy to die in the process. Lonnie tossed it in the trunk, happy to feast on choice cuts of venison for the next while. The following day he noticed the damage to the car, of course, the blood and fur glued to the broken headlight, but he had no memory of the accident. By the time he discovered the carcass in the trunk a week later it was covered in a squiggling film of maggots, and he had to scoop the goopy remains out with a shovel.

Anyway, a run-in with a suicidal deer wasn't the only reason Lonnie was driving cautiously. He needed time to react, slow down, block the road, if those out-of-towners came his way. Lonnie didn't know why Cleavon couldn't tell him whether they were lookers or not, but Cleavon was like that, a rancorous old crabapple who'd bitch if you hung him with a new rope. Still, if any of the does were half as pretty as the last one—Betty Wilfried, according to her driver's license—he'd be a happy man. It was a shame pretty Betty had gotten so beat up in the crash. Weasel had been too aggressive, scared her a bit too much, because she'd smashed her car bad enough to break half the bones in her body and face. Still, Lonnie hadn't complained. A fuck was a fuck, and broken or not, Betty Wilfried had been a great fuck.

Noah knew Steve was wrong, he couldn't fess up, they had to get rid of the body. Otherwise he was facing prison time—and what was the prison sentence for manslaughter? Five years? Ten? Hell, even one year would be too long. He'd be locked up with murderers and rapists, people who'd been in the slammer before, knew the system, knew how to work the guards. He'd know nothing. He'd be alone, surrounded by sheetrock and iron bars and gang members aligned from the housing projects they came from. They'd each want a piece of a young, straight kid like himself. Some big black or Latino dude trapping him in the shower and telling him how much he was going to love their good time up his sugah ass. And when he wasn't getting raped he would likely be getting the piss beat out of him in the exercise yard, or the cafeteria, maybe even in his own goddamn cell. Because he'd be a kid killer, pretty low on the totem pole. It wouldn't matter that the boy's death had been an accident. The lowlifes he was locked up with would believe what they wanted to believe, rumors would swirl, accounts would become embellished. He'd be finished. Hell, he likely wouldn't make it to the end of his sentence alive.

And in the off chance he did...what then?

He could kiss his career in sculpting goodbye. No respectable gallery owner would display his work. He'd be a kid killer in their eyes too, only they wouldn't need to turn him into some depraved pedophile to feel superior. Smashing in the skull of a little boy while drunk and high would be bad enough on its own in their civilized circles.

So what would he do? Get a nine-to-five job? Then again, who would hire him? He'd have to check that little box on all his future employment applications that asked if you had a criminal record.

Why couldn't Steve just cut him a break? All he had to do was turn a blind eye to what had happened, let him hide the body in the forest. Was that so much to ask? The kid was gone. Why ruin a second life?

"What the fuck were you doing?" he said quietly to the dead boy. "Why the fuck were you attacking us, you stupid shit?"

Suddenly, before his eyes, the boy's jeans darkened around his crotch. Noah stared, incredulous, terrified. He bent close and detected the acrid odor of urine.

He was *peeing?*

Feeling suddenly sick, Noah hurried to the front door, threw it open, and stepped onto the veranda. Cool air caressed his face, but this did little to calm him. He stumbled blindly to the banister and leaned over the railing. His stomach slammed his esophagus, acid burned a trail up his throat, and he vomited a jet of watery gunk. This went on for five or ten seconds, one abdomen contraction after the next, a biological pump, until there was nothing left to spew.

Groaning, Noah wiped the heel of his hand across his lips—and made out two headlights approaching along the highway. Instead of continuing past, however, the vehicle slowed, then turned onto the driveway.

"Steve?" Noah shouted in a rubbery voice. "*Steve!* Get down here!"

Steve took the steps downstairs two at a time and saw Noah standing outside on the veranda. He stopped next to him and stared in surprise at the car coming toward them through the fog. He recalled the kid's words: *Pa's coming back right now, and you're gonna be in deep shit.*

"What should we do?" Noah said. He had gone white as a ghost.

"I'll tell them," Steve said.

"I killed their kid," Noah said.

"I'll tell them," Steve repeated.

The car shuddered to a stop next to Noah's Jeep. The door flung open and a smallish man appeared. He had warthog hair sprouting from a balding crown, a turned-up nose, and a sallow complexion. He wore sagging jean and a hounds-tooth jacket over a faded red T-shirt.

He scowled at them. "Who s'hell you?" he said, slurring his words.

Steve said, "We've had an accident—"

"It's just the two of you? No one else? No girlfriends?"

Steve and Noah exchanged confused glances.

"Well?" the man demanded.

"We've had an accident," Steve continued. "Two of our friends are injured. We saw this house, a light was on, we thought we could use the phone and call the police."

The man's eyes glinted suspiciously. "Well, did ya?"

"Do you live here?"

"What's that to ya?"

"A boy lives here."

"My son, Scottie. And I'll ask you again—what's that to ya?"

"You son told us you don't have a phone."

The man smiled triumphantly, revealing stained, barnacle teeth. "That's right," he said. "Don't got no phone. Who the hell I need to call?"

"Your son," Steve said, swallowing the tightness in his throat, "started to attack us with a hockey stick. My friend tried to take the stick from him. There was an accident."

The man squinted. "What kind of accident?"

"Sir, I'm sorry. Your son is dead."

"He's *what?*"

"It was an accident. He bumped into a radiator. It fell on him."

The man stood there, staring at Steve like he was speaking Klingon. Then he clicked back to reality and bounded up the steps. "Scottie?" he shouted. "Scottie?"

Steve and Noah stepped aside as the man shoved past them, leaving a trail of cheap cologne in his wake. He went inside the house. "Scottie? *Scottie!*"

Steve stared at his feet as he listened to the man wail and blubber and finally break down in sobs. Then he went quiet. Steve glanced at Noah. He was staring off into the trees. Moonlight glinted off his tear-streaked cheeks.

The man appeared in the doorway. His eyes were bloodshot. Snot hung from his nose, stringing off his chin. "Who did that?" he barked hoarsely.

"I did," Noah said.

"You killed my boy?"

Noah didn't answer.

"*You killed my boy?*"

"It was an accident," Steve said.

The man whirled on him. "An accident? An accident! He don't got no head no more!"

"I'm sorry—"

"Sorry? You're sorry? I'll show you sorry." He hastened down the steps to his car.

Under his breath Steve said, "I think we should get out of here."

Noah rubbed his eyes and nodded.

In the next instance, however, the man withdrew a rifle from his car. He locked it into his shoulder, pressed his cheek to the side of the stock, and took aim at Noah through the open sight. "I'll see you in hell, boy," he said.

Noah's hands shot up. "Wait wait wait—"

The man rocked the bolt to and fro, feeding a round into the rifle's chamber, and fired. The report was like a canon blast. Noah flew backward against the house. His left hand crashed through the living room window, and he crumpled to the ground.

"Noah!" Steve shouted, dropping to his knees. "Noah?" He tilted his friend's head back. A circular hole rimmed with abraded skin and leaking blood marked the center of Noah's forehead like a bulls-eye. His eyes were open and unseeing.

He had died instantly.

Heart pounding, barely able to breathe, Steve bumbled backward like a crab, trying to stand but finding his legs uncooperative. The man tromped up the steps, pointing the rifle at him. He cycled the bolt, ejecting the spent casing. It struck the lumber planking with a plaintive clink.

"Fuck you!" Steve shouted in crazy defiance. "You fucking redneck piece of shit! You killed him! You killed my friend!"

"And you're next, boy," the man snarled as he closed one wild eye, taking aim through the rifle's sight once more.

Chapter 12

"I warned you not to go out tonight."
Maniac (1980)

Panting, her throat flayed raw, Mandy stumbled to a stop before a small butte overgrown with vegetation. She glanced behind her, saw nothing but the dark outlines of tree trunks in the ethereal fog, and sagged to all fours. She crawled forward and pressed her back against the rock wall, wanting to blend into it. She was so deep in shock her brain and lungs felt encased in ice. She couldn't think or make sense of anything.

She waited, listened, every nerve ending tingling, alert. The night was graveyard silent. She didn't hear any sound of pursuit. She considered continuing on, putting as much distance between her and the freaks as possible, yet she didn't think she could coax her body into getting up. She'd only been running for one minute, two at most, yet she was out of breath and exhausted. She might be thin, and look fit and healthy on the outside, but her insides were a different matter altogether. The last time she'd gone for a run—a real run with warm-up stretches and Lycra tights and Nike joggers—would have been as a junior in high school. She'd been nothing but skin and bones then. Her mother had told her this countless times at the dinner table when she refused to finish her meals. "You're nothing but skin and bones, Mandy," she would say, looking over the top of her bifocals at her in an uncanny impression of a cross librarian. "No man is going to take a stick-and-bones woman for a wife. Men want femininity, fertility, and that means breasts, hips. Even a nice round tush wouldn't hurt. Now, eat up." Whether it was from eating more, or family genes (her mother had been a buxom, curvaceous woman—until the last stages of the cancer, that was) Mandy had definitely developed the breasts, hips, and tush. But in those younger days, as a twelve-year-old girl, it wouldn't have been hard imagining a strong gust of wind picking her up and blowing her halfway down the block.

Healthy on the outside...rotten on the inside.

Nevertheless, Mandy had gotten away from Cleavon and his brothers. She was safe. As long as she remained still and didn't make any noise, they wouldn't find her—

She made out a distant yellow light arcing back and forth in the fog. Her lungs shucked up in her chest.

For a few moments the light seemed to be angling away from her. Then, to her horror, it bee-lined back in her direction. It came closer, growing larger and brighter.

Mandy watched it, hypnotized. Her muscles stiffened as she prepared to flee. She eased herself onto her knees but froze when the leaf litter crackled beneath her weight. It sounded as loud as a gunshot in the still forest.

She couldn't run, she realized. The person with the flashlight was too close. He would hear her, then see her. He would catch her.

The light came closer.

She pressed her back flat against the rock wall. The person—Floyd? Earl? Cleavon?—was now so close she could hear him. He was stepping heavily, batting branches, making no effort at stealth.

Abruptly he stopped. An unbearable silence ensued. Mandy was sure he had spotted her. But then he aimed the flashlight into the canopy. Maybe he'd heard an animal, a raccoon or possum, or maybe he thought she'd climbed a tree.

He lost interest in the leafless boughs a moment later and started forward once more, sweeping the flashlight beam to his left and right, methodically searching the mist-shrouded night. He couldn't be any more than twenty feet away. If he kept his path he would spot her. She was certain of that. A few more steps and he would cry out in triumph and charge her. She should have run when she had the chance. She should have ignored her exhaustion. What were a few minutes of discomfort when your life hung in the balance? Surely she could have pushed on, gotten a second breath—

"Cleave?" the man who was now only fifteen feet away shouted. It sounded like Earl. Mandy's stomach dropped as she waited for him to say, "Found her!" Instead he added, "She's gone!"

There was no reply for a long moment. Then Cleavon's voice, gruff and distant, told him to come back.

Mandy said a silent prayer of thanks even as Earl bounced the flashlight beam back and forth a final time. It stopped directly on her, blinding her. She felt as lit up as a fly on a television screen.

If she could have worked her lungs, she would have screamed. If she could have moved her limbs, she would have fled. But she could do neither. She was paralyzed with fear—and it was this instinct that ultimately saved her. Because Earl hadn't seen her after all. The beam moved off her, the footsteps started away.

Mandy expelled the breath she'd been holding and shook uncontrollably.

Mandy remained where she was for another five minutes, making sure Earl's departure wasn't a trick to lure her out of hiding. When she didn't hear or see anything more of him, she decided she was safe.

She sagged with relief. She had never contemplated dying before. But while frozen there, pinned in the flashlight beam, she'd been convinced it was the end. She was going to die.

Mandy—no more.

She couldn't get her mind around this possibility. She couldn't grasp the concept of not being. Maybe older people could. Maybe the longer you lived, the more familiar and understanding you became of whatever awaited you. You came to accept it, the way you came to accept aging.

Nevertheless, Mandy was too young for all this. It was as alien to her as the starving African children on those TV infomercials. She'd watched the LiveAid concert with Bob Geldolf and Michael Jackson a couple years before. She knew about the famine and disease over there. But she hadn't been able to relate to the images she saw. Babies were supposed to be chubby and gay, not emaciated and buzzing with flies. It had been too far removed from her world. She'd acknowledged that it happened, but tuned out immediately, just as she had always tuned out thoughts on death when they became too philosophical. Even when her mother died, she had not allowed herself to dwell on what became of her soul. Of course she had been overwhelmed with sadness, but at eleven years of age, it was the sadness of loss, of loneliness, nothing deeper.

Slowly, carefully, Mandy stood. She felt strangely energized, like she could run a marathon. *She was alive.* Suddenly the concept of living was as invigorating as the concept of death was frightening.

She took a deep breath and tried to figure out what to do next. She couldn't remain where she was. Cleavon and his brothers might resume their search for her in the morning when, without the cover of nightfall, she would be much more exposed and vulnerable.

She contemplated finding her way to the highway. She could flag down a passing car, get a ride into town. Then again, wasn't that what Cleavon would expect her to do? What if he collected his car from the "ol' McGrady house" and prowled the roads for her. She could unwittingly flag him down, just as the distressed damsel always flagged down her tormentor in the movies.

Could she walk all the way to town then? She had no idea how far Boston Mills was, but right then she was determined to walk all night if she had to. She could keep to the verge. If a vehicle came along, she could duck into the woods and hide until it passed—

She nearly slapped her hand against her forehead when she realized what she'd overlooked.

Steve and Noah!

They were likely already on their way back with help. Paramedics, police officers, firefighters. She had to get to the road, wave them down, warn them about Cleavon and his brothers. She wouldn't be fooled. She'd recognize a police cruiser, or an ambulance. Their lights would be flashing, their klaxons blaring.

With fresh determination, Mandy went searching for the road.

Chapter 13

"That cold ain't the weather.
That's death approaching."
30 Days of Night (2007)

Cleavon was pacing back and forth in the middle of the road when he spotted a pair of headlights beyond the veil of fog. He moved to the gravel shoulder so Jesse didn't run him over and waved his arms above his head. The two orbs of white grew brighter until Jesse's Chevy El Camino appeared and hunkered to a stop before him. Jesse left the engine running as he hopped out one door, Weasel the other.

Jesse was an owlish looking man who always had his head stuck forward and always looked like he had a question on his mind. His big-framed, thick-lensed eyeglasses made his eyes look bigger than they were, while his perpetually puckered kisser made the rest of his face look smaller. He was freshly shaven and wore a beige jacket zippered to his chin against the chill. He liked to tell people he was the CEO of his own company, and he was, technically. What he didn't tell people was that the company was a one-man operation called JG Outhouse Kleanin Kompany. He also didn't tell people, if they asked, how he got the third-degree burns on his arms. He probably wouldn't have told anybody, ever, had Randy not read about it in the *Akron Beacon Journal.* According to the story, which was now framed behind glass and hanging on the wall of Randy's pub, Jesse had been working on an emergency toilet hole cleanup job in the middle of the night and had decided he'd needed light and lit a match while down in the hole. He was only lucky he'd been wearing a half-face respirator and goggles, or his face would have gone the way of his arms.

Weasel was still a kid, twenty-one next month, ferret-faced and thin as a rail. God knew why he grew that long-ass goatee, because it made him look all the more feral. He was bushy eyed and eager to please and more times than not dumber than a bucket of coal. He wasn't a retard like Earl or Floyd, but he was prone to doing stupid shit—like what he did earlier this evening. Cleavon didn't think Spencer should have given him so much responsibility in the first place. But nobody else wanted the job of skulking Stanford Road for does. High speed chases were dangerous, even if you were the chaser.

Weasel's folks ran a café and restaurant over in Peninsula. It was successful enough they opened another larger restaurant in Akron, where they moved to a few years back. Weasel remained behind in the family house, receiving a comfortable allowance every month for doing nothing but sitting on his ass all day. Why someone so stupid got such a lucky break in life, Cleavon didn't know. Cleavon himself had worked like a son of a bitch for most of his miserable life, and he'd never once been given a break.

"That them?" Jesse said, looking at the bodies lying on the ground some twenty yards away and illuminated by the fire from the blazing wreckage: Cueball, the mocha-skinned girl, Cherry, and the handsome cripple. The way they were lined up side by side, they resembled corpses waiting for their coffins.

"'Course that's them," Cleavon said. "Who the fuck else they gonna be?"

"What I meant is, where's the rest of them?"

"Already gone when me and the boys arrived." Cleavon scowled at Weasel. "You see how you fucked up, Weasel? You see what you did now?"

Weasel stared at his boots. "I know I fucked up, Cleave, and I said I'm sorry."

"Sorry, huh? They get to town, if Lonnie don't stop them and they get to town..." He shook his head. He wasn't going to entertain that thought right now. "Jess, you bring the fire extinguisher?"

"Ayuh. On the back seat."

"Weasel, go put out the fire. You can do that, can't you?"

"Yeah, Cleave." He started toward the burning car.

"You gonna put it out with your fuckin' hands? Get the extinguisher!"

Weasel blushed. "Right, Cleave." He opened the back door, grabbed the red fire extinguisher, and trotted toward the burning car.

"That boy got about as much sense as God gave a goose," Cleavon muttered.

"Ayuh," Jesse said, though he was still looking at the three bodies. Given the hungry glint in his eyes, Cleavon suspected he was looking more at Cherry than the other two. Sprawled how she was, her denim skirt pushed up her thighs, she was showing more than leg.

Just then Earl and Floyd emerged from the forest, their flashlights pointed at the ground ahead of them, their heads lowered. They knew they were in trouble and trying to play ostrich. Fucking retards.

"Earl!" Cleavon shouted, cupping his hands around his mouth. "Get your ass over here."

"The hell they doing in the woods?" Jesse said.

"Looking for the one that got away."

Jesse raised his eyebrows. "The one that got away?"

"I had the bitch by the throat, I *had* her, then she goes and kicks me right where it hurts and got away."

"Shit, Cleave, how we gonna find her?"

"We're not, not now," he said. "Where she gonna go? It's the others we need to think about right now. We gotta deal with them first. Then we can worry about finding the bitch."

Earl approached in his lumbering size-sixteen-boot gait, red-faced and out of breath. Floyd was behind him, also huffing and puffing. Unless you gave Floyd a direct order—one he could understand, mind you—he'd simply follow Earl everywhere.

"We couldn't find her, Cleave," Earl said shyly, staring at his boots. "She took off like a rabbit, and we couldn't find her. If you didn't let her go, if you didn't do that, we woulda had her, we woulda had everyone. Why'd you let her go, Cleave? She's nothing but a girl."

Cleavon wanted to kick Earl in the nuts and see how quickly he reacted afterward, but he didn't dare. Earl had a temper like you'd never seen. You get him worked up, you better be faster than a striped-ass ape. It wasn't that Earl got it in his head to kill you; he simply might do it unintentionally. He didn't realize his own strength, or if he did, he forgot about it when he got worked up and emotional.

Back when Cleavon was twenty or thereabouts he'd been feuding with Earl over some fucking thing and had gone into Earl's room and took his pet mouse from the aquarium and cut off the thing's head with a straight razor. Earl, only fifteen but already huge, caught Cleavon red-handed and went crazy, tossing the bed out of the way to get at him. He slammed Cleavon against the wall hard enough to knock all the pictures to the floor. Then he heaved Cleavon up like he weighed nothing and launched him straight out the second-floor window. Luckily it had been winter then, and a couple feet of snowfall had cushioned Cleavon's fall. Still, he'd broken his left arm and split open his chin against his knee. When Cleavon came back from the doctor's with a cast on his arm and stitches in his chin, Earl had been profusely apologetic, said he hadn't meant to hurt him, wouldn't do it again. Since then he had lost his temper only a few other times. This wasn't due to discipline on his part as much as everybody else having the good sense not to provoke him. You could call Earl a shithead all you wanted, but you didn't go kicking him in the nuts, no matter how much he was smarting off, not if you wanted to be walking the next day.

"Shut your yabbering and listen to me, Earl," Cleavon said, feeling as though time was getting away from them all too fast. "You, Floyd, and Weasel are going to take those three there back to the house. Then you come back here with the wrecker and get what's left of the bimmer to the garage. You got that?"

"Sure, Cleave. That's easy. And back at the house, can I, I mean, I've been thinking, and I'm wondering, I know you're gonna say no—"

"Spit it out, man!"

"Can I give the bucks to Toad and Trapper."

Cleavon stared at him. "To your *snakes*?"

"Can I, Cleave, please? They just shed, they're real hungry—"

"Judas Priest! You must be dumber than you look! There ain't no way those snakes can eat a full-grown man."

"Sure they can, Cleave, they can easy. Trapper's twenty-six feet now. Toad's only a bit shorter, I just measured them last month. They can eat the bucks easy."

Cleavon frowned, thinking about that. They were damn big snakes. Monsters. If they could eat fully grown humans, well, that would be two less graves to dig.

"Also," Earl went on, "it'd mean they don't need to eat no rabbits for a couple months, and more rabbits equals more money for us, that's what you always say—"

"All right, all right, enough yabbering, for fuck's sake! You wanna feed baldy and the cripple to your snakes, feed them to your snakes. Just don't lay a hand on the girl. That means no 'playing' with her either. I swear to God, Earl, I find one mark on her when I get back, I don't know, but I'll tell Spence it was you this time, no more covering, and he'll kick you out of the club forever. You got that, Earl?"

Earl nodded solemnly. "I won't touch her, Cleave. I promise."

"Your promise ain't worth shit," Cleavon said. "You just remember, you touch her, no more does, never." He turned to Jesse. "C'mon."

They climbed in the cab of the El Camino just as a light rain began to fall, and within moments they were speeding north along Stanford Road, on their way to Lonnie's place.

Chapter 14

"Be afraid... Be very afraid."
The Fly (1986)

When Jenny came around on the back seat of Noah's Jeep, she couldn't make out whether what she was hearing was animal or human. It took her a good fuzzy three or four seconds to realize it was the latter—the warbling, forlorn cries of a man suffering great anguish. Thinking of Jeff, his broken back, she sat up quickly and cried out herself as a bomb seemed to go off inside her head. She moaned and sank back in the seat, afraid to move for fear of setting off another bomb. She remained like this, stationary, until the pain receded and her vision cleared.

The horrible wails, she noticed, had ceased. She leaned forward gingerly and peered through the rain-specked windshield. Steve stood next to Noah on the veranda of some house. A grimy little man pushed between them and stomped down the porch steps. Jenny barely had time to wonder who he was before he reached into the car parked next to the Jeep, retrieved a rifle, and aimed it at Noah.

Jenny didn't scream a warning, didn't jump out of the Jeep and tackle the man from behind. She didn't do any of this because everything inside her had ceased to work. Fear and confusion and disbelief had shut her down, made her a spectator in what was about to play out.

The man fired the rifle. The report was a toneless bang, like a firecracker. Noah collapsed. Steve shouted his name. The man started toward them.

Jenny broke her paralysis and fumbled with the door handle. She thrust the door open and fell out of the vehicle, landing on her hands and knees on the damp gravel driveway. The air reeked of cordite smoke. Light raindrops plinked off the nape of her neck. For a split second she considered turning toward the road and fleeing, running as fast and far as she could, because she didn't know what was going on here, only that it was bad, really bad, and Noah might be dead and she might be too if she stuck around. Yet even as she contemplated this she was scrambling forward. She hit the porch steps on all fours and used the banister to pull herself to her feet.

The man had stopped a few feet ahead of her, oblivious to her presence, rifle pointed at Steve. He was saying something, but Jenny didn't know what, couldn't make sense of words right then, and it didn't matter, because he was about to shoot Steve in cold blood.

"No!" she cried, throwing herself at the back of the man. She grabbed him by the shoulders and used her weight to drag him backward off balance. The rifle swung skyward as he fired. The bullet spit a chunk of wood from the porch roof.

Jenny crashed to her side. The man came down on top of her. He elbowed her in the gut, knocking her down the steps. She brought her arms up to protect her head, but still smacked her cheek against one tread hard enough to see stars and taste blood in her mouth. At the bottom she rose on her knees, expecting to hear another gunshot and to feel a round tear through her.

Instead she found Steve grappling with the grimy little man for the rifle. Bellowing like a caveman, Steve tore the gun free, shoved the barrel into the man's stomach, and squeezed the trigger. The bullet passed straight through the man, exiting his back in a jet of blood. The man clutched his gut and fell facefirst to the deck.

Jenny scrambled up the steps toward Steve. He jerked the rifle at her. His eyes were glassy and sightless, like a doll's, empty of whatever made him him.

"Steve! It's me! Jenny!"

Steve returned his attention to the now dead man, who lay on his stomach, blood pooling around him. He tossed the rifle away, as if it had burned him.

"He killed Noah," he said softly.

Jenny glanced at Noah, crumpled against the wall, his head bowed against his chest, as if he were snoozing. But he'd never be snoozing again, would he? He'd never be doing anything again. She hadn't known any of Steve's friends well, had met them for the first time this evening, but Noah had seemed most normal of the bunch. Jeff was a shmuck who thought he was God's gift to women. Austin was immature, and from what Steve had told her, a borderline alcoholic. Mandy was funny but an airhead. And Cherry, well, she was named "Cherry" and dressed like a prostitute to boot. It was only Noah—soft spoken, dark, brooding, Noah—whom she had thought she would be happy getting to know better in the future, especially if he found a nice girlfriend and the four of them could double date.

"Are you sure he's dead?" she asked, the words coming out wooden.

"The fucker shot him right in the forehead." He drove a foot into the man's side.

The man groaned.

"He's alive!" Jenny said, and felt his neck for a pulse. "Steve, he's alive!" She slipped her hands beneath the arm closest to her and flipped the man onto his back. His red T-shirt was saturated with blood. "Give me your pullover."

"Why?"

"To stop the bleeding!"

Steve came back from wherever he'd been. "Stop the bleeding?" His brow knit. "Let him bleed! Fuck, Jen! He killed Noah! He tried to kill us!"

"You're a medical student, Steve. You have a duty to—"

"Don't give me that bullshit."

"You want to have his death on your hands? Is that what you want?"

"It was self-defense."

"That's not what I meant. Christ, Steve!" She tugged her black elastic top over her head. She had nothing on beneath but her bra. The cool air bit her bare skin.

"Okay, Jesus, okay, Jen, here..." Steve removed his pullover and held it out for her.

She put her top back on, accepted the pullover, and pressed it against the man's abdomen. "This is only going to give him a bit more time. You have to go call an ambulance."

"There's no phone."

She stared at him. "What?"

"Noah and I already checked. That's what started all this..." He shook his head. "Anyway, we checked. And the kid said they didn't have one—"

"The kid? Where—"

"He's dead. It was an accident."

Jenny felt as if she'd been slapped. *A dead child?* But she didn't have time to wonder about this. The medical student inside her had taken over. The man before her was still alive. He could still be saved. He was the priority. It was her duty to help him.

"Get Noah's keys," she said. "We'll drive him to the hospital ourselves. We'll tell them about this child, and Jeff, and— Jesus, just get the keys!"

Nodding, Steve stood and said, "Oh shit."

"What?" But she saw what he did.

A car had turned off the highway and was bumping down the driveway toward them in one heck of a hurry.

Steve picked up the rifle and held it across his chest so it was clearly visible. Jenny was asking him what he was doing. He wasn't listening. Every instinct in his body was telling him that this wasn't right, that he was in danger. He couldn't say why this might be the case, not right then, not keyed up on adrenaline and stressed out of his mind with horror and grief. But now was not the time to question his instincts.

The approaching vehicle sported the roofline of a sedan and the flatbed of a pickup. It skidded to a halt behind the Jeep and Buick. Both front doors opened and two men emerged. The driver was bookish and harmless looking, and Steve might have let down his guard had it not been for the other man. He was tall, maybe six feet. Beneath shoulder-length greasy black hair he had a hard, no-bullshit face, and beneath a protruding brow he had hard, no-bullshit eyes to match. The muttonchops and handlebar mustache shouted "redneck," and he might have been a comical stereotype had he not been so...hard. That was the word that kept coming back to Steve. Hard.

Steve tightened his grip on the rifle.

"Jesus Mary!" the bookish man exclaimed. "Lonnie? That Lonnie? You shot Lonnie, you sumbitch!"

"Who are you?" Steve demanded.

"Who'm I? Who'm I? You shot Lonnie, you motherfucker!"

The hard man held up his hand, signaling the other to calm down. "We're from next door," he said. His manner wasn't pleasant, but it wasn't angry or disapproving either. It was like a cop's: cool but alert, aloof but calculating. "We heard the gunshot, came to see what happened. He dead?"

"He's alive," Jenny said. "He needs to get to the hospital."

"Right-o." He took a step forward.

Steve pointed the rifle at him. "Stop."

The man stopped.

"Steve!" Jenny said. "They can help!"

"Jenny, get inside."

"Steve—"

"Get inside!"

"Whoa there," the hard man said. "That's no way to speak to a lady."

"How many gunshots did you hear?"

The man didn't smile, not quite, but his face twitched, as if he were smiling to himself, and Steve knew right then it didn't matter the answer he gave, he was dangerous. The man's eyes flicked from Noah to the man named Lonnie and he said, "Two."

"Jenny, get inside," Steve repeated.

This time she didn't argue. She stood and backed up slowly. Steve backed up also.

"Now, say," the hard man said. "What's the matter?"

"I don't know who you are or why you're here," Steve said, "but you come any closer, I'll shoot you." He pulled the stock tighter against his shoulder.

"Hey, okay, take it easy—"

Stumbling backward across the threshold into the house, Steve slammed the front door shut, flicked the thumblock, and shot the bolt.

Chapter 15

"Good Ash, bad Ash. I'm the guy with the gun."
Army of Darkness (1992)

Beetle turned off the shower taps and dried himself with the towel he'd draped over the curtain rod. He wrapped the towel around his waist and stepped over the lip of the bathtub. Steam had turned the mirror above the sink opaque. He cleared a circle with his hand to view his reflection. He ran his fingers over a few of the shrapnel scars that tattooed his chest and right shoulder. He hated the sight of them, the feel of them. They reminded him that he should have died with the rest of his platoon on the beach in Grenada. He wished he had too. Sarah would have remembered him fondly, with love. She would not have grown to hate him. They would have avoided all the pain and suffering of the last two years.

It could have been different, of course—Grenada, his life with Sarah, everything. If the chopper hadn't missed the designated beach drop-off in front of the university campus, if it hadn't set down hundreds of yards away in the middle of enemy territory, the mission to rescue the American students could have gone as planned. But that was the thing with life: there were no second chances, no rewinding time.

Burt Jackson and Big Dave died within seconds of each other. Small arms fire erased their faces, flinging them to the ground and knocking off their helmets. Shortly after this a mortar round blew Oklahoma Eddy to confetti. The detonation was close enough to Beetle it charged the air around him and splattered him with Eddy's blood and guts.

The rest of the platoon was slaughtered in a similar fashion. In the chaos and confusion only Beetle and two other Rangers made it to the shanties beyond the shoreline, where they escaped into the zigzag of back streets and hunkered down in a derelict café. Otter, an anti-tank gunner, had been shot in the back, Pips, a sniper, in the leg. Beetle put pressure on Pip's wound and told him he was going to be okay, lies, he knew, because the bullet had severed a main artery or vein. Pips died listening to those lies a few minutes later. Knowing Otter was next if he didn't receive proper medical attention, Beetle set off on his own to the nearby abandoned Russian Embassy in the hopes of finding a two-way radiotelephone. He killed two Cuban soldiers he came across with his bare hands so as not to raise an alarm and reached the embassy undetected. Inside he discovered the power was out and retrieved a first-aid kit as consolation. While leaving he turned a corner and bumped chest-to-chest into a lone Russian diplomat.

Beetle recognized him immediately. The day before the man had driven alone to Point Salines to deliver an official message from his government to the senior American commander at the recently captured airfield. Beetle and another Ranger had searched him and his car. He had been polite and respectful and thanked them when they finished their search and handed him back his wallet, inside of which he carried a photograph of two daughters, one attractive, the other not so much.

The diplomat didn't recognize Beetle, not bloody and dusty, his face painted in black camouflage, his eyes alight with the craziness of watching several of his brothers die and killing two men with his bare hands, all within the last hour.

The diplomat tried to run. Beetle caught him easily and tied him up with telephone cord. It took him ten minutes of agonizing before he worked himself up to kill the man. It had to be done, he told himself. He didn't know how long he and Otter were going to have to hide out on the small island, behind enemy lines. It could be weeks or months. The man might be a civilian, and a father of two, but he was still allied with the enemy.

Beetle killed him as he had the Cubans, wrapping his arms around the man's head from behind and twisting sharply to the right. Back at the café Beetle disinfected Otter's wound and bandaged him up. They spoke of their families until they fell asleep, but when Beetle woke in the middle of the night, Otter was dead.

The following day US Forces took control of Grenada, the leader of the rebellion was captured, and just like that the invasion was over—and Beetle was sent home to resume life as normal.

A knock at the door caused Beetle to jump. He realized he'd been staring at his reflection for five minutes or so. Long enough, at any rate, for the mist to clear from the mirror.

Beetle exited the bathroom. The door to the hallway didn't have a peephole.

"Yeah?" he said.

"Open up." The voice was rough, deep.

"Who is it?"

"Open up!"

Beetle went to the bed. He tossed the towel onto the mattress, then pulled on a pair of laundered boxers from his rucksack.

"Hey!" the man shouted. "This is your last warning!"

Beetle dressed in the same pants and woodland camouflage shirt he'd had on earlier. He slipped the Beretta into the waistband of the pants, fitting it snugly against the small of his back.

He returned to the door. On the other side of it he heard at least two people conversing in low tones. A moment later a key turned in the lock. The door swung inward.

Two large men wearing wool sweaters and reeking of BO stood shoulder to shoulder in the doorway. The one on the left had a shaved head and a bulldog face with flaxen, almost nonexistent eyebrows. The one on the right had dark hair and a matching goatee. The family resemblance, however, was unmistakable. Behind them, scowling, was the shylock from the reception.

"This him, Dad?" Bulldog said.

"That's him," Shylock said.

Bulldog's scowl mimicked his father's. "So, you like beating up old men, do you?"

"He tried to rip me off," Beetle said simply.

"It don't matter what he did. You don't go beating on old men, especially when it's my dad."

"Would you prefer me to beat on you?" Beetle asked.

Bulldog's eyes widened in surprise, then narrowed in anger. "Is that a threat, you piece of shit?"

"You come to my room, you bang on my door, you get in my face. If you don't want a beating, what the fuck do you want?"

"I want you out of my motel!" Shylock crowed, wiping his red nose with the back of his hand. "And don't even think about asking for no money back."

"You're kicking me out?" Beetle said.

"Damn right I am."

"I don't think that's going to happen."

"I don't care *what* you think, asshole," Bulldog said, reaching for him.

Beetle swatted his hand aside and stepped backward, luring him into the narrow entryway.

Bulldog took the bait, lunging forward. He grabbed Beetle's shirt with both meaty fists. Beetle—who was trained not to think in a fight, only act or react—instinctively kicked Bulldog's right kneecap, causing him to cry out and sink to his other knee. Beetle curled his hand into a rock and drove his fore knuckle and middle knuckle into the bridge of Bulldog's nose. There was an audible crunch. Blood gushed.

"My nose!" Bulldog cried. "Owww! My fucking nose! Owww!"

Beetle struck him again in the same spot. He shut up and fell to his side, cupping his nose and rocking in agony.

Goatee was trying to get to Beetle without stepping on his brother. Beetle backed into the room proper, giving them both space to maneuver.

Goatee came at him, swinging a haymaker. Beetle stepped into the attack, blocking the blow with his left arm while chopping Goatee across the ribs with his right hand. Goatee grunted. Beetle drove a straight right into his gaping jaw, probably dislocating it. Goatee made a noise that sounded like "Oh?" and dropped to the floor.

Beetle moved purposely toward Shylock, who stood statue-still in the hallway, as if rooted there by fear. Beetle withdrew the Beretta and shoved the barrel against the man's forehead. He didn't say anything. He didn't trust himself to speak. His breathing came in quick, rough snorts. His trigger finger quivered.

Beetle waited for Shylock to give him a reason to pull the trigger, but the old cheat only made a pathetic, whimpering sound, and just like that Beetle came back to himself. He blinked away the red haze that had crept over his vision, and he heard himself growl: "You're going to go into my room, you're going to collect your sons, and the three of you are going to get out of my sight. You come back, you bother me again, I will kill you. You and whoever you bring. I will end all your miserable, meaningless lives right then and there. Do you understand that? Do you believe me?"

The old cheat bobbed his head.

Beetle lowered the pistol—reluctantly. "Then get to it before I change my fucking mind."

Chapter 16

"Who will survive and what will be left of them?"
The Texas Chainsaw Massacre (1974)

"They have guns," Steve said. He had turned off the foyer light and was peering through the front window. The Jeep's and utility coupe's high beams allowed him to see in the black night clearly enough. The bookish man had retrieved a rifle from the car. The hard man had produced a machete—*a goddamn machete*—from where it had been tucked against the small of his back. The rain had begun to fall harder, but neither of them seemed to notice or care.

"Who are they, Steve?" Jenny said in a frightened voice. She stood a couple feet behind him.

"I don't know," he said.

"Why are they here? If they were lying about hearing the gunshots, how'd they know to come? *What the hell's going on?*"

"I don't know," he said.

"Maybe we should, I don't know, maybe we should—"

"Shit."

"*What?*"

"They've backed into the fog. I can't see them anymore."

"Wait—that's good, right?" she said hopefully. "Maybe that means, maybe they're going?"

"Without their car?"

"Well, what then? What are they doing then—"

"I don't know!" Steve snapped.

"Steve, don't yell. I'm scared, okay? I'm freaking terrified. Are we going to die? *Are we going to die?*"

"Jenny, shut up!"

"Don't yell, Steve! Don't!" He could hear her hyperventilating. "I, we, God, we need to call the police—"

"There's no phone."

"There has to be."

She began fussing around the room, yanking open drawers, tossing boxes aside. Steve didn't move from the window. He assumed the two men had retreated out of sight to converse privately. It seemed pointless, considering he couldn't have heard them anyway. Maybe they thought he could read lips.

Jenny crossed the hallway to the dining room.

She screamed.

For a moment Steve was convinced she'd been shot. But when he turned, she was standing in the entranceway to the dining room, both hands covering her mouth. He went to her, put his arm around her shoulder, and led her away from the dead boy.

"What did you *do*, Steve?" she whispered, her eyes glistening with tears. "What did you and Noah *do*? That's why they're coming after us, isn't it? They know you killed that boy, and now they're going to kill us for payback."

"That's impossible, Jen. The boy died, it was an accident, the radiator fell on him, but that only happened ten minutes ago. The old man came home minutes later. He didn't call anybody. Nobody called anybody. Nobody could have known."

"Then why are they here?" She was whispering hoarsely.

"Go upstairs," he told her. "Keep searching for the phone. You're right. There has to be one. I must have overlooked it."

Steve guided her toward the staircase. Jenny hesitated, then tromped up the steps, zombie-like. Steve didn't believe he'd overlooked the phone, but if she didn't do something to occupy her mind she was going to have a nervous breakdown right then and there.

He returned to the window, pulled the floral-patterned curtain aside, and peered outside.

Nothing but fog and rain.

What were they doing? he wondered. What could they be discussing at such lengths? Were they hiding from him? Did they think he was going to pick them off with the rifle? Would he attempt that given the chance, without knowing who they were or what they were doing here? Would he even be able to hit them? A few years ago he'd fired a handgun at a friend's cottage in the Pocono Mountains. They'd set up beer cans as targets and shot at them with the cheap .25 caliber Saturday Night Special his friend's father kept in the cabin. Steve had missed the cans more times than he'd hit them, and he'd only been twenty feet away. So, rifle or not, how would he fare striking a mobile target at fifty yards?

Not good, he suspected.

Abruptly the man with the muttonchops and handlebar mustache emerged from the mist into the headlights. He held his hands over his head, the machete gripped in the right one. "Don't shoot, boy!" he called. "I just wanna talk about this."

"Talk about what?" Steve shouted.

"We don't wanna hurt you, y'hear? We only wanna get our friend some help."

Steve hesitated. Could this be true?

In a show of peace the man turned and set the machete on the hood of the utility coupe. He turned back, smiled, and stepped forward.

"Hold it!" Steve said. "You can get your friend, I'll let you get him, you can take him to the hospital, I won't shoot. But first tell me what you're doing here."

"I told you, we heard—"

"You heard nothing! There were three shots, not two!"

"That's what I said earlier. Three shots."

"Stop bullshitting me!"

"I ain't bullshitting—"

Steve sensed movement to his right and dropped to the floor just as a gunshot boomed and a bullet whizzed past his head, so close he heard it. In the second it took the bookish man to cycle the rifle's bolt and fire again, Steve had moved fast and far enough to avoid the second shot. He charged the man, driving him into the dining room table and chairs. They collapsed in a tangle of limbs, dropping their rifles. They were roughly the same size and their struggle became a grappling match that had them rolling back and forth. Steve gained some leverage and kneed the man in the groin and shoved apart.

Steve considered scrambling for one of the rifles, but the man got to his feet just as Steve did. His eyeglasses sat askew on his nose. Blood smeared his mouth and chin. He raised his fists like a boxer, taunting Steve, then launched a punch. Steve dodged it and kicked him in the right knee. The man buckled. Steve went for the nearest rifle and grabbed it just as the man wrapped his arms around Steve's midsection. Steve jammed the rifle's stock into the man's gut. They stumbled backward and crashed into the dining room table a second time. The impact knocked the wind from Steve's lungs but also broke them apart. Spinning, Steve swung the rifle with all his might. It cracked against the man's shoulder. He cried out in pain and sank to his knees, holding onto the table to remain upright.

Steve raised the rifle over his head. He was going to bring it down on the fucker's head, he was going to crush him like an insect, he didn't care if he killed him, he was half insane right then and in a fight to the death, and he was going to—

Steve sensed someone behind him. He spun to find the hard man a foot away, machete at the ready. The man didn't say anything. He didn't smile. He showed no emotion at all.

Steve opened his mouth, to plead for his life, but the blade ended it first.

Jenny heard the reports of two successive gunshots. At first she thought it was Steve firing through the window, but then she made out the commotion of a scuffle. *They're inside!* Her first impulse was to rush downstairs and offer Steve whatever assistance she could. Yet reason nixed that idea. The men were both armed. She was five-foot-five, one hundred twenty pounds. She couldn't help. She could only die, and she didn't want to die. More than anything she'd ever wanted in her life, she didn't want to die.

Glancing frantically around the bedroom, Jenny searched for a place to hide. There was nowhere—nowhere but under the bed. She contemplated returning to the hall, fleeing down the staircase, out the front door. But it was closed and locked. She wouldn't be able to escape before the men captured her. She had to hide.

She dropped to her chest and wormed beneath the bed. She lay perfectly still. She was so afraid she felt simultaneously flushed and chilled, headachy and nauseous, almost as if she were in the initial stages of the flu.

Something loud crashed downstairs. Steve cried out, what sounded like a roar.

Of triumph? she wondered. *Was Steve winning the fight? Should she return and help him after all?*

She listened, but heard nothing except the blood pounding in her head. No—she heard footsteps. Coming up the staircase, quickly. Only one set of footsteps.

Please be Steve, please let it be Steve, please God please.

The footsteps stopped outside the bedroom. They moved away, into the room across the hall. Jenny's hope was already curdling into doom. If it were Steve, he would have called her name by now. So it wasn't Steve. Steve was dead. Just like Noah was dead and she was going to be dead next. As soon as the man finished searching the room across the hall he was going to come into this room and he was going to—

The footsteps returned to the hall.

"Darlin'?"

The word iced her blood. It wasn't spoken with singsong cockiness but softly and monotonously, almost as if it were a scolding.

The man entered the bedroom where she hid. Jenny's left cheek was pressed flush to the floorboards. She could see his black boots. He took three steps into the middle of the room and stopped.

Jenny became acutely conscious of her breathing. It sounded far too loud. It was going to give her away. She bit her lip and tried not to go insane as she waited for the man's face to appear upside down, peering under the bed at her. He would grab her by the hair and drag her out and kill her.

Abruptly Jenny found herself praying for a quick death. She didn't want to experience it. She didn't want to lie there, bleeding out, in excruciating agony, *waiting*. She didn't want to see her life flash before her eyes. She didn't want to think about never seeing her mother or father again, her two older brothers, her friends. She didn't want to think about everything that could have been. She wanted a painless bullet in the head—

The black boots shuffled in a circle, then left the bedroom.

Jenny knew she couldn't remain beneath the bed. It had been stupid to hide there in the first place. She had trapped herself. She needed to get out of the house, make for the trees.

She wiggled out from the small space and went to the window. The upper sash appeared fixed in place. The lower one, however, slid vertically in grooves in the side jambs. She tried to shove the sash upward. It didn't budge. Had sloppy paint sealed it shut? Had the wood swelled or distorted? Fighting frustration and terror, she felt along the top of the sash and found some kind of metal latch. She worked the keeper free and shoved the panel upward. This time it slid easily.

She climbed through the opening.

Having checked all four bedrooms, and not finding the thin blonde in any of them, Cleavon suspected she would be behind the last door on the right. What he discovered instead was a steep set of stairs leading to the main floor.

He took the steps three at a time and emerged in the kitchen.

A back door led outside.

Cursing, he hurried to the door and found the deadbolt engaged.

Which meant the girl couldn't have left through it.

Jesse appeared in the hallway, eyeglasses busted, face a bloody mess.

"Where is she, man?" he asked. "Where'd she get to?"

"Go wait by the front staircase," Cleavon told him, then returned upstairs.

Arms and legs spread wide, back pressed against the house's weatherboards, Jenny inched away from the window along a thin horizontal strip of molding. Blinking rain from her eyes, she glanced to the fog-frosted ground twenty-five feet below and suffered a moment of vertigo. It was too far to jump. She'd break her legs. Fifteen feet to her right, though, a tall maple tree grew close to the house. She thought if she could reach the branches, she could climb safely down.

She continued inching sideways, her fingernails clawing the wet wood for a grip that didn't exist. With each small step she half expected to lose her footing and plummet to the ground. Still, she pressed on. She didn't have a choice.

"Well, fuck me blue!"

Jenny was so startled she pitched forward. For a sickening second she was convinced she was going to fall. But then she flattened her back against the weatherboards once more.

She turned her head to look the way she'd come. The man with the mutton chops and handlebar mustache was leaning out the window, leering at her.

"Come back inside, darlin'. You gonna kill yourself out there."

"Leave me alone!"

"Come on back. I ain't gonna hurt you."

She resumed edging sideways.

"Shit, darlin', I wanted you dead, I'd shoot you right now with this rifle. Now come on inside."

That was true, she realized. He could shoot her easily. So why didn't he?

Because he wants to rape you first.

Swallowing a moan, she continued her progress.

"Jess!" the man shouted.

"You find her?"

"Get outside! To the side of the house. She's gone out the window."

"Okay!"

Jenny glanced at the tree. She wouldn't reach it in time. The other man would be down below her any moment, waiting for her.

She only had one option remaining.

She jumped.

Cleavon stared in disbelief as the stupid cunt jumped off the small ledge. She hit the ground with a hundred-pound thump. For what seemed like a long moment she didn't move, didn't make a sound, and he thought she was either unconscious or dead, and it served her right—

She began to scream, high pitched and glassy, like a stuck pig.

"What did you expect, darlin'?" he muttered, then went downstairs to see how badly she was hurt.

Jesse was bent over her when Cleavon got to them. She was still screaming and crying at the same time. It wasn't doing his headache any good. But he didn't think she'd quiet down no matter how nice he asked, and he didn't have a sock to stuff in her mouth, so he ignored the noise the best he could.

"It ain't pretty," Jesse said, his owlish face frowning.

Cleavon studied the girl. She had large blue eyes and what would have been a pretty face when it wasn't wet with tears and rain and twisted in pain.

"You see what you did?" Cleavon told her. "You went and broke your goddamn legs. I told you I wasn't gonna hurt you."

Jesse said, "What we gonna do, Cleave?"

"Give me a hand getting her to the car."

"I mean, about all this." He swallowed. "Lonnie's dead, for fuck sake, Cleave. Both Lonnie and his boy. How we gonna cover this up?"

"Just give me a fuckin' hand getting her to the car." He crouched next to the girl and set Lonnie's rifle and his machete in the mud. "You take her left arm. I'll—"

"We gotta call Mr. Pratt."

Cleavon paused, one hand on the girl's shoulder. She was moaning now, which was better than screaming. "What the fuck is Spence gonna do?" he snapped. "He some sort of clean-up man, Jess? He gonna come out here and clean up this mess? What's calling him gonna do?"

"He might think of a way to explain all this."

"What needs explaining, Jess?"

"Lonnie's dead, Cleave! Lonnie and his boy. How're we gonna explain that?"

"We're not."

"We're not?"

"We were never here."

"We were never here?"

"Do I have a fuckin' echo? No, we weren't never here. Whatever happened, happened between some out-of-towner and Lonnie and his boy. We weren't here. We don't know nothing."

"But won't the sheriff wonder where that buck inside, where his friends went? Surely they told people where they were going, people're gonna know they were travelling together, they'll wonder what happened to the rest of them."

"Let them wonder, Jess. No one took a picture of us, did they? We weren't never here. That's all that matters. Now give me a fuckin' hand with the girl."

Jess set his rifle aside and took her left arm, Cleavon her right arm, and they hefted her upright. She shrieked but there was little else she could do with no good legs. They carried her between them to the Chevy El Camino and set her in the flatbed.

"Why...?" she said between sobs, propping herself up on her elbow. "Where...what are you...doing to me?"

"Keep your hands and feet inside the vehicle for the duration of the ride, darlin'," Cleavon told her. "And if you try another jumping stunt once we get going, and don't break something fuckin' else, you better believe I'll do it for you."

He slammed the tailgate shut.

Chapter 16

"These are godless times, Mrs. Snell."
Carrie (1976)

"Would you like any more potatoes, dear?" Lynette asked Spencer Pratt, her husband of seventeen years—who, she was nearly positive, was cheating on her with another woman.

He dabbed his lips with the cotton napkin. "Thank you, no," he said.

"Are you going to the hospital this evening?"

"Are you so eager to have the house to yourself?"

"Of course not. I was just wondering," she said, collecting her dishes and taking them to the kitchen. "You've been spending a lot of time there this year."

"Yes, well, work's work, isn't it?" he said, following her with his dishes. He set them in the sink and rinsed them with hot water. "These two new patients I have require...extensive work."

Lynette placed the jug of milk in the refrigerator. "Work that can't be done during regular working hours?"

Spencer didn't reply, and Lynette wondered whether she'd said too much, overplayed her hand. Smiling kindly, she turned around, assuming the role of the doting, naïve housewife. Spencer was scribbling something in a notepad he had taken from his pocket, apparently oblivious to her question.

Lynette went to fetch the rest of the dishes from the dining room table. They'd had roast pork, vegetables, and mashed potatoes with gravy. As usual, Spencer finished off most of the pork and potatoes but barely touched the vegetables. When she returned to the kitchen, Spencer was still scribbling notes.

He was the Psychiatrist-in-Chief of the Boston Mills Psychiatric Hospital, which had once been called the Boston Mills Lunatic Asylum. Lynette still thought of it as the latter. She had grown up in Boston Mills, and her first memory of the asylum had been overhearing her parents talking about a lunatic who'd gone on a rampage and killed a caseworker and two nurses. At six or seven she didn't know what a lunatic was, but she could tell by the way her parents were acting that she should be scared. Her mother would use this fear to keep her in line with ominous sayings such as, "You better be good or the lunatic will get you." She would also threaten to ring up the director of the asylum to have Lynette committed, telling her, "It's a rat trap, very easy to get in, impossible to get out." These threats were made all the more real and frightening because Lynette's father, a gardener at the hospital, brought home any number of stories about what went on there. Patients who would be forced to eat everything on their plates at mealtime even if it made them vomit it all back up. Patients who would be tied to their beds with wet sheets layered in ice in the pit of winter. Orderlies who would beat patients to within inches of their lives with wiffle ball bats before locking them away in solitary confinement. An old woman who wandered into a closed-down ward and died, her corpse remaining undiscovered for so long it left a permanent body-shaped stain on the floor. And then of course there was the debacle in 1962 when a man escaped the asylum and murdered a local woman and lived in her house for a week, eating her food and dressing in her clothes, before being discovered by the mailman. After this the community came together to form a civic association that convened with hospital administrators on how to keep the community safe, an association that existed to this day.

Given how terrified Lynette had been of the lunatic asylum growing up, it was ironic she would wind up working there. But when you grew up in a small town, and had no ambitions of leaving it, you took whatever work came your way. After graduating high school, Lynette was hired as a part-time receptionist at the local doctor's office to cover for a woman away on maternity leave. When the woman returned a short month later, Lynette worked the odd shift at a dairy bar before hearing about a position for a medical transcriptionist at the asylum. Thankfully most of her father's horror stories proved to be false. The lunatic asylum was by no means paradise. There were metal doors that locked behind her everywhere she went, most of the patients wandered in circles, and only a few had teeth due to the psych meds that dried out their mouths. However, there were no sadistic orderlies or rotting bodies or murderous patients—none that she came into contact with, at least.

When Spencer began working there as a psychiatrist, Lynette fell for him right away. He was not a particularly attractive man. He was stout and had a weak chin. But he had a full head of glorious red hair, and he was positively charming. They went steady for six months before he proposed to her. They married soon after and tried for years to conceive a child but were never successful. Eventually, after several consultations with their doctor, it was determined that Lynette was infertile.

Over the next decade they grew apart. Lynette stopped working at the asylum and became something of a lonely spinster, while Spencer did the opposite, immersing himself in the community and his work. Their relationship deteriorated to such an extent she now sensed he privately resented her, as if she were his ball and chain, preventing him from fully enjoying his life. She no longer thought of him as a husband but more of a stranger—a stranger living in her house and sleeping in her bed. This was accentuated by the fact that Spencer, physically, barely resembled the young man who had swept her off her feet. Some years ago he'd gotten into bodybuilding, and he could no longer be described as stout; he was a wrecking ball, with a bull neck, barrel chest, and bulging biceps. Also, he'd grown a beard. It had been her suggestion, because she'd known how self-conscious he'd been about his weak chin. But he continued to grow it out until it reached its current length, which stopped just short of his waistline.

Lynette dumped the remaining dishes she'd collected in the sink and filled the basin with hot water and dish soap. Spencer stuffed his notepad back in his pocket just as the telephone on the nearby table rang.

Spencer picked up the receiver and said hello. He listened for a few seconds, turning his back to her. "Stay there," he said finally in a low voice. "I'm coming right now." He hung up.

"Has something happened?" she asked.

"Yes," he told her curtly. "You'll be fine by yourself?"

"I think I'll draw a bath, then retire early. I've been a little tired recently."

"Can't imagine why," he said. "You never leave the house." He cleared his throat. "I didn't mean it that way."

"No, you're right. I should look into a hobby of some sort."

"Why don't you join that book club at the library? They meet every Tuesday, I believe."

"I'll think about it."

He nodded, took the car keys from the pegboard, then left through the back door.

Without his briefcase, she noted.

Lynette watched Spencer through the window over the sink as he hurried through the rain to the garage, pulled up the roller door, and stepped inside. A few moments later headlights flooded the gravel driveway and his silver Volvo sedan appeared momentarily before disappearing from her line of sight.

Lynette dried her hands on a dish towel, then hurried to the front of the house. She pulled aside a blind in the darkened foyer and peered through the small beveled window as the Volvo continued down the driveway and turned left, disappearing behind the forest of trees.

Lynette went immediately to Spencer's study. She'd been contemplating divorcing Spencer for some time now, but she'd been reluctant to file the necessary paperwork. She knew Spencer would be furious at the embarrassment it would cause him, at the hit his sterling reputation would take, and he would paint Lynette as a disillusioned, raving housewife. The small community would turn against her. She wouldn't be able to go to the supermarket without someone talking about her or snickering behind her back. She would be ostracized from the town in which she had grown up, the only home she knew. However, if she could produce proof Spencer was having an extramarital affair, nobody would believe the lies he whipped up. She would be viewed sympathetically. She could live out the rest of her life in relative peace and quiet. A fly on the wall, a nobody. And that was fine by her. Better a nobody than the target of scorn and ridicule.

Lynette stopped before the door to Spencer's study. She turned the brass knob and found it locked, as she knew it would be. Last year Spencer began locking it whenever he went out. The reason, he told her, was to protect confidential patient information he kept in his filing cabinet in the rare chance the house was broken into and burglarized. Initially Lynette accepted this explanation. But when he started spending more and more nights at the "hospital," she decided there was another reason altogether why he locked the study: to hide evidence of his affair.

She had been tempted on several occasions to search the study while he was in the shower or outside planting in the garden. However, she could never bring herself to do this, fearful she wouldn't have enough time to conduct a proper search, or Spencer would appear unannounced and catch her in the act. Instead she decided to remove the study key from his keychain and search the study while he was at the asylum. This carried risks as well, as she didn't know whether he would notice the missing key while at work, or whether he would head straight to his study when he returned home, before she had a chance to replace the key. Nevertheless, it was the best option she could think of.

So earlier today, when Spencer informed her that he would be going to the asylum later, she slipped the study key from his keychain while he'd been in the garage changing the oil in the Volvo. She kept it in her pocket all evening and was irrationally convinced Spencer knew it was there, could see it through the cotton of her dress. But of course he couldn't, he was none the wiser, and now he was gone, and it was time.

Lynette removed the key from her pocket and stuck it in the keyhole. She half expected it not to work, or for it to break in two. It turned easily. She eased open the door. The study was dark. She reached a hand inside and patted the wall until her fingers brushed the light switch nub. She flicked it on.

The room resembled something you might see in a men's club. Maplewood paneled walls, stodgy button-tufted furniture, a wall-to-wall bookcase. Two stuffed gray wolves stood on either side of the stone fireplace, trophies from one of Spencer's hunting trips. She had always hated them. They reminded her of that three-headed dog in Greek mythology that guarded the gate to the underworld.

Lynette went directly to the oversized desk and opened the top drawer. She sifted through the sundry items, careful not to disturb their positions. She uncovered nothing more interesting than stationary supplies and hospital memos, certainly nothing incriminating. The contents of the three smaller drawers proved equally unremarkable.

She went to the antique wardrobe next and opened the mirrored doors. Several starched white shirts and dress pants hung from the clothes rack. Spencer kept these here instead of the bedroom closet so he could change without waking her if he had to leave for the asylum early. She checked the shirts for lipstick, smelled them for any trace of perfume. They were all freshly laundered. She stuck her hand into each pant pocket. They held nothing.

There was a shelf above the hanging space, but it was too high for her to access. She dragged a wooden chair over, climbed onto the seat, and discovered three shoeboxes. The first contained several envelopes bursting with receipts, though none from jewelry purchases or expensive out-of-town dinners. Most, if not all, were utility bills from AT&T, the Ohio Edison Company, and Aqua America. The second shoebox contained stacks of aging photographs wrapped in rubber bands. Lynette's chest tightened with nostalgia as she shuffled through photos taken when she and Spencer were twenty years younger, smiling, in love. She promptly moved on to the final box. It held nothing but miscellaneous junk Spencer hadn't been able to throw out: broken watches, a torn wallet, a faded issue of *Playboy* magazine, a suede brush, a personal grooming kit, a toy pistol, a silver napkin ring, a bottle of still-corked glycerin.

Lynette stepped off the chair, closed the wardrobe doors, and looked around the study. Where next? she wondered with a growing sense of desperation. Her eyes paused on the bookcase. Could Spencer have hidden a telephone number or a love letter inside one of the books? She gritted her teeth in frustration. This would have been much easier had she known what she was looking for. Still, she wouldn't quit; she would make the most of this opportunity while she had it.

The first three bookshelves contained hardback tomes on psychiatry and psychology and science and medicine. She found nothing inside them any more interesting than a bookmark or an underlined passage that was meaningless to her. She retrieved the chair and climbed on it again so she could reach the uppermost shelf. She frowned at the first book she examined. It was bound in leather and titled: *The Book of Baphomet.* She flipped through the pages and discovered shocking illustrations of grotesque demons and people wearing animal heads and naked women in submissive poses. Her revulsion turned quickly to confusion, then fear as she realized all the books on the shelf were dedicated to the occult, books with titles such as *The Left-Hand Path*, *Arcana*, *The Infernal Text*, *Blood Sorcery*, *The Lost Art*, and so forth.

Why did Spencer have books on devil worship?

Why so many?

Was he—could he be—?

While stretching her arm for a large red book just out of reach she lost her balance and leapt off the chair. She stumbled when she landed and collided into the ottoman, bumping it across the floor. Something inside it rattled.

Kneeling, Lynette discovered the padded, upholstered top lifted away to reveal a hollow storage space. She frowned at the contents it held. There was a silver chalice, black candles, incense, what might have been folded black robes, and a stack of photographs bound by an elastic band like those in the shoebox.

Lynette swooned, momentarily lightheaded. What did all this mean? Was her husband a *Satanist?* And if so, what did he do with this stuff?

Sacrifice virgins to his dark god? For a moment she experienced a strange mix of relief and disappointment. Was there no affair after all? Was this the reason he went out at nighttime, to play dress up and *Dungeons & Dragons* with a group of like-minded associates at the asylum? Yet this seemed so unlike Spencer...

The stack of photographs was facedown. She picked it up and turned it over—and gasped.

The top one was a headshot of a young woman. Her eyes were open and unseeing, her skin pale. She appeared to be lying on a slab of stone.

She almost looked dead.

Heart suddenly pounding, Lynette removed the elastic band and cycled through the rest of the photos. There must have been three or four dozen, all females, all headshots, all closed-eyed, all pale-skinned, all—

Dead, she thought as the photos fell from her fingers. *Not almost. Definitely. Definitively. Dead. All of them, dead, dead, dead.*

And then she recognized one of the women: the teased hair, the heart-shaped face, the beauty mole on her chin. She had gone missing from Boston Mills the year before. What was her name? Debra? Darla? Her fiancé, Mark Evans, owned the auto repair shop in town—or had owned it. After he admitted to police that Darla went missing the same evening she caught him having sex with an employee from the ski resort, rumors swirled that he'd murdered her. Although no evidence could convict him of any crime, none could clear his name either. His clientele stopped patronizing his shop. The townsfolk whispered about him behind his back and avoided him on the street. Children invented stories of how he fed Darla into a woodchopper, or buried her dismembered body parts in the national park, or tossed her off the top of Brandywine Falls, where you could see her haunting at midnight on a full moon. Eventually Mark sold his business and moved out of state. No one had heard from him, or Darla, since.

But Spencer has a photograph of her face—her dead face.
Had he killed her?
Had he killed all these people—?

CHAPTER 16

Lynette buried her face in her hands and found herself wishing her husband had been having an affair after all.

Chapter 17

"Somebody once wrote, 'Hell is the impossibility of reason.' That's what this place feels like. Hell."
Platoon (1986)

In the current nightmare, Beetle was back on the beach in Grenada. However, there were no bullets whizzing past his head, no Marine Corps Sea Cobras decimating the quaint beachfront hotels and cafés with machine gun fire, no fighter-bombers flying gun runs overhead. Instead the beach was ominously deserted. He stood there alone, the sun burning in the sky, the surf foaming at his feet, the palm trees waving in the breeze. He began to walk, pretending not to see the blood staining the bright sand, or the drag marks where the tide had ferried bodies to their watery graves. Eventually the beach tapered to an end. Sarah stood where the sand met the jungle, waiting for him. At the sight of her his heart raced. He wanted to embrace her and tell her he was sorry and promise her he would change. But she wouldn't let him get a word in. She yelled at him for being covered in blood, for killing the Russian diplomat, for drinking so much, for becoming a stranger to her.

He became enraged. Didn't she understand what he'd been through? Couldn't she understand that and empathize with him? No, no she couldn't. All she could do was yell and accuse, yell and accuse—

Suddenly the USS Caron, a destroyer armed to the teeth, towered beside him, an impossibility in the shallow water, but there nonetheless. His lieutenant, a brown-noser who looked like a dentist and often pulled rank, yelled to him to put down the pistol, to turn himself in. Beetle pressed the barrel beneath his chin and squeezed the trigger—

Beetle jerked awake bathed in sweat, disorientated, gutted, afraid. It took him a moment to realize he was sitting on a rickety wooden chair on the balcony of the room at the Hilltop Lodge. The full moon hung in the black sky, a moldy white disc poking out from behind a smudge of dark clouds. It had started to rain, which had cleared away some of the fog, or at least thinned it, so he could see much of the forest stretching away below him. He swallowed, discovered he was parched, and picked up the bottle of vodka on the ground next to him. He took a three-swallow belt.

"Yuck!" a woman's voice said. "That would make me puke."

Beetle fell sideways off the chair, though he somehow managed to keep the bottle from spilling or breaking. He looked to where the voice had originated and found the woman leaning on the wooden banister that separated the two balconies.

She was tall and had lidded, amused brown eyes beneath arched eyebrows. Her features were too long, her face too gaunt, to be considered beautiful, but she had an unusual attractiveness. "I'm so sorry!" she exclaimed. "I didn't mean to startle you so much." She had a strong German accent.

"It's okay," Beetle said, pushing himself to his feet and returning the chair upright. He remained standing, looking at the woman, waiting for her to go away.

"What terrible weather," she said. "It reminds me of the weather in Bavaria. That's where I'm from, in Germany. My name's Greta." She stuck her hand out over the banister.

Beetle hesitated, then shook. "Beetle." His head was spinning from the booze. He had to concentrate on standing straight and enunciating clearly.

"Like the..." She made a crawling motion with her fingers.

"Yeah, like that."

"Better than earthworm, I suppose," she said, smiling. "No, I'm kidding. So what's going on? You're having a big party by yourself?" Her eyes went to the bottle in his hand, then back to his face.

"I think I'm going to go inside."

"Is that an invitation?"

He blinked at her.

She laughed. "I'm kidding, Herr Beetle. But don't go inside. Help me smoke this." She produced an elegantly rolled joint from her pocket.

Beetle's eyes came awake. He didn't merely want to get high; he suddenly realized he needed to.

"I'll take that as a yes?" She lit up, took a couple short drags, and passed the joint to him.

Beetle inhaled, pulling hard and closing his eyes. His mind rode the smoke as it tickled down his throat and floated in his lungs. He exhaled in a long stream.

"Hey," Greta said. "Did you see the blood on the carpet?"

"No," Beetle replied, thinking about Shylock and his sons for the first time since waking. The knuckles of his right hand, he realized, ached dully. He took another, longer toke from the spliff, then handed it to the woman.

She accepted it and said, "Yeah, there is. Blood. There's a trail leading all the way to the stairs. And I swear it wasn't there before I went to dinner." She offered him a sly smile. "Maybe it has something to do with the legends?"

Beetle frowned, wondering what legends she was talking about, and why he thought he should know.

"The legends," she repeated, seeing his confusion. "Like the church." She pointed.

Beetle followed her finger. The fog had continued to dissipate even as they spoke, eradicated by the rain, and all that remained of it were whiffs of white condensation drifting up here and there through the roof of the moonlit forest. Squinting, he could make out a white structure atop a small rise some distance away.

Beetle remembered the two kids in town telling him something about upside down crosses. He mentioned this.

Greta nodded. "Creepy, right? Everybody says the church was built by Satanists to perform black masses in the basement."

"Who's everyone?" he asked, eyeing the joint. She held it between her fingers, letting it burn, wasting it.

"Well, just these two English backpackers I bought the pot from. I met them last night in a hostel in Cleveland. They said this place is called Helltown. It sounded neat, so I drove down this morning to check it out for myself. But the fog was so bad I decided to stay overnight and try again tomorrow." She finally took a drag of the joint and passed it to him. "Finish it," she said, and retrieved a paper cup from the table behind her. She held it up for him to see. "Wine. Classy, I know. But it was the only glass in the room. I think you're supposed to use it to rinse toothpaste out of your mouth."

Beetle puffed away, and he realized he wasn't just drunk or high. He was ripped. He wasn't going to be able to walk let alone think in a minute—and that was a-okay with him.

He flicked the roach into the night and gripped the railing so he didn't fall over.

"Anyway," Greta said, and he heard her light a cigarette, smelled the burning tobacco. "The church is just one of the legends. There's so much other stuff." She gestured to the forest. "Like all the abandoned houses. There're dozens of them, just sitting out there, empty. It's true. The English guys showed me pictures they took. And there's a cemetery at the end of a dead-end road that's filled with kid graves. The English guys said a serial killer waved down a school bus years ago and murdered everyone on board. It's in the woods, the bus. They showed me pictures of it too. The trees have grown up around it. Hard to find, but I have a map. The English guys drew it for me. The English guys—that sounds so stupid, doesn't it? I don't know why I keep calling them that. Anyway, they said they met someone who slept overnight in the bus, and he said he heard all these strange noises. Hey, are you sleeping? Open your eyes."

Beetle opened them. The world canted. He gripped the railing tighter.

"Wow, you're trashed," Greta said, dropping the cigarette to the ground and stubbing it out with the toe of her shoe.

"I think I'm going to watch TV," he said, moving to the door. He tripped trying to get around the chair, but stayed on his feet.

"Hey, wait up! What about tomorrow? Do you want to come with me to check out the church and cemetery and stuff? It will be more fun with someone."

"Can't," he told her. "Thanks for the smoke."

Greta said something more, but Beetle was already stumbling inside his room. The warmth from the heater made him realize how chilly it had been outside. His hands were stiff and numb. He set the vodka on the Formica table and withdrew the Beretta from the waistband of his pants, comforted and numbed by its cold, heavy weight. Then he remembered he'd told Greta he was going to watch TV, so he powered the thing on.

It was bizarre, he thought, he was going to kill himself in a moment, blow his brains out all over the ugly floral wallpaper, she would hear the gunshot, she would be the one to discover his body, and he was concerned about hurting her feelings?

Sitting carefully on the bed, his back against the headboard, Beetle clicked off the pistol's safety, pressed the barrel into the soft flesh beneath his jaw, and counted to ten.

Chapter 19

"Humans are such easy prey."
From Beyond (1986)

Jeff's eyes snapped open. He sucked back a sharp intake of air. His arms shot out from his sides, as if to prevent himself from falling.

Where was he?

He tried to sit up and pain flared in his back. He cried out, a twisted, tormented howl.

What the hell had happened?

He thought back. The crybaby bridge. Tossing the baby shoes he'd brought with him beneath the bridge to scare the others. The hearse—*oh shit the hearse!* Swerving off the road at the last second. Punching through the forest. Steve kneeling beside him, asking him to squeeze his hand, which he could do, asking him to move his legs, which he could not do.

An icicle of fear skewered his heart.

You're paralyzed, a jolly, manic voice told him. *You can't walk. You can't even tie your own shoes anymore. How about that? Try getting someone "more on your level" now, buddy old pal. You would be lucky to find a hooker who won't feel sorry for you. Speaking of sex—can you even get an erection? Or is your dick as gimped as your legs?*

Clenching his jaw against the pain radiating from his back, Jeff maneuvered himself onto his elbows. He tried moving his legs. They didn't respond. He tried harder, focusing all of his concentration on them. Nothing. It was like trying to move a third arm.

He swallowed the panic that wanted to explode from his mouth in a needle-sharp scream.

"Steve...?" he said instead, his voice rusty, barely a whisper.

No answer.

He felt rough wooden floorboards beneath his palms. He moved his right hand, exploring blindly for his legs. He found them where they should be, though they didn't register his touch; they felt like someone else's legs. Nevertheless, they were there. They weren't amputated.

Jeff's eyes adjusted to the dark, and he discovered that the blackness was a little less black to his right. He stared in that direction until he understood he must be looking at a door. Dim light was seeping through the crack at the bottom of it.

So he was in some sort of a room. But why were the lights off, and why was he lying on the fucking floor? Shouldn't he be in a hospital? Had Steve and the others gone to get help? Why would they all go? Wouldn't someone stay behind with him?

"Mandy...?" he said.

Nobody replied.

Jeff squinted. There was something in the far corner of the room, something large and lumpy. A piece of furniture? Or someone else?

"Noah...?"

Jeff sniffed, detecting the putrid odor for the first time, though he suspected it had been there all along. Urine? Yeah, urine. But not his own. His pants were dry.

Urine and...something musky.

Swallowing fresh panic, Jeff eased himself to his side as gently as he could. His back screamed in protest at the movement. It was as if his vertebrae were being held together with razor blades.

"Ignore it," he mumbled to himself, blocking out the pain.

Using only his arms, he began to drag himself forward on his belly. His body felt as though it weighed a ton, and it took all of his upper strength and willpower to move inch after excruciating inch. He didn't stop once, fearing he wouldn't be able to start again, and then he was close enough to make out the shadowy shape in the corner.

"Austin?" he croaked in relief at seeing his friend's face—though it seemed strangely puffy, especially his lips. "Austin—"

Jeff froze in terror.

A gigantic snake was coiled around Austin's body, from his feet to his shoulders. Its jaw, unhinged and opened impossibly wide, was attached to the top of Austin's skull in a toothless smile as it worked on swallowing him headfirst.

Austin was having the nightmare again, only this time it was different and somehow worse than all the others. He was in his bar. It was late, long past closing. He was alone. From the back office came the now familiar sneaky, scuffling sound. He knew what was causing it from past dreams. It was his grandmother. He would go back there, like he did every other time, and he would find her rifling through the filing cabinet in which he kept all his receipts and bills. She would tell him she was looking for the inheritance money she'd given him. She would say it had been a mistake leaving it for him, he didn't deserve it, he was going to blow it all on a stupid investment.

Austin reached for the handle of the door to the office, intent on confronting his grandmother, telling her purchasing the bar wasn't a mistake, it was doing all right, but his arm didn't respond. He glanced down, certain he would see a stump where it once existed. His limb was intact. He simply couldn't move it.

"That's my stuff, Nana!" he shouted. "Leave it alone!"

The door swung open.

Across the threshold his grandmother lay on the floor, on her back, swaddled in what looked like spider silk. She was missing her eyes.

"Nana?" he said. "What happened? What's wrong? What happened to your eyes?"

From the darkness Jeff appeared, stopping behind Austin's grand-mother's head. He was all blond hair and smiles and dressed in the maroon golf shirt and grays slacks of his Monsignor Farrell school uniform. "Hey, dickweed," he said, buddy-buddy. "How's it hanging?"

"You can walk?" Austin said.

"How 'bout that?"

"You were in an accident, and you couldn't move your legs." He frowned. "What happened to my grandmother?"

"Hell if I know. It's your dream."

"I can't move my arms."

"It's not so bad. You'll get used to it."

"Get used to what?"

"Being a paraplegic or quadriplegic or whatever you are now."

"How did you fix your legs?"

"Don't you know what's going on?" Grinning easily, the way he would grin when chatting up women he wanted to take back to his place, Jeff stuck his fingers in his mouth and whistled. "Dinner time, 'lil buddy."

Slowly, almost ponderously, Steve slithered from the shadows. But it wasn't Steve, not completely. He was green and fat and he just kept coming. His tongue flicked in and out of his lipless mouth.

"Jesus, Steve!" Austin said. "You're a snake!"

Steve headed straight for Austin's grandmother.

"No!" Austin shouted. "Steve, stop! Don't touch her!" He tried to intercept his friend, but he still couldn't move.

Steve reached Austin's grandmother and slinked around her torso, one loop, then two.

Austin screamed, or at least he tried to. He no longer had any air in his lungs, and nothing came out of his mouth.

Then he was awake, his mouth open, still trying to scream, though the sound remained sunken within his chest.

Something tight and solid squeezed his body, pinning his arms against his sides. His first thought: he'd been locked up in a straightjacket. It took all of one second for his waking mind to equate what his sleeping mind had already surmised.

A snake! A fucking snake's wrapped around me! Where's its head? Where's its fucking head?

Then he saw Jeff. He was a few feet away, on his side, staring at Austin with an expression alien to his usual cocky confidence: helplessness.

Austin wanted to beg him to help, but he couldn't get any words out, so he begged with his eyes.

Help me, goddammit! It's suffocating me! It's crushing me!

Suddenly he became aware of something wet on his head. It felt like an ill-fitting cap, though he knew it was no cap.

Overcome with dismay and repulsion, Austin struggled madly but futilely before giving up and exhaling from the wasted effort.

The snake squeezed tighter.

Jeff hated snakes. They disgusted and terrified him on a primeval level. He couldn't hold a harmless garter in his hands without shivering. Regardless, this was not the time for phobias.

Austin was dying. Hell, he was being eaten alive.

Steeling his nerves, Jeff dragged himself forward, toward the snake's tail. He'd once read that's where you started if you wanted to uncoil a snake that somehow got wrapped around your arm or leg.

The snake's tail was exposed, not buried beneath its tubular body. It trailed away from Austin's feet in lazy curlicues, terminating in a tip no thicker than a banana. However, that was not the case where it began to coil around Austin's ankles. There, it was already a foot in circumference.

Jeff gripped the plump length with both hands, grimacing at the dry and satiny feel of the skin. He pulled. He couldn't budge it, not an inch. He punched the thing with his fists, more in frustration than in any hope of causing it harm. It was like punching a sandbag.

Jeff changed tactics and dragged himself toward the snake's head. Austin's eyes, he noticed, were bloodshot and bulging and crazed.

The snake's eyes, on the other hand, were black, beady, emotionless.

Jeff hesitated, thinking he didn't have the balls to do what needed to be done.

"Do it, goddammit!" he told himself.

Grimacing, he wedged his fingers into the corners of the snake's mouth.

A moment later he cried out and yanked his hands back. Teeth he hadn't seen had pricked his fingers. He thought about bashing the serpent's head with his fists or elbows, but that would injure Austin as well.

Then, with a pelican-like gulp, the snake's grinning mouth jerked over Austin's eyes and nose, so only his mouth and chin remained visible.

"No!"

Jeff stuck his fingers in the snake's mouth again, one hand gripping the upper jaw, one the lower. He pulled with all his strength but still couldn't pry them apart. As if to prove it was undaunted by his effort to steal its prey, the snake's coiled body undulated and its mouth moved farther down over Austin's face, all the way to his neck.

With a moan, Jeff rolled away from the demonic thing, unwilling to watch it devour the rest of his friend. He closed his eyes, gripped his hair with his hands, and touched his forehead to the floor.

He wasn't aware of the second green anaconda slithering silently through the darkness toward him.

Chapter 20

"Something came out of the fog."
The Fog (1980)

According to Mandy's gold wristwatch—a gift from Jeff—she had been wandering through the ghostly forest for a little over an hour, though it seemed much longer than that. She had started away from the small butte in what she'd thought had been the direction of the highway, but she'd never arrived at it, and now she had to admit she was completely lost. She wasn't surprised. The forest would have been difficult enough to navigate correctly in the daytime. The thick, soupy shadows and coalescing fog made it near impossible. It seemed every five or ten feet she had to circumvent another tree, ducking beneath the low sprouting branches, each time veering more and more off course. To make matters worse, it had started to rain twenty minutes ago. This had cleared some of the mist, improving her visibility, but it had also soaked through her silly Cheetara costume, making the Spandex cling uncomfortably to her cold and clammy skin.

Nevertheless, despite all this, Mandy had to remind herself she was lucky. She had escaped Cleavon and his brothers. God knows what the others were going through right then. She could still hear Cherry's screams in her head. What had Cleavon or his brothers done to her? And why? Moreover, why had they attacked Mandy and the others in the first place? What was their motivation? Were they a bunch of sick, depraved rednecks that ran some sort of torture operation back at the "ol' McGrady place?" Or were they simply psychopaths, who killed for the sake of killing?

She tried to convince herself that Steve and Noah had returned to the scene of the accident with the police and paramedics in time to rescue Cherry and Austin and Jeff. But something told her they would return to find nobody there. They would think Austin and Mandy and Cherry had carried Jeff off in the hopes of finding help. They would organize some sort of search party, but they wouldn't find them. And this was why Mandy felt so frustrated she hadn't reached the road. She wouldn't be able to tell the police about Cleavon and his brothers—and by the time she made her way out of the forest and contacted them, it would likely be too late.

A branch clawed Mandy's face. She cried out at the burning sensation in her right cheek. She touched the cut and felt warm blood.

Suddenly tears welled in her eyes and threatened to spill down her cheeks in great torrents. This wasn't fair. This shouldn't be happening. This was supposed to have been a fun weekend, a chance for she and Jeff to rekindle what had been lost in their relationship. She shouldn't be wandering around wet and lost and...hunted...in some god-awful national park. She should be in the cozy hotel room in town that Jeff had rented for them, warm, the TV on, snuggling with him under the bed covers.

It's all your fault, Jeff, she thought with a hot-blooded surge of anger. If you hadn't felt the need to play chicken with that hearse, we wouldn't have crashed. We wouldn't have run into Cleavon and his brothers. Everything would have been as we'd planned it—

Mandy stopped on the spot. Ahead of her, visible between the crosshatch of branches, illuminated in the cold light of the autumn moon, an old derelict school bus sat in the center of a small glade.

She remained unmoving for several long seconds, trying to comprehend what a bus would be doing out here in the woods, and when no answers came to her, she approached it cautiously, quietly, half convinced it might disappear at any moment, like a mirage.

It didn't disappear, of course. It was as real as the cedars, firs, and pines that had grown up around it. Judging by its beat-up, weathered condition, it had been there for a very long time. It rested on flat tires and canted to one side, perhaps a result of a broken axle. Many of the windows were cracked or missing altogether.

What was it doing here in the middle of the forest? she wondered again. A car, she could understand. This land might have once been someone's property. The owner might have abandoned a broken-down sedan when he moved away, leaving it for nature to claim as its own.

But a school bus?

As Mandy ventured closer she made out graffiti scribbled along the vehicle's shadowed flank. It was similar to the stuff they'd seen beneath the bridge: inverted pentagrams, upside down crosses, crude drawings of Satan, a goat's head sprouting evil-looking horns. In blue spray paint: "DANNY WAS HERE, 82!" In red: "look behind you..."

Despite herself, Mandy glanced over her shoulder. She found nobody lurking there.

She stopped before the bus's bi-fold door, conflicted. It was cranked open, allowing entrance. It would be dry inside, out of the rain. She could curl up on a seat, wait until the rain stopped, maybe wait until morning arrived.

Then again, was the bus safe? What if the floor had rotted out and she fell through it, her legs shredded by rusty metal? Or what if the ceiling collapsed on her?

She folded her arms across her chest and glanced to her left, to her right, seeing only the thin veil of slanted rain, the dripping trees, the bent, water-sopped tall grasses and saplings.

She climbed the steps that led inside the bus. The metal groaned beneath her weight but seemed solid enough. At the top she gripped the stanchion by the driver's compartment and detected a sickly smell, like something had died inside the vehicle. This almost made her turn around and head back outside, but she didn't. The odor wasn't overpowering; she could deal with it for a few hours.

She turned to face the passenger area. The shadows there were plentiful, but she could make out that all the bench seats had been removed.

She started down where the aisle once would have been. Cobwebs dusted the ceiling while others filled out the spaces where windowpanes had once resided. Soda cans and candy wrappers and other trash littered the floor. Three fluorescent green tennis balls sat incongruously next to a paperback novel swelled to twice its original size, as if it had been dunked in water and dried out. She found no decomposing wood mouse or other small rodent. Whatever was causing the smell must be beneath the bus.

Somewhat relieved by that conclusion she settled down next to a raised wheel well. She pulled her legs against her chest and wrapped her arms around her knees. Rain plinked steadily against the roof. Every so often a frigid gust of wind whistled through the missing windows.

Suddenly Mandy felt extremely small and insignificant—and alone. She could die out here, her body never discovered, and who would miss her? Her mother was dead, she had no siblings, she wasn't close to any of her relatives, she hadn't spoken to her father since he'd kicked her out of the house when she was eighteen. Her friends would be shocked at her disappearance, she supposed, but would they miss her, really *miss* her? She doubted it. Their lives would go on as usual, and they would forget about her. Maybe her name would come up now or then, something like, "Hey, did you used to know Mandy?" or "You know they never found out what happened to Mandy?" But that would be all. She would become a memory, then a name, then a girl they once knew, then nothing at all.

To Mandy's surprise, she yawned. She wasn't tired, she realized; she was bone weary with exhaustion. She lay down on her side, curled into a ball, and rested her cheek on her forearm. The galvanized steel floor was hard and cold but more comfortable than she would have guessed. The strain and tension seemed to seep out of her weary muscles. Her eyelids drooped, batted, then closed. She wondered if any of those spiders that had spun the webs above her might crawl into her hair or her ears while she slept. However, she didn't really care one way or another. She was too tired, too comfortable. She would wake in the morning and it would be bright and sunny and warm outside. She would find her way to the highway. She would wave down a passing car. She would find everyone waiting for her at the police station or the hospital. The cops would have arrested Cleavon and his brothers during the night, and Mandy and Jeff and the others would return to New York City, and everything would be back to how it had been before. They would joke about what happened, laughing at how Cleavon had said he was as country as a baked bean sandwich. They would joke and laugh at all of this because it would be behind them.

Mandy heard a scuffling noise outside the bus. She wanted to ignore it, she likely would have, if she didn't hear it a second time. It sounded very close. It sounded like footsteps—

Mandy hauled herself out of the black pool of sleep she had been sinking into. Wide awake, she lay on the floor of the school bus, unmoving, listening. She heard nothing. Had she imagined the scuffling noise? Or had Cleavon and his brothers found her?

Pulse pounding in her ears, she eased herself into a crouch. She wanted to run, bolt out of the bus, into the trees. But she was too afraid to do that, too afraid Cleavon would be waiting for her in the night.

Maybe they didn't know she was there? she thought. Maybe if she remained quiet, they would move on, leave her alone?

Mandy raised her head to peek out the nearest window. A strong wind was blowing, bending the saplings and rattling the branches of the larger trees. She didn't see anyone. Nevertheless, that didn't mean she was alone. It was dark, she couldn't see far—

Footsteps again, now on the other side of the bus.

Mandy yelped in surprise and fear and bumped backward into the bus's wall panel. A commotion sounded outside. She shot to her feet, ready to run, even as she glimpsed the powerful hindquarters of a deer bounding away into the darkness.

Mandy's hand went to her chest, and she forced the trapped breath from her lungs. "My God," she whispered to herself.

She sat back down, pulled her knees to her chest once more, and rocked back and forth, wanting the night to be over, wanting morning to arrive, wanting to leave the miserable forest.

Reluctantly she glanced at her wristwatch and discovered it was still as early as she'd dreaded, 11:42 p.m., leaving her another six or seven hours until dawn broke.

Chapter 21

"Wanna play?"
Child's Play (1988)

Cherry lay in the corner of the smelly room, hot, dizzy, nauseous, her hands and ankles bound with coarse rope. The giant named Earl kept guard less than ten feet away, lounging in a ratty upholstered armchair, farting and burping and mumbling to himself as he drank beer and watched television. He didn't know she was conscious, and she wanted to keep it that way. Who knew what he would do to her? He and his brothers were monsters. He had nearly killed her.

Everything that had followed her beating in the forest was blurry and muddled in her mind, like a long-ago memory, or a vague dream. Earl had carried her back to where Jeff and Austin both lay unconscious on the ground. Shouting followed, then talking, then nothing for a while, then a vehicle arrived, and there was more talking. Then Earl was carrying her once again. She was flung over one shoulder, Austin over the other.

Finally she lost consciousness, and when she came around a few minutes ago, she was dumped here in the corner of the smelly room, bound by rope, in more pain than she'd ever been in her life.

She didn't remember Earl kicking her in the face, but he must have, because her jaw was swollen. Her probing tongue had found several gummy gaps where her teeth had once been. And her chest, God, that's where she hurt the most. Each breath was torturous, as if her lungs were encased in an iron maiden with nowhere to expand but into razor-sharp points.

Cherry couldn't know for certain why Cleavon and his brothers had attacked them, but she had a pretty good guess. She had seen the lustful look in Cleavon's eyes while he'd been talking to them and pretending to be civilized. It had taken her back to her days as a masseuse in Daveo. At the end of each massage she would finish massaging her customer's head, and she would say, "Finished, sir," and he would open his eyes and look at her how Cleavon had looked at her and say, "How much for extra service?" and she would giggle and say, "No, sir, I don't do that," because that's what they wanted to hear, and he would grin and say, "Come on, just a hand job," and she would pretend to think about it and give an exorbitant amount like two thousand pesos, and sometimes the customer would pay no questions asked, or sometimes he would work her down to one hundred pesos, which was as low as she would go, and then she would jerk him off and, afterward, ask to use his bathroom to wash the semen off herself, and then she would collect her money, tell him to request her the next time he called her company, and she would wait out front his building for the driver on the Honda motorbike to arrive, who would take her back to the housing where she and the other massage girls lived, and she would try not to think about what she'd done, she would tell herself it was just to pay for nursing school, and she would do it all over again the next day.

Nevertheless, as much as Cherry had detested that period of her life, at least she had been in control then. She had been the one setting the rules. She had never agreed to intercourse, no matter how much money was offered. To this day she remained a virgin, and she vowed to uphold her chastity until she married. Austin had not been happy by this declaration, but he'd accepted it. Maybe he thought he could change her mind at some point, or maybe he wasn't planning on sticking together with her for long enough for it to matter, but whatever the reason he had accepted it.

Now, however, Cherry was no longer in control. Now there were no rules, and that terrified her like nothing else, because if Earl or Cleavon or Floyd wanted to fuck her, they would fuck her, they would fuck her and take her virginity, and they would likely kill her when they were done and bury her body in a shallow hole somewhere.

Earl burped and scratched his groin. He reached into the cooler next to his recliner, retrieved a fresh beer, and twisted off the cap. Judging by the empty bottles on the floor next to him, this was his fifth one. Cherry didn't think that would be enough to get him drunk. It would probably take ten or twelve to get someone his size drunk, maybe more than that. So it wasn't likely he was going to pass out any time soon. It wasn't going to be that easy to escape.

Cherry knew she needed to free her legs. If she could do that, she was confident she could outrun Earl. He was big and would have a large stride. But he was also fat, and she was confident she could escape.

He glanced at her suddenly. She squeezed her eyes shut. Too late. She heard him push out of the recliner, cross the room, the floorboards protesting beneath his girth.

"Hello?" he said, and she could almost feel his shadow looming over her. "Excuse me? Little girl, wake up. I know you're awake, I saw your eyes, and they were open, so open them up again."

She didn't.

"Hey," he said, angrier. "Did you hear me? I said open your eyes." He kicked her in the side. He didn't put much force behind it, but she had three or four broken ribs, and if felt as though he'd stuck her with a hot poker.

She cried out and opened her eyes and stared up at him.

"Hi," he said, smiling.

"Hi," she managed.

He sat down before her and crossed his legs. He smelled rancid, like he'd soiled himself two days ago and hadn't gotten around to cleaning himself yet. He reached out a massive hand and patted the top of the head, the way you pat a dog.

He didn't say anything. She didn't either.

Then, abruptly, Cherry began to cry. She couldn't help it.

"Hey," he said, and he sounded alarmed, almost scared. "Don't do that, I didn't hurt you, so don't cry, don't do that."

"I wanna...go home," she said between sobs, throwing herself on his mercy.

"I can't let you go, I'd get in trouble, I'd get in real trouble, my brother would be madder than...he'd be really mad."

He was still patting her head. It was driving her crazy.

"Stop!" she shrieked. "Stop touching me!"

"Hey!" he said, recoiling from her. "I didn't hurt you, I was just petting you, there's nothing wrong with petting, I'm allowed to do that."

Cherry forced herself to calm down. The crying was making her lungs heave inside the iron maiden. She half expected to begin vomiting blood at any moment.

"I didn't do nothing," Earl grumbled, getting to his feet.

"Wait..." she said. "Wait..."

He frowned down at her.

"I need...the bathroom..."

"You gotta hold it in until my brother gets here."

"I can't."

"You gotta."

"Please?"

Earl twisted his mouth indecisively. "A deal?" he said. "Okay? I let you go, I let you use the bathroom, you let me kiss you, that's the deal. Okay?"

Cherry didn't know if he was joking or not.

"Okay?" he said.

"Okay," she said.

Grinning hideously, he bent over, gripped her beneath the arms, and lifted her as if she weighed nothing.

She resisted the urge to cry out; she didn't want to scare him off.

"I can kiss you?" he said.

"After...I go."

"I wanna kiss you now." Without waiting for her to answer he knelt before her, tilted her chin upward with his hand—on his knees he was still taller than she—and pressed his lips against hers. They were wet with beer. The stubble around them prickled her skin. She kept her mouth squeezed shut until he pulled away. He grinned at her proudly.

"Bathroom?" she said.

"Can we do it again? Can I kiss you again? Just one more time, real quick, can I?"

"After I go to the bathroom," she said.

"Okay, after you go, but you promised, you promised I can kiss you again." He heaved himself to his feet and got all the way to his armchair before realizing she wasn't following him. He glared at her. "What's wrong? The bathroom's this way."

"I can't walk," she told him. "You need to untie my feet."

"I can't do that, I'm not allowed, but you can hop, like a rabbit."

"I can't."

"Then I gotta carry you, is what I gotta do, I gotta carry you, that okay?"

"No!" she said, and began to penguin-walk. When she waddled past Earl, he placed his hand on her shoulder, gently, the way one might guide a young child, or a blind person.

They left the living room this way, the captured leading the dumb, and followed a hallway barren of pictures or any other décor. A 1960s-looking kitchen opened to the right. The bathroom was across from it. The hall ended another ten feet or so farther on at a windowless door she hoped led outside.

Cherry extended her arms in front of her so Earl could untie the rope. He stared at her.

"You need to untie my hands," she told him. It felt as though she were speaking between sausages instead of lips. Even so, she was feeling better, stronger, more clearheaded. She suspected the adrenaline coursing through her veins had something to do with that.

Earl shook his head. "I told you, don't you listen, I said I can't untie you, not your feet, not your hands, I'm not allowed."

"How am I supposed to use the toilet?"

"You can still use your hands, they're just stuck together, that's all. You can still pull up your skirt. Look." He demonstrated, pressing his wrists together, as if they were handcuffed, and groping for her skirt.

"Stop it!" she told him, alarmed. She shuffled into the bathroom and elbowed the door closed. "Don't look."

Earl stuck his foot between the door and the jamb. The door bounced off his boot. "I have to watch," he said. "My brother, he said tie her up and don't let her outta your sight, so I can't let you outta my sight, I gotta watch."

"I need privacy."

"My brother said—"

"I won't kiss you again. Not if you watch me."

For a brief moment it was as though a black veil had lowered in front of Earl's face, and she feared he was going to strike her. But then the veil lifted and he said, "If I don't look, you'll kiss me?"

"Yes."

"Two times?"

"Once."

"Two times?"

"Fine."

Earl removed his foot. Cherry elbowed the door closed again. To her dismay she discovered there was no lock. She voiced this.

"So?" Earl's voice came back.

"Don't peek! If you peek, I'm not kissing you."

"You promised!" He tried opening the door.

She pressed her body against it. "If you don't look!"

"I told you I wouldn't, didn't I?" He gave up his effort to get in. "Now go on, go pee, go quick, my brother, he'll, he'll be back soon."

The bathroom, Cherry observed, was no more than six feet in length by four feet in width. Hunkered into the small space was a sink marred with toothpaste gunk, a toilet with a partially unhinged seat, a shelf lined with half-used toilet paper rolls and two bars of withered soap in a shallow ceramic dish, and a medicine cabinet.

Cherry caught her reflection in the medicine cabinet's mirrored front. Her hair was disheveled, her naturally tanned skin so pale it was almost white. Mascara streaked her cheeks like black tears. Blood smeared her mouth, as if she had just finished a strawberry pie eating competition.

She opened the medicine cabinet door, praying the hinges didn't squeak.

They didn't. Inside she found a bottle of Aspirin, two cans of Gillette shaving cream, three toothbrushes all poking out of the same glass caked with green grime, and—*thank you, Lord*—a straight razor with a rust-free blade.

She snatched the razor by the wooden handle, eased the medicine cabinet closed, and lowered herself onto the toilet seat.

A moment later Earl shoved open the bathroom door and stuck his head in.

"Don't look!" she cried.

"I'm not, I'm just checking, that's all—"

"Get out!"

He obeyed. Cherry said another silent prayer of thanks, because although she was sitting on the toilet seat, she hadn't lifted her skirt, or pulled down her panties.

Quickly, not trusting that Earl wasn't going to stick his head in the bathroom again, she used the razor to saw the rope binding her ankles. In her haste she sliced the pad of her left thumb open. Blood squirted to the floor. She bit her lip but kept sawing until the last of the twine snapped apart.

She unwound the length of rope and tossed it aside. Then she unbuckled her stilettos and left them next to the discarded rope. She stood, barefoot, and flushed the toilet. She went to the door, terrified yet at the same time oddly calm. She cupped the razor with her bleeding hand.

"I'm done," she said, opening the door.

Earl smiled down at her, no doubt in anticipation of his two kisses. The smile turned into a frown when he noticed the blood dripping off her hand.

"Hey," he said, "what happened? And where's the rope for your feet—"

Cherry slashed his throat with the straight razor. His eyes bloomed; he tottered backward, his hands going to the wound. She ran toward the windowless door. For a moment she was positive it wasn't going to lead outside, it was going to open to a cellar, she would be trapped, Earl would recover, catch her, kill her—

The door handle turned easily in her hand and then she was outside. A cry of elation escaped her as she fled down the porch steps into the night, through the rain, through the mud.

Her eyes were searching for the best path to take into the forest when she spotted a wood-paneled pickup truck parked at the end of the gravel driveway.

She risked a glance behind her, didn't see Earl, and made for the vehicle. She didn't think she'd be lucky enough to find the keys inside it, but this wasn't the city. She had to check.

Just as she reached the truck she heard Earl exit the house behind her. She opened the driver's door with her bound hands. The overhead light blinked on.

A key was inserted into the ignition lock.

Cherry's heart sang. She heaved herself up onto the bench seat and she turned the key. The engine vroomed to life. She tugged the column shifter into drive and was about to tromp the gas when Earl appeared next to the open door, one hand pressed against the bleeding tear across his throat.

Shrieking, Cherry swiveled in the seat, brought her knees to her chest, and kicked as hard as she could. Her left foot breezed past him. Her right connected with his gut. He grunted—more of a bloodied gurgle—and stumbled away.

She stepped on the gas. But Earl managed to snag her hair. The truck lurched forward; her head snapped backward. Her foot came off the pedal.

The truck jolted to a stop.

Earl tugged her head, hard, as if trying to pull her from the vehicle. Her toe, however, found the pedal. The truck shot forward. Earl released her hair but kept pace next to the door. She stamped the gas at the same moment Earl fell and grabbed the steering wheel. His weight yanked it to the left.

The pickup truck arced on a dime, the cornering force tipping it onto two wheels. Cherry's stomach lurched. She thought of bracing herself, grabbing hold of something, but she couldn't with her bound hands.

The truck crashed onto its side. She heard the juxtaposition of crunching metal and shattering glass, followed by a dead silence.

Pain. Nowhere. Everywhere.

Cherry had no idea how long she laid in a crumpled heap in the crashed pickup truck, half cognizant, but then the pain sharpened, becoming more localized, coalescing inside her head and chest. She opened her eyes and tried to push herself upright. She cried out as sharp teeth bit into her hands. She glanced down and saw she lay on a bed of gummy safety glass. Where the driver's side window should have been was jagged gravel.

Earl, she thought, and her fear of the man mobilized her into action.

Grimacing—not thinking about how broken her body was right then, though "smushed" seemed an appropriate description—she stood and became perpendicular to the seats. The engine hadn't shut off. The dashboard clock read 12:11 a.m. The steering wheel protruded from the dash at her face level. A pair of sunglasses had somehow remained clipped in place to the sun-visor.

Cherry tried to shove open the passenger's door above her head with her bound hands. She cracked it a foot or so but didn't have the height or leverage to push it all the way. She wound down the window—the simple action of turning the crank took a Herculean effort—but she accomplished it. Then she climbed, using whatever she could for purchase: the driver's seat, the center console, the dashboard, the steering wheel.

With a final groan she pulled herself atop the door. She didn't rest or congratulate herself. Carefully, slowly, she slid to the ground. Her knees buckled on impact and she collapsed.

She wanted to remain there, on the prickly gravel, on her side. She wanted to close her eyes, go to sleep, forget the pain. But she couldn't do that, of course.

Focusing, steeling her determination, she regained her feet and shuffled around the pickup truck's hood. She stopped.

Earl lay on the ground, next to the exposed undercarriage. His ugly, piggy face was turned toward her, his eyes closed, his expression slack. Blood covered his pasty-white neck and singlet.

Was he unconscious or dead?

Cherry glanced about for the straight razor and realized with dread it must be somewhere inside the truck. For a moment she contemplated jumping up and down on Earl's skull with her bare feet. But she didn't. Because what if he was faking, playing possum, waiting for her to come close enough he could spring awake and snatch her?

Earl's body hiccupped. A moment later his eyes opened. Cherry wasn't sure whether he could see her or not—then his sightless eyes fell on her. They thundered over. He pushed himself to his knees, weakly, wobbly, like a calf minutes out of the womb.

Cherry stumbled back around the pickup truck's hood and limped down the driveway. She glanced over her shoulder. Earl was up and loping after her, weaving back and forth like a drunk, one hand to his throat. They were both moving with the speed and grace of geriatric patients, and the scene likely would have been comical had the consequences of getting captured not been so horrifying.

Cherry forced herself to move faster and concentrated on not falling over. She barely felt the sharp crushed stone beneath her bare feet.

Earl, she noticed when she glanced back yet again, was no longer weaving and was closing the distance between them.

Knowing he would soon catch her, Cherry veered left, into the thicket that lined the driveway. Her feet sank into the wet leaf litter and she lost her balance but didn't fall. She pressed forward blindly, recklessly, batting her way through the spindly branches with her bound hands.

Finally, when she could go no further, she stopped to recuperate. She listened. She could hear Earl behind her, panting, cursing.

Getting closer.

Cherry pressed on. She should have been focused on survival, getting as far away from Earl as possible, and she was, but at the same time her mind was also lecturing her for detouring to the pickup truck. She should have made a straight break for the trees. She might have been alone and wet and lost, but she would have been in a better predicament than she was in right then.

Cherry stumbled into a patch of thigh-high bush. Instead of backing out and feeling her way around, she waded through it. The scratchy shrubbery snagged her skirt and blouse and held her captive. She tugged her clothing, heard the fabric tear, and freed herself.

She only made it another ten feet, however, before she rammed her forehead against a tree trunk and buckled to the ground. She listened for Earl but couldn't hear anything over her ragged breathing and the drone in her ears.

She didn't know how long she lay there for, waiting to be discovered, drowsy with pain and despair. Maybe one minute, maybe ten. The cool October air had slipped its icy hands beneath her skin, caressing her bones, whispering for her to relax, to give up the struggle, to slip away—

No!

Consciousness returned with bright urgency. Everything that had occurred over the past ten minutes exploded inside her head in a collage of images—and even as she fought for clarity—*Where was she now? Why was she on the ground? What happened?*—she found Earl towering above her, his face slabs of fat and severe shadows, his eyes dusty white and gleeful.

"Gotcha," he said, and reached for her.

Chapter 22

"They strike, wrap around you. Hold you tighter than your true love. And you get the privilege of hearing bones break before the power of the embrace causes your veins to explode."
Anaconda (1997)

After Jeff's failed attempt to rescue Austin he dragged himself to the door, gripped the knob, and found it locked. Of course it was locked. What had he expected? Someone to open it and tell him, "Golly, what a mix-up! How did you end up in here?" Nevertheless, this understanding didn't prevent him from shouting as loud as he could, begging for someone to get him out of there, off the fucking slaughter floor. When his throat became raw from this effort, he slumped against the door—and thought his eyes were playing tricks with him. The room was black but not pitch black thanks to the light seeping beneath the door sweep, and in that light he swore he could make out the snake directly ahead of him, perhaps ten feet away. The longer he stared the more convinced he became he was right. But it couldn't be the snake that had eaten Austin; that nightmare creature wouldn't be moving for the next few months while it digested it's man-sized meal.

So a second snake?

Jeff's heart pounded. The snake—yes, there was no mistaking it for shadows now—lay curled upon itself like a giant garden hose, watching him watch it.

Then it began to move.

Its improbable bulk slinked back and forth, propelling it across the floor

174

toward him. Jeff wanted to scream, but he had no voice. He wanted to run, but he had no use of his legs. All he could do was sit there and watch it come for him.

It went for his legs first. Its serpent head nosed beneath his ankles, lifting them with ease. It looped itself over his shins, then beneath his calves, then back over his shins again. It was one big muscle, he could *feel* its power, and it manipulated him as if he were nothing but a stuffed doll.

As the snake wrapped itself around his waist, it corkscrewed him onto his chest. Screaming now, Jeff thrashed his upper body and pounded the snake with his fists, but none of this did any good.

The eyes! he thought desperately. *Where are the eyes? Claw the bloody eyes!*

But by then it was already too late.

Jeff was floating in a perfect void—perfect because in the void there was a rule, and that rule was no thinking or reflecting or regretting or worrying. All you could do was float and be. Then, he didn't know when exactly, only at some point during his floating and being, he realized he was thinking after all. But he wasn't thinking about Austin's purple and puffy face. Nor was he thinking about the second snake that had slipped itself around his own body and was now in the process of working its monstrous mouth down over his skull. All he was thinking about was his childhood, and that, he decided, was okay, that he would allow.

Specifically, he was thinking of all the Saturday mornings when, after the cartoons had finished, he would go to his garage, stuff a basketball into his backpack, hop onto his BMX dirt bike with the yellow padding around the middle bar so you didn't smack your balls on it, and ride to the neighborhood school, where he would meet his three closest friends and play whatever game they were into. Bernie Hughes always preferred box ball because he had a curveball you couldn't help but chase out of the strike zone. Alf Deacon liked Checkers because he was fat and lazy and you didn't have to run playing Checkers. Chris Throssell always picked basketball because he was taller than the rest of them and could get most of the rebounds.

Jeff, on the other hand, never cared which game they chose. He was equally good at all of them. He hit the most home runs in box ball. He was always one move ahead of them in Checkers. And despite being a few inches shorter than Chris, he scored the most baskets in basketball, zipping around the beanpole, layup after layup.

Jeff didn't know why he excelled so naturally at sports. He didn't have the ideal build for them, not then at least. He'd been one of the shortest kids in all his classes up until grade eight when his growth spurt kicked in. It was true he'd always been coordinated. That helped, he supposed. But it wasn't only athletics he'd excelled at. It was everything. Schoolwork, conversation, visual arts—it all came naturally to him. And being coordinated surely didn't help with math problems or vocabulary quizzes. So it was something else.

Ironically enough, he got off to a slow start in life. He didn't start walking until he was well into his first year, and he didn't start speaking until he was nearly three. Originally his mother feared this might be indicative of some intellectual disability. But their pediatrician assured her that Jeff was in perfect health. And he was right. In his fourth year Jeff was not only speaking but reading fluently. When he entered school at five and a half he found the games and activities of his age-peers babyish and showed little interest in their company. His teacher recommended he skip grade two, though his mother didn't allow this, fearing it might cause him emotional difficulties down the road.

Nevertheless, in the following years Jeff continued to impress his teachers with his mature questioning, intense curiosity, desire to learn, and advanced sense of humor. In grade five his physical precocity kicked in, and he was constantly picked first for teams during recess or gym. In grade six he was the runner-up for the state's science fair competition. In grade seven he won first place in the same competition. Whenever his teachers told the class to pair up, everyone wanted to be his partner. Part of this was because he was popular, but it was also because he'd do all the work himself, or at least figure it out, then explain it to the others.

He never paid much attention to when his parents and teachers called him "gifted." He simply took for granted he was smart and talented and athletic. That was his life, it was easy, and it would always be easy.

Yet now, drifting in the void, Jeff understood how foolish and naïve his worldview had been. Because life was never easy, not for anybody. It threw you curveballs much more devious than Bernie's had ever been. Models were disfigured in freak accidents, millionaires lost their millions in bad investments, celebrities had their deepest secrets exposed in the tabloids. People like Jeff, who'd won the genetic lottery, lost the ability of their legs and were fed to grotesque-sized snakes.

If Jeff could have, he would have laughed at the absurdity of it all, and by "all" he meant life. But he couldn't, his lungs were just about crushed to nothing, and as the blackness of unconsciousness and death closed around him, these last thoughts faded from his mind, and he let himself float and be.

Chapter 23

"All work and no play makes Jack a dull boy."
The Shining (1980)

Boston Mills Psychiatric Hospital was an imposing Victorian structure composed of staggered wings, pointed roofs, and a bevy of turrets. When Spencer Pratt first began working there, doctors were performing lobotomies and electroshock therapy on a whim and sending the unruliest patients into comas with large doses of insulin and metformin. Today, of course, that no longer occurred. Today, in the great and noble year of 1987, you were held accountable for your actions, and accountable people didn't perform sadism and torture on others—at least not in public anyway.

Spencer parked the Volvo in his reserved parking spot and shut off the engine. He climbed out and darted through the rain across the lot, spotting four other cars. They would belong to the nightshift orderlies and nurses. He skipped up the front steps of the main administration building and pressed a four-digit code into a metal box affixed to the brick wall. A beep sounded, the locks unclicked, and he stepped inside.

He shook the water from his blazer and proceeded down the drab hallway, his rubber-soled loafers squawking on the polished laminate flooring. He was greeted by the usual smell of cleaning solutions, antiseptic, and laundry starch.

Spencer enjoyed coming to the hospital at nighttime to work. One, it got him out of the house and away from Lynette. Two, it was serene, peaceful even, the opposite of the controlled chaos that reigned during the day.

At the end of the hall he stopped before the nurse's station. The duty nurse, a twenty-four-year-old local named Amy who had albino skin, horse teeth, and blowfish lips, looked up from the trashy paperback romance novel she was reading.

"Good evening, Dr. Pratt," she said, flashing an ugly smile that made Spencer wonder if she had ever been laid. "Burning the midnight oil again?"

"Work keeps you young. Isn't that what they say?"

"I don't know how you do it, Doctor. All of your late hours, I mean. I think it would make me go crazy." She pressed her hand to her mouth and looked about, as if fearful she had insulted eavesdropping patients. "Oops, I didn't mean it that way."

"Quite all right, Amy. We're all a little crazy, aren't we? If you need me for anything, I'll be in my office."

"Thank you, Doctor. But it's pretty quiet here at night, as you know."

Spencer continued to his office, which was located at the end of the adjacent corridor. He withdrew his keys from his pocket, opened the door, and flicked on the overhead light. Without entering, he locked and closed the door again. A window opened to the hallway. The sheers were drawn, but you could see that a light was on inside. He didn't think Amy would need to contact him for any reason, but if she did, she would see the light and assume he was somewhere else in the building.

Spencer exited the hospital through a side door that led to manicured gardens bordered by neatly trimmed hedges. He made his way back to the parking lot and his car.

Satisfied with the alibi, he started the engine, turned up the heat, and continued on his way to Mother of Sorrows church.

Spencer Pratt had not always been a Satanist, but he had always been a killer. He'd grown up in Shaker Heights, an affluent suburb of Cleveland. His father had owned a shoe factory, which made him a wealthy man when it became one of the manufacturers and suppliers of boots to American soldiers fighting in World War Two. Spencer, Cleavon, Earl, and Floyd had all attended the same prestigious private school. While Spencer was a stellar student, and Cleavon a mediocre one, Earl and Floyd were both born with chromosomal abnormalities linked to inherited mental retardation and were enrolled in the special education program. They weren't trusted to walk home unsupervised, so at three o'clock each afternoon either Spencer or Cleavon—they rotated the responsibility every other day—would escort them. There were two routes you could take. The first kept to the sidewalks. The second cut through a hundred-acre swath of undeveloped woodland. The latter was quicker and more scenic, but a group of bullies often hung out along the path and would throw rocks and sticks at Spencer if he were by himself. That's why he only cut through the woodland when he had Earl and Floyd tagging along. Everyone in school knew Earl was not only big and strong but also a lunatic. They knew if you teased him he would break your arms or legs if he could catch you. He earned this reputation when he was in grade four and beat up a kid two years his senior so badly the boy didn't return to school for a month. Kids would taunt Earl and pelt erasers at him from a distance because they knew they could get away with that; Earl could never remember faces long enough to hold grudges. But no one risked getting up close and personal with him.

On the day Spencer committed his first murder at thirteen years of age, he was walking through the woodland with Earl and Floyd. It was warm, sunny, June, a few weeks before summer vacation commenced. They didn't run into the bullies but instead came across a girl named Genevieve. She was in special ed with Earl and Floyd. Whenever Spencer stopped by the special ed classroom to pick up his brothers, he would try to tap Genevieve on the head because it set her off yelling and banging around the room like a human tornado.

Spencer spotted Genevieve in the long grasses off to the sides of the path, her shirt held in front of her like a pouch, holding a dozen or so freshly-picked wild berries. He called her name in a singsong way which also drove her nuts. Earl and Floyd joined in, repeating everything he said and chuckling stupidly at their ingenuity. Genevieve shouted at them in the inarticulate gibberish that passed as language for her. Hands held up, palms facing outward, as if he were an ambassador of peace, Spencer got close enough to tap her on her head. She threw her arms into the air, dropping all her berries at the same time. She spun in circles swatting the air and herself until she tripped on her feet and fell. Spencer stood over her, watching her dissolve into a blubbering mess on the ground. He didn't feel guilt. He didn't feel pity. He didn't feel disgust. He didn't feel anything but curiosity—curiosity at what it would be like to kill her. That's all he remembered thinking in that moment.

He knelt beside her and plugged her snot-dripping nose with his thumb and index finger. She wailed and tried to pull away. He placed his other hand over her mouth, pressing her head into the ground. She flailed her arms and legs and was surprisingly strong. Earl and Floyd shouted at him to stop. He ignored everything except Genevieve's eyes. He stared into them and saw that she understood she was dying. This gave him a great satisfaction. Then, eventually, her eyes glazed over and she went still.

That's when Spencer returned to himself, when his nerves kicked in. He wasn't remorseful at what he'd done; he was scared white at getting caught.

He told Earl and Floyd that they would all be in really big trouble if they didn't help get rid of Genevieve's body, and so they obeyed him without question. The three of them carried her to a waterhole where Spencer had gone swimming once, and where his mother had banned him from going ever again, telling him swimming unsupervised was how little boys died. The waterhole was the third the size of a baseball field and filled with sludgy brown water. They loaded Genevieve's pockets and backpack with rocks and sank her in the middle of the pool.

For a few weeks it seemed as though her disappearance was all anybody talked about. Spencer often overheard his parents speculating what might have happened to her, while the kids at school had their own more fantastical theories. Yet after a month or so Genevieve became old news. She was gone, she would never be seen alive again, she was best left forgotten.

Spencer didn't kill again for six years. He thought about doing so on most days. He might see a girl in the supermarket, or riding a bicycle on the sidewalk, and he would imagine getting her alone somewhere and suffocating her to death as he had done to Genevieve. He never followed through with these fantasies, however, because he was too afraid of getting caught. Killing Genevieve had been a spur of the moment action. He knew he had been very lucky. Someone could have seen him and Earl and Floyd cut through the woodland that June afternoon, or seen them while they were disposing of her body. The waterhole could have dried up and revealed her skeleton and perhaps some link to Spencer. Earl or Floyd could have talked.

In the end it was the move from home to his dorm at Case Western Reserve University which kicked him into action. The freedom he found living on his own at college intoxicated him and gave him the confidence he had until then been lacking. He had a private room. He had no curfew. He could come and go as he pleased, no questions asked. He could do anything and everything he wanted.

Spencer found the person he would kill in the classified section of *The Plain Dealer*. Her adult-services advertisement read: "Sensual massage to forget your stress and worry. Black, busty, 24 y/o Monique will make all your desires come true." He chose Monique over the other illicit masseuses after consulting the Rand McNally Cleveland Street Guide and confirming her address was a residential property far away on the other side of the city.

Spencer's parents had bought him a brand new Mercury Comet as a high school graduation gift—this was still several years before his father would lose all his savings in a series of bad investments and declare bankruptcy—but he left the car in the college parking lot and instead opted for public transit. He had grown into a cautious man—perhaps because of so many years of waiting for the police to knock on his door and haul him off for the murder of Genevieve—and he was determined not to leave any evidence that could point back to him.

After getting off the bus at Detroit Avenue and West Fifty-eighth Street, he started along a quiet tree-lined street, his head down, his face hidden by his hoodie. The masseuse's home-cum-workplace was a bungalow with a knee-high stone property fence. A white sign on the front lawn read, "Oasis Massage Clinic," and below that in handwritten letters, "Please use side door."

Spencer turned down the driveway. A placard on the side door invited him inside. The reception was dimly lit and smelled of lavender incense. A cash register and a telephone and some pamphlets sat on six-foot-long counter. Given that it was unmanned, Spencer figured the masseuse was with another customer. He was about to leave when Monique pushed through a beaded doorway. She was indeed black, but she was only busty because she was twenty-five pounds overweight. She wore a short skirt and tight top that did little to cover or support her braless breasts. She was definitely older than twenty-four, maybe early-to-mid thirties. Spencer, however, didn't care. This wasn't about what she looked like. It was more intimate than that.

"Hi," she said pleasantly though with little enthusiasm. "I'm Monique. You can come this way."

She led him to a dark room and told him to take off all his clothes and lie facedown on the table. Spencer never had a massage before, but he didn't think Monique was adequately skilled at what she professed to do. She mostly trailed her fingernails across his back and along his legs like a bored student doodling in her notebook. The massage was advertised as an hour, but fifteen minutes into it she tickled her fingers up and down the inside of his thighs and said, "Time's up, hon. Do you want something extra?"

He didn't and told her so. She seemed surprised by this, but then shrugged, replied curtly that it was his loss, and left the room. He got dressed again and pulled on a pair of leather gloves he'd kept in his pocket until then. Monique was behind the reception counter waiting for him. He walked up to her, ignoring her protests that he was on the wrong side of the counter, and seized her around her plump neck. He was still skinny then, having not yet discovered weight training, and it took all of his strength to wrestle Monique to the ground. He pinned her shoulders with his knees and continued to squeeze her throat, preventing her from breathing or screaming for help.

Throughout this he stared into her eyes and saw in them the same understanding she was dying as he'd seen in Genevieve's eyes, and once again this brought him a great satisfaction. Afterward he took a Polaroid of her lifeless face, so he wouldn't forget it as he had Genevieve's, then left her for someone else to clean up.

After earning his MD, Spencer wanted out of Cleveland and chose to perform his residency at UCLA. While in his first year there a friend invited him to a party in San Francisco. The venue turned out to be a strange little black house in which the owner, a man named Anton LaVey, kept a lion and a leopard as household pets. Spencer had no idea who LaVey was then, but according to the other guests he was a local eccentric: ghost-hunter, sorcerer, organist, psychic. He was also an intellectual who spent much of the evening ranting to those gathered about the stagnation and hypocrisy of Christianity. In place he argued for a system of belief, or black magic as he called it, that emphasized the natural and carnal instincts of man without the nonsensical guilt of manufactured sins.

Spencer left the party that evening a different man, for he had found in Anton LaVey all the answers he had been seeking for much of his adolescent life. He was not an outcast, a deviant, a sexual predator—or if he was, there was nothing wrong with any of that. Life was not about self-denial and the hereafter; it was about pleasure and the here-and-now.

Over the course of the next six months Spencer attended all of LaVey's soirees, mingling with artists, attorneys, doctors, writers, and even a baroness who'd grown up in the Royal Palace of Denmark. LaVey continued his rants against Christianity, though he was not a soapbox preacher. He wanted to start a real revolution, one that would free people from the blind faith and worship that life-denying Christian churches demanded.

To accomplish his goals he knew he could not simply present his ideas to the world as a philosophy, which could be too easily overlooked. He needed to do something shocking, and so he ritualistically shaved his head in the tradition of medieval executioners and black magicians before him, formed a new religion he called the Church of Satan, nominated himself as the high priest, and declared 1966 Year One, *Anno Satanas*—the first year of the reign of Satan.

For a while LaVey's Friday night lectures and rituals continued as cathartic blasphemies against Christianity. But then LaVey, drawing upon Spencer's expertise in psychiatry, began to focus more on self-transformational techniques such as psychodrama, encouraging his followers to enforce their own meaning on life. This proved hugely popular with the masses, and within two years LaVey was getting coverage in major magazines such as *Cosmopolitan*, *Time*, and *Newsweek*. By the time he published *The Satanic Bible* in 1968, the Church of Satan had ten thousand members and he had become an internationally-recognized Satanist labeled the Black Pope by the media.

Over the next couple years, however, LaVey allowed himself to become charmed by his own hype and grandiosity, causing Spencer to lash out at him one evening in September of 1971, accusing him of turning the church into a cult of personality. The following day Spencer discovered just how much he had overestimated his position and influence within the Magic Circle—or underestimated how crypto-fascist LaVey had become—because LaVey kicked him out of the church, what had become his family.

Disillusioned, lost, Spencer returned to Cleveland and did his best to get on with his life. He often consoled himself with the knowledge that LaVey was a lie and a phony. The man wrote and preached that Satanism was about becoming one's own god and living as one's carnal nature dictated, but he never had the balls to move beyond the conformities of the masses and follow this teaching through fully. He never raped or killed or indulged in any other of the most basic of human desires—desires repressed inside everyone—which made him as hypocritical as the hypocrites he professed to hate.

Spencer, on the other hand, indulged more than anybody ever knew. During his time in LA he killed seven women, while over the next sixteen years he killed dozens more, experimenting with everything from necrophilia to cannibalism to human sacrifice. What kept him from getting caught, he believed, were two simple rules: he never killed anyone he knew, and he never killed anyone in or around Summit County.

He broke both those rules in the winter of 1985.

Her name was Mary Atwater. She was committed to Boston Mills Psychiatric Hospital during a blizzard three days before Christmas day. As Psychiatrist-in-Chief it was one of Spencer's responsibilities to interview each incoming patient. Based on the photo in her files he knew Mary was attractive, but he wasn't prepared for her extravagant beauty. Armenian-American, she had glossy jet-black hair and piercing chestnut-brown eyes and a wide, handsome mouth. She wore a blue silk kaftan with a silver-and-turquoise necklace and an armload of silver bracelets. She had been born in Chicago where she enjoyed a normal, stable childhood. She became a cello prodigy in her teenage years and married her former college professor. They relocated to Cleveland when she was twenty-five, where, quite out of the blue, a combination of heritability and her daughter's birth precipitated a catastrophic mental breakdown from which she never recovered. It's what landed her in Ward 16 of Boston Mills Psychiatric Hospital, an "acute admissions" ward meant for patients in highly disturbed states who needed around-the-clock care and medication. They were all sectioned, a euphemism for legally detained (hence the hospital's barred windows and locked doors), and most were never discharged, instead withering away in the long-stay wards until they died and were no longer burdens on the system.

Mary was deeply and irremediably psychotic with the most extreme form of what used to be called manic depression and is now known as bipolar disorder. On the day Spencer first met and interviewed her, she was in relatively good spirit and mind. She spoke with an educated accent and, had you not known better, you would have thought she was a perfectly healthy young woman.

But Spencer had treated enough patients with bipolar disorder to know this was a deceptive calm in what would be a stormy, unforgiving life.

Indeed, the very next day Mary sank into her depressed state and refused to get out of bed. She simply lay there unmoving, unspeaking, barely eating or drinking. She would be torturing herself inside her head, Spencer knew, rehearsing every bad thing she had every done, every bad thought she'd ever had, telling herself she was trash, filth, perhaps contemplating killing herself. This terrible low continued for several days until her manic state took over and she became wild, uncontrollable, ripping off her clothes, screaming obscenities at the orderlies and other patients, and once attacking the charge nurse, taking a bite out of her arm.

Seven weeks after she was committed she escaped from the hospital while under the influence of one of her manic phases. The Ward 16 nursing station sat between both the male and female dormitories, with a twenty-four-hour lookout spot. After ten o'clock only one nurse remained on duty. That night it was Ron (the night nurses were always male), who admitted to falling asleep for what he called in his statement to the police a "brief spell." Spencer, who had been working late at the hospital as usual, alerted Alan Humperdinck, the Summit County sheriff, to Mary's disappearance, and an impromptu, sleepy search of the hospital grounds commenced. When Mary wasn't found, the search was called off until first light. Spencer left the hospital at 3 a.m. that morning—and discovered Mary when he pulled out of his parking spot. She had been hiding beneath his Volvo, presumably to get out of the wind and snow, and had fallen asleep.

Instead of installing her back in her room, Spencer set her in the backseat of his car. The situation was too serendipitous to pass up. The police knew she was missing; Ron had already copped blame. The weather being how it was, everyone would assume she'd died from exposure to the elements and was buried by the snow.

While Spencer drove her to one of the abandoned houses that littered the national park—now wide awake and buzzing with the adrenaline and excitement that always preceded a kill—Mary woke and went into a psychotic episode, screaming at him, clawing his face with her sharp nails, pulling his beard.

Spencer lost control of the car and plowed into a tree. He struck his forehead on the steering wheel and incurred a three-inch-long gash that gushed blood dangerously. Mary hadn't been wearing a seatbelt and flew into the windshield, her head smashing through the reinforced glass up to her shoulders.

Holding onto consciousness by a thread, Spencer nevertheless understood he was in serious trouble. If he'd been heading in the direction of Boston Mills, he could have explained he'd been returning home when he spotted Mary alongside the road and picked her up before she went ballistic on him. But he hadn't been returning to town; he'd been driving in the opposite direction, into the national park. He couldn't lie about this fact. The police would want him to take them to the scene of the accident. Nor could he dump Mary's body somewhere and pretend nothing happened. Scratches raked his cheeks, Mary's blood coated his windshield, and he was in no condition right then to clean up himself or the car.

With a desperate, half-formed idea in mind, Spencer reversed onto the road and drove to what he thought simply as The House in the Woods. In fact, his father had built the house years ago after the bank took his Cleveland residence. It had been little more than a two-room shack then. His mother and father lived in one room, Earl and Floyd in the other. This arrangement, however, only lasted a few months. That was how long it took their father to work up the nerve to fill his wife with buckshot before turning the shotgun on himself. Cleavon, who'd been living in a trailer park in Akron and working the odd construction job, moved into the shack to look after Earl and Floyd, for it was either that or commit them to Boston Mills Psychiatric Hospital. Over the next several years he collected wood and materials from the nearby abandoned houses and enlarged the shack until it resembled some post-apocalyptic hideout with eight or nine ramshackle additions in total.

Spencer didn't remember the drive to the house, or his arrival there. He woke the next morning in a bed with Earl sitting on a stool next to him, patting the top of his head gently. He batted Earl's hand away and explored the gash in his forehead, finding it had been sewn closed with stitches.

"Where's the girl?" he asked hoarsely.

"She hasn't woke up yet," Earl said, and put on a sad face. "We got her out of the car, and fixed up her neck, but she didn't never wake up, and Cleave, he says—"

"Where's Cleavon?"

"He's in the garage, fixing up the Mustang. That's what it's called, ain't it, Spence? It's a Mustang, ain't it?"

"Get him."

Cleavon arrived a short time later grease-covered and cranky as usual, though his eyes were alight with a shit-eating grin.

"Who did this?" Spencer said, touching the gash in his head.

"Hell if I know, Spence. I thought it was from the car accident."

"The stitches."

"That was Lonnie," Cleavon said, wiping his greasy face with a greasy dish towel. "You were bleeding a fuckin' river, and Lonnie said he'd fixed up his boy a couple times when he'd cut himself. He said he just needed some fishing wire and a hook."

"You called Lonnie Olsen?"

"Nah. Lonnie was already here, Lonnie and Jesse and Weasel. We were playing cards earlier and they got shitfaced and passed out. Well, that was until you came driving your car right into the fuckin' porch. The girl's okay. Breathing at least." Cleavon cocked an eyebrow. "Say, Spence, what was she doing in her pajamas? Rather, what were you doing driving her around in the middle of the night in her pajamas?"

Spencer didn't reply. He was numbed with dismay as he imagined Lonnie Olsen sitting in Randy's Bar-B-Q right then, telling all the other drunks how Spencer had ploughed his car into Cleavon's porch with some girl's head poking out of the windshield like a crudely mounted game trophy—

Lonnie Olsen appeared in the bedroom doorway, rubbing his eyes as though he'd recently woken up. Jesse Gordon and Weasel Higgins crowded behind him.

"Hiya, Spencer—Mr. Pratt," Lonnie Olsen said awkwardly, clearing his throat. "Or is it 'Doctor?'"

"Everyone's still here?" Spencer said, surprised.

"Where else would we be?" Lonnie said.

"So what the fuck happened last night, Spence?" Cleavon said. "We won't say nothing."

"Speak what you want to whom you want," Spencer said poker-faced, though his mind was racing, for he thought he might be able to dig himself out of the mess after all. "The woman's name is Mary Atwater. She's a patient at the hospital. She believes she's possessed by a demon."

"A demon?" Earl said in awe.

Spencer said, "I wanted to try a kind of psychodrama therapy—"

"Psycho-what?" Cleavon said.

"A type of role playing. It employs guided dramatic action to help individuals examine issues they might have. I was taking her to one of those abandoned houses where we were going to perform a black mass to ask Satan to deliver the demon from her body. It's all in her head, of course, but acting her fears out rather than just talking about them can reap substantial results. However, on the way there she had a psychotic episode and attacked me."

Spencer paused, reading their reactions, and decided they bought it. After all, why wouldn't they? He was the psychologist-in-chief of a large hospital and one of the most respected men in all of Summit County.

"Now, I'm still prepared to carry out this black mass," he went on confidently, swinging his legs off the bed and standing upright. "And I don't mind an audience, if you gentlemen care for a once-in-a-lifetime spectacle? Come, truly, you'll find it...engrossing."

Spencer gathered the supplies he would need for the black mass—a can of primer paint and a paintbrush, a hammer and nails, a carving knife from the kitchen, a bottle of bourbon, a candle and matches, a wilted carrot, a beer stein—then he led Cleavon and the others on a half hour hike through the forest, with Earl carrying Mary over his shoulder. At the first abandoned house they came to he painted an inverted pentagram on the floorboards of a dirty, moldy room to serve as an altar. Cleavon constructed a six-foot-tall crucifix with two pieces of scavenged timber, which he positioned upside down against the wall behind the altar. Earl placed Mary, who was still unconscious, in the middle of the pentagram. Spencer cut her pajamas from her body with the kitchen knife, to the muted delight of those gathered.

Then, when Spencer had everybody's full attention, he crossed himself in a counter clockwise direction with his left hand and began the black mass. Channeling the intonation and charisma of Anton LaVey, he recited a collection of passages from the Satanic Bible from memory, moving from the Introit to the Offeratory to the Canon to the Consecration. Cleavon and the others watched him in an enraptured state, saying nothing, not even when he inserted the withered carrot/host into Mary's labia—but he saw the lust in their eyes. It burned like black fire.

During the fifth and final segment of the mass, the Repudiation, Spencer passed around the beer stein/chalice filled with bourbon. When everyone had drunk from it he said in a commanding voice, "Brothers of the Left-Hand Path, the penitent has proved a worthy neophyte in our high order. It is now time to free her from the bonds of ignorance and superstition. Cleavon, come forth and partake in your desire."

"Huh?" Cleavon said, as if coming out of a trance.

"Do you desire this woman?"

"I, well...I guess."

"The Dark Lord Lucifer has granted you all that you desire. Now take her!"

"I don't know—"

"Lonnie? Quick! We must conclude the mass. Take her!"

"Hell ya!" Lonnie Olsen said, coming forward, unbuckling his belt. He was fully aroused as soon as his pants hit his ankles. Then he was on his knees before Mary's prone body, his pasty, pockmarked buttocks clenching in rhythm to the thrusting of his hips.

"*Eva, Ave Satanas!*" Spencer chanted. "*Vade Lilith, vade retro Pan! Deus maledictus est! Gloria tibi! Domine Lucifere, per omnia saecula saeculorum. Amen!*"

Moments after Lonnie removed himself from Mary, Cleavon took his spot, then Jesse, then Weasel, then Earl, and finally Floyd. When they had all been sated, Spencer knelt next to Mary with the kitchen knife. Before anyone could protest, he sank the blade into her chest, into her heart. Her eyes popped open at this, and he watched as her life drained from them.

"And so it is done," he said softly.

Afterward, in the guilty, bewildered silence that followed, Spencer held each man's gaze in turn and said, "Thank you, gentlemen. It is as she wanted. She is at peace." He hesitated before adding, "And you all must know, of course, that in the name of your self-preservation, what happened here this morning can never be spoken of to anyone, ever."

Two months later Spencer read a story in the Boston Mills *Tribune* about a young couple who had disappeared while visiting "Helltown" in the hopes of spotting the mutants said to inhabit the national park (the Satanist rumors wouldn't begin in earnest for another year or so). Nevertheless, Spencer didn't think much about it. When he read a second story two months after the first about another missing couple, he had his suspicions. These were confirmed a week later when Sheriff Humperdinck discovered a number of makeshift crosses and Satanic graffiti at several different abandoned houses in the national park, which he attributed incorrectly to "troublesome out-of-town folks coming here and giving our town a bad name."

Spencer thought long and hard about what to do before visiting Cleavon at the House in the Woods and telling his brother, "If you and your friends are going to keep this up, you may as well learn to do it right."

Since that encounter Spencer had inducted the six of them—Cleavon, Earl, Floyd, Weasel, Jesse, and Lonnie—into his "club" and had led them in eight other black masses, all of which he had enjoyed tremendously, especially the psychodrama involved, which he'd never incorporated into his private killings but which was proving to be wonderfully erotic. As an added bonus he no longer had to leave Boston Mills to find his victims. Weasel took care of this in the ugly black hearse Cleavon had picked up from some junkyard.

Even so, Spencer had always understood this convenient arrangement wouldn't last forever. There were too many people involved, too many chances for something to go wrong.

And that something had gone wrong tonight, very wrong.

Ever the cautious man, however, Spencer had prepared for this eventuality from day one, prepared and planned, and he knew exactly what needed to be done.

Ahead, through the gray drizzle, he spotted Mother of Sorrows Church jutting from atop the small rise on which it had been built, and he went over for the final time the massacre he was about to commit.

Chapter 24

"I think people should always try to take the bad things that happen to them in their lives, and turn them into something good. Don't you?"
Orphan (2009)

Mandy crouched next to the bus's window, peering out into rain-swept forest, searching for the source of the scuffling she'd heard again. Seeing no animal or person, she made her way quietly to the front of the bus and exited through the bi-fold doors. She wanted to run, disappear into the mix of evergreens and deciduous trees, but then she spotted eldritch blue cigarette smoke drifting out from behind the end of the bus. She started along the flank of the rusted yellow relic, suddenly, happily, convinced she would discover Noah back there. He and Steve had returned from the hospital with the police. They had come looking for her. Noah found her sleeping inside the bus, didn't want to disturb her, and so decided to hang around outside it until she woke.

"Noah?" she said.

Noah didn't answer.

Perhaps he was listening to his Walkman through a set of headphones? Or perhaps it wasn't Noah but Austin. He had escaped from Cleavon and his brothers after all, and he was ignoring her because she told him to stop slapping Jeff's cheek.

"Austin?"

No answer.

Collecting her nerves, Mandy peered around the bus's rear quarter.

A man sat on the jutting metal bumper. He was looking away from her so she could only see the back of his head. He raised the cigarette to his turned-away face.

Mandy noticed blood dripping from his hand—and just like that she had an epiphany. This man had slaughtered the children who'd once occupied the bus. She didn't know how he did this, or why, but he did it, he butchered them, then he killed himself, and now she was seeing his ghost, haunting the spot of his passing, as ghosts tend to do.

The apparition turned to face her. Where its face should have been was a spiraling black void, and that spiraling black void terrified Mandy more than anything had in her life, because it wanted to suck her into it, and this would be worse than death, for she would not merely disappear, cease to exist, she would be *undone*, erased, so she had never been born.

Mandy turned to flee, but her legs had become elephantine. She managed to lift one, to take an impossibly slow step. Her foot sank into the ground all the way to her knee. She glanced over her shoulder, through her stringy bangs and the falling rain, and saw the ghost floating toward her. The black hole that was its face was expanding, cannibalizing its neck, then chest, then arms and legs, consuming its entirety. Then it slipped over her, silently, painlessly, consuming her too, *undoing* her—

Mandy heaved awake, her breath trapped in her throat. She lay on the floor of the bus where she had fallen asleep. Rain drummed on the roof. The wind howled.

A dream, she told herself, exhaling all at once. *Just a dream, a horrible, horrible dream—*

Her relief wilted.

The car accident wasn't a dream. Jeff paralyzed from the waist down wasn't a dream. Nor was Floyd playing baseball with Austin's head, or whatever happened to Cherry to make her scream the way she had.

Despair swelled inside Mandy, despair as cold as the bony finger of death. She fought the tears that once again threatened to burst from her eyes, because if she started crying, she wouldn't stop, not for a long time. Instead she tried to think about something nice, but this proved impossible, like trying to look at the positive side of a funeral. She had no nice thoughts inside her right then.

In her bleakness Mandy sought refuge in her childhood memories. They were neither good nor bad. They occurred too long ago to pass judgment on. They were merely a distraction, a picture of a simpler world when all that mattered were toys and candy and the love of her parents. This was all she'd needed to be happy, day after day, year after year—until when? When had the innocence ended and the real world kicked in? Probably around the time she became interested in boys. That's when "important" things began to matter, like the clothes she wore, or how she did her hair, or who in her grade was developing breasts first, or who was cool and who was uncool.

Nevertheless, the *real* world didn't kick in until her mother's death. Tragedy matures you, ages you, makes you wiser, and thus more cynical. At least it does when it strikes at such an early age.

All of Mandy's priorities went out the window. Her wardrobe became a triviality, boys a nuisance, popularity—she couldn't care less. In fact, she stopped caring about everything. She became petty, self-centered, and bitter. She was miserable, and she wanted everyone else to be miserable too.

But I changed, she told herself defiantly. *I got over all that. I'm a different person now.*

But was she? Was she really?

Because if she had changed, why was she still not speaking to her father? Why was she still angry at him for kicking her out of the house, out of his life—when she had known for some time now that while he had indeed kicked her out of the house, she had deserved it, and he had certainly not kicked her out of his life. It was the other way around. *She* had kicked *him* out of her life. After all, he was the one making the effort to get back in touch. He sent her a letter every month, asking her how she was doing, telling her what he was up to. She kept them all in a folder beneath her bras in her dresser drawer. But she never replied to any...because she was still that selfish little girl who after all these years still wanted someone to blame for her mother's death, something to which no blame could be attributed.

"I'm sorry, Daddy," she mumbled softly to herself, and now the tears came. They flooded her eyes and streaked her cheeks. Yet they were good tears. She had wanted to say those words for a long time, but she always told herself there would be time enough in the future, naively believing there would always *be* a future.

As Mandy wiped the wetness from her cheeks, the despair inside her withered into a profound loneliness, and she wanted nothing more than to see her father again, to tell him the words she had just spoken, to ask forgiveness for being a terrible daughter, for rebelling against him when she should have been mourning with him.

Mandy closed her eyes, steepled her hands together, and for the first time in memory, she began to pray.

Chapter 25

"You gotta be fucking kidding."
The Thing (1982)

Beetle thought he heard knocking and opened his eyes. He was right. Someone was at the door to his motel room. *Rap, rap, rap.* Pause. *Rap, rap, rap.*

Shylock and his sons? he wondered groggily. Would they be stupid enough to return? Or had they called the police? Shit, the cops were the last thing he needed. They'd run his name, he'd come up AWOL. He'd be shipped back to Hunter Army Airfield where he'd face a court-marshal and likely get tossed in the brig.

Beetle sat up on the bed and swooned with lightheadedness. A dull pulse thumped inside his left temple. The Beretta, he was surprised to find, was gripped in his sweaty hand. The last thing he remembered was thumbing off the safety, pressing the barrel beneath his chin, and counting to ten. Apparently, however, he never reached ten. Or if he did, he wasn't willing to squeeze the trigger. And despite feeling sick and shitty, like he'd just woken up the morning after the bender to end all benders, he was relieved this was the case, otherwise he wouldn't have woken up at all.

But that's what you want, my friend. That's the point. Goodbye, goodnight sweet world. You're a coward, that's all. You don't have the balls to do what you know needs to be done—

"Hey!" a woman's voice called. *Rap rap, rapraprap.* "It's me! Beetle? Are you sleeping?"

Beetle frowned. Me? Who was "me?"

The girl from next door. The tall German with the lidded eyes and the long face who was backpacking through the country to LA.

What the hell did she want?

Beetle stuffed the pistol beneath a pillow and stood, grimacing as the dull pulse in his head became a wicked pounding. For a moment his stomach turned and he thought he might be sick. The queasy sensation passed.

Breathing deeply, he unlocked and opened the door and squinted into the bright light of the hallway. The German—Gertrude? Greta?—stood two feet away from him. Her face appeared flushed, her eyes as wide and round as they'd been, now exaggerated, either in fear or excitement, and for a split second Beetle wondered if maybe the motel was on fire.

"You were sleeping," Greta said, more statement than question. "I woke you."

"No, yeah—sort of." His voice sounded thick and slow in his ears. He cleared his throat.

"I thought so," she said. "You were pretty drunk on the balcony. I would have let you sleep, but I know you would want to see this."

Beetle waited expectantly. He was trying to remember what they'd spoken of out on the balcony and was drawing a blank.

"There are people at the church!" Greta told him in an unnecessary whisper, given they were likely the only two guests in the entire motel.

"Huh?" Beetle said.

"The church! With the upside down crosses."

"Ah..."

"Three cars just arrived. Right now."

Beetle frowned, struggling to make sense of the meaning and significance of this. Who would attend church at this hour, and why the hell did it matter?

Greta read the confusion on his face and said, "The legends! Remember?"

The legends. Right. What had she told him? Something about mutants...and a graveyard? Or a school bus? He shook his head.

"Satanists!" she blurted. "They're there right now!"

Beetle almost smiled—almost.

"You don't believe me," Greta said. "I can see that in your eyes."

"What time is it?"

"Two in the morning. Who visits a church at two in the morning?"

"You really think there're a bunch of Satanists over there?" His eyes shifted to the door.

"What?" she said.

"Huh?"

"You want me to go?"

"I'm a bit tired, and I have a headache..."

"You want to go to *bed*?" She seemed incredulous.

"I'm sure you'll be safe," he assured her. "Just lock your door—"

"I don't want to hide. I want to *see* them—and you have to come with me."

"To the church?" Beetle was already shaking his head "I'm not going to the church."

"You'd let me go by myself?" She became indignant. "What if they kidnap me? What if they *sacrifice* me?"

"No, I don't think you should go either. It's late. Go to bed. In the morning you can check it out, see if they left anything behind."

"And miss a real Satanic mass? No way! This is why I *came* to Helltown. Now come with me, Beetle. Please? We're wasting time standing here. They might finish soon and leave."

"I'm sorry, Greta. Not tonight. Maybe in the morning."

"I have a car. We can drive there. It won't take long."

Her persistence was trying Beetle's patience. He'd made up his mind; he wasn't changing it. "I'm not going," he told her firmly. "That's that. Okay?"

Anger flared in Greta's eyes, and for a moment she wasn't uniquely attractive; she was beautiful. Then she clenched her jaw and returned to her room, slamming the door behind her.

Beetle eased his own door closed, relieved to be alone again.

He stepped into the bathroom and urinated into the toilet bowl without bothering to lift the seat, fearing the simple act of bending over might ratchet up his headache. Afterward he filled the paper cup on the counter with tap water and drank from it greedily, spilling water down his shirt. He refilled the cup and drank again, albeit more slowly. His parched throat thanked him.

Back in the room proper he sat on the end of the bed, facing the TV. A news anchor was reporting on a tsunami that had struck Japan's eastern shoreline. Beetle's eyes shifted to the bottle of vodka next to the TV. Roughly a third remained. He was about to fetch it when he realized the idea of drinking more booze right then made him feel more nauseous than he already was.

Then, quite abruptly, a weight settled over Beetle. Not the suicidal depression—that was still there, pressing down on his shoulders like an invisible lead cloak—but something else that made him stare stupidly at the television and fidget with his hands repeatedly.

Boredom. He was bored out of his fucking mind.

He wasn't going to kill himself tonight. He'd already decided that. He wasn't going to continue drinking either. Ideally he would have liked to go to sleep, but right then he felt not only wide awake but wired. If he attempted sleep he would lie there, thinking thoughts he didn't want to think.

"Fuck it," he grunted, getting up and snagging the motel room key.

Beetle knocked a second time on Greta's door. When she didn't answer he realized she wasn't ignoring him; she had likely already left for the church. Beetle started along the hallway, noting the zigzagging line of blood that stained the carpet. He passed the clicking ice machine and took the stairs to the first floor. The reception was deserted. The old cheat was likely in bed sleeping, or at the hospital with his sons. Beetle stepped through the front doors, into the rain and wind.

While he was halfway down the steep staircase that led to the parking lot he heard the rev of a car engine. He took the steps two at a time, ignoring the knot of pain bouncing around inside his head.

At the bottom he stepped into blinding headlights. Brakes screeched. Shading his eyes, he went to the car.

Greta rolled down the driver's window and stuck her head out, beaming. "You changed your mind!" she said.

"Yeah, but I think we should walk," he told her. "Because if there really are Satanists at the church like you think, we're going to need be discrete about this."

Chapter 26

"Oh yes, there will be blood."
Saw II (2005)

As Spencer drove through the gate in the split-rail fence and down the gravel driveway toward to the House in the Woods, he frowned as he passed Cleavon's pickup truck, which was tipped over on its side like a toy that had been tossed to the broken pile. He parked the Volvo and hurried through the rain to the sagging front porch where everyone was waiting for him: Cleavon, Jesse, Earl, Floyd, and Weasel. There were also two women at Cleavon's feet. They were hogtied and gagged and staring up at him with red, terrified eyes.

"So," Spencer said heartily, "having some car trouble, are we, Cleave?"

"Don't get me started," Cleavon growled.

"I told you, it was an accident," Earl said, holding a bloodied dish towel against his neck. "I didn't mean to, I told you that, she was just too quick."

"What happened to you neck, Earl?" Spencer asked.

"He almost let the tiny bitch get away, that's what," Cleavon said. "She sliced him with my razor, jumped in my truck, and almost got away."

"But she didn't," Spencer said.

"No, she didn't. But look at my fucking truck, Spence! I'm gonna need all new side panels, a new headlight, and a new window. And you think Earl got the money to pay for that? You think his rabbits gonna pay for that?"

"Aw, Cleave," Earl complained. "I told ya, I told ya a hundred times, I didn't mean it."

Spencer held up his hand to command silence. "The truck's not important right now. What I want to know is what exactly went on here tonight. Who would like to explain this to me from the beginning? Weasel? Cleavon tells me this is all your doing?"

Weasel Higgins had his scrawny arms folded across his chest, the beak of his cap pulled low over his forehead, as if he were trying to hide. "No it wasn't, Mr. Pratt, I wasn't even here when the truck crashed—"

Cleavon whacked him across the back of the head. "He's talking about Stanford Road and all the shit that's happened 'cause of your stupidity, stupid."

Weasel swallowed. His Adam's apple bobbed up and down like a quickly moving elevator. "I don't know it's fair to say that, Mr. Pratt, to say it's all my doing. Cleave, he's the one who let that redhead get away."

"She wouldn't have gotten away," Cleavon told him, scowling, "if you hadn't gone messing with two cars in the first place." He took an angry drag of the cigarette he was smoking and flicked what remained into the night.

"I'm not blaming anyone," Spencer said calmly. "I merely want an explanation. The account you told me on the phone, Cleave, was brief, to say the least."

"Yeah, well, okay then," Weasel said, lifting his cap and clawing his hand through his oily hair. "Well, I was patrolling Standford Road, like we talked about last meeting. It being Halloween and all, there was gonna be some does, right? So eventually I come to these two cars parked next to Crybaby. Problem was, I drove by so fast I didn't get a good look inside them, didn't know there were so many people. That was the problem." He studied the others warily, as if to see if anyone would challenge this claim.

Cleavon jumped on the opportunity. "That's not what you told me on the phone, you lying shit. You told me—and Jess, mind you—you told us there were seven people inside 'em."

"I did not."

"Jess?" Cleavon said.

Jesse Gordon stood off on his own, chewing bubblegum. "Ayuh, Weasel," he said, looking at his feet. "You said seven."

"What the fuck?" Weasel said. "You two ganging up on me?"

"Now, now, Weasel, what's done is done," Spencer said, holding up his hand again. He felt like a school teacher mediating aggressive children. "There's no point arguing about this. Now please continue."

"Yeah, that's right," Weasel said, shooting Cleavon a triumphant look. "What's done is done." He pulled at his goatee, a nervous habit of his. "Anyway, what happened? Well, what happened was, I turned the meat wagon round and high beamed the first car, the Bimmer. It high beamed me back. So it's on, right? So I come straight at it. The driver in the Bimmer was ballsy, but I was ballsier. I kept my cool. Didn't blink. At the last second the Bimmer swerves and shoots off the road faster than a cat can lick its ass."

"Were they screaming?" Earl asked earnestly. "Did you hear them screaming?"

"Naw, Earl, like I said, it happened too fast." He swept his hands together while making a whistling noise. "Now you see 'em, now you don't, just like that. Anyway, I knew they wasn't going nowhere. So I burned rubber all the way home and got on the horn to call Cleave, but he was already talking to Jess, so I told 'em, I told 'em both, what happened. That's when Cleave, that's when he took over. So you see, Mr. Pratt, I didn't have nothing to do with the girl getting away, that was Cleave—"

"There were four of them and only three of us," Cleavon snapped. "Me and the boys took care of them the best we could—"

"Three," Weasel corrected. "One was a cripple. And he was out cold. So there was only three, and two of 'em were girls—"

"I've had about enough of your smarting off, boy," Cleavon said, and shoved Weasel, knocking him into Earl. He shoved him again, this time to his knees.

"Cleavon!" Spencer said. "Leave Weasel be."

"Ehhh," Cleavon spat next to where Weasel cowered. "The little drink of water ain't worth it." He took out his cigarettes and lit up a fresh one while Weasel regained his feet and moved a safe distance away from him.

"So what happened at Lonnie's, Cleave?" Spencer asked, doing his best to appear empathetic. Lonnie Olsen had been one of Cleavon's better friends. "How did he die?"

Cleavon shrugged, showing no emotion—if you didn't know him better. Spencer could tell he was holding back a whole lot of hurt and anger inside. "Happened before me and Jess got there," he said. "But looked like one of the bucks got hold of his rifle and shot him point blank in the chest."

"And his boy?"

"Got it bad, real bad, brains all over the floor. You ask me what happened, I reckon the bucks got into it with the boy before Lonnie arrived for not letting them use the phone. They killed him accidentally, 'cause that's what it looked like with the radiator and all, an accident, and Lonnie came home and went ape shit, killed one of the bucks, then got served himself. But don't take my word for it. Ask the flying princess here. She was there." He kicked the blonde in the side of the ribs.

She moaned and squeezed her eyes shut.

"No, that won't be necessary," Spencer said. "Your account sounds logical to me. Where had Lonnie returned from?"

"Randy's," Cleavon said.

"You called him at Randy's?"

"First thing I done when I hung up with Jess and Dumbass." Cleavon eyed Spencer apprehensively. "What? What's the problem?"

"There's no problem," Spencer said. "You did well."

"Don't bullshit me, Spence," Cleavon said. "You don't think the sheriff... Motherfuckingshitter! The sheriff, he's gonna find out I called Randy's, ain't he? He's gonna know I was the last person to speak to Lonnie. He's gonna think I had something to do with what went down at Lonnie's. He's gonna put it all together."

"Put what together, Cleave?" Spencer said amiably, carefully. "You just tell Sheriff Humperdinck, if he asks, that you called Randy's to see if Lonnie was going to be around for a while because you wanted to join him for a drink. Lonnie, however, told you he was calling it a night and heading home."

Cleavon screwed up his lips as he thought about this. Then he nodded. "Yeah, that makes sense, don't it? I was just calling to see if Lonnie wanted to stick around for a beer. But what if Randy was standing next to Lonnie? What if he heard something different?"

"Like what?" Spencer asked. "What did Lonnie say to you?"

"Shit, I don't remember his exact words."

"And neither will Randy, even if, by some rare chance, he wanted to snoop in on a call between Lonnie and yourself when he has a bar to run. No offence, Cleave, but you're not the President of the United States." Spencer held his brother's eyes until Cleavon nodded his agreement. "You have nothing to worry about, Cleave," he added. "None of us do. Some out-of-towners crashed their car. On their way to find help they came across Lonnie's place. Something happened, it doesn't matter what, and his son died. Lonnie shot two of them, but not before he got shot himself. The five others fled into the woods. The sheriff will conduct a search, of course. But the national park is twenty thousand acres of dense woodland. It will be like looking for needles in a haystack. When no one turns up, the conclusion will be they got lost and died. And that's it. All we have to do is sit tight and wait this out."

"You're forgetting 'bout the girl who got away, Mr. Pratt," Jesse Gordon said, blowing a purple bubble and swallowing it again. "She saw Cleavon and Earl and Floyd. If she gets to town tonight, tells the sheriff about them..."

"Jess's right," Cleavon said. "And we're wasting talk standing round here shooting the shit. Jess, me and you, we'll take the El Camino. The bitch hasn't seen it. She'll think she's flagging down help. By the time she finds out it's us, it'll be too late."

They were correct, Spencer knew. The young woman getting to town would be a disaster—but this was a disaster Spencer wanted. "You're overreacting, Cleave," Spencer told him in a calm, rational, slightly patronizing tone. "It's highly unlikely she could make it to town on foot. That would be a good ten mile hike—"

"She could—"

"She won't. Not in the middle of the night. Moreover, she'll know you'll be out there looking for her. As soon as she hears a vehicle approach, she'll duck into the woods. You'll drive straight past, never the wiser." He shook his head. "No, she'll bunker down somewhere until morning, when she feels safer. She won't think you'll still be looking for her then. That's when you'll get her."

"I don't know," Cleavon said. "She gets to town—"

"She won't."

"But if she does—"

"She won't," Spencer said with enough decisiveness to signal the discussion was over. "Besides, we have other matters to attend to. We have to get rid of the other out-of-towners in case Sheriff Humperdinck comes by questioning you boys about Lonnie. Speaking of which, where are the other two? There should be—"

"I gave 'em to Toad and Trapper," Earl said in his giddy, booming voice. He shifted his bulk from one foot to the other, almost as if he had to urinate. "Cleave said I could, I asked, and he said I could, 'cause they'd just shed, and they were real hungry, and it would save us giving 'em rabbits."

"You fed them to your *snakes*?" Spencer said skeptically.

"Yeah, Spence," Earl said, obviously tickled blue by the idea. "They're two happy snakes right now, I'll tell you that, you should see them—"

"Show me."

Earl led Spencer through the ramshackle house, down one cracked-plaster hallway, then another, until they stood before a solid oak door.

Earl had purchased the snakes from a pet store in Akron some ten years ago. They were green anacondas, the largest species of snake in the world, though they had only been a few inches long then. They grew fast. After two years they were nine feet in length and devouring a couple rabbits each a fortnight. When they became too big for the timber and wire-mesh melamine cage Cleavon had built for them, Earl demanded they be relocated to the room he and Spencer stood before now. Cleavon put down linoleum tiles to make cleaning the floor easier—they defecated like horses—and he installed a thermostat and humidifier to keep the temperature at eighty-five degrees with ninety degrees humidity. It was a lot of work, and Cleavon wasn't happy about doing it, but when Earl got something in his mind, there was no talking him out of it. There was no ignoring him either, not unless you were prepared to deal with four hundred pounds of single-minded, unreasoning fury.

And then, of course, there was the time one of the snakes tried to make a meal of Cleavon. He especially wasn't happy about *that*. This wasn't long after the snakes moved from the cage outside into the house. Earl would often plunk down in the rocking chair he set up in one corner of the room and sit there watching the snakes even when they weren't doing much of anything, which was their usual state of affairs. On the occasion in question he had been drunk and didn't close the door properly when he left to go to bed. Cleavon woke in the middle of the night shouting. One of the snakes—Toad, Spencer believed—had curled itself around Cleavon's left arm and ankle, swallowing his arm nearly to the elbow. Even Earl, with all his strength, couldn't unwrap the thing. Cleavon wanted him to cut it in half, but Earl wouldn't hear of it. In fact, Spencer wouldn't have been surprised if, had it come to it, Earl chose the snake's life over his brother's.

Fortunately the situation didn't devolve to this. Instead Cleavon had Earl ring Spencer and explain what happened. The telephone call had been chaotic, with Earl blabbering incoherently and Cleavon cursing in the background. Spencer didn't know the first thing about snakes, but he had once read about a boy who had been bitten by a pit bull. The quick-thinking owner of the dog got it to release the boy's arm by dumping half a liter of alcohol down its throat. So that's what he told Earl to do. Amazingly it worked. The snake regurgitated Cleavon's limb and released its death grip from his arm and leg.

Now Earl took the key dangling on a string from around his neck and unlocked the door. He stepped fearlessly into the room, hit the light switch to the left, and said proudly, "See, Spence, I told you, they ate them, they ate them good, didn't they?"

Spencer wrinkled his nose at the sudden stench of feces and urine, and beneath this, the pungent, musky odor the snakes emitted from their anal glands to keep the poisonous organism found in the marshes and swamps of South America at bay.

The two anacondas lay curled in opposite corners. They were both over twenty feet long—nearly twice their length when Toad attacked Cleavon. Their glossy olive bodies dwarfed their heads, which were marked with prominent red stripes. Black oval-shaped markings spotted their backs, tapering down to black spots with yellow centers along their flanks.

Spencer's eyes went immediately to their grotesquely extended middle sections. He stared, fascinated. Despite the massive sizes of the animals, he'd had no idea they could consume fully grown humans. But why not? he thought. Surely if anacondas could swallow caiman and deer in the wild, they could work their mouths around human shoulders.

Spencer wished he had arrived earlier so he could have witnessed the spectacle of the two men's deaths, so he could have looked into their eyes and seen the understanding of their impending doom. Now that would have been something.

"Did I do good, Spence?" Earl asked.

"Wonderfully," he said softly.

"Can I feed 'em more bucks and does in the future? We'll save on rabbits if I do, and all those does and bucks, they just go to waste where we bury 'em out back, so this way we make use of them, and we save on rabbits. I'm right, Spence, am I right?"

Spencer told Earl he could do whatever he wished in the future—an easy proclamation to make considering Earl would not live to see the morning—and they returned to the front porch where they found Cleavon in a heated discussion with Jesse and Weasel. Cleavon was still lobbying to go find the missing woman, while Jesse and Weasel seemed okay with leaving the matter until first light.

"So what we gonna do till morning then?" Cleavon challenged. "Get pissed and hit the sack like this was any old Friday night? You think any of you gonna sleep knowing that bitch is on the loose out there?"

"Why don't we hold a black mass, gentlemen?" Spencer suggested. "My mistake," he added, casting the bound women a glance. "Why don't we hold *two*?"

All eyes turned toward him.

"Huh?" Cleavon said.

"A black mass," Spencer repeated. "Earl's snakes have taken care of the two bucks nicely. That leaves these two does. It's either bury them out back right now, which would be a shameful waste, or have some fun first. Given we have the time…"

The women moaned and flopped around on the porch like fish out of water. Their struggles only earned the attention of the men present, whose eyes began to burn with primitive hunger and lust.

"I don't wanna waste them," Earl said, squatting next to the small woman and patting her on the head. "I wanna have some fun? Please? Can we, huh? Can we have some fun?"

"Given all the trouble we've gone through to get them…" Jesse said, nodding. "Yeah, I think it would be a mighty shame not to get our due."

"I'm in," Weasel said with alacrity.

"Cleavon?" Spencer said.

"You four go have your fuckin' orgy," Cleavon griped. "I'll search for the girl myself, like I do every goddamn thing else myself round here."

Spencer clenched his jaw. "Weren't you listening to me? She's—"

"Hiding. Right."

"Tell you what, Cleave," Spencer said, playing his final card, "this being our last mass in a while—we're going to have to lay low for several months after this—I was contemplating holding it in Mother of Sorrows church."

"Inside the *church*?"

"That's right. Do a proper mass for once. Also, if that young woman somehow makes it from the forest—and that's a big if—Stanford Road will take her straight past the church. She'll see our cars parked out front and come to *us* for help."

"She'll come right to *us*!" Earl parroted. "Then we'll have her, we'll have her good!"

"Smart thinking, Mr. Pratt!" Weasel exclaimed.

"Hell of an idea, Mr. Pratt," Jesse said, nodding sagely. "Hell of an idea."

Cleavon, however, was ever the pessimist. "Or she might walk right on past the church."

"Would you?" Spencer said. "If you were terrified and alone and you'd just been through what she'd been through, would you pass up the nearest help you came across? Anyway, Cleave, to alleviate your concern, we'll rotate a sentry outside the church while the masses are proceeding, to keep an eye on the road."

Cleavon scratched his stubble. "Well, now we're getting somewhere, boys." He nodded. "I s'pose that might be okay. But the church, it's a bit public to hold a mass, ain't it?"

Spencer shook his head. "There's nothing for miles save that little motel." He made a show of glancing at his wristwatch. "And who's going to be peering out their window with night-vision goggles in the middle of the night? Now, are we all agreed?"

To Spencer's immense relief, they were.

They drove to Mother of Sorrows church in three separate cars. Cleavon, Weasel, and Jesse in the El Camino; Earl, Floyd, and the two women in Earl's old nuts-and-bolts jalopy; Spencer in his Volvo. They parked at the top of the hill on which the church was built and dashed through the rain to the abandoned building.

The sanctuary was pitch black and dusty. The air smelled stale, with the faintest traces of myrrh and spikenard. Spencer turned on his flashlight and led the way down the center aisle to the small nave. The others followed, carrying the supplies they would need for the black mass: the cast iron chamber pot, the brass Chinese gong, the cased ceremonial sword, black and white candles, and a rusty bucket filled with chicken blood. Weasel usually brought his Casio keyboard to the black masses they held at the scattering of abandoned houses they frequented, but Spencer assured him the church had a full-sized organ that was in working order.

Earl dumped the two struggling women on the stone floor, next to the altar, and said, "Can we do the small one first, Spence? Lookit her go! She's like a rabbit that knows what's coming for it. So can we, Spence, can we do her first?"

"I'm in the mood for the blonde," Jesse said. "See if she really *is* a blonde."

"I'm with Jess," Weasel said. "We haven't done a real blonde yet, have we?"

"Cleave?" Spencer said. "Your call."

"The fuck does it matter?" he grumbled. "We doing both of them, ain't we? So it don't matter two flying shits to me what order we do them in."

"The blonde it is then," Spencer said.

Jenny was nearly insane with fear. She didn't know how anything could have been worse than lying beneath the bed in that house, knowing Noah and Steve were dead, knowing someone was coming for her. But this was. Because at least when she was beneath the bed she'd had an inkling of hope she might yet get away. Not now. Now she was strapped down on an altar, stripped naked, the number 666 painted across her breasts with what smelled like sour blood. Now... God, now she was being *sacrificed.* These men were going to sacrifice her to their dark lord. They were going to rape her. Then they were going to bury her in a hole somewhere.

How is this happening? her mind screamed hysterically. *I'm a second-year medical school student. I'm supposed to be attending microbiology and pathology on Monday. I'm supposed to be studying all week for Dr. Mann's exam on Friday. I'm supposed to be a doctor one day, helping people, saving lives. I'm certainly NOT supposed to be strapped to an altar and sacrificed to the devil.*

A gong rang, reverberating loudly. Then organ music began to play, what sounded like corrupted church hymns.

God, it's happening, it's started, it's really happening!

Jenny thrashed so violently the rope securing her limbs sliced into her skin. Warm, syrupy blood spilled down her wrists, her ankles.

Abruptly two of the men appeared before her. One wore a black hooded robe that concealed his face, the other the habit and wimple of a nun.

Jenny shook her head from side to side, screaming, but the gag in her mouth turned the screams into a muffled whimpers. Sobs wracked her body.

A third man appeared between the other two—the leader with the beard. He wore the same navy blazer, crisp white shirt, and red and yellow striped necktie he'd had on before.

The hooded man rang a bell nine times. The leader raised his hands, palms downward, and began chanting in Latin.

And right then something inside Jenny snapped with a dry, delicate *whick*, and she believed this to be the sound of one losing their mind.

Cherry could close her eyes but she couldn't close her ears, and she was forced to listen to the horrible organ music and chanting and wild shrieks—and near the end of the ceremony, the grunts of pleasure from the men as they mounted Jenny one after the other.

And Cherry knew she was next. They were going to gang rape her like she was a piece of meat. The irony of the situation was not lost on her. She had spent her entire life following the Roman Catholic decree to abstain from sexual intercourse before marriage. She had upheld this edict even as she worked for a sleazy massage company with men propositioning her on a daily basis. Yet now she was going to be violated a half dozen times within the span of minutes—all on the altar of a Roman Catholic church.

If God had a sense of humor, He would surely be laughing at this. And suddenly Cherry was furious. How could He sit by and let this happen to her? If He was so omniscient and omnipotent, how could He let horrible acts of savagery like this occur in His creation?

She knew the answer. The last several hours of horror had pulled back the curtain on life and shown her the cruel truth.

God was not sitting on His throne in heaven in all His glory, surrounded by His angels, beckoning for her to join Him at His side.

God didn't exist, He was dead, and very shortly she would be too.

After Spencer plunged the ceremonial sword into the blonde's chest to conclude the black mass, he turned to the assemblage and said, "I must admit, gentlemen, I have enjoyed myself thus far immensely."

"And we still got one more," Earl said excitedly.

"That we do." Spencer stroked his beard thoughtfully. "Cleave, what would you think about leading the next mass?"

"Me?" Cleavon said, surprised.

"You don't want to?"

"It ain't that. It's just...I don't know none of that Greek mumbo jumbo."

"Latin mumbo jumbo. And the mass doesn't have to be led in Latin. You can recall most of the English parts can't you?"

"Sure...probably." He shrugged. "I guess."

"Then you'll do fine."

Cleavon cocked an eye suspiciously. "Why you offering to let me lead the mass?"

"It seems in our excitement we forgot to post a sentry out front the church." A brief uproar followed this announcement, which Spencer promptly cut off. "Calm down, gentlemen. Calm down. We simply won't make the same oversight twice."

"I'll go, Mr. Pratt," Jesse Gordon said. "I don't mind. The old pecker's not what it used to be, and I'm not sure I could get it up for another go anyway."

"Thank you, Jesse," Spencer replied, "but my libido isn't what it used to be either. Also, to be perfectly frank, without my robes and headgear I don't feel comfortable leading the mass. The psychodrama is not at the level it should be." He started walking toward the double front doors. "Collect yourselves, gentlemen," he added over his shoulder. "Take your time with her, enjoy her, for she will be our last sacrifice for some time."

"You holler you see that girl!" Cleavon called.

"You'll hear me."

Outside, beneath the black, weeping sky, Spencer went to the Volvo, popped the trunk, and retrieved the two lengths of half-inch chain and the two heavy-duty padlocks he'd kept there since deciding on Mother of Sorrows church as the venue for his contingency plan.

He secured the doors on the east side of the church first, looping one chain through the sturdy brass handles several times before attaching a padlock. He repeated this procedure with the front doors. Both times he tested his handiwork, tugging the handles quietly.

Spencer had always been curious as to how he would feel when the occasion inevitably arose when he would have to murder his brothers. They weren't nameless, random women. He had grown up with them, went to school with them, opened presents on Christmas day with them. They were blood. He had hoped he would feel regret or sadness—those would be the appropriate emotions one should feel in such a situation—but as it turned out he didn't feel anything. Their deaths would be meaningless to him.

Back at the Volvo's trunk Spencer withdrew the red jerry can, unscrewed the cap, and walked the circumference of the church, splashing a line of gasoline behind him. When he met up with where he'd begun, he lit a match and dropped it in the gas. Flames whooshed to life and chased the flammable fluid around the wooden building like a line of falling dominoes.

A sense of accomplishment filled Spencer. It was done. Everyone inside the church would meet their fiery deaths shortly. There would be no one left who knew about the Mary Atwater incident. Moreover, they would take the fall not only for the murders this evening, but for each and every murder over the past twenty-four months. The police would raid the House in the Woods and find eight skeletons buried out back. They might not be able to explain who was responsible for locking and burning the church to the ground, but they wouldn't have any reason to suspect Spencer. It would remain a mystery, which, in the big picture, wouldn't matter anyway—because the main culprits were dead, justice was served.

Spencer, of course, could not continue with the Satanic masses on his own, at least not in Boston Mills. This would be a shame. He had become comfortable with the arrangement he'd orchestrated. Nevertheless, a return to his old ways would be its own relief. He would no longer have to worry about other people talking, other people screwing up. He would once again be wholeheartedly in control of his fate.

"Goodbye, gentlemen," Spencer said as the heat from the quickly escalating fire rose against his face. "Be sure to give our fair Lucifer my salutations when you see him."

Chapter 27

"It's been a funny sort of day, hasn't it?"
Shaun of the Dead (2004)

The storm continued to strengthen, the torrent of driving raindrops turning the surface of Stanford Road into a furious boil. The first peal of thunder rumbled ominously in the dark sky, almost directly overhead.

Greta, more skipping than walking, said, "How are you feeling?"

Beetle rubbed rainwater from his eyes. "Wet."

Greta laughed, tilted her head to the heavens, and stuck out her tongue, to catch the raindrops on it. "I love walking in the rain."

"You're in the minority."

"Then you should have brought an umbrella, Herr Beetle." She smiled crookedly at him. "Are you still drunk?"

Yeah, he was. Drunk and stoned and a bit squishy inside. But walking in the midst of a storm had a way of sobering you up. "I'm fine," he said.

"You don't talk much, do you?"

"We're talking right now."

"Because I'm talking to you. I think if I never said anything, you might not either."

Beetle wondered about that. He supposed she was right. He'd never been much of a talker, especially with strangers. And although Greta was no longer really a stranger—more like the talkative girl at a party who wouldn't leave you alone—he was in no mood for chitchat. In fact, he was already beginning to second-guess his decision to come along on this witch hunt or whatever it was.

He hunched his shoulders against the rain and dug his fists deeper into his pant pockets.

"See!" Greta said.

"Huh?" he said, glancing sidelong at her. Her eyes were sparkling, her wet face glowing. She was really getting off being out in a storm.

"I didn't say anything, to see if you would say something, and you didn't."

"What do you want to talk about?"

Greta rolled her eyes. "Nothing. That isn't the point. Talking doesn't have to be about something. You can just talk to talk."

Beetle nodded, realized this didn't qualify as speaking, didn't want to get reprimanded again, and so said, "Got it."

"Do you have a girlfriend?"

The question surprised him—and angered him. "No."

"I don't either," she said. "A boyfriend, I mean. I'm too tall."

"To have a boyfriend?"

"No man wants to date a woman taller than themselves. Only movie stars don't seem to care. Unfortunately, I don't know any movie stars."

Beetle glanced at Greta again. She must have been six feet, maybe six-one—his height, though likely two thirds his weight. She wore a red rain slicker over a white T-shirt. The slicker was unzipped, the tee soaked through. She wasn't wearing a bra.

"You know," she said, "it's nice walking next to someone as tall as I am. I don't feel like a freak."

"You're not a freak."

"I was at a zoo last week, the one in Toronto. There were these young children there with their teachers on a school field trip. You should have seen how they all looked up at me, with these big, curious eyes, the same way they looked at the animals. I stick out like a blue thumb."

"A sore thumb."

"A blue thumb doesn't stick out?"

"I guess. But the saying is a sore thumb."

"I like blue thumb. I think a blue thumb sticks out more than a sore thumb."

"Why would you have a blue thumb?"

"Hey," she said, "do you think if we had babies, they would be tall too?" Her eyes shone with bright mischievousness. "Don't worry," she added, "I'm not proposing we have a baby. I don't even know you. And you're too quiet to be my husband. I'm just wondering if you think we would have tall babies."

Beetle shrugged. "Babies aren't tall."

"Some are."

"No, they're not—inherently not. The same way ice isn't warm."

"Are you making a joke?"

"I'm pointing out a truism."

"No, I think you made a joke." She clapped her hands. "I can't believe it! Herr Beetle has a sense of humor. Tell me something else funny."

"It wasn't a joke—" Beetle stopped abruptly. Aside from the machinegun-like patter of rain he thought he could hear the sound of an approaching engine. "A car's coming," he said.

"So?" Greta said.

Headlights appeared from around a bend ahead of them. Beetle took Greta's arm and steered her into the vegetation lining the verge until they were concealed behind a large tree.

"Kinky, mister," she said.

"It's coming from the direction of the church."

"Oh!" she whispered. "You think...?"

The headlights merged into a blinding white light. For a moment Beetle felt unacceptably exposed. He pressed his body against Greta's, wanting to blend further into the shadows. The car roared past, the sound of the engine faded, then they were alone once more.

Beetle realized his lips were inches from Greta's, his chest pressed against hers. Embarrassed, he led her back to the road. Her cheeks were flushed. Her erect nipples pressed against the fabric of her drenched shirt. She noticed him notice this.

Beetle looked away. "Guess we missed it," he said.

"What do you mean?" she asked.

"The mass," he said. "If that was one of the Satanists, it seems the party's over."

"We don't know who that was. It could have been anyone."

"At this hour—?"

"*Sue dumm fuhrt!*" Greta said. "Don't give up so easy on things, Herr Beetle." She took his hand in hers. "Now come on! There still might be time."

Chapter 28

"Sometimes dead is better."
Pet Sematary (1989)

Cleavon had been the first to smell the smoke. They had replaced the blonde with the Asian on the altar—she'd been a bitch to tie down, fighting as if she really did have a demon inside her—and as Cleavon stood in front of her, trying to think how to begin the black mass, he detected the unmistakable smell of smoke. For a moment he wondered if someone was burning leaves before remembering the nearest neighbor was the motel some two miles away. He said, "Can you smell that?"

"That ain't how you start the mass, Cleave!" Earl said. "First you gotta cross yourself backwards, that's what you gotta do first—"

"Jess," he said, "you smell that?"

Jesse was sniffing the air. "Sure do, Cleave."

"Something's burning, I reckon," Weasel said.

"What the fuck's Spence doing?" Cleavon growled. "Starting a fuckin' signal fire for the girl?"

Tossing aside the little bell he'd been holding—it landed on the altar with a small *ding!*—he snatched the flashlight and marched up the aisle to the front doors. Jesse and Weasel followed close behind him, with Earl and Floyd bringing up the rear. He gripped the brass door handle and immediately released it, crying out in pain. He spun in a clumsy pirouette, flapping his scorched hand in the air. "*Jeeeeee-zus!*"

"What is it, what happened?" Earl asked, reaching for the handle next.

"Don't touch that!" Cleavon said, slapping Earl's hand clear. "It's hot!"

"Why the hell's it hot?" Jesse said.

Cleavon kicked the door hard with his right foot. It didn't budge.

"It's stuck?" Weasel said, kicking the door himself to no avail.

"Mr. Pratt?" Jesse called. "Hey-o! Mr. Pratt!"

There was no answer.

Understanding dawned on Cleavon, and a body-wide coldness slipped beneath his skin. "The motherfucker!" he mumbled.

"Who?" Jesse asked, staring at him with eyes expecting the worst.

Cleavon, however, barely heard him. He was numbed. His goddamn bastard of a brother had double-crossed them all! No wonder he hadn't given a damn about finding the bitch who'd gotten away. She'd never seen *him*.

"Cleave?" Earl said, worried. "What's happening, Cleave? *Cleave?*"

"Bust them down, Earl!" Cleavon told him, pointing at the doors. "Bust them hard as you can!"

Earl shoved Weasel aside and raised his massive boot and slammed it into the crack where the doors met. The doors shook but held.

"Again!" Cleavon shouted.

Earl kicked a second time, and a third, and a fourth.

"It ain't working, Cleave!" he cried. "They're too strong!"

Cleavon's shock and anger was quickly giving way to blistering fear.

They were trapped.

They were going to roast alive.

Spencer wouldn't have attempted something like this had he not been convinced it would work.

My brother! he thought, his mind reeling. *My own fucking brother!*

Then again, was he really surprised Spencer could orchestrate something so heartless? Two years ago he would have been, back before Spencer showed up at the house with that Mary woman, both of them bloodied and smashed up. Because before then Spencer might still have been a holier-than-thou asshole, but that had been all. After that night, however—that's when Cleavon began to see his older brother in an entirely new light. It

223

wasn't the revelation that Spencer was okay with killing. Hell, as it turned out, the whole merry lot of them were okay with killing. Life was a spiteful whore, and you had to do what you had to do sometimes to make yourself happy. So it wasn't that Spencer was okay with the killing; it was that he actually *enjoyed* it. Jesse and Weasel, Earl and Floyd, himself too, they were in this devil worship stuff for the sex. That first woman, that Mary, she got them hooked on the black masses like junkies on heroin. This was not so much the case with Spencer, who always seemed more interested when he was looking in the women's eyes in those last few seconds before they died, as if he were seeing something there no one else could see.

So, no, maybe Cleavon wasn't surprised to discover Spencer had it in him to murder his own brothers. Maybe he wasn't surprised at all.

Cleavon directed the flashlight beam around the church's sanctuary. Three stained-glass windows lined the east wall, three the west wall, each a dozen feet tall, two feet in diameter, tapering to pointed tips. Earl could boost Cleavon up to one, but it would do no good. They were all secured with steel mesh on the outside to protect against vandals and the elements.

"Well don't just stand there looking pretty, boys!" he quipped. "Get looking for another way out!"

They searched every dark corner of the church. The only other set of doors they found turned out to be locked as tightly as those at the front.

Think, Cleave! he told himself, turning in a circle, panicking. *Think!*

But how could he? The scene was chaos. Earl wailing like a little kid. Floyd holding his ears and making that retarded deaf sound he made. Weasel and Jesse both shouting for instructions.

"Shut up!" he exploded, wiping sweat from his brow. It was as hot as hell in summer. "The lot of you! Earl! Shut the fuck up!"

They went quiet.

Cleavon's eyes fell on the dead blonde. A great sadness welled inside him. Not for her. For himself. Because shortly he was going to be dead too. Dead and crisped so black the sheriff will be identifying him by his teeth.

And I just unloaded two hundred bills on a new carburetor for the Mustang in the garage, and I ain't even gonna get a chance to install it. Ain't that a bitch, ain't that just a goddamn, motherfucking bitch.

His eyes drifted to the pew the blonde was lying on, then the pew's clawed wooden feet.

They weren't bolted into the floor.

An idea forming in his mind, Cleavon rushed to the pew, shoved the woman's body to the floor, and gripped the pew beneath the seat. He managed to rock it back an inch. "Boys!" he rasped in the dry air. "Give me a hand here! We got ourselves a battering ram!"

With Cleavon and Earl on one side, Weasel and Jesse and Floyd on the other, they lifted the pew between them, swung it perpendicular, and carried it up the aisle. On Cleavon's instruction they set it down still some distance from the front doors.

"This is it, boys!" he said, shaking his spaghettied arms. "On the count of three we charge those doors like it's nobody's business! Y'all ready? *Y'all fuckin' ready?*"

"Ready, Cleave!" Earl said.

The others concurred with equal enthusiasm.

"On the count of three!" Cleavon said. They lifted the pew simultaneously. "One! Two! Three!"

They rushed the double doors, shouting like a pack of crazies.

The front of the pew crashed into the doors straight on—and came to a bone-jarring stop. Everyone's momentum caused them to release the pew and torpedo into the doors themselves. Cleavon and Earl bounced backward, lost their balance, and collapsed to the floor in a mix up of limbs.

"Shoot, Cleave," Earl said after a dazed moment. "That didn't work real good, did it?"

Chapter 29

"We all go a little mad sometimes"
Psycho (1960)

Beetle and Greta stared in disbelief at the white wooden church with the upside down crosses incorporated into its architecture. It was engulfed in a glowing red fire that blazed against the black night. The flames, undeterred by the downpour, licked as high as the overhanging soffits, crackling and popping as they consumed the buckling weatherboards. Clouds of thick, acrid smoke streamed upward into the sky.

Beetle and Greta had frozen at the sight of the inferno when they'd breasted the summit of the hill on which the church had been built. Now they rushed past the two parked cars toward the front doors, where they stopped and stared again at the chain wound through the door handles and cinched together by a large bronze padlock.

"What the hell?" Beetle said.

"Hey!" Greta shouted, cupping her mouth with her hands. "Hello in there! Hey! Can you hear me?"

A chorus of weak croaks erupted from the other side of the doors, followed quickly by an equal number of gut-wrenching coughs.

"We need to help them!" she said as thunder crashed overhead, so loud it seemed to shake the ground. Forked lighting flashed moments later, searing the sky a blinding white.

Beetle was already reaching for the Beretta tucked into the waistband of his pants. "Step back," he told Greta, aiming the pistol at the padlock.

"You have a gun!" she exclaimed. "Why—?"

"Stand back!"

Greta backed up.

Beetle squeezed the trigger.

The first bullet ricocheted off the padlock, pock-mocking the metal but otherwise leaving the lock intact. He fired two more rounds—*pop, pop*—both direct hits. The second smashed the tumblers inside the lock to pieces and left the lock dangling by the hook.

He tucked the pistol away, snapped a branch off a nearby sapling, and poked it through the ribbon of flames, lifting the dangling padlock free of the chain. The padlock struck the cement pavers with a metal clack. He worked on the chain itself next, unraveling its length loop after loop until it was free from the handles and dropped in a slinky coil beside the lock.

"Try opening the door now!" he shouted to those trapped inside the burning structure.

For a long moment nobody replied, nothing happened, and Beetle feared he and Greta had arrived too late. Then, abruptly, the right door swung open. In the hazy gray smoke that filled the church a man stood hunched over, the hooded black robes he wore pulled up over his mouth and nose to form a crude mask so only his eyes were visible. He leapt through the flames, took several drunken steps, as if he'd forgotten how to walk, doubled over, and vomited.

A second man clad in black robes—he must have been close to seven feet tall—followed the first. He carried two unconscious men as if they weighed nothing.

"Nuh...nuther..." the big man said between poleaxing coughs. The two men slipped from his grasp like ragdolls. One landed on his back, his arms spread out at his sides, the other on his chest, his arms folded beneath him.

"Another inside?" Beetle said.

The man's head bobbed.

"Help them," he told Greta, nodding to the unconscious men. Then he covered his mouth and nose with the crook of his elbow and ducked inside the burning church.

The heat hit him like a physical force. The cloying gray smoke stung his eyes, causing them to blur and water. He dropped to his knees, so he could see in the space where the smoke had risen off the floor. He spotted the last man. He was several feet to the right, lying motionless on his side.

Beetle seized him by the wrists and dragged him toward the door. At the threshold he scooped him into his arms, stood—and heard coughing from deep within the church.

"Shit!" he mumbled. Leaping through the flames, Beetle deposited the man next to Greta and returned inside the church, thinking, *So this is what a firefighter feels like—only firefighters have fire retardant suits and oxygen masks and powerful water hoses.*

Crouched low, he scrambled on all fours down the main aisle, and discovered a woman atop a candle-lit altar. She was naked. Her wrists and ankles were bound with rope secured to the eyelets of four iron stakes hammered into the floorboards.

Ignoring the questions banging around inside his head, he untied the ropes and carried the woman outside. He set her down on the ground, then collapsed next to her. His eyes itched maddeningly. His throat felt stripped raw. Each breath was equally glorious and excruciating.

"Greta..." he rasped. He might not know what happened here, but he didn't think it was an innocent sex game gone wrong. "Go..."

"Not so fast," the first man out of the church said, standing straight and wiping puke from his mouth. "No one's going nowhere."

Still on his knees, squinting against the rain, Beetle whipped out the Beretta and aimed it at the man with the muttonchops and handlebar mustache. "Get back!" he said. "Now!"

The man, who had been approaching them, froze. "Whoa, hold up there, hoss." He raised his dripping hands. His hair was plastered to his head like a helmet.

"Get back!"

"Listen—"

"Get back!"

He took a single step backward.

Greta helped the naked woman into a sitting position. "Can you stand?" she asked her, taking off her jacket and draping it around the woman's shoulders.

Still coughing, the woman nodded. Greta eased her to her feet.

"Get behind me," Beetle told them.

"Now wait just a sec—" Muttonchops said, his words drowned out by an explosion of thunder. "You don't understand," he went on a moment later. "We weren't doing nothing wrong. The little lady there, she's here of her own free God-given will."

The woman shook her head vigorously. Lightning shattered the sky. The succession of brief flashes illuminated her face starkly, gouging deep shadows beneath her saucer-wide eyes. "He's...he's lying...he killed them...he killed everyone..." Her coughs turned into sobs that wracked her body.

"Who's everyone?" Beetle demanded.

"Everyone!" she blurted, fixing the man with a murderous glare. "Noah! Steve! Jeff! Austin! You fed Austin to a snake! *You fed my boyfriend to a snake!*"

"Listen to her!" Muttonchops said. "Too much smoke got into that tiny pinhead of hers—"

"It's true! I heard you! And Jenny..." She issued a low moan, as if reliving some terrible moment inside her head. "I saw you...you raped her...all of you...she's in there...the church..." She devolved into inarticulate noises.

Beetle glanced at the church. His stomach sank. It was nothing but a gigantic fireball now. If anyone were still inside, they were dead. He didn't know what was going on, but even if half of what the woman was saying was true, it was something much bigger than either he or Greta had imagined, or were prepared to deal with.

"Greta," he said without taking his eyes or pistol off Muttonchops, "take her back to the motel, call the police, get them out here."

The big man, who had been slowly getting his coughing fit under control, now wiped a meaty paw across his slobbering mouth and pushed himself to his feet. He glanced at Beetle's pistol, then at Muttonchops. Beetle didn't like the dumb, cruel look he saw in his eyes. It reminded him of a dangerous dog awaiting an order from its master.

"Greta," Beetle said. "Get going, now—"

Muttonchops tipped his head in a barely perceptible nod. The next moment he and the Goliath charged Beetle simultaneously. Beetle fired a round at Muttonchops, clipping him in the shoulder, sending him to the ground. He swung the pistol at Goliath and fired two more rounds, point blank into his chest. Goliath stiffened and slowed but didn't stop, and then he was right in front of Beetle. He batted the pistol into the flames. In what seemed like the same instant his huge hands were around Beetle's throat, lifting him clear off the ground. Beetle straight chopped him on either side of the neck. It was as effective as striking stone. He dug his thumbs into the brute's eyes. Goliath roared in pain and launched Beetle through the air. He landed on the wet gravel, the sharp pebbles tearing the skin off his chin and both elbows. He rolled over to find Goliath rushing toward him. Rage had transformed his ugly, blunt face into something inhuman.

Beetle scrambled backward, splashing through shallow puddles, away from the impossibility barreling down on him—*I shot the fucking guy point blank*—but he was too slow. Goliath reached him in a few strides and lifted his booted foot, as if to squash him like a bug.

Beetle slipped his legs around the man's ankle, locked his own ankles, and corkscrewed his body. Goliath fell like a tree, stiffly and inelegantly, issuing a strange womanly yelp when he struck the ground.

Beetle climbed onto Goliath's back and locked his arms around his neck in a chokehold. Despite Beetle's size and strength, Goliath lumbered to his feet with monstrous ease. Beetle squeezed his arms tighter, in an equal effort to subdue the man and hold on. His feet dangled in the air.

Goliath reached a hand over his shoulder and swatted Beetle with powerful blows. Then he staggered, and Beetle filled with hope. Either the gunshot wounds to his chest were finally exacting their toll, or the chokehold was cutting off sufficient airflow to his brain.

Goliath spun left and right, trying to shake Beetle free. Beetle felt like a cowboy, riding a maddened bull. He held on with all his willpower and strength.

The blows became weaker. The spinning lessoned.

Then Goliath staggered again, this time dropping to one knee.

His calloused fingers pried at Beetle's arm in a final, desperate attempt to free himself. He was making a dry, wheezing sound that was almost lost in the drumming rain.

Beetle wondered if he was trying to speak, to beg for his life.

Finally he shuddered, then collapsed to his chest, dead.

While the stranger wrestled with the giant, Cherry attacked the man named Cleavon, shrieking like a woman possessed. She had never wanted to kill another person in her life, but she wanted to kill Cleavon right then. She would claw his eyes from his face if she could, she would spit in their bloody sockets, and she would laugh while doing it.

The man lay on the ground, cupping his injured shoulder where he had been shot, trying to rock himself to his knees. He saw her coming and kicked. She dodged his foot and fell on top of him, unleashing a fury of blows.

"Bitch!" he growled, shoving his hand in her face.

She bit his fingers to the bone.

He wailed, tried to yank his fingers free. She bit harder and tasted sweet, coppery blood. She shook her head, trying to sever the digits.

"Cunt!" he gasped and walloped her in the face so hard he might have broken her jaw. She seemed to fall through space, seeing stars.

Greta had picked up the wet, slimy branch Beetle had used to work the chain free from the church doors. Now she stood indecisively with it raised in a threatening gesture, unsure whether to help Beetle or the naked woman. When the man with the muttonchops walloped the woman in the side of the head, Greta made up her mind, rushed to the woman's aide, and began striking the man with the stick. He shouted obscenities at her and tried to protect his face. She got three solid licks in before he grabbed hold of

231

the end of the stick and tugged it free from her grasp. He struck her with it across the shins, flaying the bare skin below the hem of her dress. She cried out and fell as he rose to his feet. He whipped her several times before the stick snapped in two. He tossed what remained away, then started toward one of the vehicles.

Wiping blood and rain from her eyes—the stick had sliced a gash across her forehead—Greta staggered after the man. She didn't know what she was doing. He was obviously fleeing the scene, and maybe it would be for the best to let him do so. But she was filled with adrenaline and hate, and she grabbed his hair from behind, yanking it as hard as he could.

"Aiyeee!" he said, stumbling backward.

She released his hair and gripped his injured shoulder, digging her nails into the bloody bullet wound.

He shrieked louder.

Nevertheless, he was not only muscular and wiry, but resilient, and he didn't go down. Instead he grabbed a fistful of her hair, bending her sideways, and growled, "Eat this, bitch!" He dragged her to the nearest car and slammed her face against the hood, smashing teeth loose from her gums and knocking her senseless.

Chapter 30

"Trust is a tough thing to come by these days."
The Thing (1982)

Spencer made a left onto Grandview Lane, an unpaved rural road that switch-backed to the top of Eagle Bluff. The posted speed limit was twenty miles an hour, but it was wise to slow to half that when rounding the hairpin corners, especially in a full-blown storm.

The Volvo's windshield wipers thumped back and forth like a metronome, yet even on the fastest setting they barely cleared the water gushing down the windshield. Inside the vehicle, however, it was comfortable, with heat humming softly from the dashboard vents, warming the chill air. Paul McCartney sang of yesterdays on the tape cassette.

Spencer had been a fan of the Beatles since he saw them on their 1965 North America tour at the Cow Palace in San Francisco. This was a year before the official inauguration of the Church of Satan. He had gone with Anton LaVey, who had used his connections to get them backstage passes, and while LaVey had been tripping out on acid with Ringo Starr and George Harrison, Spencer had spent an hour speaking to Yoko Ono. They'd been alone, sipping wine in a room with comfortable sofas, but aside from this all he could recall of their time together was the nearly uncontrollable urge he'd had to strangle her to death. Although he had these urges often, the reason for the intensity of that particular urge, he suspected, was because she was famous—or at least famous by association to someone famous by merit—and he had never killed a famous woman before. But of course killing her had been out of the question. He would never have gotten away with it. So he parted her company with a pleasant farewell and a kiss on the cheek.

When John Lennon was murdered fifteen years later, Spencer had liked to think he was indirectly responsible for the man's death. Because if he'd killed Yoko Ono that day in 1965, John Lennon's life would have followed a different path. He might never have purchased the apartment at The Dakota. He might never have returned from Record Plant Studio on that fateful night. And even had the delusional man who shot him tracked him down elsewhere, the bullet he fired might not have been fatal.

Time, Spencer thought, was like a coat with an infinite number of pockets containing an infinite number of futures: you never knew what lay hidden within each.

A reflective yellow road sign warned of an upcoming turn.

Spencer slowed to fifteen miles an hour and reminded himself to return the jerry cans to the shelf in the garage, and to wash his hands in the first-floor bathroom, to eliminate any trace smell of gasoline. He and Lynette no longer shared the same bed. He had taken to sleeping in the guest bedroom some years ago, so now it was no longer the guest bedroom, he supposed, but his bedroom. Even so, when the news of Mary of Sorrows church burning to the ground during the night reached her tomorrow, he didn't need her wondering if she could smell gasoline as she puttered about the house. She wouldn't be able to, of course, he was being paranoid, but being paranoid had served him well throughout the years.

At the summit of Eagle Bluff, Grandview Lane flattened out and continued for another half mile. He passed only two other residences, both impressive country estates with gated drives and three-car garages. Grandview Lane was the most desirable address in all of Summit County, offering sweeping views of Boston Mills Country Club far below.

Spencer's home sat on two lush acres at the end of the road. It was a modern design made of reinforced concrete and glass, oval in shape, the second floor off-centered from the first in an avant-garde sort of way. He had designed it himself and had collaborated with the architects during the planning phase, then with the builders during the construction phase, making sure no corners were cut. It had been an expensive project, but money had not been an issue. He'd been investing in the local real estate market for nearly twenty years. He had a savvy knack at finding diamonds in the rough, and knowing when to cut his losses. Consequently he'd amassed an impressive portfolio of properties, all of which were occupied with long-lease renters, providing him a substantial cash flow on top of his regular income.

The Volvo's headlights fell upon a rain-whipped police cruiser parked in the roundabout driveway in front of his home. Lights burned behind the Levolor blinds in several of the first floor windows.

Spencer was so surprised he almost slammed the brakes. His immediate impulse was to turn around and get the hell out of there. He didn't do this. His headlights might have already been spotted. Moreover, whatever business had brought the police to his home at this late hour couldn't be related to Mother of Sorrows church. He had set the fire all of ten minutes before. This had to be an unrelated visit—but concerning what?

Had something happened to Lynette?

Yes, that had to be it. She'd had a stroke, or a heart attack.

Spencer wanted to believe this was the case. He wished fervently it were so. Yet he couldn't convince himself of it. The timing was too coincidental.

Spencer parked behind the black and white—"Sheriff" stenciled next to the police department shield—and cut the engine. He retrieved his briefcase from the passenger seat, climbed out, and hurried through the downpour to the front stoop. He took a moment to collect himself at the door, then swung it open and stepped into the marble foyer. The house was silent. "Hello?" he called.

Alan Humperdinck, the Summit County sheriff, and a young deputy, both wearing gray rain slickers over their uniforms, stepped from a doorway a little ways down the hall. They had been in the living room.

Humperdinck was in his sixties, on the cusp of retirement. He had a sun-weathered face and hard gray eyes, cop's eyes, suspicious, wary. Spencer had been introduced to him a half dozen times over the years at community gatherings and festivals. However, they'd never exchanged more than passing pleasantries. The deputy couldn't have been more than twenty. Beneath his wide-brimmed Stetson, his face was gaunt, white, anemic.

"Sheriff Humperdinck," Spencer said, allowing his genuine confusion to inform his tone. He took a step forward and extended his hand in greeting.

Humperdinck merely looked at it with an expression equal parts surprise and loathing, and right then Spencer knew Lynette was fine. They were here for him. Somehow they knew about the church. It was impossible, but there was no other explanation for the frosty—no, the downright rude—reception.

Spencer lowered his hand and adopted a concerned expression. "What's happened, Sheriff? Is it Lynette? Is my wife all right?"

"She's okay," Humperdinck said tightly. "She called us."

Spencer frowned. "She called you? Why? What's happened?"

"Where were you just now, Mr. Pratt?"

"I was at the hospital."

"At this hour?"

"I often stay late, to catch up on work. Now, Sheriff, I must demand to know what's happened."

Humperdinck reached a gnarled, liver-spotted hand into the back pocket of his trousers and withdrew a card. He began to read from it. It took Spencer a moment to realize he was citing a variation of the *Miranda* warning: "You are a suspect in several capital crimes. You will accompany us to the Boston Mills police barracks. You have the right to remain silent—"

"Now hold on a minute, Sheriff—"

"You have the right to legal counsel. If you cannot afford legal counsel, such will be provided for you—"

"I'm not going anywhere with you," Spencer interrupted more forcefully. "Not until you tell me what in God's name is going on."

"You're coming with us one way or the other, Mr. Pratt," Humperdinck said. "If you refuse to come willingly, Deputy Dawson will wake Judge Pardy and get a warrant for your arrest. Given what your wife has shown us, that would be very easy."

"Lynette? Where is she?" Spencer stepped forward.

The two officers blocked his path.

"Get out of my damn way," he snapped. "This is my bloody house, isn't it?"

For a moment Spencer didn't think Humperdinck was going to concede. His old body seemed to tremble with a barely constrained hostility. But then, reluctantly, he stepped aside. The deputy did so as well, his eyes downcast.

Spencer turned his bullish body sideways to slip between them in the narrow hallway. He stopped at the entrance to the living room, from where they had emerged. Lynette sat on the buffalo-hide chesterfield, staring up at him with wet eyes.

Dozens of Polaroid photographs were spread out on the coffee table before her. Spencer stiffened in surprise. This morphed into panic, then rage. The dumb whore had gone snooping when he was out! She had somehow gotten into his locked study. She had discovered the false top on the ottoman, what he kept *within* the ottoman, and she'd called the police on him.

Spencer's mind raced, searching for excuses, but there were no excuses to be found, there was no way to explain the photographs, nor his collection of Satanic paraphernalia, which alone would link him to the massacre at Mary of Sorrows church.

"Lynnette?" he said, stepping into the living room, his eyes searching for a weapon. "What's going on? What are these photographs? Why did you call these gentlemen?"

She didn't answer.

"Mr. Pratt," Humperdinck said. He and the deputy had stuck close behind him. "You need to come with us. Now."

Spencer whirled on him. "Not until you tell me what the bloody hell is going on here, Sheriff! What are these purported capital crimes of which I have been accused?"

"Murder," Humperdinck said coldly. He moved next to Spencer and

237

pointed at the photographs on the coffee table. "These were discovered in your study."

"My study?" he repeated, though he was thinking: *A chair? No, too unwieldy. The bronze bookend on the bookshelf? But how did he reach it without drawing suspicion?* "Impossible," he added. "I've never seen these photos before in my life."

Humperdinck gripped Spencer's right biceps. "We'll continue this discussion at the barracks."

"Just a moment, Sheriff," Spencer said, reaching into the inside pocket of his blazer. "I need my eyeglasses."

"He doesn't wear—" Lynette began.

Spencer's fingers curled around the gold-plated ballpoint pen in the pocket. He plunged it into Humperdinck's right eyeball, driving the shaft three inches deep, into the man's brain. Humperdinck spasmed, almost as if he had been zapped by an electrical shock, then fell to the floor, where he continued to convulse.

Lynette screamed. The deputy cried out and faltered backward.

Already moving, Spencer tore open the buttoned clasp on Humperdinck's leather holster and withdrew the .357 Magnum. He swung the service revolver toward the deputy, who was fumbling with his own holstered weapon. He squeezed the trigger. The kickback rocked Spencer onto his rear. The hollow-point slug blew straight through the deputy's chest, punching him backward into the hallway. Spencer fired a second time. The bullet hit the already dying deputy in the gut. The kid slid to his ass, leaving two blood-splattered, plate-sized holes in the wall behind him.

Spencer leapt to his feet, shot Humperdinck in the chest to end his suffering, then aimed the gun at Lynette, who had turned white as a sheet.

"Spencer..." she whispered. "I'm your wife..."

"Not anymore," he said.

He blew her brains out the back of her skull.

Spencer went to his bedroom on the second floor, tugged his suitcase off the top of his bureau, and tossed it onto the queen bed. He unzipped the main pocket and filled it with his clothes, not bothering to remove the wire hangers. He selected items mostly from his summer wardrobe, shorts and golf shirts, given that the **Yucatán Peninsula** enjoyed a year-round tropical climate. Next he went to the master bathroom, retrieved his leather travel case from the cupboard beneath the sink, and filled it with toiletries. Back in the bedroom he upended the contents of the studded oak box that sat on the dresser—cufflinks, watches, rings—onto the clothes he had hastily packed. Finally he zipped the bulging suitcase closed and lugged it downstairs. He left it by the front door while he went to the basement gym. He glanced about the room, at all the Life Fitness exercise equipment which he had used every day for much of the last decade. Today his workout would have been chest and triceps and quads.

No matter, he thought. He would choose a hotel when he reached Kentucky tomorrow, or even Tennessee, that featured an exercise room. Perhaps one with a swimming pool as well...and maybe a heated hot tub. Yes, why not? If you're going to live life on the lam, you may as well do it as comfortably as you could.

Adjacent to the floor-to-ceiling mirror was a glass-and-steel fire ax case. Spencer depressed the two screw heads on the underside of it. The case with its false backing swung away from the wall on hidden hinges, revealing a safe. He swiveled the knob left and right, entering the correct number combination, then opened the thick door. He tugged a black duffel bag out. It dropped to the floor with the heavy thump of two hundred sixty-three thousand dollars.

Contingency plan two.

Spencer returned to the first floor. On the way to the front door he found he had a slight bounce in his step. He had wanted to leave the life he had become a slave to for a long time now: the hospital, Summit County, Lynette. But he always felt he had too much invested to simply pack up and leave. Nevertheless, necessity was not only the mother of invention, but also of motivation. Getting ratted to the cops by his duplicitous wife was, ironically, the best thing that could have happened to him.

He had become untethered, unconditionally free.

239

In the living room, stepping over the sheriff's body to retrieve the Polaroids from the coffee table, Spencer's gaze fell on Lynette. Although slumped backward on the chesterfield, she had remained in an upright position. She could have been knitting, or watching television, except for the fact she was missing her head from her mandible up.

Had he ever loved her? he wondered. Yes, he thought he had. He had been lonely in those early years after being kicked out of the Church of Satan, he had needed companionship, and she had offered it to him. She was never a great conversationalist, and she didn't have many original ideas of her own, but she was a good listener. And he supposed that's what he'd wanted. Someone to listen to him, to agree with him, to admire him.

Spencer slipped the photographs into his blazer pocket and went to the front door. He paused on the front porch to watch a magnificent display of lightning, then he carried the suitcase and duffel bag to the Volvo, loading both onto the backseat. He was about to return to the house, to collect the contents of the ottoman from his study—the police might eventually piece together his role in all that happened this evening, but he saw no need to make it easy for them—when a voice said, "Not so fast, Spence."

Spencer whirled around. Squinting against the onslaught of rain, he made out a shape emerging from the nearby trees. Thunder boomed and lightning flared almost simultaneously, and in the brief heavenly illumination he recognized Cleavon. His brother held a long, thick branch in his hand.

"Cleave...?" Spencer said in disbelief.

How the hell had he gotten free of the church?

"Who blew the whistle on you, Spence?"

"My, er—my wife, Lynette, if you can believe that."

"So you killed her, did ya?"

Spencer cleared his throat. "There was no other choice."

"And the sheriff too?"

"Again, there was—"

"No choice." Cleavon nodded. "Just like there wasn't no choice but to burn everyone alive in the church, that right?"

"This was your mess, Cleave. Weasel, Jesse—they were your friends. They screwed up, not me. Someone had to take the fall."

"And Floyd and Earl? They were your *brothers.*"

"It's...unfortunate, yes... I certainly didn't want to—"

"And me, Spence? What about me?"

"Christ, Cleave! Don't—" Thunder drowned out the rest of the sentence. "Don't get all maudlin on me," he repeated. "You left me no choice. You would never have agreed to—"

"That woman wasn't your first, was she? That Mary? How many people you killed, Spence?"

"What does it matter?"

"It don't. But I'm curious."

"Forty one," he said. "Plus Mary and the eight you know about."

"What's that? Fifty?" Cleavon whistled. "You're slicker than greased goose shit, Spence. That's gotta be a record or something. And I didn't never suspect nothing. Not 'till that Mary anyhow."

"Yes, well, now you know," Spencer said impatiently. "Your older brother is a serial killer. And so are you. Now, I have a long drive ahead of me..." As he spoke he reached into the blazer pocket for the sheriff's revolver.

Cleavon was unexpectedly fast. He covered the distance between them almost instantaneously, swinging the branch in his hand as he came. The business end struck Spencer in the face with bone shattering force, spinning him about. He landed on the macadam, on his chest, dazed. He rolled onto his back, blinking stars from his vision, wondering what happened to the revolver.

Cleavon loomed over him, backlit by a burst of lighting that electrified the black sky, turning it a deep-sea blue. He raised the branch with both hands.

Spencer opened his mouth but choked on the blood pooling inside it. Nothing came out but a garbled, incomprehensible plea.

Cleavon felt no pity as he brought the tree branch down with all his strength across the top of his brother's skull. He repeated this action again and again, payback for Earl, for Floyd, for Jesse, even for that dumb shit Weasel.

Then, panting hard with exertion, his eyes tearing from sweat and rain, he tossed the blood-covered tree branch aside and stared for a long moment at what remained of his brother's head. He spat on his lifeless body and turned to leave, to head back to the El Camino he'd parked up the road, when his eyes fell on the Volvo. The back door was ajar. A suitcase and duffel bag rested on the seat. The duffel was unzipped, and a brick of cash wrapped in an elastic band poked out the top.

Cleavon blinked twice, then went to the car. He tugged the mouth of the bag open wider. "Judas Priest!" he whispered. "*Judas fuckin' Priest!*" Then he turned his face to the heavens and danced in the rain and laughed like he had rarely laughed in all his miserable life.

Chapter 31

"We came, we saw, we kicked its ass!"
Ghostbusters (1984)

Beetle discovered a set of car keys on Goliath's body, which turned out to be for the rusted old banger parked in front of the church. He set Greta gently in shotgun and the small woman across the backseat. They were both unconscious but breathing. Then he got behind the wheel and sped to town. Given the late hour, and the full-throttled tempest, the rain-slicked streets of Boston Mills were deserted. However, he came across a twenty-four-hour gas station, where a clerk told him directions to the hospital. He arrived at the emergency entrance of the Boston Mills Health Center a few minutes later. Medical staff wheeled the two injured women away on stretchers while Beetle remained behind in the reception to explain what happened. He was then led to a private room where he changed into a dry paper frock and was checked over by a grandfatherly doctor who, upon finding no serious injuries, advised him to rest until the police arrived to take his statement.

Exhausted and emptied, Beetle fell immediately asleep, waking some eight or nine hours later at eleven o'clock that same morning. He was surprised to find a pretty redhead in the previously empty bed opposite his. She was watching him with haunted green eyes.

"Hi," she said hesitantly.

"Hi," he said.

"The police were here for you."

"When?"

"Three hours ago? I was just admitted then. They questioned me. They wanted to question you too, but they weren't allowed to wake you up."

"They questioned you?" he said.

"My friends..." Her face dropped. She looked like someone who had just been told they had a week to live. "You saved one of them. Cherry. The doctor told me she's going to be okay."

"She was your friend?"

The woman nodded. "The police told me about you. What happened at the church. I told them I had never met you before."

"Who were those men at the church?"

"Crazies."

"Satanists?"

"I don't know. They attacked my friends and me in the woods. I got away and hid in a school bus. Then when it became light I found the road. I followed it out of the national park. I came to the church—or what was left of it. There were police and firefighters. They brought me here. They said they didn't know what happened to the rest of my friends. But I think...I think..." She rubbed tears from her eyes, shaking her head. "Where could they be?"

Suddenly Beetle remembered the small woman shouting off the names of three or four people who the man named Cleavon had apparently murdered, along with something about a snake...feeding her boyfriend to a snake?

He decided it was not his place to break this news to the already distressed woman. Instead he said simply, "I'm sorry."

She nodded, still rubbing her eyes.

He said, "Did you hear anything about someone named Greta?"

"The doctor mentioned her. He thought she was my friend. He said she was also in stable condition."

Beetle felt a bit of the tightness in his chest loosen. Then he wondered where the police were, when they would return to question him. And after they did, would they contact the army, tell them they had an AWOL soldier in their custody? Or would they release him, let him go...to where?

Beetle frowned. It was a valid question. Where was he going to go? Not back to Savannah. The recent events hadn't changed his relationship with Sarah; there was nothing left for him in Georgia. However, something else *had* changed. He found he no longer had a desire, a need, to kill himself. Although the night before he had been so sure it had been his only recourse, his only way out from the nightmare his life had become, he no longer felt that way. He didn't know why this was the case. He wasn't going to philosophize over it either. Because perhaps this feeling was only a temporary reprieve, perhaps the darkness and despair would return in a week, or a month...perhaps...but he didn't think so. A switch had been flicked inside him. He felt different, not ebullient—not like he had as a kid on his birthdays, or on the day he wed Sarah—but different. Alive. He had almost forgotten how pleasing, how natural, a feeling that was.

The door to the room opened. A portly man with salt-and-pepper hair and a too-tight tweed jacket appeared. His eyes fell on the redhead, and his face lit up with joy.

"Mandy!" he said.

"Daddy!" she blurted.

The man rushed to her bedside and wrapped her in an embrace.

"They told me they called you..." she mumbled into his shoulder.

"I came as fast as I could."

The redhead said something more, though Beetle couldn't hear what, not that he was listening anyway, for he was suddenly thinking of his own parents, how nice it would be to see them again, and he knew he had a place to go to after all.

Chapter 32

"Boy, the next word that comes out of your mouth better be some brilliant fuckin' Mark Twain shit. 'Cause it's definitely getting chiseled on your tombstone."
The Devil's Rejects (2005)

School had only finished one week before, but eight-year-old Danny Kalantzis was already anticipating the best summer of his life. Most past summers he stayed in Cincinnati and didn't do much of anything and then September came around and it was time to start school all over again. This year, however, his best friend Roy Egan had invited him to his family's cottage for a full week. Danny's family didn't have a cottage, and he had never been to one before, so he wasn't sure what to expect. But apparently it was on a small lake in northeastern Ohio, and they could go swimming every day and take rides in the motor boat. He could even try water skiing if he wanted to. He wasn't sure he did. It sounded difficult. Roy told him there was also a rope hanging from one of the trees along the shore, and they could swing from it into the water. That was probably good enough for Danny.

Nevertheless, what made this week really great was the fact Roy's sister, Peggy, had come along as well. She was a year older than Danny and Roy, and Danny thought she was the prettiest girl in school. Originally she was supposed to attend summer camp for ballerinas, but then her friend backed out, so she did too.

Because Roy didn't want to sit beside her during the car trip, Danny got to, and he was fine with that arrangement. In fact, he had been thrilled every time his knee touched Peggy's, or his shoulder brushed hers.

Ten minutes ago they had pulled into a picnic spot in Cuyahoga Valley National Park. Roy's mother had packed a cooler full of egg-salad sandwiches. Roy had wolfed his down, along with a cold can of Pepsi, then told his parents he and Danny were going to go ahead to check out Brandywine Falls. Danny had wanted to stay behind, so he would be close to Peggy, but he couldn't say this, of course, and he obediently jogged after Roy, still finishing off his sandwich as he went.

Halfway to the falls, however, Roy left the trail and began making his way through the forest.

Danny hesitated. "Where are you going?"

"Come on!"

Danny followed.

When Roy found a glade suitable to his liking, he plopped down on his butt and took a sad, bent cigarette from the pocket of his shorts, along with a book of matches.

Danny's eyes widened. "Where'd you get that?"

"My dad. Don't worry. He doesn't know."

Roy stuck the cigarette expertly between his lips.

"You smoked before?" Danny said, impressed.

"A few times," Roy said proudly.

He lit the cigarette with a matchstick and sucked hard. His face turned gray, then he bent forward and began coughing up a lung.

Danny bust a gut laughing. Roy must have kept coughing for a full thirty seconds. He was holding the cigarette toward Danny, telling him to try it.

"No way," Danny said.

"Don't be a chicken!"

"Look what happened to you."

"Chicken!"

"I don't want it."

"You're such a wimp."

"*You're* a wimp."

"At least I tried it."

"Try it again."

Roy contemplated the cigarette, then tossed it away.

"Seriously, Danny," he said, "you're such a wimp."

"I know you are, but what am I?"

"Oh jeez." Roy rolled his eyes, then jumped to his feet. "I gotta take a dump."

"Right here?"

"No, not right here, you perv. What, you wanna watch?"

"Then where?"

"In the trees."

"I think there were toilets back at the picnic area."

"Those things are disgusting. You can get diseases from the seats."

"You don't even have toilet paper."

"You can lick my ass."

"You're so gross."

"I'll be back."

Danny watched Roy forge a path through the trees until he was out of sight. Then Danny lay down to get comfortable, folding his hands behind his head and staring up at the sky. Much of it was blocked by the canopy of branches overhead, but he could see bits and pieces, all bright blue, not a cloud anywhere.

He closed his eyes and wondered where he would be sleeping tonight. Would he have his own bedroom? Or would he share a room with Roy? That would be fun. They could stay up late, talking or reading comic books, like they did when they had sleepovers. Roy's parents were pretty cool with curfews and stuff like that. They let Roy do a lot of things Danny's own parents would never let him do. And besides, it was summer break. It wasn't like they had school the next day.

And what about Peggy? he wondered. She was a girl, so she would have her own room, obviously. Danny wondered if he should try to kiss her at some point. He was a year younger after all. He was only going into grade six. She probably still thought of him as a little kid. Then again, she'd laughed at some of his jokes in the car. Didn't that mean she liked him? Maybe if he could keep making her laugh, *she* would kiss *him.* Maybe they would even get married one day. That would be pretty neat. Then Roy would be his brother, or half-brother...

As Danny unwittingly drifted into a light sleep, his thoughts turned to what Roy's dad had told them about Helltown during the car ride. The place was right around here somewhere. Supposedly there had been a bunch of devil worshippers a few years back who lived in the woods and kidnapped people. But then some army guy, Special Forces or something like that, tracked them all down and burned them alive in some church. Roy's dad stopped there because Roy's mom told him he was going to give "the kids" nightmares. Roy and Danny protested, they wanted to hear more, but Roy's dad changed the topic. Sometimes it seemed to Danny that Roy's mom ruled Roy's family. It was true she was stricter than Roy's dad (which was still pretty lenient by Danny's parents' standards), and she could be scary sometimes when she got angry, but for the most part Danny liked her. He just better make sure he stayed out of her bad books for the next week...

The twenty-six-foot-long green anaconda slithered silently through the deadfall toward the sleeping boy, forked tongue flicking in and out of its lipless grimace, collecting the sleeping boy's scent particles from the air and the ground. It had devoured a similar creature years before, on the night it had escaped the House in the Woods, and like all the raccoons and deer and foxes and rodents it had subsisted on since, it knew the creature to be easy prey.

When the snake came to within striking distance, it opened its mouth one hundred eighty degrees and sunk its rear-facing teeth into the boy's shoulder. The boy awoke, jerking then thrashing, trying to flee, but the snake was already coiling its body around its prey, constricting and wrapping, around and around and around, until the boy went still.

Then it ate.

II

ISLAND OF THE DOLLS

2001

The bullfrog sat on a big green lily pad in the middle of the rotten-smelling pond. Its throat expanded like a balloon as it made a rusty croaking sound.

Eight-year-old Rosa Sánchez took another careful step toward it, then another, doing her best not to disturb the scummy water. She had taken off her sandals, and the mud on the bottom of the pond squished between her toes, feeling both good and gross at the same time.

The frog shifted its fat body on the lily pad so it seemed to stare right at her, its bulging eyes glistening.

Rosa froze, one foot in the air, stork-like.

The bullfrog croaked.

"Look away, frog," Rosa mumbled in Spanish. "Look away."

It didn't, and Rosa, thinking she might topple over, get her clothes wet and stinky, set her lead foot down. Something sharp—a rock or a pokey bit of branch—jabbed the underside of her heel. She ignored the pain, keeping her eyes on the bullfrog.

It continued to stare back at her, its eyes unblinking. The air left the sack in its throat, and the bullfrog shrunk nearly in half. Still, it was a big sucker. And it was so close...

Rosa took another step and thought she might be able to grab it now if she was quick enough. She stuck her hands out before her and tilted forward slowly.

The bullfrog sprang. Rosa's hands clutched its slimy flanks. But she was too slow. It plopped into the water and disappeared from sight.

Rosa's momentum, however, kept her moving forward. One uncoordinated step, two, then she dunked facefirst into the water. She closed her eyes but forgot to close her mouth and got a big gulp of what tasted like sewage. Her hands sank into the muddy bottom of the pond, then her knees, yet she managed to arc her back and keep her head from going completely under.

She made a noise like she was crying, though she wasn't crying, she was eight years old, a big girl, and big girls didn't cry when they fell in water. Still, she *wanted* to. She was soaked, a foul taste was in her mouth, and she couldn't get back to her feet. The mud sucking at her hands and knees was too slippery—

Now her head did go under. Water gushed into her ears, her nose, but at least she'd kept her mouth closed this time. When she burst back through the surface, she crawled, moaning, toward the bank, grabbing at tall grasses, roots, anything she could reach, until she was up on dry ground.

Rosa flopped onto her stomach, her eyes burning with tears. Then she sat up. Her clothes clung uncomfortably to her thin frame. And she stank like a toilet. Worse than a toilet. It reminded her of the smell when her big brother Miguel found the dead rat in the wall of their house, and told Rosa to take it out to the street.

Miguel. He was going to murder her. He was already mad at her for walking too slow when they got to the island and went looking for a spot to make camp. Then he got even madder because he wanted to kiss his girlfriend, but he couldn't do that with Rosa around. That's why he told Rosa to go do something. Rosa didn't want to at first. The island scared her with all of the dolls hanging from the trees or sitting on the ground, just staring at her with their painted faces and glass eyes. However, you didn't say "no" to Miguel, not unless you wanted to get a slap across your head, and so Rosa went, not planning to go far...and then she saw the pond. At first she wanted to muck around in the water a bit. She didn't know there would be bullfrogs. But there sure were; they were everywhere. She spotted three right away. Yet she wasn't careful then, and they all hopped off their lily pads and vanished beneath the water before she got close enough to catch one. It took her another fifteen minutes before she found the big fatty.

And now it was gone too, and she was dripping wet, and Miguel was going to call her names and slap her across the head—

A scream shattered the quiet.

Rosa jerked her head about.

That had been her brother's girlfriend, Lucinda.

Did Miguel jump out from somewhere and scare her, as he always liked to do to Rosa? Or did one of the dolls hanging from the trees come to life and attack her? That's what Miguel kept telling Rosa: the dolls were alive but they were just sleeping, and when you weren't looking they would—

Another scream.

Not Lucinda. Deeper, male.

Miguel?

Rosa didn't know, because she'd never heard her brother scream before, or at least not for years. Miguel wasn't afraid of anything.

Rosa got to her feet, her soaked clothes forgotten.

Her eyes scanned the trees ahead of her, searching for movement, for Miguel to be sneaking from bush to bush—and that's what this all was, wasn't it? A joke, not on Lucinda, but on Rosa. Miguel got Lucinda to scream, then Miguel screamed too. As soon as Rosa went to investigate, they would jump out and scare her.

Rosa waited. The forest was silent. No wind. No crickets. Nothing.

"Miguel?" she said.

No reply.

Rosa picked up her sandals and began to walk back the way she came, toward the source of the screams. She knew Miguel was going to ambush her, but that was okay, because it would only be scary for a second, then everyone would be laughing. And that was better than how Rosa felt right now. Like she was sick, like she wanted to throw up.

Rosa left the glade with the pond. Trees closed tightly around her. She had to duck branches and watch where she stepped. The late afternoon seemed suddenly dark. She didn't remember it being this dark earlier. Was that because the branches were blocking out the sun and sky? Or had a cloud passed before the sun?

"Miguel?" she said, though not very loud this time.

Because what if something else heard her?

Like what?

The dolls?

They couldn't do anything to her. They were only dolls. Even if they came to life, she was a lot bigger than them.

But they got Miguel and Lucinda.

No they didn't! Rosa told herself severely. Miguel was joking around. He was going to jump out any second now.

He didn't jump out.

The forest remained silent and dark.

Maybe she should return to the pond and wait there for Miguel to grow bored of his game and come and get her? Then again, what if Miguel or Lucinda really were hurt? What if they needed her help?

Rosa continued forward, pushing through the thick foliage. She began to move quickly, heedless of the scratching branches and the sharp rocks and other deadfall beneath her bare feet. Then she was running. All she could hear was a thumping in her head and her loud breathing. Every tree looked the same, and she wondered if she was heading in the right direction. But she didn't stop. If she turned back, she would probably only get more lost. Besides, she was pretty sure the camp was right ahead. It couldn't be much farther.

She ducked around a tree—and ran into several dolls hanging from a low branch. She cried out and fell on her butt. Looking up, she recognized them from earlier: grimy, peeling, sinister.

That meant the camp was not very far away.

"Miguel!" she shouted. She could no longer suppress her fright.

"Rosa!" His voice came back, strangled, weak, filled with terror. "Go! Run!"

Rosa got to her feet. A sob caught in her throat, tight, painful.

"Miguel!"

"*Run—*" He was cut off abruptly.

Rosa hesitated a moment longer, then she turned and ran.

Jack

I woke up covered in my own blood. It had congealed between the right side of my head and the pillow, and I had to peel the damn pillow away, as if it were a crusty bandage. I held the pillow in front of me, staring in disgust at the brown splatter on the white slip. All the while I was trying to remember what had happened the night before.

I'd been having dinner with my fiancée, and her brother and his girlfriend. What a ball that had been. Listening to Jesus talk about himself all evening. That was Pita's brother's name, Jesus. Ironic how the one guy I'd ever met named after a god had an ego of a god to match. His girlfriend, Elizaveta, was far too good for him. Smart, down-to-earth, attractive. I didn't know how he landed her. Actually I did: money. Pita's and Jesus's father, Marco, turned a mom-and-pop restaurant and pub into a multi-million-dollar brewery, and after Marco died of a brain aneurysm the year before, twenty-nine-year-old Jesus stepped up to the top position.

Setting the stained pillow aside, I touched the cut on my head, igniting a sharp pain that until then had been dormant. The cut ran from the outside of my eyebrow straight to my hairline. Dried blood crumbed beneath my fingertips and fell to the bed like red dandruff.

Recalling what happened, I cringed in embarrassment.

We'd been sitting on the back deck, the four of us. Dinner was finished. Jesus had been smoking one of his expensive cigars and going on about a skiing trip to Chile he and Elizaveta had gone on the previous winter. I was only half listening until he launched into some ridiculous story that had him backcountry skiing outside the ski resort's boundaries, which he reached by helicopter. I chuckled loudly. It wasn't that I didn't believe him. Pita once told me she and Jesus had gone on skiing trips every year when they were younger. So I assumed he was a decent enough skier. It was the bragging. Making sure to mention the chartered helicopter, the difficulty of the off-piste terrain, his entourage, which included a famous Mexican singer.

I wasn't nitpicking or being overly critical of Jesus. Everything the guy said and did was orchestrated to make him look good, to make people want to admire him, to see him as the apotheosis of success. Yet at the same time it was all layered in humility, like he was just one of the guys. His efforts were so transparent he became a caricature, a joke. You couldn't help not laughing at him sometimes.

Jesus asked me what was funny. I told him nothing, please continue. The back and forth escalated, the insults becoming sharper, Pita and Elizaveta telling us to stop. Then the asshole took a cheap shot, bringing up the accident that ended my racecar driving career, saying I didn't have the guts anymore to break the speed limit.

I could have taken a swing at him. I should have. Instead I went inside to take a leak. I didn't return to the deck. I went to the second floor, to the balcony that overlooked the deck and the adjacent swimming pool. I climbed atop the railing so I stood precariously on the headrail, yelling that I was going to jump into the pool below, challenging Jesus, the fearless alpine skier, to do the same.

It was probably a good thing I slipped. Roughly ten feet separated the balcony and pool, and had I jumped, I might not have reached the water. But that's what happened, I slipped—or lost my balance, it was all a blur—falling backward and cracking my head on something. I have no idea what. All I remember was the exploding pain—loud was how it felt—then the gushing blood, then everyone gathered around me. They wanted to call an ambulance, but for some reason I didn't want them to. I guess I didn't want to spend the night in the hospital. Then I was in the shower. I seem to recall standing there for a very long time, watching pink water swirl down the drain.

Grimacing, I pushed myself off the bed now, to my feet. I felt momentarily lightheaded, likely due to a loss of blood. I was in the guest bedroom. Not surprising. Pita wouldn't have let me sleep in our bed bleeding like I'd been, even if it was my house. And what had she been thinking letting me go to sleep with a serious head wound? I know I said I didn't want her to call an ambulance, but she should have done so regardless. I might not have woken up at all.

Light streamed through the window, all too bright, almost audible, like a horn. I wondered what time it was. I stepped into the pine-paneled hallway and went to the bathroom because I heard running water.

I knocked on the door lightly, then opened it. Steam fogged the mirror. Pita stood beneath the shower spray, her mocha-colored back and butt to me, her hands massaging either shampoo or conditioner into her dark hair.

"Hey," I said, the word coming out brittle. My throat was as dry as if I'd eaten a handful of saltine crackers.

When we first began dating some five years before, Pita would have turned all the way around, showing off her body. Now she only turned her head slightly so she could see me sidelong. She lowered an arm across her breasts.

"You're alive," she said in her Spanish-accented English.

"Barely," I said.

"So does that mean you're not coming anymore?"

"Coming?"

"Don't you remember anything from last night?"

That irked me, but I said, "Where are we going?"

"You really don't know?"

"I wouldn't have asked if I did."

"Maybe if you didn't drink so much—"

"Forget it, Pita."

I was about to close the door when she said, "Isla de las Muñecas," and went back to washing her hair.

Man, I really had been black-out drunk. But a light switched on inside my head, the darkness shrouding my memories cleared, and the rest of the evening came back in snippets. Isla de las Muñecas. Island of the Dolls. That was the reason Jesus and Elizaveta had come by. We'd spent most of dinner discussing the details of the excursion. We'd agreed to leave at 10 a.m. Jesus and Elizaveta would pick up Pepper, then come by my house. Pita and I would follow them in my car to Xochimilco, where we would embark on a two-hour boat ride to the island.

Pepper was a host for a Mexican copycat of The Travel Channel, a basic cable show that featured documentaries and how-to programs related to travel and leisure around the country. He caught a break at the beginning of his career when he got a regular gig as a presenter on episodes featuring animal safaris, tours of grand hotels and resorts, lifestyle stuff—and in the process became a bit of a mini celebrity. Nevertheless, it wasn't until last year that things took off for him due to a documentary he hosted on El Museo De Las Momias, or The Mummies' Museum. The story went that after a cholera outbreak in the nineteenth century the city cemetery in Guanajuato was filling up so quickly that a local tax was imposed demanding relatives to pay a fee to keep the bodies interred. Most relatives couldn't pay or didn't care, the bodies were disinterred, and the best preserved were stored in a building. In the 1900s, entrepreneurial cemetery workers began charging tourists a few pesos to check out the bones and mummies—and the place has since become a museum displaying more than a hundred dried human cadavers, including murder victims, a Spanish Inquisition victim in an iron maiden, criminals buried alive, and children laid to rest dressed up as saints. Most were so well preserved that their hair, eyebrows, and fingernails were still intact, and nearly all of their mouths were frozen in eternal screams, a result of the tongue hardening and the jaw muscles slackening following death.

The documentary proved to be a huge hit, so Pepper pitched The Travel Channel an ongoing series titled *Mexico's Scariest Places*. They liked the idea, and Pepper's next project took him to La Zona del Silencio, or The Dead Zone, a patch of desert in Durango that got its moniker after a test missile launched from a US military base in Utah malfunctioned and crashed in Mexico's Mapimí Desert region. The missile was carrying two containers of a radioactive element. A big US Air Force recovery operation lasted weeks—and made the region a pseudo Area 51 ripe with myths and urban legends regarding mutations of flora and fauna, lights in the sky at night, aliens, magnetic anomalies that prevented radio transmissions, the whole works.

Pepper has since done several other episodes in the series—most of which focused on haunted mansions and shuttered asylums and the like—but the Island of the Dolls had always been his golden egg so to speak. Problem was, the island was private property. The owner had recently died, and his nephew was now in charge—and he repeatedly refused to allow Pepper and his film crew access to the island. The Travel Channel, for their part, gave Pepper the unofficial go-ahead for the documentary, telling him if he got footage, great; if he got busted doing so, they didn't know anything about it.

That was where Pita and I came in. Pepper didn't want to go to the island alone, and we didn't have any affiliation with the television network. I had been looking forward to the trip until Jesus got wind of it a few days ago and, in his blusterous fashion, insisted he and Elizaveta come as well.

Pita was rinsing her hair now. Milky white soap streamed down her back. I asked her, "We still leaving at ten?"

"Yes," she said without looking at me.

"What time is it now?"

"You have half an hour to get ready."

I groaned, wondering if I could pull myself together in time.

"You don't have to come," she told me, turning enough I could see the side of her left breast.

"I already told Pepper I would."

"I'm sure he would understand—your head and everything."

"Would you mind?" I asked cautiously, wondering whether I was walking into one of her traps. I would agree with her, only for her to pounce, accuse me of never wanting to do anything with her, of disliking her brother, something along those lines. Her machinations would have been amusing had they not always been directed at me.

"I think you should rest, Jack," she said. "That's what I think. But it's up to you."

Jesus and crew arrived forty minutes later in Jesus's brand new Jaguar X-Type. The vehicle suited him: all show, little substance. Because under the prancing cat hood ornament, and leather and wood interior, it was nothing but an all-wheel-drive Ford Mondeo. Jesus likely didn't know that. He would have purchased it because it was the type of car a young, affluent guy should be driving.

While Pita went out to greet everyone—wearing a chambray shirt with roll-tab sleeves and cutoff jean shorts that showed off the bottom curve of her ass—I went to the garage and loaded our daypacks into my three-year-old Porsche 911. It was parked next to a junked '79 Chevrolet Monte Carlo. I used to own the same make and model as a kid in Vegas. I'd worked in an auto-repair shop for three years to save enough money to buy it. When I turned eighteen and got my racing license, I began racing four nights a week at the local tracks. I consistently finished middle to back of the pack, but I nevertheless became a fan favorite because of my name. The race track announcers thought Jack Goff sounded like a joke and took every opportunity to mention it over the PA system to the delight of the crowd. Soon nobody was calling me Jack anymore. It was always Jack Goff. Announcers, interviewers, fans, whoever. It had that two syllable cadence—and of course innuendo—that made you want to say the whole thing.

I never won a checkered flag with the Monte Carlo, but it was my first race car, and I had some of my fondest memories in it. That's why I bought the junker to restore a few months ago. It was a pet project, a way for me to fill in the days now that I was finished racing.

I got behind the wheel of the Porsche and rolled down the driveway until I came nose to nose with the Jaguar. Elizaveta, in shotgun, her face hidden behind a large sunhat and sunglasses, flashed me a smile and a wave, which I reciprocated. Jesus had his window open, his elbow poking out, as he spoke with his sister. His hair as always was impeccably neat, the sides short, the top parted to the left and slicked back. He wore Aviator sunglasses and a day's stubble he no doubt considered fashionable. The glare of the sun on the windshield prevented me from seeing Pepper in the backseat, and I was wondering if I should get out to say hi when Jesus and Pita finished their chat.

Jesus finally acknowledged me, tipping a grin and tooting the Jaguar's horn. I squeezed the steering wheel tighter and wondered why I had decided to come. But I had little choice. As I'd told Pita, I'd already committed to Pepper. I would be copping out if I gave him some excuse, especially given my head didn't hurt that much. In fact, my hangover bothered me more than the gash. I felt heavy, unmotivated, blah—but okay enough for a daytrip. Besides, Jesus's company or not, I was still interested in seeing the infamous Island of the Dolls.

Cranking up the volume of some Mexican song heavy on the bass, Jesus reversed onto the street, swung about, and started off. Pita hopped in next to me in the Porsche.

A couple of minutes into the ride she began humming to herself. She'd pulled her thick wavy hair into a ponytail, away from her face, which was sculptured with faultless features. Long-lashed, coyote-brown eyes (which she liked to say were hazel); a straight nose so unremarkable you didn't notice it, which was a plus when it came to noses; full lips more playful than pouty; angular cheekbones, and a gently rounded chin.

Pita's hums transformed into words, a Spanish song I recognized from the radio. She sang it softly under her breath. She had a throaty singing voice.

"What's up?" I asked her.

She glanced at me. "What do you mean?"

"You're in a good mood."

"I'm not allowed to be in a good mood?"

"I just mean...what were you and God talking about?"

"Don't call him that."

"I don't to his face."

"He calls you Jack."

What she meant was, he didn't call me Jack Goff. And she was right; he didn't. Not to my face anyway. I said, "What were you and your brother talking about?"

"Nothing."

"You were chatting for five minutes."

"He's my brother, Jack. We were just talking."

"About the weather? The trip?"

"What does it matter?"

"I'm making conversation, Pita."

"No, you're making it sound like we were conspirating or something."

I didn't correct her mispronunciation. She sometimes got certain English words mixed up or wrong altogether. Conspirating/conspiring was one I'd never heard before though.

"How's Pepper?" I asked, changing topics.

"Excited."

"Does he still want to interview you?"

"Yes, he will give me what he wants me to memorize on the boat. He wants you to say some things too."

"I'm not going on film."

"He really wants you to."

"Why doesn't he ask Jesus?"

"Because Jesus is too well known."

"And I'm not?"

"We're not in America anymore, Jack," she said. "I'm talking about Mexico. People here know my brother. They don't know you."

It was true. I only stood out in this country because I was white, and because of my height. That anonymity was the initial appeal of moving down here. Having said that, my exit from racing had been a pretty big deal, and I could only imagine ESPN getting their hands on a copy of Pepper's "Island of the Dolls" episode and airing a clip of me with the headline: "NASCAR Rookie of the Year, Jack Goff, Turned Paranormal Investigator for Mexican TV."

"I'm not going on film," I repeated.

Jesus stopped at a red light. I pulled up beside him. I was staring ahead at nothing in particular, going over the directions to Xochimilco in my head, when I heard the Jag's engine rev.

I looked past Pita and saw Jesus grinning at me. He revved the engine louder and longer.

"Is he serious?" I said.

"Don't you dare think about racing him," Pita said.

"I'll cream him," I said, grinning myself.

Jesus started blipping the throttle, making the Jag go vroom vroom and sound sporty.

I depressed the clutch, shoved the Porsche into gear, and brought the engine up to 5k RPM.

"Jack!" Pita shouted above the noise. "You're not racing him!"

"The road's clear."

"Jack—!"

Jesus jumped the start before the light changed. I dumped the clutch and nailed it. The tires let out a brief squeal, the revs went to redline. My head snapped back. Jesus's head start had given him a fender length on me, but I gained it back on the shift to second.

We remained side by side through to third gear. I wasn't worried because I knew I would out-per-mile him when I hit fourth.

And sure enough, by the time we were both in high gear, I'd put a car length on him with no trouble.

"Slow down, Jack!" Pita said.

Given I was doing ninety in a forty zone, and now two car lengths ahead of Jesus, I figured I'd proven my point. I let off the throttle.

Instead of backing down, however, Jesus ripped past me.

"Little prick," I grunted, gunning it again.

"Jack!" Pita said.

We were approaching an onramp to the freeway that ran east-west across the middle of Mexico City. Jesus hit it without slowing. I did too.

Pita was still shouting over the roar of the flat-6—only now she sounded more scared than angry, her shrieks punctuated with "Stop!" and "We're going to die!" But there was no way I was backing off. Not until I put the poser in his place.

Jesus and I moved into the left lane, passing traffic at more than a hundred miles per hour. I parked myself on his ass, riding his slipstream.

I veered slightly to the right, to see ahead and to make my move to overtake—when I noticed one of the cars we thundered past had lights on top and "Policia" written down the flank.

A moment later the cop swung into the left lane behind me, siren wailing.

"Jack, you have to pull over! You're going to get us arrested! Pull over! Jack!"

Jesus overtook a red sedan in front of him, swinging back into the left lane. I stuck with him for the next five hundred yards, whipping around several more vehicles.

"Jack!" Pita all but wailed. "Please!"

And I conceded.

Speeding down the far side of an overpass, I glanced in the side mirror, didn't see the police car, and locked up the brakes, squeezing in between two freight semis in the right lane to the tune of bovine air horns and flashing high beams.

Several long seconds later the cop blasted past me none the wiser.

Jesus's problem now.

When we reached Xochimilco an hour later, I followed signs that read "*los embarcaderos*"—the piers—to Cuemanco, one of nine locations that offered access to the ancient Aztec canal system. It was where we had agreed to meet the others. I parked in a busy parking lot, retrieved our daypacks from the trunk of the Porsche, and handed Pita hers. She took it silently and started toward the strip of ramshackle buildings that separated the parking lot and the waterfront. I fussed through my bag for a minute, checking the sparse contents. It wasn't necessary. I knew what I'd packed. But Pita and I needed a bit of space.

After we had evaded the cop, Pita had spent the next ten minutes yelling at me in a mix of English and Spanish, saying I was crazy, I could have killed them, all because of my ego. I didn't argue with her. She was right. Street racing was stupid and reckless. So I listened stoically to her tirade, which seemed to incense her all the more. Eventually, however, she ran out of fury and called Jesus on her cell phone. As it turned out, he ended up pulling over and paying off the cop. I didn't pick up any more details than that, and Pita refused to speak to me, let alone elaborate, after she hung up.

Nevertheless, the outcome was what I'd expected. This was Mexico after all, and just about every cop could be bought. Some actively searched out bribes. I'd learned this firsthand my first week in the country. A cop pulled me over on some empty stretch of road and told me I'd been speeding, which I hadn't been. He took my driver's license as a "guarantee" and said I could either get it back on the spot if I paid him one hundred fifty American dollars, or I could follow him to the police station, where I would have to pay two hundred fifty. It was clearly a scam, I got pissed off, and tried to swipe my license from his clipboard. He accused me of being *aggressivo* and doubled the fine. We continued to argue until I gave up. I paid him one hundred sixty—all I had on me—which he was more than happy to accept.

I closed the Porsche's trunk with a heavy thud, slung my daypack over my shoulder, and went to the docks.

The boardwalk along the canal was filled with people and a general air of festivity. Gondola-type barges called *trajineras* lined the bank for as far as I could see. Most were the size of a large van, featuring a roof for shade, open-aired windows, and tables and chairs for picnicking. They were painted a spectrum of colors, ornately decorated, and for some reason bore female names.

I scanned the crowd for Pita—I had little trouble seeing over all the dark-haired heads—but I didn't spot her anywhere. I wasn't too concerned. I had my cell phone. If I didn't bump into her sooner or later, I could call her, or she could call me.

I started along the boardwalk. Merchants called to me from their market stalls, hawking wares that ranged from handicrafts and T-shirts to embroidered clothing, linens, sandals, and other souvenirs.

A walking vendor fell into step beside me. He was short and wore white pants and a white shirt over his padded frame. Smiling, he asked what I was looking for.

"My friends," I said.

"You want watch? Rolex? You want Rolex?"

"No, thanks."

"What you want? Marijuana? Pills? I get you anything."

I shook my head, pulling away from him.

"Hey, man!" he called after me. "Girls? You want girls? I give you my sister! Cheap!"

Another fifty yards on I came to two old women selling banana-leaf tamales. I realized I hadn't eaten anything all morning, and I bought two, one stuffed with chicken and salsa, the other with refried beans.

I found a bench to sit on and dug into the tamales. Two of the best things about living in Mexico, I believed, were the weather and the food. It was pretty much spring-like year round with zero humidity, and the greasy street meat was made with crack or something it was so addictive.

I gave the last bite of my second tamale to a flea-riddled mutt that had been eyeing it hungrily, and I was thinking about getting a third when the vendor who tried to sell me his sister spotted me and came over.

"My man!" he said, sitting next to me. "How's the tamale? Good, yes? You like Mexican food?"

"I'm not a tourist," I told him. "I live here."

"You live here? Where?"

I wasn't going to tell him my neighborhood, as it was one of the pricier ones in Mexico City, so I simply told him the name of the general borough.

"So what you do?" he asked.

"Listen, I don't want to buy anything."

He smiled. "No problem. No problem. But where're your friends? Maybe they want a watch? I have Cartier too. Anything they want."

I stood and continued along the boardwalk again. The tout caught up to me.

"So you and your friends going down the canals, huh?" he said. "You need a boat? I get you good price."

"My friend already organized one."

"Your friend, huh?" I felt him looking at me like he didn't believe me, or like I was brushing him off, which I was.

"Yeah, my friend. He's filming that island with the dolls. He's organized everything. The boat. The tickets. We don't need anything."

"You go Isla de las Muñecas?" he said.

I realized I'd said too much, and I was planning to ignore the tout, keep walking, but the expression on his face caused me stop. I couldn't tell if it was fear or anger.

"What?" I asked.

"You go Isla de las Muñecas?" he repeated.

"No," I said. "We're not going *to* it. We're going around it." I made a curlicue gesture with my finger. "Take some pictures, come back. Just tourists, okay?" I started away, but his hand seized my wrist tightly.

"You don't go there."

"Let go of me."

Passersby were looking curiously at us, and I was starting to get angry myself. I tried pulling my arm free from his grip. He wouldn't let go.

"Why you film there?"

"Let go of me."

"Why you film there?"

"Last warning."

"You go," he said, lowering his voice to a threatening whisper, "you die."

I stared at the guy, wondering if maybe he was crazy. Perspiration had popped out on his forehead. The cheerfulness was gone from his face, replaced with tension. He black eyes held mine.

My cell phone rang, breaking the terse moment. I yanked my arm free and took the phone from my pocket.

"Yeah?" I said, moving again, blending into the flow of traffic on the boardwalk.

"Where are you?" It was Pita.

"I just got something to eat."

"Everyone's waiting for you."

"Everyone's here? Where? I didn't know where you went."

"About four hundred meters east of where we parked. You'll see a restaurant with a green awning. The *trajinera* is out front."

"I'll be there soon."

We hung up.

Stuffing the phone back in my pocket, I glanced over my shoulder, expecting to see the nut job staring after me.

He was gone.

1950

María Diaz was born premature at thirty-two weeks via an emergency caesarian section. She weighed three pounds thirteen ounces. She passed all the typical tests and was deemed a perfectly healthy baby. When she was one week old, however, her heartrate skyrocketed. Her parents rushed her back to the hospital, where she suffered twenty-two seizures over the next twelve hours. As epilepsy was not well understood then, her pediatrician assumed hemorrhaging in the brain and confidently told her parents she wouldn't survive the night.

María was now four years old. She knew nothing of what happened during that eventful first week of life, of course. Like most four year olds, her knowledge was largely restricted to her immediate environment, which included her house and the street out front of it.

Currently María stood before a shelf in the house's playroom, deciding which dolls would participate in her morning tea party. Her first choice was Angela, who was dressed in a lacy blue dress and bonnet. She was a Rock-a-bye Baby, which meant at nighty-night time you had to rock her until her eyes closed and she fell asleep. María carried her carefully to the small table and set her in a chair. She flopped forward, her heavy rubber head clonking the tabletop. "No more sleeping," María told her sternly and sat her upright. She waited to make sure Angela wouldn't move on her own again. Satisfied, she returned to the shelf. Eight dolls stared back at her, but there were only two available seats at the table. After some contemplation, María decided on Miss Magic Lips. She was wearing her pink dress with glitter-net trim, and she was smiling, showing her three front teeth, which meant she was happy. When she was unhappy she pressed her lips together and cried.

Not wanting to make a third trip to the table, María also grabbed Teddy, who wore nothing but an apricot-colored sweater. He was a bear and not a doll, but he was a friendly bear and got along with everyone.

At the table she sat Miss Magic Lips to the left of Angela, and Teddy to her right. They were better behaved than Angela, and neither of them tried to go to sleep. Pleased, María went to the chest in the corner and mussed through the toys for the necessary saucers, tea-cups, and kettle. She set the table, then said, "Thank you everyone for coming to my tea party. Who wants some tea?"

"I do!" Angela said, though it was really María speaking in a higher pitched voice.

"Here you go, Angela," María said, reverting to her normal hostess tone. She poured imaginary tea into her cup. "Who else?" she asked.

"Me!" Miss Magic Lips said.

"You're happy today, Miss Magic Lips," María observed, pouring tea into her cup.

"I want a cupcake," Angela said.

"I don't have any cupcakes."

"Can you bake some?"

María looked at the pink stove by the wall and said, "Well, maybe. But Teddy still needs his tea. Right, Teddy?"

"Yes, please."

She filled his cup.

"Can I have honey with it?" he asked.

"I only have sugar. Is that okay?"

"Yes, please."

She picked up an imaginary cube of sugar and dropped it in his cup.

"I want a cupcake!" Angela said.

María sighed and went to the oven. She turned some knobs and said, "Okay, they're baking."

Back at the table, she took her seat opposite Angela, poured herself a cup of tea, then raised it to her lips. "Oohh. It's very hot! Be careful every—"

She never finished the sentence.

María's mother knelt before her, a worried expression on her face. María blinked, slowly, torpidly, like a housecat after it had been fed. When did her mother arrive? Was she here for the tea party too? She was speaking to her. "Answer me, María," she said. "Are you okay? Can you hear me?"

"I'm having a tea party, Mom," she said.

"I see that, sweetheart. But just now, what were you thinking?"

María frowned. "That the tea was hot."

"That's all?"

She nodded. "Why?"

"You didn't answer me when I came in the room. You were staring off into space."

"I was thinking the tea was hot."

"That's all?"

"That's all."

Her mother seemed relieved and hugged her.

"Are you here for the tea party?" María asked into her shoulder.

Her mother released her. "No, honey. It's lunchtime. I made you tortillas."

"I *love* tortillas."

"Then let's go eat."

"What about my tea party?"

"You can finish it later. Your dolls won't mind, will they?"

"Angela might. She doesn't like waiting."

"That's part of learning how to become a little lady. Sometimes you have to be patient."

"Angela," María told her, "you have to be patient."

Angela stared back at her.

"Be good while I'm gone," she added. Then she followed her mother from the playroom to the kitchen for lunch.

Jack

I saw Pepper first, then Elizaveta. They were standing next to a tree on the bank of the canal.

"Jack!" Pepper said, opening his arms wide. "*Bienvenidos Xochimilco!*"

He was smiling broadly at me, and I couldn't help smiling back. He was one of the merriest people I knew with a cherub face and sparkling eyes to match his go-happy personality. He was also one the most fashionable people I knew. Today's statement was a banana-yellow Oxford shirt open at the throat, a purple blazer draped over the shoulders, a polka dotted handkerchief poking from the blazer pocket, fitted purple slacks creased and rolled up at the cuffs, and a white belt and matching loafers, sans socks.

We embraced, patting each other on the back.

Pepper always liked people commenting on his outfits, so when I stepped away I said, "I like the jacket, just on your shoulders like that. Very Ralph Lauren."

"Jack," he said, clearly thrilled with the compliment, "the chicest way to wear a coat is not to, don't you know that?"

"Hi, Eliza," I said, pecking her on the cheek. She smelled of flowers and still wore the sunhat and oversized sunglasses. Combine those with her pink top, white shorts, bangles, wedge heels, and leather shoulder bag, and she and Pepper could have just come straight from lunch at the St. Regis.

Elizaveta slapped me lightly on the chest, then waggled her index finger. "You are crazy," she said in her Russian accent, which was slightly masculine, broad and bold. She dropped the cigarette she was smoking and toed it out. "Do you know that? Very crazy."

"So I've been told already."

"You want to kill us?"

She was trying to be mad at me but failing. She clamped her lips against a silky smile.

"Jesus challenged *me*," I said. "Did you get mad at him too?"

"Very mad. I think he's crazy too." *Very med. I zink ees crazy too.*

"Where is he, by the way? And Pita?"

"They went to restroom." Elizaveta frowned in concern at the bandage on my forehead. She took off her sunglasses to see it better. She had emerald-green eyes, aristocratic features with prominent cheekbones, thin lips, and long dark hair. While she was likely white as a snowflake when she'd lived in Saint Petersburg—or "Sankt Peterburg," as she would pronounce it—her skin was now brown from the tropical sun.

She'd been in Mexico for four years or so. She worked as a governess for a wealthy Russian family, homeschooling their two daughters. Her employer, a consultant for a Mexican state-owned oil company, ran in the same circles as Jesus, who she met at a neighborhood picnic. Jesus spent several weeks wooing her before they started dating roughly one year ago.

Sometimes I thought Elizaveta and I would have made a good couple had I not been engaged to Pita, and she not seeing Jesus. She was smart, fun, cheeky—my type, I suppose. I felt guilty when I caught myself contemplating the two of us together, but they were thoughts, that was all, I couldn't control them. I had never cheated on Pita, and I never would.

"Is your head okay?" Elizaveta asked me, frowning at the bandage on my forehead.

I lifted my baseball cap and ran a hand through my hair. "I'm fine," I told her.

"What happened?" Pepper asked.

"He tried jumping from balcony to swimming pool last night and fell," Elizaveta said. "See, he is crazy."

"I agree with Eliza," Pepper said. "Anyone who chooses to drive a car around a track filled with other cars at two hundred miles an hour has to be crazy."

I switched the topic and said, "So this place is pretty spectacular. I had no idea it would be so busy."

"Weekdays aren't," Pepper said. "But weekends, yes, especially Sunday."

"So which one is our boat?"

We turned to face the canal, the gondolas lining the bank. With their garish colors and kitsch decorations, they were the amphibious equivalent to the Filipino Jeepney. Pepper pointed to the one directly before us. "Lupita" was painted on the back arch.

"What's up with the female names?" I asked.

"Some refer to someone special," Pepper said. "Maybe a wife or a daughter. But some, I think, are just the name of the boat."

"I never knew there was anywhere so green in Mexico City."

"We call Xochimilco the lungs of the city. Xochimilco means 'flower fields.' Wait until you see some of the *chinampas*. They are beautiful."

I frowned. "Chin what?"

"The island gardens that separate the canals. The Aztecs made them."

"To grow flowers?"

"And other crops. There used to be many more *chinampas*, but after the Spanish invasion, and the lakes dried up, these canals are all that remain."

I looked at Pepper skeptically. "Lakes?"

"Oh my, Jack," he said. "Didn't you know Mexico City was once surrounded by five lakes?"

"I had no idea."

"You Americans," Elizaveta said.

"You knew?" I asked her.

"Of course. I am Russian, and Russians are not ignorant Americans. I learn about the country where I choose to live."

I rolled my eyes. "So where did the lakes go?" I asked Pepper, still not sure he wasn't having me on. "How did they just dry up—?"

"There he is!" a voice called from behind us, cutting off my question. "Mr. *Days of Thunder* himself!"

I turned to find Jesus and Pita approaching—along with Jesus's new best friend, Nitro.

To say Nitro and I didn't get along was a gross understatement. The animosity between us started because of a screen door. One of Pita's friends threw a party a couple of months back, and as expected at any decent party, there had been a copious amount of boozing going on.

Around 2 a.m., after most guests had left, roughly ten of us remained behind. Pita's friend was renting the penthouse unit in some old Art Deco building. We'd moved to the patio to take in the city views. At one point I went inside to the kitchen to get another beer, and when I returned to the patio I walked straight into the screen door, knocking it off its track. I picked it up and set it aside, given I wasn't in any condition to figure out how to replace a screen door. No harm done, I thought. But Nitro seemed to take the whole thing personally. He started railing on about me in Spanish. I didn't know what he was saying, but it was clear he was insulted. I asked him what his problem was. He told me to fix the door. I told him to mind his own business. He got up in my face, reeking of testosterone, so I clocked him. He came back at me like a loosed pit bull. We pin-balled around the patio, toppling plants, smashing bottles and glasses, breaking a glass coffee table—in other words, causing much more damage than a dislodged screen door.

When people pulled us apart, Nitro had a busted lip, and I had a black eye. Pita and I took a taxi home, and I figured it was the last I'd see of the guy. But the fight seemed to have endeared him to Jesus, because Jesus began inviting him everywhere after that. He even showed up to Pita's birthday party in July. I did my best to ignore him when we crossed paths, but he was as adept as Jesus at pushing my buttons, and we've come close to blows on a few more occasions since.

Looking at Jesus and Nitro now, you'd think they were complete opposites. Jesus was his typical preppy self with a tweed jacket over a white button-down shirt, khaki chinos, and oxblood penny loafers. Nitro, on the other hand, was dressed like me in a tank top and shorts and flip-flops—the difference between us being his arms were brocaded with ink and his hair was tied back in a ponytail.

It was Nitro who'd called me "Mr. *Days of Thunder.*"

"You know, chavo," Nitro went on, "for a race car driver—a *former* race car driver—Jesus totally left you in his dust on the highway."

"Who got pulled over?" I said.

"Who wimped out?"

"You really need to get over that screen door, Muscles," I told him. He didn't react to the pejorative nickname, but I knew it got to him, which was why I used it. "You know what I don't get?" I added. "It wasn't even your place."

"Jack," Pita said. "Drop it."

But I didn't want to. This trip was getting to be too much. First, Jesus invites himself. Then he invites Nitro—and no one bothers to tell me?

"Anyone else coming I don't know about?" I asked.

"We mentioned Nitro was coming last night," Pita said.

"Not to me you didn't."

"I'm sure we did," she said.

"We did," Jesus assured me with bullshit sincerity. "Maybe you just don't remember—?"

"Guys! Guys!" Pepper interjected brightly. "What does it matter? We're all here, and we're going to have a great time. That's all that matters." He flourished his arm toward the *trajinera.* "Now all aboard!"

A long yellow table ran down the center of the gondola. Fourteen chairs accompanied it, giving everyone plenty of room. Pepper and I sat across from each other near the bow while Jesus and Nitro sat near the stern. Pita and Elizaveta settled smartly in the middle of the boat, acting as a buffer between Nitro and me. The boatman or oarsman—or whatever you called the guy who steered the gondola with the long pole—was two boats down, playing cards with two other boatmen. He was middle-aged with a grizzled moustache and wiry salt and pepper hair. Dark salt stains dampened his shirt around his neck and beneath his arms. When he saw us boarding, he jotted across the boardwalk, disappearing into the crowd, returning a few minutes later carrying a large bucket of ice filled with beers, sodas, and an assortment of juices. I asked him how much for the lot. He told me three hundred pesos, which worked out to twenty pesos a drink, or roughly one dollar. I passed money to Pita, who passed it to Jesus, who paid the guy. Then Jesus plunked the bucket on the table. Elizaveta and Pepper each took a soda, Jesus and Nitro and me a beer. Pita declined everything. She was on some strict diet, and I rarely saw her indulge in anything that contained more calories than a stick of celery.

The boatman expertly guided us away from the crowded dock and into the waterway, then we were on our way.

The canal was crowded with other flat-bottomed gondolas like ours, most filled with Mexican families, couples on dates, and Caucasian tourists. A flotilla of merchants in smaller canoe-like boats tooled between them all. Their wares were similar to their brethren's on the docks: jewelry, candied apples, corn, toys, ponchos, flowers. Jesus waved over a floating *tortería* restaurant and ordered a variety of sandwiches. While we were eating—despite the two tamales I'd consumed earlier, I was still hungry—a boat carrying a Maríachi band in *charro* outfits sidled up next to ours, serenading us for the next while at what worked out to be a few bucks a song.

Soon we pulled away from the congestion and moved deeper into the ancient network of maze-like canals. The floating gardens Pepper mentioned earlier replaced the historic buildings and markets and general hustle and bustle of Cuemanco. Tall semi-evergreens lined the banks. Many had developed multiple trunks that formed expansive canopies of dark green pendulous foliage. A few were absolutely monstrous, as thick as a living room in diameter, and I suspected they had been planted by the Aztecs hundreds of years before. Complimenting these were coral-red flame trees and purple-blue jacaranda and colorful flowering plants such as bougainvillea, poinsettia, oleander, and hibiscus.

As we glided down one channel after another, I glimpsed old farm-houses, flower nurseries, and other cottage industries. Birds and farm animals grazed on green pastures. Kids swam in the water, men and women toiled in fields, and older folks sat stoically on rocks or logs or other makeshift seats, not doing much of anything. Pita and Elizaveta waved at them. A few waved lazily back.

Pepper, I realized at one point, was saying something to me. I blinked, looked at him. The warm sun and pastoral scenery had lulled me into a hypnotic state.

"What did you say?" I asked him, tilting a beer to my lips.

"Where do you go sometimes, Jack?" Pepper said in his ebullient manner. "I asked you if you can now see why the Spanish dubbed Xochimilco, 'The Venice of the New World.'"

"It's nice," I said.

"You'd never know these canals were a mass grave."

I frowned. "What are you talking about?"

"A mass grave," he said. "During the revolution, the army dumped the bodies of hundreds of opposition fighters into the canals."

"You're kidding?"

He shook his head. "Not long ago many skeletons were discovered all throughout the channels."

We were floating over dead people? Suddenly the place was not so Eden-like.

I said, "You should mention that in your documentary."

"I intend to.

I sipped my beer, thinking about this, letting it gather weight in my mind, when Pita flicked the cigarette she'd been smoking into the water. She was chatting with Elizaveta, telling her how she and Jesus used to come to these canals at nighttime when they were younger. They'd rent a large gondola with their friends and turn it into a floating nightclub with music, dancing, drinking.

Pita, and Jesus for that matter, were colloquially referred to as "Juniors"—the sons and daughters of Mexico's elite ruling class, whose wealth was only matched by their sense of entitlement. Pita and Jesus weren't so bad—they actually worked (Pita was the PR specialist for the family brewery)—but I couldn't stand some of their friends. They were the type who bragged about having four hundred pairs of shoes, or two hundred suits—and keeping them stashed away in swanky homes abroad.

I considered sliding Pita my beer bottle, telling her to put her cigarettes out in it instead, but that seemed like a jackass thing to do, especially given the fact we were still fighting. She'd think I was starting something, and she'd continue tossing her butts in the water, to make a point. Lately she'd become adept at making much of nothing.

I shifted on my too-small chair to get more comfortable. My headache was returning. Maybe it was the onset of one of my migraines, or maybe it was just the heat, or the beer, but a locust-like thrumming had started in my frontal lobe, beneath the vertical gash that likely required stitches. I massaged the area around the bandage with my fingers.

"Jack, look there," Pepper said. He was pointing past me to a glade in the trees along the bank, where a twenty-foot Aztec pyramid stood. It appeared to be a stage prop, painted in bright shades of purple, pink, and green. "That's the set for a show that has been put on there for the past ten years," he added.

"What kind of show?" I asked.

"It's called 'La Llorona.' It's based on a famous legend in Mexico of the same name. Basically, a beautiful woman drowns her children to get revenge on her husband, who cheated on her with a younger woman."

"Hell hath no fury—"

"Yes, yes, Jack," Pepper said. "Anyway, this woman, she's so filled with guilt, she ends up killing herself. But she's held up at the gates of heaven. She's not allowed to enter until she finds her children. So she ends up trapped between this world and the next, doomed to search for her kids for all eternity."

"Hence the reason you should never murder your kids to spite someone." I swatted at a fly buzzing around my head, missed it, and said, "So why's it called 'La Macarena'—?"

"'La Llorona,' Jack. That's Spanish for 'The Weeping Woman.'"

I furrowed my brow. "Does this legend have anything to do with the

Island of the Dolls? You mentioned the hermit who used to live there, Don Juan—"

"Don Javier Solano."

"He found a body of a little girl in the canal?"

Pepper nodded. "The locals around here believe there is a connection, definitely. Because on nights when the *chinampas* are shrouded in fog, La Llorona is believed to roam about, kidnapping other children who resemble her missing children, drowning them in the hope she can take them to heaven instead of her own."

"I don't know if you can really pull the wool over God's eyes like that, you know, with Him being omniscient and everything."

"It's a legend, Jack. But that's what the locals think happened to the little girl."

"La Llorona drowned her?"

Pepper nodded again. "You know how superstitious Mexicans are."

I did. And this didn't apply to only the poor and uneducated. Superstition seemed to be built into the collective unconsciousness of the entire country. Pita, for instance, was about as Americanized as you could get, but she one hundred percent believed in ghosts.

"What about you, Jack?" Pepper went on. "Are you superstitious?"

"Hardly."

"I'm not surprised," he said. "You look like an atheist."

"What does an atheist look like?"

"Like you. They have a hard edge. How should I say this...always looking a bit pissed off."

"I'm not always pissed off."

"I didn't say that, Jack. I said, *looks* pissed off. I know you're a very nice guy."

"Thanks, I guess." I finished the beer, set the empty bottle aside. "So I still don't see how all the dolls work into the story? Why did this guy, this Solano, begin stringing them up all over his island? Were they some sort of offering to the drowned girl's spirit?"

Pepper nodded. "She began contacting him at night, communicating with him in his dreams. She told him she was lonely. So the dolls were his gift to her, to keep her spirit at peace."

"This might sound like a stupid question, Peps, but where did he get all these dolls?"

"Didn't your teachers ever tell you there's no such thing as a stupid question?"

"Only because they were the ones always asking the stupid questions."

"An atheist *and* a pessimist—oh joy." Pepper beamed a smile at me. "To answer your question, Jack, Solano got most of his dolls from Mexico City. He would go there occasionally to search the trash heaps, or the markets. But then later in his life, about ten years ago, Xochimilco was designated a national heritage site. A few years after that a civic program to clean up the canals was implemented, and the island was discovered. At first the locals thought Solano was an old crackpot and steered clear. But then a few of them began to trade him dolls for produce he grew."

I swatted at the fly that kept taunting my slow reflexes and thought about what Pepper had told me—and I had to admit I was now more curious than ever to see the island.

"Pretty cool, Peps," I said. "Sounds like you have one hell of a documentary on your hands."

"I agree, Jack. I think it will be my best one yet. And with the way Solano died recently, it all just comes together."

I raised an eyebrow. "How did he die?

"Didn't I tell you?"

"You only told me he died, which is why we're able to trespass on his island."

Pepper folded his hands on the table and leaned forward conspiratorially. "He drowned in the same spot where he found the girl's body, fifty years to the day."

"Bullshit!" I said.

"It's true, Jack."

"What did the police say?"

"They couldn't determine anything. Solano had been dead for too long.

The fish and salamanders got to him long before they did."

I dreamed I was in a gondola with Pita. Not in Xochimimco. Maybe Venice, though I had never been to Venice before. It was dusk, what daylight remained was washed out, otherworldly. A mishmash of old buildings decorated with friezes and columns and broken pediments lined the banks of the wide canal, though they all seemed deserted.

I had the sense we had been in the gondola for a very long time, hours, days even. Pita kept telling me we were almost there, and by "there" she meant heaven. She was excited to see her younger sister, Susana, who'd died when she was five years old. Susana and Pita had been playing hide-and-seek with some other neighborhood kids. Susana climbed into the fountain out front their house and drowned in the shallow water.

Pita never talked to me about Susana. She'd mentioned her when we first began dating, but that was it. Now, however, she seemed more than happy to talk about her sister, and she began listing off all the things they were going to do when they were reunited. When I mentioned that Susana might still be five years old—how do you age if you stop existing?—Pita went quiet, contemplative.

I was grateful for the reprieve. I had enough on my own mind. Specifically, I was worried I wouldn't be allowed into heaven because I was an atheist. I kept wondering what I would do if Pita got in and I didn't. She would probably tell me it was my fault for not believing in God. She would do the whole I-told-you-so routine. She would leave me there, outside the gates, on my own. And that's the last thing I wanted: to be stuck by myself in limbo, if that's where we were right then.

The daylight continued to fade quickly, as if time was being fast-forwarded. The air cooled, becoming frosty with the prescience of death.

As if on cue, a corpse appeared in the water, starboard. It floated face up, a few feet from the gondola. The eyes were ivory orbs, sightless. Skin was missing in places, revealing vellum-hued patches of skull.

I pointed out the body to Pita. She looked the other way, playing ostrich, believing if she didn't acknowledge it, then it wouldn't exist. But then another body appeared, then another. Soon they filled the canal for as far as I could see in the gloom. Heads and limbs bumped against the hull of the gondola as we cleaved through them, but instead of slowing down, we seemed to be speeding up, as if the dead were ushering us along.

I was telling Pita this couldn't be the way to heaven, it was too morbid, too sad, when a thundering roar, like a waterfall, sounded in the distance. It was accompanied by a thick, wet mist, which wrapped around us, blinding us.

Pita began to scream. I turned to face the boatman, to tell him to stop, to take us back.

The boatman was a skeleton, its empty orbits gazing past me, its mouth fixed in a permanent rictus, its impossible arms pushing us forward with that long pole, rhythmically, inexorably.

Pita had stopped screaming, and it took me a moment to realize why. She had become a doll. Life-sized, but definitely a doll, molded from polymer clay, painted bright colors, with glass eyes and synthetic hair.

I tried to stand, to jump ship, to swim through the corpse-infested water to safety, yet I couldn't move, and I wondered whether I was a doll too.

Suddenly the mist parted and a black disc on the surface of the water appeared. Doom filled me as I knew this was a one-way trip, I was seconds away from dying, and there was nothing I could do to prevent it from happening.

The gondola plunged over the edge of the void, into a bottomless abyss, and I was falling, falling, falling.

I woke up and knew I was still dreaming because now I was in the ER room of the Florida hospital where I'd been airlifted to by helicopter after the racing accident. My heart wasn't beating. I was in cardiac arrest, effectively dead in both brain and body. Then I began to float, or my consciousness began to float, up toward the ceiling of the room, and then I was looking down, watching the medical staff work the defibrillator on my bare chest, watching them inject me with a cold saline solution to hopefully save my brain and organs, hearing their discursive conversations, hearing "Hotel

California" on the stereo, hearing the lyrics about checking out but never leaving.

Everything was just as it had been when this happened to me for real eleven months before...and then the dream took on a mind of its own. A hole opened in the ceiling, and I found myself being pulled into it, down a tunnel of white light. Yet this wasn't the comforting white light you hear about from people who'd had near-death experiences. There was no feeling of overwhelming transcendent love, no sense of connectedness to all of creation. Instead there was only terror like I had never experienced and never knew existed, terror that stripped me to my bones. Because there was a presence in that white light. It was waiting for me. I couldn't see it, hear it, or smell it, but it was there, and it was waiting. And it wasn't God, or at least not the benevolent one to which Christians and Muslims and Jews prayed. It was pure evil. And when I reached it, when it enfolded me in its embrace, it would never let me go. I would spend all eternity—the afterlife, heaven, hell, whatever you wanted to call it—in absolute, unrelenting pain.

I came awake with a start. *I wasn't dead.* I was in the gondola in Xochimilco, seated at the long picnic table, my head on my arms.

I sat straight, still waking up, and rubbed my eyes. I was shaken from the nightmare, disorientated. The first part of it—when I was in a gondola, and maybe a doll—wasn't too bad. That was almost fun in a trippy sort of way. But the second part, when I was dead in the ER, floating down the tunnel of white light, toward whatever it was that awaited me, that was not fun at all.

I'd been having similar dreams two or three times a week since the accident. Sometimes I'd just float around the ER watching the doctors and nurses work on me. Sometimes I'd leave the ER and zip around the hospital, invisible to the patients and staff. Sometimes I'd watch my physical body wake up in the ICU, and I'd freak out because I realized there was no getting back into it; I was going to be trapped outside of it forever, doomed to haunt the hospital. And then there was the dream I'd just had, which was the worst by far.

The tunnel. The white light. The thing in the light.

I shuddered—and berated myself. I didn't believe in out-of-body experiences. I mean, I think something weird happened to me in the ER. I had a top-down view of my body while on the operating table after all. But I didn't think this was my spirit stepping outside my body, preparing to travel to the other side. It was more along the lines of neurons in my brain dying, doing whatever weird shit they do when they die. Maybe even some sort of astral projection.

The day, I noticed, had become overcast, tinged with the scent of ozone. The clouds were unusually low and dark. I picked up the beer bottle before me but found it empty.

"Welcome back," Elizaveta said to me, cocking her head waggishly. *Velcome beck.* She still sat next to me, though everyone else had moved to the gondola's stern, where it appeared Jesus and Pepper were discussing something of importance with the boatman.

"Why'd we stop?" I asked, looking down the table for an unopened beer.

"The boatman thinks there will be tropical storm," she said. "He doesn't want to leave us on island, because maybe he cannot come back, get us."

It was Mexico's rainy season, which meant almost daily afternoon showers. They were brief but intense, capable of filling streets with rainwater in a matter of seconds. Tropical storms were a different matter altogether, reaping destruction and often lasting days.

"Didn't anyone check the forecast before we came?" I reached for the metal bucket and tilted it to see inside. Two sodas and one orange juice floated in water that had once been ice.

"Did you, Jack? But do not worry. Probably he only wants more money. Jesus will fix everything."

"Perform one of his miracles?"

"You know, Jack, he hates—he *hates*—when you compare him to that Jesus."

"That's the thing," I said. "There should only be *that* Jesus. Nobody calls themselves Buddha."

"He didn't choose this name. So you should stop making jokes. Besides,

Jack," she added, "you should know what it's like having unfortunate name."

Giving up on finding a beer, I pushed the bill of my cap a little higher and prodded the bandage on my forehead with my fingers. The headache had receded, but it was still there, hiding, ready to pounce if I moved too quickly. "How long was I out for?" I asked.

"A long time," she said. "And you snore."

"No, I don't."

"I heard you." She made exaggerated snoring noises.

"I don't snore," I insisted.

"How would you know if you were sleeping?"

"I just know."

"Don't be ashamed. Everybody snores."

"Do you?"

"No."

Just then Jesus dug his wallet out of his pocket and withdrew several bills from the sleeve. He handed these to the boatman, who took them with reluctance.

"See," Elizaveta said happily. "I told you Jesus would fix it."

"Hallelujah."

She gave me a severe look. I pretended not to notice and said, "I'm going back to sleep. Wake me up when we get there."

"When we get there?" Elizaveta seemed amused. "Look behind you, Jack. We are already here."

I wasn't sure what I was seeing at first. My brain didn't register the dolls. There were too many; the sheer number overwhelmed me. But then I was seeing them, registering them, because there they were, everywhere, an entire midget army clinging to trees and dangling from branches. There must have been hundreds of them—and these were only the ones lining the bank. "Holy shit," I said.

"I know," Elizaveta said.

The gondola started moving, the boatman pushing us forward with that long pole of his through the overgrown wetland flora. Pita retook her seat and began talking with Elizaveta. I kept my attention fixed on the island.

The dolls were every shape and size and color. They were clothed, naked, broken, weatherworn, grungy. And opposed to the beatific dolls that had lined every shelf in my sister's bedroom up until she was eight or so, the decrepit state of these made them appear to be demonic. Like they'd been to hell and back and couldn't wait to return.

I was still trying to get my head around the uncanny spectacle when the gondola bumped against a short pier with a jolt. Then everyone was getting to their feet, gathering their stuff, preparing to disembark.

1952

María woke to her mother shouting at her from the kitchen: "María, get up! You don't want to be late for your first day of school."

María buried her face in her pillow.

"María! Get up now!"

Reluctantly she poked her head out of the covers. The blinds were open. It wasn't dark, but it wasn't light either.

"María!"

María forced herself out of bed. She took off her pajamas and dumped them in the laundry basket. Then she pulled on the clothes her mother had laid out for her: a beige dress, white underwear, and white socks. She scooped up Angela, who had been sleeping with her, and went down the hall to the bathroom. She peed, then brushed her teeth. She'd had a bath the night before in her mother's bathwater, so she didn't have to have another one this morning.

"I don't want to go to school," María confided in Angela, speaking around the toothbrush in her mouth. She listened to Angela's reply, then said, "I don't want to leave my mom. And I don't want to meet my teacher." She listened again. "Of course you can come. You're my best friend." She spit, rinsed, then went to the kitchen.

Her mother stood at the sink, washing dishes. She was starting a new job as a seamstress today, and she was wearing her uniform. She glanced over her shoulder. "Eat up, sweetheart. We have to leave soon."

María sat down at the table, but she only ate a few of the beans before her. She didn't touch the sweet roll or piece of tamarind.

Then, out of the blue, she began to cry.

"Oh, baby," her mother said, drying her hands on a dish towel and crouching before her. "What's wrong? Are you worried about your first day of school?"

She nodded.

"Just remember, it's everyone's first day. Everyone feels just the same as you."

"What if nobody likes me?"

"Don't think that. You'll meet plenty of friends."

"Do you promise?"

"Cross my heart. Now go put on your shoes."

María went to the door, took her book bag from the hook on the wall, and she slid her feet into her Mary Janes.

Her mother frowned at her. "Angela has to stay home today, sweetheart."

María clutched the doll tighter. "I want her to come with me."

"You're five years old now, María. You're a big girl. And big girls don't take their dolls to school."

"I want her to come!"

"No one else will have a doll."

"I don't care!"

"Some of your classmates might tease you."

"I don't care!"

"María, please..."

"I want her to come! I want her to come! I want—"

"Okay! Okay!" Her mother shook her head. "If you want to take her, take her. But don't say I didn't warn you."

The school was a huge two-story yellow-brick building with a playground on one side and a farm on the other side. The sight of it made María's heart beat faster. She wanted to turn around and go home, but she knew her mother wouldn't allow this, so she followed her through the iron gate, up a set of steps, and to the office where a gramophone was playing music.

Her mother spoke to the woman there, signed some papers, then led María through a maze of hallways that smelled of floor wax and wood polish and chalk. Some of the classroom doors they passed were open. The students were seated at wooden desks, and they all seemed to be older and bigger than her.

María hugged Angela more tightly.

They climbed a set of stairs and stopped in front of a classroom. Her mother knocked on the door, even though it was open. "Good morning, Mrs. **González**," she said. "I'm Patricia Diaz, María's mother. I'm sorry we're late. This is María."

The teacher consulted the clipboard in her hand and said, "That's all right. Come in, María."

María stared up at her mother, begging her with her eyes not to leave her.

"It's all right, sweetheart," she said, bending over and stroking the top of her head. "Go on and meet everyone. I'll be back at two-thirty to pick you up at the front doors." She turned and walked away.

"María?" Mrs. **González said. "Come inside now, please."**

María shuffled hesitantly into the classroom, taking in the new sights: the paintings of animals on the walls, the large blackboard, the bookcase filled with books, the globe mounted on a metal meridian.

Her classmates were all looking at her. They weren't seated at desks like the bigger kids but at small tables in groups of four.

"You can sit right here, María." The teacher indicated an empty seat at a table near the front of the room.

María went to it, wishing everyone would stop staring at her.

Before she could sit down and become invisible, Mrs. **González said, "Please remain standing, María. We're introducing ourselves**. Can you introduce yourself to the class, María?"

She shook her head.

"You can tell us your name, can't you?"

"María," she said quietly.

"I can't hear her!" a student said.

"Please speak more loudly," the teacher said.

"María," she said.

"I still can't hear her."

"That okay, **Raúl**." Then, to María: "What else can you tell us?"

"Nothing," she said.

"Surely you can tell us something?"

She shook her head.

"How about we ask you some questions then. All you have to do is answer them. Does anyone have a question for María?"

A boy stuck up his hand. "Why are you so small?"

Everyone laughed.

Mrs. **González** cracked her meterstick against a desk. "Quiet, children. Everybody grows at their own pace. María may end up being taller than all of you in a few years."

A girl raised her hand. "Why do you have a doll?"

"She's my friend," María said.

"I still can't hear her!"

Another hand. "What does your dad do?"

"He's a construction worker."

"What does he build?"

"He puts up street lights."

Another hand. It belonged to a funny looking boy with large teeth and eyeglasses. "Do you want to be my friend?"

"Okay."

Someone shouted: "He loves you!"

"Do not!"

"He wants to *marry* you."

"Do not!"

The class began making eewwing noises.

Mrs. **González** cracked her meterstick again. "That's quite enough, children. Quite enough. María, you can sit down now."

Thankfully, she sat.

After everyone introduced themselves, Mrs. **González** explained the rules of the classroom the students were to follow for the duration of the schoolyear, then she read a story from a picture book. At lunchtime María ate the lunch her mother had packed her and drank the milk that was delivered to the class in small bottles. Most of the kids spent the break playing games and making friends. María was too nervous to join them and remained quietly in her seat. When two girls asked her why she was sitting by herself, she told them because she wanted to. Then Mrs. **González rang a brass bell with a wooden handle, and everyone returned to their chairs. She set a large piece of paper displaying the outline of a house on each table. She also distributed packs of crayons and explained what sharing meant. Finally she instructed each group to** color their house. There were two rules. The first was to color inside the lines. The second was to only use up and down strokes.

María chose a green crayon and began coloring the grass out front the house. The girl sitting beside her—María couldn't remember her name—started yelling at her, saying she was doing it wrong. Mrs. **González** came over and asked what the problem was.

"She's doing it wrong," the girl said, pointing at María's green scribbles.

"Did you understand my instructions, María?" Mrs. **González asked.**

"Yes."

"What did I say?"

"Color the house."

"Yes, but what were the rules I mentioned?"

She couldn't remember.

"You must color only inside the lines, and your strokes must be vertical. That means up and down." She demonstrated with her finger. "Do you understand now?"

María nodded and went back to coloring, now using up and down strokes. When a boy at her table finished with the brown crayon, she snatched it up and began coloring the front of the house.

"Teacher!" the girl beside her said, sticking her hand in the air. "She's doing it wrong again!"

Mrs. **González** returned and said, "What did I tell you, María?" She sounded angrier this time.

"Color the house."

"Yes, but what were the rules?"

"I don't know."

"I've explained this twice now"

Tears warmed her eyes, then spilled down her cheeks.

The girl beside her said, "She's crying!"

Another student: "She's a baby!"

"She's stupid!"

"She's a stupid baby!"

Bawling, María threw her crayon down and raced out of the room.

Jack

Pita stepped onto the island first, followed by Jesus, then Nitro, then Pepper, then Elizaveta, and finally me. Almost immediately the boatman pushed away from the pier. He didn't look back.

"Why doesn't he just wait around for us?" I asked.

"Because he is afraid of island," Elizaveta told me.

"Of course," I said sardonically. "The ghost."

"This is *so* weird," Pita said in awe. "I mean, look at all the dolls. They're everywhere."

I was looking. And they were everywhere, literally. They adorned not only the trees but fence posts, railings, clotheslines, even the collection of ramshackle huts—*especially* the huts. They were almost buried beneath the dolls.

"They're like...dead babies or something," she added.

"Hey, I like that one with no shirt," Nitro said. "She got curves just the way I like them." He made a slithering motion with his hands.

I said, "Can't get any living, breathing women, Muscles?"

"Shut up, Jack Goff."

"Ugh," Jesus said, pointing to a doll nailed to one of the pier's timber piles. "Are those maggots?"

We shuffled closer for a better view.

"They're ladybugs," I said.

"They're not ladybugs, Jack," Jesus grumbled.

They weren't, I realized. But they definitely weren't maggots. They were black, beetle-like, with red diamonds on their backs. However, I could see why Jesus might have thought they were maggots from a distance. They were a squiggling mass that covered much of the doll's torso and half its face. They were clumped together particularly thickly over the doll's right eye. In fact, I think the eye might have been missing, and they were spilling out of the empty cavity in the head.

Pepper produced from his bag an SLR camera with a big lens and told us to give him some room so he could take a picture.

We started down the dirt path. After a brief congress in Spanish, Jesus, Nitro, Pita, and Elizaveta turned right over a crude bridge. I continued straight ahead, glad to be on my own.

Birds chirped and squawked all around me from hidden roosts, while cicadas put up a wall of cryptic noise. The heat had left the afternoon, and now I found myself almost cold. The forest was still and dark. I walked slowly, swatting absently at flies and turning my head this way and that, as if it were on a swivel. Dolls decorated nearly every tree. Most appeared to be secured to the trunks with nails or wire, though some were tied to branches by their hair.

I shivered. I couldn't help it. Dolls in general were inherently creepy. Their inexpressive eyes and knowing smiles, their lifeless limbs and outstretched hands that seemed to be beckoning to you. Yet these rejects took the cake. Even in the gloomy light of day they were menacing. The sun had bubbled and scabbed their "skin," while the rain had eroded much of their paint, leaving behind waxy skull-like faces the color of bone meal. Pita's description had been quite apt: they really did look like dead babies—horribly mutilated dead babies with black-rimmed eyes and tufts of wasting hair. And aside from their state of dissolution, many were decapitated or missing arms and legs, while others were nothing more than butchered torsos, or disembodied heads impaled on broken boughs.

As I progressed through their ranks, I found it rather unnerving to have so many sets of soulless eyes trained on me. They might be nothing more than glass orbs, unseeing, lacking consciousness or menace, yet I couldn't shake the sensation of being watched, of the dolls twisting their heads and limbs unnaturally to follow me after I'd passed them by.

I stopped beside a sagging timber hut with a corrugated iron roof. The majority of the dolls attached to the warped wood were the porcelain-faced variety—these had dominated the island thus far—but among them I was surprised to see a Cabbage Patch Kid, a troll doll, and several nude Barbie dolls.

Footsteps sounded behind me. I turned just in time for Pepper to snap a picture of me.

"That better not be for your documentary," I said.

"It's only a photograph, Jack. It's for my private collection."

"Private collection? You sound like you have a trunk full of body parts somewhere."

He assumed feigned hurt, hand on hips. "You know me, Jack, I'm a pacifist."

Actually, I didn't know Pepper was a pacifist, and the revelation surprised me. I'd always considered anyone who felt bad about stepping on a bug once in a while a bit of an oddball—unless, of course, you went out of your way to step on bugs, and if that were the case, you had a whole different set of problems.

I said, "So you've never flushed a spider down the toilet?"

"What are you talking about, Jack? I *hate* spiders. I kill them all the time. I'm opposed to violence. People-against-people violence."

"I thought pacifists were opposed to violence categorically because of the karmic consequences and all that."

"You're thinking of Ghandi, Jack. You can definitely be a regular pacifist and kill spiders." He stopped next to me and studied the wall. "Wow, Barbies!" He raised his camera, adjusted the focus, and snapped consecutive shots. "What do you think happened to that one? I've seen a few like it." He indicated a doll that appeared charred, as if it had been set on fire.

"Maybe it came to life and Solano had to torch it."

"Oooh, Jack, that's good. I have to remember that."

"Get a photo of that pissed-off one too." I pointed to a doll with an onion-domed head that seemed to be scowling at us, one plump arm outstretched.

Pepper aimed the lens inches from the evil thing's face. The camera clicked.

I adjusted the doll's arm so it was now reaching above its head.

Pepper seemed shocked I touched it. "What are you doing?"

"Take some more photos. You can tell people it moved on its own. It will make good TV."

He was nonplussed. "The documentary will make good TV regardless."

"Even if nothing spooky happens?"

"Patience, Jack. We only just got here. Let's wait and see."

"For what? *Night of the Living Dead*—only with dolls?"

He huffed. "Okay, fine. You don't believe in spirits, or an afterlife. I'm not going to try to persuade you otherwise. You are too stubborn."

I raised my eyebrows. "I'm stubborn?"

"You're the most stubborn person I know."

"I beg to differ."

"See, you won't even admit I might be right."

"Because I'm not stubborn."

Pepper sighed melodramatically. "Yeesh, Jack."

"Tell me, Peps," I said, "in all your TV shows, all your investigating, have you ever seen a ghost, really?"

"Not in the sense you might be thinking."

"What sense is that?"

"Not a white sheet that goes 'boo.'"

"So what have you seen?

"Things that cannot be explained. I've recorded cold spots, abnormal ion counts in the atmosphere, photographic anomalies—"

"With your *Ghostbusters* equipment."

"*Scientific* equipment, Jack. Electromagnetic field detectors, infrared cameras—"

"I hate to point out the elephant in the haunted room, Peps, but if any of that stuff actually worked, wouldn't it have proven the existence of a ghost already?"

"There's no more scientific evidence to support the existence of black holes than there is to support the existence of spirits. But you believe black holes exist, don't you?"

"You're talking apples and oranges."

"Why, Jack? Parapsychology is not a pseudoscience, or at least it shouldn't be classified as one. There are plenty of respected institutes and universities investigating paranormal phenomena. There was a particularly important experiment done a couple of years ago. A person with a terminal illness volunteered to die in an air-tight glass box. At the moment he passed away the glass, which was thirty centimeters thick, cracked in numerous places. The amount of energy needed to accomplish this would be tremendous." Pepper paused dramatically. "Now with this in mind, remember what Einstein said. All the energy of the universe is constant. It can't be created or destroyed. It just gets transferred to a different form. So what happens to the electrical energy in you and me, the energy that makes our hearts beat, when we die? It continues, just in another form. And that form is..."

"Ghostly," I said.

"Right, Jack."

"Well, whenever you get more proof of this than cracked glass, or a fleeting electromagnetic field, let me know, will you? Beers on me."

"I figured for someone who's had an out-of-body experience, you would be a little more open-minded to what may lie beyond this life."

"Neurons firing, Peps. Hallucinations."

"Look, Jack. We might not yet have the means to conclusively prove spirits exist, but that doesn't mean they don't exist either."

"What about clothes then?" I said. "If our energy gets converted to a different form after we die, why do our clothes, a manufactured convention, come with us? You know, the manifestation of the butler in the old British mansion. Why's he always wearing a petticoat and bowtie?"

"Close your eyes and picture yourself. What are you wearing?"

"What I'm wearing now."

"You're not naked?"

"Sorry to disappoint you."

I opened my eyes. Pepper was smiling triumphantly at me.

"See, Jack," he said. "When you see yourself, you see yourself clothed. The same could be said for ghosts. If they have any control over the energy which they're comprised of, then it's quite likely they would manifest themselves how they saw themselves as a living person, wearing clothes."

I shook my head. "I don't get it, Peps," I said. "Why do you want to prove ghosts exist so badly?"

"Why? Because it would prove your life continues beyond this one, Jack! It would change the way we think about everything. It would be revolutionary."

"But you're presupposing that there being an afterlife would be a good thing."

"How could life everlasting not be a good thing?"

I thought of my dream earlier. "Because what if that life everlasting was eternal suffering? Would you really want to know that's what awaited you?"

"You mean hHHell?"

"Call it what you want. But, hell, fine, why not. Would you want to prove the existence of hell?"

"Well, sure, because if there's hell, then there's heaven."

"Maybe not, Peps," I said. "Maybe there's only hell, and that's why death is so mysterious, so unknown. Maybe it's not supposed to be understood or unraveled. Maybe it's so cloaked in secrecy because what lies beyond is so terrible that life would cease to be livable if we knew what awaited us after we died."

"Damn, Jack!" he said. "How do you ever get out of bed in the mornings?"

"Because life is what it is. There's either something waiting for us after we die, whether good or bad, or there isn't anything. Overthinking, even proving, what might be or not be won't change a thing." I clapped him heartily on the back. "On that note, let's go see what's lurking inside this hut."

Unsurprisingly, there were no ghosts inside the hut. There were, however, dolls. Best guess, a hundred, probably more, crammed into an area the size of a small bedroom. For a moment I thought of those carnival midway booths with prizes overflowing the walls and ceiling—only these weren't cute stuffed animals or toys. They were like all the other dolls we'd already seen: decrepit, sad, mottled, cobwebs spun inside their mouths and eyes sockets. Yet they were different too. They all had their heads and limbs intact, while many were bejeweled with necklaces, bracelets, and strange handcrafted headgear. The result was an incongruous mixture of neglect and love.

I said, "Seemed Solano had special affection for these particular guys."

Pepper was moving from wall to wall, camera stuck to his eye, taking close-up shots of several of the most disturbing dolls. "Look at this one, Jack," he said excitedly. *Click, click, click.*

I joined Pepper at the support post to which the doll was attached, wrinkling my nose at the almost sickening musty smell that permeated the air. At some point the doll had been painted flesh-colored, but now most of it was covered in a gray grime that made me think of a necrotizing disease. Clumps of tangled black hair fell in front of its face, though it was parted almost deliberately so one black eye could peer out. A dozen colorful bracelets encircled its wrists, while a stethoscope dangled from its neck.

"Oh, and this one," Pepper gushed, moving on to a doll whose bald head was studded with nails and nose rings and anything else that could pierce the plastic. *Click, click.*

I said, "I wouldn't have guessed Solano as a *Hellraiser* fan."

"Hey, is that a shrine?" Pepper was already moving on once more. *Click, click.* A step backward to frame the shot better. *Click.* "Can you take a picture of me in front of it?"

"Don't you want to get all this stuff on film?"

"I like to take photographs first, to get a feel for the locale."

He passed me his camera, then crouched next to the shrine, which featured two wood-carved cranes atop a hand-painted sign that read "XOCHIMILCO." Beneath this sat what might have been the most bizarre doll yet. She wore some sort of hat from which dangled ribbons, rosaries, and large hoop earrings. She also wore sunglasses, a necklace with a large silver pendant, and a white and pink dress with two teddy bears embroidered on the chest.

"You guys make a good pair," I said, squinting through the camera's viewfinder and taking several pictures. "Any idea what her deal is?"

Pepper took the camera back and twisted his lips in a thoughtful expression. "I can't say for certain, but I would guess she was Solano's favorite. Maybe it was the first doll he found?"

"She doesn't look old enough."

"Since when do dolls age?"

"They do here, on this island. Some look like they're a hundred years old."

"Maybe the spirit of the little girl chose it to serve as her medium."

"To speak to Solano? I thought you said she spoke to him in his dreams?"

"And perhaps she spoke to him through certain dolls too."

"Are you making this all up as you go?"

He feigned hurt. "Please, Jack. Can you at least try to keep an open mind?"

"I am, Peps. It's all going in one side and coming out the other." I indicated a large wood-framed photograph hanging on the wall to the left of the shrine. "So is that the great Solano himself?" It showed a man with thinning black hair, kind black eyes, an unkempt handlebar mustache, and a wispy goatee. He was smiling, revealing yellowed teeth. He wore a sleeveless jacket beneath a poncho. "Looks like a nice enough guy."

"Nobody said Solano wasn't nice."

"Just crazy."

"Spiritual—"

"...*MA-MA*..."

I started. Pepper seemed as surprised as me.

I said, "Which one—"

"...*MA-MA*..."

The voice was loud, whiny, effeminate.

Pepper began backing up toward the door.

"Where are you going?" I said.

"A doll just *spoke*, Jack!"

Ignoring him, I moved along the wall, trying to figure out which doll was speaking—

"*...MA-MA...*"

My eyes paused on a clown doll directly before me: brown shaggy hair, white face, pink nose, pink dimples on the cheeks, pink lips.

Was it smiling at me?

The kid inside of me that had once been afraid of the dark and wondered what slept under my bed wanted to follow Pepper's lead and get the hell out of the claustrophobic room. Nevertheless, the rational adult wouldn't allow it.

It was just a doll. An inanimate chunk of plastic. Battery-powered, programed to speak every now and then.

I reached for it, to turn it around, to peel off its pajama top, to check for the on/off switch and battery compartment—

A thunderous *bang!* shook the wall, accompanied by an ear-splitting shriek.

I cried out, stumbling backward. I collided into a support beam and fell down, dragging several dolls with me. At the same time laughter erupted from the other side of the wall.

Embarrassment burned me from the inside out. I pushed myself to my feet, scooping up the dolls on the floor. I'd snapped the strings holding them in place, there was no way to reattach them to the beam, and I was still cradling them in my arms when Nitro and Jesus appeared in the doorway to the hut, both grinning like pigs in shit.

Nitro said, "You scream just like a little girl, Jack Goff!"

Jesus assumed a straight face that barely disguised his look of hauteur. "I hope you're okay, Jack," he said with the proper air of civility. "You didn't hurt yourself, did you?"

I dumped the dolls at the base of the support beam and went to the door. "Funny, dickheads," I told them. "Now how about getting the fuck out of my way?"

Jesus stepped aside. Nitro seized my forearm as I passed him. "You just going to leave those dolls there on the ground, chavo? That's disrespectful."

"Let go of me," I told him.

He squeezed tighter. "You got to learn some manners, my friend. You can't just go around busting everything—"

I shoved him hard enough he nearly fell over. I would have gone after him but Jesus grappled me from behind, pinning my arms to my side.

I ran him backward, crushing his body between mine and the doorframe. His hold on me slackened, though he didn't let go.

Nitro, recovering, eyes storming, charged. I spun around, using Jesus as an unwitting shield. Nitro's fist whizzed past my right ear.

Then Pepper leapt into the skirmish, shouting, telling us to break it up.

"Jesus!" Pita said a moment later, appearing from nowhere. "Nitro! Stop!"

Jesus released me. I turned back around, tensing to attack Nitro, but Pepper and Jesus were in the way.

Nitro was pushing against Pepper, letting Pepper hold him back.

"Jack, Nitro!" Pita shouted. "What the heck is going on?"

Nitro ran the heel of his hand over his mouth. "Your boyfriend got scared and spazzed out, that's what."

"Don't touch me again," I told him quietly.

"Or what, chavo? You gonna sissy-push me again?"

I shoved Jesus and Pepper out of the way and lunged at Nitro. He threw a punch that deflected off my chin, dazing me. Nevertheless, I got my shoulder into him. We smashed through a railing and tumbled down a gentle slope. We struggled all the way to the bottom, flipping back and forth. Nitro was strong, all muscle. But I was bigger, probably had thirty or forty pounds on him, and when we came to a stop I got my weight on top of him—only to realize I didn't know what to do next. He pissed me off, but I wasn't going to smash in his face. That's when I heard Pita and Elizaveta. They were talking frantically. Something had happened.

I got off Nitro. I expected him to leap at me. He didn't.

I climbed the slope, clawing at long grasses and ferns. At the top I saw Jesus sitting on the ground, Elizaveta and Pita and Pepper crouched in front of him.

"What happened?" I asked, going over.

"He twisted his ankle," Elizaveta told me.

They'd rolled up Jesus's left pant cuff. Elizaveta gently pulled off his penny loafer. He wasn't wearing socks. There was a large red bump where there shouldn't be on his ankle.

Elizaveta probed it with her finger. Jesus hissed in pain.

"Sorry," I said. "I didn't mean to—"

Pita glared at me. "You pushed him over."

"He was in the way."

"In the way of what?"

I shrugged. "Nitro."

"Nitro—right. Why were you attacking Nitro? What's wrong with you, Jack?"

"With me?" I said. "Are you serious? Nitro—"

"You heard her, chavo," Nitro said. He'd climbed the slope behind me.

"Fuck you, Muscles."

Pita said, "You've gone over the board, Jack."

I blinked. "Over the board?"

"You know what I mean."

"Over the board?"

Her face flushed. "Jack!"

"Why don't you take a hike, Jack Goff?" Nitro said.

I faced the joker. He was grinning, his barrel chest puffed out like a turkey's. His eyes drilled into mine, black, taunting. He wanted to start something again because he knew everyone was on his side.

I walked away.

I'd met Pita some five years ago when I was twenty-three. Her father, Marco Cuhna, had put together a self-sponsored racing team to compete in the '96 Busch Series Grand National Division, NASCAR's minor league circuit, and he wanted me to be his driver. I'd come a long way from the back-of-the-pack kid racing the Monte Carlo on local tracks. The previous year I'd won the American Speed Association rookie title, while the current season I'd finished fourth in standings with two wins. Nevertheless, the big corporate sponsors didn't want to touch me. I wasn't fit enough to compete at a more elite level, they said. I bumped too much on the track and drank too much off it. In other words, I wasn't the whitewashed, polished driver you could put on the front of a Wheaties cereal box. Yet none of that bothered Marco Cunha. "They're stupid," he told me simply during our first meeting. "They want someone with perfect hair, perfect teeth, perfect personality. Why? Who watches NASCAR? I tell you, Jack. Beer-drinking, blue-collar young men. And they want someone they can root for. An underdog, a hothead, an anti-establishment figure." He smiled. "So now you tell me, Jack. Know anyone who fits that bill?"

Driving the No. 11 Conquistador Brewery Chevrolet, I finished the '97 season sixteenth in the point standings with zero wins. Not exactly statistics to celebrate, but Marco had faith in me, and I had become sort of family, as by then Pita and I had begun dating seriously. She was in her final year at UCLA and came one Sunday to watch me race at Irwindale Speedway. She, Marco, and I went for dinner afterward, and when Marco retired to the hotel, she and I stayed out partying well into the morning, parting with a goodnight kiss. After that, we kept in touch via telephone every now and then until she graduated in June—then she was accompanying her father to every race. I hadn't wanted a girlfriend. I was too busy. A typical day had me putting in fifteen hours at the racetrack. Pita, however, was persistent, she was always around, and she was a lot of fun. At first we were spending one or two nights a week together. Then it was three or four. Then it was every night, falling to sleep together, waking together. She didn't know much about stock car racing, but she learned quickly. Moreover, she was a people person by nature, and she fell in love with the glamor of the industry. The buzz of the press conferences, the socializing at the press dinners, the race day parades and post-race functions. What she didn't like so much were the pit lizards, or groupies, who always seemed to know where I hung out away from the track. Pita was a confident, attractive woman, but seeing these girls throwing themselves all over race car drivers drove her crazy, and it was the source of our first few fights. So to prove to her I wasn't interested in any of them, I proposed to her in Charlotte, South Carolina, on a clear night in the center of an asphalt oval.

The following season I recorded my first win at the Chicagoland Speedway and finished seventh in the point standings. Sadly, that was the year Marco died from a brain aneurysm and Jesus took over as Chairman and CEO of Conquistador Brewery. His first order of business was to disband the racing team and sell the operation. He argued the costs of sponsoring a race car outweighed the publicity generated, as the company's three varieties of beers had yet to receive a significant boost in sales. I didn't know what a "significant boost" entailed, and I didn't care much. Aside from not wanting to be under Jesus's thumb—we'd enjoyed a healthy dislike for each other pretty much right off the bat—I had a slew of new offers from other teams.

In the end I signed with Smith Motorsports for the '99 season and began racing fulltime in the Winston Cup Series, NASCAR's top-level circuit. I earned my first career pole position for the Daytona 500, but then crashed at the Las Vegas Speedway, finishing forty-first. However, I rebounded with consecutive wins in the Coco-Cola 600 and Pocono 500. All said, it was a breakout season. I won four races, two poles, twelve top five's, and fifteen top ten's. I also took NASCAR's Rookie of the Year—and just like that I became a household name. I was being interviewed by *Motor Week Illustrated*, *Sports Illustrated*, *SPIN Magazine*. The guys on SportsCenter were always talking about me (and cracking jokes about my name). I received two lucrative endorsement deals, I bought a private bus to travel in, a gated house in Vegas, the Porsche. It was all beyond my wildest imaginings.

Then the accident happened, and everything changed.

It took me close to twenty minutes to reach the far side of the island, which made the island larger than I'd originally guessed. My beer-filled bladder felt ready to burst, so I unzipped and aimed at a patch of elephant ear plants, careful to avoid the backsplash. My urine was bright yellow due to dehydration. I hadn't brought any water, and I wondered if anyone else had. Jesus, probably. He was so obsessive compulsive it wouldn't surprise me if he organized in advance which ties and cufflinks to wear for each day of the week.

I shook, zipped, then slipped the daypack off my shoulders. Mosquitos and other bugs had joined the cloud of flies hovering around my head, all of them buzzing and biting, causing me to repeatedly smack myself. Then a kamikaze fly shot up one of my nostrils. I snorted and waved my arms angrily, my hands striking a couple of the annoying fuckers.

I opened the pack's main pocket and withdrew a liter bottle of vodka. Yup, I had my priorities right. Forgot the water but remembered the booze. I twisted off the cap and took a small sip, ladylike, to acclimatize my palette. Then I took a long belt. The vodka burned a trail down my throat and hit my stomach with a warm punch. As an afterthought I glanced the way I'd come, to make sure nobody was coming looking for me.

Nobody was.

Bottle in hand, I wandered from the shadows beneath the deciduous and coniferous trees to the marshy edge of the bank. There wasn't a patch of blue left in the sky, and it was no longer a question of if it would storm but when. I wondered what this meant for us. Would the boatman return early to pick us up? Or would he wait out the storm...which could last...how long? One day? Two? Surely he wouldn't leave us stuck on the island for that long? On the other hand, if the rain and wind and flooding were bad enough, he might not have a choice.

Oddly I found I wouldn't mind being stranded on the island. I'd always been a nature person. When I was five years old my father sold the patent to one of his inventions for a good chunk of cash and bought an RV to travel the country. Most of what I remembered from my childhood involved national parks and campfires and breakfasts at interstate McDonald's. I didn't attend grammar school. My parents homeschooled me—or RV-schooled me, I guess you'd say—though this involved less arithmetic and history and more hunting, fishing, and basic survival skills. Only when I was old enough to attend high school did my parents settle down in a trailer park in Vegas, where they still lived today.

So, sure, as far as I was concerned, roughing it for a day or two on the island would be a bit of an adventure. Pepper and Elizaveta were good company. Pita and I would likely make up by nightfall. I'd have to put up with Jesus and Nitro, unfortunately, but whatever. And this place would be something else at nighttime, wouldn't it? The Island of the Dolls in the dark—how you were supposed to see it.

Three dolls to my left caught my eye. They were tied to a tree, one at chest level, the other two much higher. How Solano got them up there, I didn't know. I doubted he had a Craftsman ladder tucked away somewhere. Then again, living fifty years on an island by yourself, you had time to build yourself a ladder.

The doll at chest level was one of the more normal looking ones on the island as it hadn't yet been disfigured by the elements. It had a button nose and chubby cheeks and a frisky smile. Actually, it sort of resembled Pepper. It even had short black hair, which I thought I could style into a pompadour.

I took another drink of vodka and decided Pepper might like a souvenir of the island. I set the bottle at the base of the tree and withdrew my keys from my pocket. Attached to the keyring was a Swiss Army knife I'd purchased at La Merced, a public market on the eastern edge of Mexico City's historic center. I used to go there to buy chili peppers and other vegetables, and to stuff myself with the street food. There was one particular stall that sold what might have been the best quesadillas and tostadas in the world. Nevertheless, I hadn't been back to the market in a while because I got tired of the underage prostitutes propositioning me at ten bucks a pop.

Anyway, I bought the pocket knife because, given how much I'd started drinking over the last year, always having a bottle opener handy was a no-brainer.

I opened the knife's sharp blade, gripped the doll, and was about to cut the string securing it to the tree when its eyes blinked open.

I started, looking around for Jesus or Nitro. They weren't anywhere in sight, of course. This was not another prank. I'd caused the eyes to open when I gripped the doll. I'd disturbed the pendulum inside it, or whatever mechanism was responsible for controlling the eyelids.

I used my fingertips to close the doll's eyelids, the way you might close the eyelids of a recently deceased person. As soon as I ceased contact, however, they flipped up again, so the doll stared at me with its disturbingly lifelike eyes.

Cutting the little monster free, I stuck it in my pack, collected the vodka, then started back the way I'd come.

I chose a different route back which I believed would reveal more of the island while offering up a whole new freak show of dolls. I wasn't disappointed, as Solano's obsession seemed contained by no boundaries. As the forest closed around me, the canopy and understory blocked out much of the sky to create a syrupy, shadowed world. Birds cawed and chirped and beat their wings far above my head. Cicadas whirred louder than before, an angry, palpitating sound that could suddenly and inexplicably stop before starting up again. Bugs bit my legs and arms and neck, and the sensation of being watched returned, making me feel suddenly alone, isolated.

Jack, a doll to my right whispered. Its voice was like the rustle of leaves, so close and clear I turned my head despite myself, my eyes searching the cluster of dolls wedged into the various crooks of a tree. *Are you lost? You're going to die—*

"Shut the fuck up," I said, to hear my voice, a real voice.

I took a belt of vodka and pressed on, following the well-beaten path. For a while I tried to pick out a doll to give to Pita—a peace offering of sorts—but I couldn't find any that resembled her. For starters, about ninety-nine percent of the dolls were Caucasian, which I found strange. China had Chinese dolls. Japan had Japanese dolls. Weren't there any patriotic doll makers in Mexico?

Eventually I came across one doll with black hair that could pass as Pita if you ignored the pigmentation. Nevertheless, I left it where it was because it was seriously evil-looking, and if I gave it to Pita, she would likely accuse me of making fun of her.

When I was roughly halfway back to the side of the island where we'd disembarked, I came to a dilapidated cabin. Unlike the hut Pepper and I had investigated, this was much larger and featured a porch with an actual swinging door.

I tried the door, expecting it to be locked. It opened, and I stepped inside. The main room was dark and carried the forgotten smell of wood rot and age. There was a contrary feel to it, perhaps because there were no windows, though gaps between the corrugated iron roof and the timber walls allowed for some natural light.

When my eyes adjusted to the murkiness, I found myself in what you might call a living room. There was no TV or stereo or anything resembling modernity. But there were two rattan chairs, a table, and a bookcase, all of which appeared to have been rescued from a trash heap. More junk littered the floor, or at least what I considered to be junk, though Solano would have likely begged to differ. Some of the detritus included glass bottles, tires, an umbrella, a lunch box, a handsaw, a hammer, even a very old car seat.

And of course there were dolls—a riot of them, thirty, forty, more. Most were like those outside, discolored and blistered and boiled from the tropical sun. They were affixed to the walls, a cornucopia of creepy, crawly, bump-in-the-night abominations, and once again the sight of so many of them filled me with a niggle of trepidation and sadness.

I wondered why they made me feel like this, and some Freudian mumbo-jumbo I read once came to mind, something regarding an inherent contradiction. Dolls are inanimate objects, they're lifeless, but because they look like us, they appear alive—and when something that's not alive appears *too* alive its familiarity turns to unfamiliarity, our brains reject it as unnatural, and our feelings for it sour toward revulsion.

A roundabout way, I guess, of saying dolls are just plain spooky.

I crossed the room to the table where one doll sat alongside what might have been a shoebox. The wooden floorboards creaked beneath my weight. My heartbeat thudded in my ears, likely because even though Solano was dead, I felt as though I was trespassing, invading his privacy—which was exactly what I was doing.

I peered in the shoebox.

I wasn't sure what I'd been expecting to discover—spare doll parts?—but certainly not makeup. Yet that's what I found, loads of it, far more than any woman would ever need. I selected a metallic tube of lipstick, removed the cap: Firetruck Red. I dumped it back in the box and examined the doll. Its face was painted with eyeliner, eyeshadow, blush, and lipstick. Moreover, it was in much better condition than its outdoor cousins. Limbs intact, dressed in clean clothes, free of cobwebs and filth. The word "groomed" came to mind.

I picked up the doll. Its eyes were dark, reptilian, almost calculating, its earlobes pierced with bronze hoop earrings, its fingernails sporting vermillion nail polish. I sniffed its hair—a pleasant citrus scent.

Did Solano bathe the thing?

I wished Pepper were here to see it, because it was proof I was right. Solano had been a crazy bastard. Maybe even a raving lunatic.

I pictured him sitting at this table at nighttime, an old man worn down by time and aged by the weather and hardship of living off the land, working by candlelight, brushing the dolls hair, or carefully applying blush to its cheeks, or lipstick to its lips, or polish to its nails, mumbling incoherently to it as he did so, maybe asking how her day was, or what she was going to do tomorrow, or, hell, had she met any Ken dolls lately.

Yet why? What had he been thinking? That it was a flesh-and-blood child?

Did he fuck it?

This question startled me. He wouldn't, couldn't—it was a *doll*, for Christ's sake. Then again, some people had pretty sick fetishes, and he was lonely as a cloud out here, no human company...

I was tempted to lift the doll's dress, pull down its knickers, see if Solano had altered the space between its legs in any way. But I didn't. I didn't

314

want to know.

The sight of a gaping hole would make me sick.

Suddenly I didn't want to touch the thing any longer, and I set it back on the table. I moved on to an adjoining room, the floorboards once again creaking beneath my weight. I poked my head into what turned out to be a kitchen. I wrinkled my nose at the smell of something rotten. Dishes were piled on the top of a roughly hewed counter. Alongside these were a knife, a spoon, and a fork. Staples such as pasta, salt, rice, and sugar occupied a single shelf. A basket on the floor was filled with dry corn which Solano likely ground into flour. There was no sink or stove because he wouldn't have had running water or electricity. I assumed there would be a fire pit nearby where he would have boiled water from the canal and cooked his food. Pepper mentioned the locals traded him dolls for produce he grew. I hadn't seen a vegetable garden anywhere, but then again I had only seen a small slice of the island.

My eyes swept the floor, the shadowed corners, for a dead mouse or small animal, something that had crawled in here to die and was responsible for the stench. I didn't see anything.

Back in the living room I went to one of the two rooms I had yet to explore. It was a Spartan bedroom: bed, dresser, window, that was all.

The door to the second room was closed. I gripped the doorknob and was about to twist it when a sneeze originated from the other side of the door.

I froze, dumbstruck.

Please, Jack—first a doll opening its eyes, then another talking to you, and now one sneezing?

But then what had I heard?

I pushed open the door, half-expecting a Chucky doll to scuttle toward me on its small child's legs, a big knife gripped in one hand.

The room was empty save for a bed and a dresser.

"Hello?" I said, regardless.

No reply.

I didn't want to check beneath the bed. It was something a child would do, to assuage their paranoia and superstition. Nevertheless, I knew I couldn't avoid doing so, because I'd heard something after all. I hadn't imagined that.

I touched a knee to the floor and looked.

The little girl was on her belly, hands at her sides, fingers splayed on the floor, like a sprinter about to bolt from the starting blocks—or come straight at me. Matted black hair obscured much of her face. She wore an embroidered cheesecloth top and pastel-colored jeans.

When I regained my wits, I cleared the lump in my throat and said, "Hi." This sounded not only lame but, given the circumstances, sinister as well, what a stranger says to lure an unsuspecting child into his car. "I'm Jack," I added.

The girl didn't reply. I guessed she was seven or eight. She had a round face with small features that suggested she would one day grow up to be an attractive woman.

I wondered if she could be Solano's daughter. Had he had an affair with a local woman and been charged with raising the illegitimate child? Or was it more sinister than this? Had he kidnapped her and held her prisoner here until he died? If so, how long had she been on the island? Her clothes weren't in tatters, but they weren't clean either.

I opened my mouth, then shut it. I wasn't good with kids, wasn't one of those people who could converse with them using falsetto voices and fake laughs.

I thought about getting Pita, but I discarded this option immediately, knowing the girl would be gone when I returned.

"What are you doing under there?" I said—then realized she likely didn't speak English. "Er... *Que haces...haciendo?*"

The girl swallowed. Her eyes darted to the door, then back to me. She was going to make a run for it. And what would I do? Let her go? Grab her? Close the door, trap her in the room, and shout for help?

No, no shouting. Jesus and Nitro would never let me live that down.

"Umm... *Puedes entender? Mi español... mal...*"

The girl said something so softly if I hadn't seen her lips moving I might not have believed she'd spoken.

"*¿Qué?*" I said.

"Yes," she said louder, but still not much more than a skeletal whisper.

"You understand me?"

She nodded.

"So you speak English?"

"We study it at school."

I hadn't known English was studied in Mexican schools at such a young age, and I said, "Where's your school?"

"Balcones de San Mateo."

"Is that in Mexico City?"

"Naucalpan."

Which was north west of the city. "So what are you doing way down here on this island?"

"I—" She bit her lip. Tears shimmered in her eyes, then spilled down her cheeks.

"Hey, hey," I said. "It's okay. It doesn't matter." I lifted my baseball cap with one hand and ran the other through my hair. "What's your name?"

"Rosa," she said.

"Okay, look, Rosa. Why don't you come out of there?"

"I don't want to."

"You can come meet my friends."

"Your friends?"

"Yeah, I'm here with..." I had to mentally count. "Five of them."

She sniffled, then rubbed her leaking nose and eyes with the back of her hand. "Are they nice?"

"Two of them are tools. But the other three are nice."

"Tools?"

"Like, uh... Do you know what a dork is?"

She nodded.

"Well, they're like that. Dorks. One's called Muscles."

"Is he strong?"

"He thinks he is."

"Maybe he can protect us?"

"Protect us?"

She bit her lip and didn't say anything.

"Is there somebody else on this island, Rosa?"

She remained silent.

"Come out, Rosa," I said. "Come meet my friends. You can't stay under there all day."

"What's the other dork's name?"

I laughed. I couldn't help it. Rosa smiled hesitantly, as if unsure what was funny.

I said, "God."

"No it's not!"

"What a stupid name, right?"

"He can't call himself God."

"Hey, I agree totally."

"What about your other friends? Do they have stupid names too?"

"Their names are Pita, Pepper, and Elizaveta."

"Those are better."

"I agree."

"Why are *you* here?"

"The island? One of my friends—Pepper—he works for a TV show."

Rosa's eyes widened. "Really?"

I nodded. "Do you know what a documentary is?"

"Not really."

"It's like a real-life movie. You know, like those animal shows and stuff? Only Pepper's shows are about ghosts."

She seemed surprised. "He knows about the ghost?"

I frowned. "What ghost?"

"The ghost on the island. The ghost that..." She bit her lip again.

I studied her silently. I had a dozen questions, but there would be time to ask her them later. Right now I needed to get her out from under the bed, to the others. They'd know how to talk to her, get her to open up. I said. "Are you hungry, Rosa?"

She nodded.

"We have water. I think we might even have a candy bar. Do you want a candy bar?"

She nodded again.

"Okay. But you have to come out of there first."

I offered my hand to her. After a long moment, she took it.

We walked side by side, holding hands. I would have felt awkward doing this with a child back in the city, and I felt equally uncomfortable now. But the girl—Rosa—didn't want to let go. She really was spooked by something. Which was what I was trying to figure out. What was the ghost she thought she'd seen? Shadows playing tricks with her eyes? A glimpse of a doll in the dark? A figment of her imagination?

Moreover, why was she on the island in the first place? Someone brought her here from Naucalpan obviously, but who? And where were they now? The island wasn't big enough that you could lose someone on it. Sound carried out here precisely because there was little sound of anything to begin with. All Rosa had to do was yell and whoever she came with would hear her.

Which meant something had likely happened to her guardian. But again I was stumped. Because if the person slipped and cut their head open on a rock, or had a heart attack or some other serious medical emergency, you'd think Rosa would tell me. Yet the fact she was mum on this, as well as the so-called ghost, led me to conclude the two were related. Something happened to Rosa's guardian, and for whatever reason Rosa believed a sinister spirit was responsible.

"You don't believe me."

Her voice startled me. "Huh?" I said, even though I knew what she meant.

"You don't think there's a ghost on the island."

"Did you actually see one?"

"No..." She frowned, struggling with what to tell me. Then she blurted, "It killed my brother."

I stopped. She did too. She looked up at me, and she seemed so small, so afraid.

I said, "Your brother brought you here to see the dolls?"

"To show his girlfriend the dolls."

His girlfriend? I crouched next to Rosa. "How many people did you come here with?"

"Just them. My brother, Miguel, and his girlfriend. He wanted to show her the dolls. We made camp, and then...then he wanted to be alone with Lucinda, and he told me to go away."

"Lucinda is his girlfriend?"

She nodded. "So I went away. I found a pond. I was trying to catch frogs. And then I heard my brother scream, and he never screams."

"What happened to him?"

She scrunched up her face, fighting more tears. "I don't know."

"You don't know?"

"He told me to run. He sounded like..."

"Like what?"

"Like he was dying."

"What about his girlfriend? What happened to her?"

"I don't know. I ran away until I found that house." She pointed back toward Solano's cabin. "I fell asleep on the bed. But when I woke up, it was dark, and I was scared, so I hid underneath it."

"You've only been here for one day?"

She nodded.

I stood, took her hand again. One day, I thought. Which meant if what she was telling me was the truth, and if someone had indeed attacked her brother, then the person could still be around. I recalled the feeling of being watched earlier. The dolls—or a living person? I looked past Rosa, then over my shoulder, my eyes searching the trees.

"Come on, Rosa," I said. "Let's get to the others."

1954

It was a warm spring day. María, now in the third grade, spent recess walking in the field behind the school. She held Angela in her right hand, the doll's feet dragging on the ground. Her mother often tried to stop her and Angela from being friends, but she would always throw a temper tantrum, yelling and crying, until her mother gave in.

She passed a group of kids in her grade playing a game with a ball. The boy with the ball threw it up into the air and all the other kids ran. When the ball came down he caught it and yelled a country name, and all the kids stopped. Then he went after the closest one and threw the ball. It hit a girl on the head, and everyone cheered.

María continued on. She didn't understand the rules. Besides, it didn't look very fun. She was much more interested in her present activity: collecting leaves. She didn't know why they fell off the trees, but she liked to pick them up in case the trees ever needed them back.

Eventually she came to the wooden split-rail fence that separated the school from the farm. On the other side of it was an open-air stable that consisted of a corrugated iron roof on posts. A black horse and two cows stood inside it. The horse saw her and came over.

"Hi, horsey!" she said. "What are you doing today?"

"I like horses," Angela said.

"I do too. But I don't like how they smell."

"That's manure."

"I know. Horses don't have toilets like we do, so they go on the ground."

"Do you like cows?"

"Yeah, but they smell even more than horses."

She continued her conversation with Angela and didn't notice the two girls in her grade approach until they were right behind her.

"Hi, María," Lydia said. She was a bit fat and mean, and María tried to avoid her if she could. A few days ago Lydia told her she was going to tie María to a chair and kill her mom and dad in front of her. "What are you doing?"

"I'm petting the horse."

"I'm petting the horse," Devin repeated in a dumb-sounding voice. She was tall and thin and had dark skin. "Why are you so stupid?"

"I'm not stupid."

"Yes, you are," Lydia said.

"No, I'm not."

"What's it like to be stupid?"

"I'm not stupid."

"You are. You're a stupid head. You're a stupid head who carries a doll around. Everyone thinks so."

María's eyes became hot and wet.

"Are you going to cry?" Lydia said.

"No."

"Go on, crybaby. Cry. That's what crybabies do."

"I'm not a crybaby."

"What's in your hand?" She grabbed the stack of leaves María had been holding.

"Those are mine!"

"Why are you carrying leaves?"

"They're mine!"

Lydia ripped the leaves into little bits and threw them up in the air, so the wind scattered them about.

"Ewww!" Devin said, covering her mouth with her hands. She pointed at the horse.

Lydia shrieked in amusement.

María turned to see the horse, but she didn't know what she was supposed to be looking at.

"Is that...?" Devin said.

"Gross!"

"So gross!"

Lydia whispered in Devin's ear. Devin listened, then began nodding and giggling.

"Look, María," Lydia said, pointing. "The horse has five legs."

María noticed the fifth leg for the first time. It was pink and crusty and peeling. Also, it was shorter than the other four. It didn't even touch the ground.

"Do you see it, María?" Lydia asked.

"Yes."

"It needs help."

"Huh?"

"You need to pull it down so it touches the ground."

"I don't want to."

"If you don't, the horse will fall over. It will die. It will be your fault."

"I don't want to touch it."

"We'll tell Mrs. Ramirez you killed the horse."

She looked at the leg. Maybe she could just pull it quickly. Then the horse would be okay, and Lydia and Devin would leave her alone.

She stepped to the fence.

"Go on!" Lydia urged. "Pull it down."

"I can't reach it."

"Climb under the fence."

María hesitated.

"Hurry up! Climb under the fence."

María went down on all fours. Leaving Angela on the ground, she crawled beneath the fence rail. Then she was right next to the horse.

"Grab it!" Lydia said.

"Pull it!" Devin said.

María grabbed the horse's leg. It was smooth and thick and warm. She pulled it. But instead of going down it went up, breaking free of her grip, disappearing into some kind of sheath.

María looked back at Lydia and Devin, confused.

They were bent over, laughing so hard tears came to their eyes.

María smiled hesitantly, wondering what she had done that was so funny, and wondering if maybe they would be nice to her now.

Jack

I heard them before I saw them. Pita was speaking in Spanish in a long monologue. By the sound of the choppy, unnatural cadence of her speech, she was reciting what she'd memorized for the documentary.

Sure enough, when the trees filtered away, she was standing before the hut that contained the shrine, over-enunciating her words and gesturing to the dolls attached to the wall, as though she were an action reporter covering a breaking news event. Pepper stood ten feet away, his video camera perched on a tripod. He was watching Pita on a small LCD screen. Nitro was behind him, arms folded, legs slightly apart, his back to me. Jesus sat against a tree, the leg with the sprained ankle stretched straight before him.

When Pita saw Rosa and me she did a double-take. She stopped midsentence, her mouth ajar.

The others turned, confused, surprised.

Rosa shied behind my legs and gripped my hand tighter.

"Who the fuck is that, chavo?" Nitro blurted.

Jesus and Pepper were both saying something to me. I didn't have time to reply to either because Pita had come hurrying over. She unclipped the microphone from her collar, squatted next to me, and starting spurting off Spanish to the girl.

Rosa mumbled something back. Pita frowned. They exchanged a few more words.

"What?" I said.

Pita looked up at me. "She says she doesn't want to speak Spanish because you can't understand."

"Sounds logical to me."

"What did you do, brainwash her?"

Rosa pressed tighter against my legs. I peeled her off me and crouched so we were at eye level. "What's the matter, Rosa? Remember, they're my friends."

"I don't like the dork," she said.

"Dork?" Pita was indignant. "Me?"

Rosa pointed past her to Nitro. "Him."

Nitro guffawed.

"That's okay," I said. "Nobody likes him. But you can talk to Pita. She's nice."

"What are you doing here, honey?" Pita asked. "Where are your parents?"

"They're at home."

"So who are you with?"

Rosa threw her arms around my neck and buried her head into my chest. I hesitated, then patted her on the back. "Where's Eliza?" I asked.

Pita looked around, as if just noticing she was gone. "I don't know."

"Nitro," I said, "go find Eliza. She shouldn't be on her own."

"Fuck you, Jack Goff."

"Do it!"

For a moment I didn't think he was going to, he was going to stand there in stupid defiance. Then Jesus gave him a godfather nod.

Scowling, Nitro wandered off into the trees.

To Pepper I said, "Do you have any more of those candy bars you had on the boat?"

"Lucky I have a sweet tooth," he said, nodding. "I have one more." He went to his bag, retrieved the candy bar, and brought it to Rosa. "Here you go."

Rosa raised her head from my shoulder. She took the candy bar and said, "Are you Pepper?"

Pepper beamed. "Have you seen my show?"

"Jack told me your name," she said.

"And did he tell you Nitro was a dork?" Pita asked.

"Who's Nitro—? Oh, you mean Muscles?"

Pita shot me a look.

"Nice, Jack," Jesus said.

"Here," I said to Rosa. "Let me do that." I unwrapped the candy bar, then handed it back to her.

She took a small bite, then another, and another, all the while chewing quickly.

"The poor thing's ravenous," Pita said.

"Rosa," I said, easing her away from me and standing. "Can you give us a sec? I'm going to tell them what you told me, okay?"

She nodded without taking her eyes from the candy bar.

I moved a dozen yards away, indicating for Pita and Pepper to join me. Jesus got up and hobbled over on his good foot. When we were out of earshot, I said, "I found her beneath a bed in what I think must have been Solano's house."

Pita frowned. "What was she doing?"

"Hiding from you?" Jesus said.

"Not me exactly," I said. "She told me she came here with her brother, Miguel, and her brother's girlfriend, Lucinda. Yesterday, by the sound of it. Anyway, she says she was catching frogs or something when she heard her brother scream. He told her to run, and she did. She hasn't seen him since."

They stared at me like I'd just told them I'd been abducted by aliens.

"That's what she told me," I insisted.

"My God, Jack!" Pepper said. "Do you think she's telling the truth?"

"Why would she lie?"

Pita said, "Maybe she's mad at her brother so she made up this fantasmal story?"

"Fantasmal?"

"Jack!"

I shrugged. "I don't know. She seems genuinely frightened. Besides, wouldn't her brother have gone looking for her? The island is big, but not that big. Wouldn't we have crossed paths with him by now?"

"We didn't know the girl was here," Jesus pointed out.

"She was hiding. If her brother was looking for her, he'd be calling out and stuff."

"Okay, hold on a minute," Pepper said. "We're jumping ahead. We need to slow down. What happened to her brother? What made him warn her away?"

I hesitated. "She thinks a ghost attacked him."

"A ghost?" Pita's eyes widened. "You mean, the ghost of the little girl who haunts this island?"

"Come on, Pita," I said.

"Come on, what?"

"This is serious. Something's happened—"

"I am being serious, Jack."

"You think a ghost attacked Rosa's brother?"

"Why not?" she said defiantly.

"She's entitled to her opinion, Jack," Jesus said.

I looked at Pepper for support. He might like to debate the existence of ghosts and spirits and whatnot, yet he was a pragmatic guy, and I didn't think he really believed what he preached. It all went part and parcel with his act.

Nevertheless, he was looking at his shoes, unwilling to back me. He knew how religious Pita was, how superstitious. He wasn't going to reveal himself as a false prophet, rain on her parade.

"Okay, whatever, ghost, no ghost," I said. "Bottom line, we know one-eighth of fuck all right now. We're just speculating. So what's important, what we have to do, is find Rosa's camp. We can figure out what happened then."

"Easier said than done, Jack," Jesus said. "This island has to be a couple of hundred acres easily. And it's all jungle."

Pita had taken her mobile phone from her pocket and was holding it up in the air. "No reception," she said.

"I could have told you that," Pepper said. "We're in the middle of nowhere. There isn't a radio tower for kilometers."

"Rosa?" I called. "Do you think you can find the way back to your camp?"

"I don't know." She looked about helplessly. "I don't think so."

"How did you guys get to the island? Did you take one of those gondolas?"

"*Trajineras*," Pita said.

"*Trajineras*," I amended.

Rosa shook her head. "We took a canoe."

"So if we found the canoe, do you think you could find your camp?"

She nodded. "Easy."

Nitro and Elizaveta returned a few minutes later—Elizaveta had gone off to take some pictures with her small digital camera—and we gave them a quick rundown of everything Rosa told us. Like the rest of us, Elizaveta was visibly agitated by the possibility a murder had occurred on the island. Nitro's reaction, however, was the exact opposite: he seemed pumped, like a Hardy Boy keen to tackle a new mystery. He even went so far as to scavenge a stick to defend us with.

We didn't want to split up given a killer might be lurking about, but we didn't have a choice. Jesus's sprained ankle made him immobile. So in the end we decided to divide the group in half. Elizaveta and Pita would stay behind with Jesus, while Nitro, Pepper, and I (with Rosa guiding us) would set off along the bank to circumvent the perimeter of the island in search of the canoe.

Nitro and his stick took vanguard. Pepper and I came next with Rosa between us, holding our hands. We followed a strip of land that ran between the tree-line and the water. The ground was mostly hardpan and scrub, occasionally overrun with huge ferns and waist-high vegetation, but it was relatively easy-going. The dolls were strung up in greater concentration here, along the waterfront, than anywhere else on the island, though no one mentioned them. The fun and games were over; our little day trip had suddenly become very serious business.

The weather continued to worsen, and quickly. A wind picked up shivering foliage and small twigs, and it started to rain lightly. The clouds blocked out the sun completely, so everything was lit in a premature, felt-gray twilight, more dusk than midafternoon.

"Great," Pepper said, holding out his free hand to verify it was raining.

"Maybe it will blow over," I said.

"I checked the forecast this morning," he said. "The meteorologist didn't say anything about rain today. I swear."

"What channel do you watch?" Nitro asked him.

"Canal de las Estrellas."

"Switch to El Trece. The weather girl on that one..." He whistled. "Major smoking hot front, you know what I'm saying?"

"Do you have a girlfriend, Muscles?" I asked him.

"What's it to you, Jack Goff?"

"I take that as a no."

"Take it whichever way you want, brother."

"Maybe the ponytail's the problem," I went on. "You should have left it in the nineties."

Nitro laughed. "We go to a bar babe-hunting, you and me, I'll outscore you ten-zero, you better believe that."

"Babe-hunting?"

"The girl I'm pounding right now, she's vaginamite."

"Vaginamite?" The guy really was a douchebag—a prurient douchebag.

"Fucking right, Jack Goff."

"Watch your language around Rosa."

"I don't mind," she piped up.

I glanced down at her. She was watching the ground where she walked, almost skipping to keep pace with Pepper and I. Suddenly I felt absurdly proud of her. She believed her brother was dead. She believed a ghost shared the island with us. She'd spent a night on her own beneath a bed. And here she was telling me she didn't mind if someone cussed around her? She was made of something tougher than the rest of us put together.

"Can I ask you something, Rosa?" I asked her.

She bobbed her head. "If you want."

"How long was Miguel seeing Lucinda for?"

"Hmmm. Maybe two months? Maybe more?"

"Did they ever fight?"

"No, not really. Why?"

"Well, I've been thinking," I said, "and maybe Lucinda got angry at Miguel yesterday and did something to him. It might not have been on purpose, not completely. It might have been an accident, sort of."

"An accident?"

"Maybe she wanted to hurt him a bit, but she ended up hurting him a lot. Maybe that's why he screamed..."

Rosa seemed to think about this, then she shook her head. "I don't think Lucinda would even want to hurt Miguel a bit. She was really nice."

"But why would a ghost want to hurt him?"

"Because this is *her* island. She doesn't want us here."

"That's what Miguel told you?"

Rosa nodded gravely.

"Hey, Rosa," Pepper said. "Do you want to be on TV?"

"She's not going in your documentary, Pepper!" I said.

"Why not? She'd be great."

"Why can't I be on TV?" she asked me.

"Because," I said.

"Because what?"

"Just because...your mother wouldn't like it," I added.

Rosa frowned at this. "You're probably right. She doesn't like me doing anything fun."

"She let you come to this island though...?"

"No, she didn't."

"She doesn't know you're here?"

Rosa shook her head. "My sister—my oldest one—is getting married soon. She and my mom went to a special party all weekend. Miguel was babysitting me."

"And he brought you all the way here?"

Rosa nodded. "Because he couldn't leave me alone."

"What about your father?" Pepper asked. "Couldn't he look after you?"

"He's living in France right now."

"He works there?"

She nodded again. "He's an *embajador*. I don't know the English."

"A diplomat?"

"I think that's it."

"What school do you go to?" Nitro asked.

"Greengates."

"The British international school?" Pepper said. "That's where Jesus and Pita went!"

"They went to my school?"

Pepper nodded. "Their dad was rich like yours. But that was a long time ago."

"How long?"

"More than ten years."

"Wow, I didn't know they were so old."

"Don't tell Pita that," I said.

"She's like as old as my mom—"

Nitro called out abruptly, cutting Rosa off.

Twenty feet ahead was the canoe.

The canoe was pulled up onto the bank so it wouldn't float away. Scuffs and dents marred the aluminum hull. Two wooden paddles lay within it, propped against the yoke.

"This is the one you came in?" I asked Rosa, using my hand to shield my eyes against the rain, which had become a steady drizzle. The once mirror-smooth canal was now a simmering boil. Waves crashed against the bank, the penumbra of their spray dissolving into fine droplets.

She nodded. "That means the campground isn't far. It's just that way, past a big pond." She pointed to the trees.

I hesitated. "Maybe it would be better if you stayed here—say, with Pepper—while Nitro and I checked it out. What do you think?"

"Why?"

I didn't want to splinter the group further, but I hadn't been thinking clearly before when I'd suggested Rosa lead us to the campground. Exposing her to whatever might have happened to her brother had not been one of my better ideas. "Pepper's a big scaredy cat," I told her by way of explanation. "He doesn't want to go to the campground. He needs someone to look after him."

Rosa studied Pepper. "He doesn't look like a scaredy cat. He looks like the Purple People Eater."

"I should tell you, young miss," Pepper said, indicating his clothing, "this is a very fashionable ensemble."

"Well, I guess I can look after him."

I said to Pepper, "You don't mind staying back?"

"As long as you two don't dawdle."

"You should find some shelter."

He pointed to a nearby magnolia, the branches of which seemed to be bending beneath the weight of its wet blooms and foliage. "We'll wait under that."

"Okay," I said. "And remember, we'll be within hearing distance. So if you see anybody, yell."

Pepper tried a smile. "That's reassuring, Jack. Thanks."

The canopy and understory blocked out some of the rain and the wind. However, there was no path like the one I'd followed across the island earlier. Instead Nitro and I were forced to circumvent the tall trees and duck low-sprouting branches. A tangle of broadleaf shrubs and palms and woody plants obscured much of the ground, so we didn't really know where we were putting our feet down. Vipers could be found across Mexico, and their bite was dangerous to humans. I hoped if there were any on this island they abided by the old adage that they should be more scared of me than I was of them.

To take my mind off snakes, I turned my attention to what might await us at the campground. I wanted to believe that Rosa was wrong, that her brother hadn't been attacked, that it was an uncanny misunderstanding.

But how could this be the case? She had heard him screaming. He had told her to run. So something had happened, something bad.

Which brought me back to the million-dollar question: Who would attack him? Rosa said Lucinda was nice, and she and Miguel didn't fight, but who knew what went on between them in private? Besides, there was no rule to say nice people didn't do bad things, especially in the heat of the moment.

Then again, if Lucinda suddenly lost the plot, why would Miguel tell Rosa to run? Wouldn't he instead implore her to help him? Telling her to run implied he thought she was in danger too. Yet why would he think she would be in danger from Lucinda if Lucinda's beef was with him?

And then there was the whole problem with the canoe. Why hadn't Lucinda taken it back to the docks? Why had she remained on the island?

To search for Rosa?

To silence the only witness?

"Nitro," I said, his name coming off my tongue awkwardly. I don't think I'd ever addressed him as anything but Muscles. "Any theories on what might have happened you're not sharing?"

"Why do you care what I think, chavo?" he said without looking back.

It was a good question. I suppose because while the others would have been content to play ostrich until the boatman returned to take us back to the docks, Nitro had been all action, gung-ho to discover answers, and that was something I respected.

I couldn't bring myself to tell him this, of course, and I was about to tell him to forget it, when he said, "Money."

"You think Miguel owed Lucinda money?"

"Think big, chavo. Her father's an ambassador. That means big bucks in Mexico."

"You mean a kidnapping?" Kidnappings were serious business in Mexico, a daily occurrence, the reason people like Jesus often had a bodyguard or two with him in public. Even I was a target simply because I was a foreigner, which was the reason I never took gypsy cabs. There were, I'd been told, roughly two thousand kidnappings a year. This was a conservative figure, as many were never reported because the police weren't trusted not to be

334

involved. "You think someone would follow him all the way here just to kidnap him?"

Nitro shrugged. "A few hours work for a potential big payoff, why not?"

"What about Lucinda then?"

"What about her?"

"If they took Miguel," I said, pushing a branch out of my way, "what happened to her?"

"Who's to say she wasn't the target? She might come from a wealthier family than Miguel. Unfortunately for him, wrong place, wrong time. Or maybe they took her too. Or maybe they offed her. No witnesses—"

Nitro came to an abrupt halt. I looked past him and saw the pond ahead and to the left.

Nitro put his finger to his lips, and we continued forward in silence. Twenty yards on he mumbled something and began moving more quickly. I stuck behind him, searching for what he'd seen.

I saw the body a moment later.

We entered the glade where Miguel and Lucinda had made camp. A dozen dolls, maybe two dozen, swayed from branches in the wind and rain, their glass eyes and evocative smiles all too lifelike. Two backpacks, one green and one orange, and two sleeping bags, both rolled up, sat on the grassy ground at the base of a cedar. Next to these items were a scattering of clothing: shorts, a T-shirt, boxers, a dress, a lacy bra, silk panties.

In the middle of the clearing lay Miguel—at least I assumed it was Miguel. He was facedown, naked, his back shredded with what appeared to be stab wounds. Red-brown blood covered his bare skin, from the nape of his neck to his buttocks.

My pulse quickened at the ghastly sight. My legs turned rubbery, as if they no longer wanted to support my weight. I opened my mouth to say something, but I didn't know what was appropriate.

He was dead, Miguel was dead, nothing now but offal and decay.

Nitro knelt next to the body, which was thick with flies. I hadn't noticed their maddening buzzing until right then, though now it seemed to fill the air, loud and angry. Same with the smell. I hadn't detected it before. But it hit me like a truck, a maggoty stench.

"Eleven," Nitro said, examining the cuts. "Someone stabbed him eleven times. Looks like they used a serrated knife."

Nitro rolled the body onto its back.

"Fuck me," I said softly. I wanted to look away, but I couldn't. The morbidity, the wrongness, transfixed me.

The man's eyes were missing.

In the next instant a startled centipede, sinuous and black with bright yellow legs and a flattened head bearing probing antennae, scurried out of the left bloodied orbit, down the once handsome face to the ground, and wiggled beneath the leaf litter.

Nitro glanced back at me, scowling. "I think we might have stumbled into some deep shit, chavo."

1955

Patricia Diaz entered through the front doors of María's school, trying to ignore the apprehension that had been churning in her gut ever since the phone call from the principal the day before. She had been summoned to the school on several previous occasions to discuss her daughter's academic development or bullying or other sensitive topics. However, these meetings had always been with María's teachers, never with the resident psychologist.

In the front office a secretary told her the directions to the psychologist's office, and a few minutes later Patricia was knocking on a door with a bronze plate attached to it that read: Dr. Lola Cavazos.

The door opened and a woman wearing a champagne-colored dress smiled at her. "Mrs. Diaz?" She had an urchin haircut and a friendly demeanor. She stuck out her hand. "I'm Dr. Cavazos."

"Good afternoon," she said, shaking.

"Please come in. I'm so happy you were able to come this morning. May I get you a cup of tea?"

"No, I'm fine, thank you."

"Have a seat." She gestured to a seat on one side of a desk, while she settled into the seat on the other side. "How are you today?"

"A little nervous to be here."

"Understandably. So let me get to the point. I'd like to talk to you about your daughter, María. Specifically, how she is coping in grade four. First, however, let me begin by saying I've had the pleasure of spending some time with her over the last week, and she is a very well-mannered child."

Patricia smiled. "Yes, she is."

"She is also sweet and helpful."

"She always has been."

"Mrs. Diaz, from what I understand, you've had several meetings with her teachers in the past. What have they told you about her academic performance?"

"That she's a little behind some of her classmates. Her last teacher, Mrs. Ramirez, said she was having difficulty concentrating and was easily distracted."

"And her general behavior?"

"She hasn't made many friends. She...keeps to herself, I guess you would say."

"Would you say, generally speaking, her behavior resembles the behavior of other eight year olds?"

Patricia wanted to say yes, but she wasn't here to deceive anybody. She was here to get María help. "No, I suppose not."

"If you were to name an age you believe her to be functioning at...?"

"Perhaps a seven year old." She hesitated. "Perhaps even a six year old."

Dr. Cavazos nodded. "From the assessments I have done, I would say she has the overall skillset of a five year old, so we are both pretty close—"

"Five?" Patricia's stomach sank.

"The point, Mrs. Diaz, is that we are in agreement that she is progressing at a much slower rate than her classmates not just academically but in all areas. Would you agree with this statement?"

"Well, yes. But *five*... Are you sure? I know she's a little shy around other students—"

"Yes, I've noticed that. Nevertheless, I don't think it's a case of mere shyness. I don't believe she can carry a two-way conversation with her peers. Also, she seems to have a difficult time remembering things. For example, she struggles to retain simple math facts that should come very easy to someone of her age. She also can't recall details of a book that she has read only minutes before."

"I've tried to help her with her math and reading at home. Her father works late. But I usually spend an hour with her each evening."

"And how has this been working out?"

"I think it's helping. I know she's a bit forgetful. But she's still very young."

"You are aware that she has temper tantrums?"

"Don't all children?" she said with a bit too much asperity. She was beginning to feel as though the psychologist was attacking María.

"They do, certainly," Dr. Cavazos said calmly. "Such outbursts arise because young children have difficulties expressing themselves, especially complex emotions. Having said that, by grade four they have usually grown beyond this stage. María, it seems, hasn't. She still can't fully express herself, what she wants to say, what she's feeling. Which, I believe, is why she isolates herself from other children. And why she has her temper tantrums. She's frustrated." Dr. Cavazos paused. "Mrs. Diaz, have you heard of intelligence quotient tests—or IQ tests?"

"I believe so. They measure a person's intelligence."

Dr. Cavazos nodded. "You can't study for them. They test how individuals solve brand new problems, both verbal and visual. Does the word 'idiot' or 'imbecile' or 'moron' mean anything to you?"

"I don't think so, no."

"In the psychiatric community, those with an IQ between zero and twenty-five are referred to as idiots. They can't respond to stimuli or communicate with any level of competency. Those with an IQ between twenty-six and fifty are termed imbeciles. They are stalled mentally at about six years of age. And those with an IQ between fifty-one and seventy are termed morons. Morons can communicate with others and learn common tasks, though they often need specific instruction or guidance." Dr. Cavazos retrieved a chart from the shelf behind her and placed it on the desk, facing Patricia. It was divided into several different sections, the bottom one labeled idiot, the top, genius. "Here is a representation of where most students score." She pointed to the range between ninety and one hundred ten. "On both visual and verbal problem-solving, however, María scored here." She pointed to seventy. "For example, when I asked her how a banana, apple, and orange are alike, she said, 'Pear.' That's not quite...it's related to what I said...but it misses the point that they are all fruit."

Patricia didn't know how much more of this she wanted to hear, and she said, "Please just say what you have to say, Dr. Cavazos."

"Well, the good news is that María isn't functioning at the level of an idiot or imbecile."

"But she's not normal either. She's...what did you say? A moron?"

Dr. Cavazos nodded. "She can take care of herself. She doesn't have any physical challenges. She has some typical life skills. But, yes, she does fall into the moron range."

Patricia swallowed the tightness in her throat. "Well, how long is this...this phase...going to last? How long until she grows out of it?"

The psychologist hesitated. "In my experience, Mrs. Diaz, it isn't a phase, and one doesn't grow out of it."

Patricia stared blankly. What was this woman telling her? María wasn't just developing slowly. She was in fact...what was the word people used...feebleminded? "I'll spend more time with her at home," she said softly, quickly. "I'll help her—"

"I'm sorry, Mrs. Diaz," Dr. Cavazos said. "What afflicts María is not something you can 'fix.' Now, don't get me wrong," she added. "María can and will continue to learn and add to her skillset. She can love and be loved—"

"But if she continues to fall further behind her classmates, how is she going to graduate? How will she cope in high school? How will she ever get a job?"

The psychologist leaned forward. "I don't think you understand fully what I am saying, Mrs. Diaz. María will never graduate. She will never attend high school, or college for that matter. And she will almost certainly never hold a job. She is going to need special care."

"For the rest of her life?"

"That's correct. But thankfully there are special schools where she can get the help she needs, and where she will be among others like her, where she will no longer be singled out and bullied."

Patricia felt all of a sudden hot and woozy at the same time. Then she began to cry. "It's my fault. Her birth, it went on for far too long. I wasn't pushing right. She was distressed. The doctor had to perform a caesarian section..."

"No, Mrs. Diaz. María's ailment is not the result of something you did or didn't do, so don't blame yourself."

"Oh dear me...my María...my poor María..."

"I know how hard all this must be for you to take in, Mrs. Diaz. I know how hard it was for me to tell you—"

Patricia stood decisively. "Where is María right now?"

"She should be in class, I imagine."

"Would you please fetch her for me? Tell her I'll be waiting out front the school. I'd like to spend some time with her."

María burst out the front doors, her book bag slung over her shoulder, Angela gripped in one hand.

That doll, Patricia thought with vitriol. *I never should have let her keep that doll. Maybe if I'd put my foot down years ago, maybe she wouldn't be...*

"Mamma!" María said, her face lighting up. "Why are you at school?"

Patricia knelt on the pavement and opened her arms wide. María crashed into her, hugging her tightly—and in that moment Patricia realized her daughter was the same daughter she had always known, and she would continue to love her, she had a duty to love her, feebleminded or not. "I thought you would like some ice cream," she said, brushing fresh tears from her eyes. "Would you like some ice cream?"

"Yes, please! Can I have chocolate? Can I have chocolate? Can I?"

"You can have anything you want, sweetheart."

"What about after? Do I have to go back to school after?"

Patricia stood and took her child's hand. "That's something we're going to talk about."

Elizaveta

Not long after Jack and the others left, a mild wind picked up, and the slate-gray sky began to spit. Then, maybe twenty minutes after that, the sky let loose, unleashing torrents of driving rain, which now plinked against the hut's corrugated iron roof, sounding like a carnival Wheel of Fortune at the height of its spin. Elizaveta sat cross-legged on the floor, her back against a support post. Jesus and Pita were seated across from her. Dolls covered almost every inch of wall behind them, their eyes glinting in the murky half-light, shadows carving hard edges into their round childlike faces.

The first peal of thunder rolled across the sky. Elizaveta glanced out the hut's door. Through the swaying trees she could see a section of the canal. It looked to be all foam and spray. No way the boatman was coming back any time soon, she thought. Which meant they would be spending the night on the island, cold and wet. She wondered whether the others had found Rosa's campground. And if so, had Miguel and Lucinda been there? Were they okay? Or were they injured, dead, or missing altogether?

Elizaveta couldn't believe their newfound circumstances. How had they gotten tied up in a possible murder mystery? This was supposed to be an easy day out. A relaxing cruise down the canals, sun and Mexican food, a lighthearted adventure, that was it.

They should have listened to the boatman, she knew. They should have shelved the documentary and returned to Cuemanco with him. If they had, she would have been back in the casita, or guesthouse, on the estate in San Angel where she worked as a governess. It was currently home for her. And home was the place you wanted to be during one of Mexico's summer tropical storms because they could be absolutely vicious. Last month she'd been in Acapulco with Jesus when a tropical storm struck hundreds of miles off Mexico's Pacific Coast. While the resort they were staying at continued to operate normally, most of the outlying neighborhoods lost access to power and water. Streets turned into gushing rivers while landslides shut down highways. On the low-income periphery of the city, steep hills funneled rainwater into neighborhoods of cinderblock homes, washing many away. During the drive to the airport, which had also flooded, Elizaveta had seen people with picks and shovels digging in mounds of mud and rubble, perhaps for buried friends and relatives.

That was one thing Mexico and Russia had in common, she thought: endemic poverty. The difference was that the poor in Mexico took it in stride and were for the most part content and upbeat, while the poor in Russia were angry, bitter, always grumbling about how bad things were.

Elizaveta had been born on Vasilyevsky Island in Saint Petersburg. Her parents were both journalists, critical of the Cold War and the oppressive authoritarian regime in power at the time. Consequently, the KGB kept them under constant watch. Elizaveta remembered a small Russian-made Lada would follow their car around the city, and a man in a dark suit would always seem to be wherever they went, keeping tabs on them. Her father told her their phones were tapped, their apartment bugged, their mail opened. He also believed their government-provided housekeeper filed frequent reports on them. Then one day when Elizaveta was ten years old she came home from grade school to find the man in the dark suit waiting for her. He told her that her parents had been taken away and she would not see them again, and she never did. The next day she was installed in a state-sponsored orphanage that was like a mini gulag for children. Many infants had fetal alcohol disorders, and it wasn't uncommon to see them sitting by themselves, staring blankly at nothing, or knocking their heads against the walls. The older children such as herself were frequently mistreated, abused, even "rented out" to local farmers to work on their farms. Needless to say, many of Elizaveta's Dickensian housemates became psychologically scarred. One girl she got to know well picked up the unhealthy habit of rocking herself to sleep each night, while another rubbed the same part of her head so frequently she went bald there over time.

Elizaveta left the orphanage at the age of fifteen, in accordance with Soviet guidelines. She moved into a room in a state-subsidized Kommunalka, or communal apartment, in which none of the floors, walls, and pipes seemed to line up right. She shared the kitchen, two toilet closets, and a single bath with six other families. Although the building was warm during winter, it was not uncommon for the heat, or hot water, to shut off without warning—which had happened to her on several minus-thirty-degree days, and which was why she kept a giant jug of water handy so she could flush the toilet or wash dishes if needed.

The Soviet Union collapsed when Elizaveta was eighteen. Retail stores were routinely empty, and you had to wait in long queues for food supplies. You never threw out a vodka bottle because you could get small change for it at a recycling point. People with PhDs drove taxis, while neighbors banded together to chase off looters.

For the next four years Elizaveta pursued a university degree in education, focusing on English, French, and Spanish. She had grown sick of her homeland—sick of the daily indignities, the endless prostitution of everybody and everything—and her plan was to move to Western Europe or the United States. Upon graduating, however, she discovered there were few legal channels for low-paid employment abroad such as teaching. Elizaveta considered simply getting on a plane to the West with the intention of never returning—the Russian Federation was not the USSR; you were no longer persecuted or imprisoned if you applied for a visa—yet she hesitated. If she violated her visa regulations, she would not have any legal status in her new country, which was why most Russian women who attempted such an escape ended up trafficked as sex workers.

In the end Elizaveta accepted a job in an elementary school in Saint Petersburg, where she taught for several years. Life in the new Russia improved slightly, but a pair of sneakers were still something you showed off, and a VCR was still a luxury far out of her reach. Then, in 1997, when she was twenty-five years old, her close friend, Olga, who worked as a nanny for a wealthy family, told her the family was moving to Mexico—and interviewing for a governess of Russian nationality who could speak Spanish.

Elizaveta folded her arms more tightly across her chest, to ward off the damp chill in the hut. She told herself to be positive. She shouldn't be thinking about being back in San Angel. They'd made their decision not to return with the boatman to Cuemanco, they couldn't change that, so they had to deal with the situation the best they could. Besides, who would have thought the weather would have deteriorated so implacably and quickly?

Pita examined Jesus's ankle, pressing her fingers to it gently. The ankle had turned a virulent purple and had swollen to the size of a melon.

"Stop it," Jesus told her. "That's not helping any."

"We need to reduce the swelling," she replied.

"Got a spare bag of frozen peas?" he remarked.

"Hopefully it will be better in the morning."

"Fucking Jack," Jesus grumbled.

"He didn't mean it," Elizaveta said. Her Spanish accent wasn't native, it never would be, but her Spanish was about as fluent as her English.

"Didn't mean it?" Jesus said to her. He'd pushed his Aviators up onto his forehead and was looking at her with incredulity. "Did you see how hard he shoved me?"

"Pepper said Nitro started it."

Jesus waved dismissively. "Pepper doesn't know anything."

"I saw you and Nitro double-teaming him."

"You're taking Jack's side?" Pita asked. Her long-lashed eyes were dark and disapproving. She shot a Camel from her pack and lit up.

"I'm not taking any sides," Elizaveta said. "I'm saying Jack didn't mean to make you sprain your ankle, Jesus. He was going after Nitro. You were in way."

"He caught me by surprise, that's all," Jesus said. "I wouldn't have fallen otherwise."

"And Jack has a bad temper, Eliza," Pita said. "He has to learn to keep it under control."

"Nitro's a bully," Elizaveta said.

Jesus chuckled. "What grade are we in?"

"To tell you truth, Jesus, I don't like him. I don't know why you like him. You two are so different."

"Nitro isn't a bully," Pita said, blowing smoke out the corner of her mouth. "He's actually a very nice guy when you get to know him."

Elizaveta didn't say anything. She knew why Pita was defending Nitro. She was fooling around with him behind Jack's back.

They'd all been at a beach house party two months or so ago. Jesus and Elizaveta picked up Pita on the way there, though Jack stayed behind. There was some important American football game on the television he wanted to watch. The beach house was packed with people when they arrived. Jesus and Pita went into mingle mode, working the room. Elizaveta poured herself a glass of wine from the bottle she'd brought, left the rest in the kitchen, and went to the deck for a cigarette. She much preferred going to bars or clubs than these private parties. There was a great community of ex-pats living in Mexico City, and she knew many of them: Russians, French, Canadians, Australians, a few New Zealanders, a lot of Americans and British. They were all intelligent and friendly, and she always had a good time with them. The people around her that evening, on the other hand, fell mainly into two groups: young Mexican socialites who didn't work and lived off their parents' credit cards, and older businessmen who drank whiskey and smoked cigars. The bratty socialites looked down on Elizaveta because she was a "salary worker," while the businessmen often treated her like a prostitute until she firmly put them in their place.

Around midnight Elizaveta asked Jesus if he was ready to leave. He wasn't. He was surrounded by admirers hanging on to his every word, most holding one of his brewery's beers in their hands. Tired of talking to strangers, she decided to walk along the beach. The night was cool and dry. The ocean droned on endlessly while waves lapped gently at her bare feet. She walked for close to thirty minutes, and she was on her way back to the beach house when she ran into Pita and Nitro. She didn't know it was them at first.

They were little more than amorphous shapes on the sand beneath a palm tree. Then she heard Pita speaking in that throaty voice of hers, and Nitro replying in that gruff way of his. Elizaveta froze, dumbstruck. She was contemplating whether to make her presence known, to ask them what they were doing out here, when she realized they weren't merely talking; they were making out. She hurried back to the party, told Jesus she wasn't feeling well, and took a taxi home.

She'd seen Pita and Nitro at parties together three times since, but Jack had been present at each one. She'd been tempted to confront Pita, or even tell Jack what she'd witnessed. She didn't, because she'd been hoping it had been a one-time thing, a drunken fling. For a while it seemed this might be the case until last night at Jack's place. Jack had been inside refilling his drink, and Pita had been trying to convince Jesus to invite Nitro to the Island of the Dolls the next day. Jesus didn't want to, given the animosity between Nitro and Jack. Pita, however, was persistent, arguing that Jack was so drunk he likely wouldn't even get up in the morning. So Jesus rang Nitro, who confirmed he would come on the spot.

Again, Elizaveta didn't confront Pita. It wasn't her business to intervene. Besides, these types of things, romantic affairs, never remained secret for long. Jack would discover Pita's infidelity on his own. It was simply a matter of time.

At least, that's what she told herself. But there was another reason she remained silent: Pita was vindictive. Elizaveta didn't want to get into her bad books for fear Pita might turn Jesus against Elizaveta herself. Pita wielded a surprising amount of control over her brother, and if push came to shove, Elizaveta didn't know with whom Jesus's loyalty would lie. If he dumped Elizaveta, what would become of her then? The twin girls she was tutoring turned fourteen this year; they would enter boarding school in autumn. Consequently, she would be out of a job, and her visa expired early next year. She would have no choice but to return to Russia...to poverty. And she couldn't do that. She'd worked too hard to get to where she was in society now. She couldn't go back to waiting an hour in line for a loaf of bread, or to teaching fifty-hour weeks for a couple of thousand Rubles—the equivalent to what she currently earned in one morning.

"What's taking them so long?" Jesus said, tugging Elizaveta from her reflections. He was staring out the door at the slanted rain and the swaying trees.

"They've only been gone thirty minutes," Pita said.

"How long do you think it takes to walk the circumference of the island?" She stubbed her cigarette on the floorboards. "Longer than thirty minutes."

"You know," Jesus said, "we're going to be stuck here overnight now. We're going to be stuck here with whoever killed Rosa's brother."

"We don't know he's dead," Elizaveta said. "All we know is he screamed."

"Eliza's right," Pita said. "He might just be injured."

Jesus shook his head. "Like Jack said, if he was simply injured, he would have gone looking for Rosa. He would have been calling her name. We would have heard him."

"What about Lucinda?" Elizaveta asked. "Do you think she was attacked too?"

"Of course," Jesus said. "Otherwise we would have come across her already."

"Unless she took canoe back to docks."

Jesus shook his head again. "If she did that, she would have gotten help. She would have returned with the police."

"So who attacked them?"

"Thugs," Jesus said.

"Thugs?" Elizaveta repeated skeptically. "Why would thugs be out here, in middle of nowhere?"

"We are."

"Well—*why* would thugs attack them?"

Jesus shrugged. "Rosa said her brother sent her away so he could be alone with Lucinda, right? So they were getting it on, these guys saw them, they got a hard on, they wanted a ride."

"You think they killed Miguel so they could rape and kill Lucinda?"

"There's a motive behind every murder," Jesus said. "And when the victim or victims are strangers, the motives are usually sex or money."

"What about a ghost?" Pita asked. "What are a ghost's motives?"

"We're not talking about ghosts," Jesus said.

"Why not? That's what Rosa thinks. She thinks a—"

"Rosa's a child, Pita. And that story about that little girl who drowned, that's all it is, a story, a legend—"

"Legends don't just materialize out of thin air," Pita said defiantly. "People don't just make them up."

"That's exactly what they do. And they tell other people, and other people tell other people. There's no such thing as ghosts, Pita. Okay?"

Pita glared at him. "What about Susana?"

Jesus opened his mouth, closed it, shook his head.

Elizaveta frowned. Susana—as in Pita's and Jesus's deceased younger sister? "What about Susana?" she asked.

Pita said, "She was our younger sister."

"I know. Jesus told me what happened."

"Did he tell you I saw her ghost when I was a kid?"

Elizaveta shook her head.

"Well, I did," Pita said. "It wasn't long after she drowned. I woke up in the middle of the night. She was at the bedroom window."

"Did she speak to you?"

"Yes—sort of. Not with her mouth. I don't know how to explain it. It was like I could feel her thoughts. They were inside me. She told me she was okay. She told me not to worry about her."

"Did you see her again?"

"No. Only that one time."

"Huh..." Elizaveta said, not sure what else to say.

"You were a kid," Jesus said.

"I didn't make it up!" she snapped.

"Fine. Say you did see Susana. That's one thing. But the ghost of a girl who died fifty years ago, haunting an island filled with dolls, killing two strangers who trespassed on it...?"

"All I'm saying," Pita said, "is that we need to keep an open mind. We don't know what happened, and we need to keep an open mind. Right, Eliza?"

"Yes, we should keep open mind," she said diplomatically. "We should also wait until the others return, hear what they've learned, before we jump to conclusions."

They returned some twenty minutes later. Pepper came first, his head ducked against the cauls of rain. Jack and Rosa followed, and finally Nitro, who carried a medium-sized canoe on his back. They were all drenched, their hair sticking to their heads, their clothes to their bodies. Elizaveta and Pita leapt to their feet and went to the hut's door, though they remained inside, out of the downpour.

"Jack!" Pita said. "Did you find the campsite? Did you find Miguel and Lucinda? What happened to them?"

Jack wiped water from his face and pointed to a different hut maybe thirty meters away. "I'm going to take Rosa there so you guys can talk. Pepper or Nitro can tell you everything."

He led Rosa away. They didn't run; the rain didn't seem to bother them as they were already as wet as they could get. Nitro dumped the canoe on the ground, then he and Pepper entered the hut. Their shoes squeaked, trailing mud. Nitro removed the elastic band from around his ponytail and shook his hair out like a dog. Pepper found a spot against the wall and sat down with a tired sigh. His complexion appeared ashen in the dying light. A grimness etched his usual merry features.

"Well?" Jesus demanded. "What happened, man?"

Pepper looked at Nitro, who was running his fingers through his hair in an effeminate manner. Nitro said, "It's not good, buddy."

"What do you mean?" Pita asked. "What happened? Are they dead?"

"Miguel's dead. Stabbed eleven times."

"Eleven times!" Pita said.

Jesus swallowed. "What about Lucinda?"

Nitro shook his head. "No sign of her—except for her clothes."

"Her clothes?" Elizaveta said.

"Her clothes were on the ground, discarded. Same with Miguel's."

"She ran away naked?"

"They took her," Jesus mumbled.

Nitro frowned. "Who took her?"

"Thugs. They killed Miguel, raped Lucinda, and took her with them."

"I don't think thugs killed Miguel," Nitro said, tying his hair into a ponytail once more. He hesitated. "His eyes were missing. Cut out, or even plucked out, it was tough to tell."

Elizaveta folded her arms across her chest to ward off the chill that suddenly reached all the way to her bones, and stared big-eyed at the others, waiting for someone to explain what this might mean. Jesus seemed equally bewildered. Pita was pacing back and forth, her head down, brooding anxiously. Pepper wouldn't look at anybody. Only Nitro seemed calm.

"Why would someone take his eyes?" Elizaveta asked.

"He's sick, obviously," Nitro said.

"You think it's just one person?" Jesus said.

"Doing something like this, cutting out the eyes, it fits the profile of someone who kills for the thrill of it."

"You mean a serial killer?" Elizaveta said.

"Yeah," Nitro said. "And serial killers act alone."

"Bloody hell!" Jesus said. "There's a serial killer loose on the island?"

Nitro held up his hands. "We don't know that. Miguel was killed yesterday. The killer might have already left the island. We only saw the one canoe—Miguel's and Lucinda's."

"Lucinda," Elizaveta said. "What about her?"

Nitro shrugged. "This guy could have chased her down and killed her somewhere else on the island. Or he could have taken her with him. Without a body, there's no way to know."

"Should we go looking for her?"

Nitro shook his head. "I said this guy *might* have left the island. But he might not have either. Best thing to do is bunker down here for the night and leave as soon as the storm dies down."

"It wasn't a serial killer," Pita said, stopping her pacing and facing them. Her voice was flat, her color drained. "It was the ghost. I know none of you believe ghosts are real, but they are. Jesus said so."

"I never—"

"Not you! The real Jesus. It's in the Bible—"

"The Bible's just a book—

"A little girl died here!" Pita exploded. "She *died* here, perhaps in a horrible, inconsolable way. Her spirit's not at rest. Solano knew this. Look around you! Look at all the dolls! They're offerings to her, to appease her spirit." She glared at each of them in turn. "But now he's dead, and she's alone, and she's angry. Isn't this obvious? She killed Miguel and stole his eyes. So isn't this pretty damn obvious?"

1956

María stood at a tall window, her nose pressed against the glass, watching as her parents drove away. Then hedges obscured them from view and they were gone.

She didn't understand why they had brought her here. Her mother had told her it was a special school. She would like it. She would meet new friends. That all sounded okay. But then she said María would have to sleep at the school too. That wasn't good. That was terrifying. She wanted to keep living in her house. She wanted her room, her bed, her dolls. She glanced at Angela, who she held by the arm. "I want to go home," she said.

"Maybe you'll go home soon?" Angela said.

"I want to go *now*."

"I don't think you can."

"Why're my mom and dad leaving me here? What did I do—?"

The door to the room opened and a nun entered. She had a strawberry pudding face framed by tufts of white hair visible beneath her funny hat. Mean eyes peered out from behind silver-rimmed spectacles. "My name is Sister Lupita," she announced.

"My name's María."

"No, it's not, you snottery pup," she snapped in a completely different demeanor than when she'd spoken to María's parents. "It's 46. From this point on, your name is the number 46. Do you understand that?"

She didn't. "My name's María."

Sister Lupita leaned toward her. María didn't know what was coming and simply stood there. The nun clapped her hands against the side of María's head simultaneously with the flats of her palms. Pain lanced through her ears, and she almost fell over.

"Ow!" she cried.

"What's your name?"

"46!"

"Remember that. Now give me that doll."

"She's mine!"

Whack. Harder this time.

"Ow!"

"Give me the doll."

María began to cry.

Whack.

"Ow!"

"There will be no crying in this school. Crying is a sign of weakness, and weakness is the work of the devil. Now give me the doll."

Biting her bottom lip to stop the tears, María thrust Angela at the woman.

Sister Lupita took her and said, "Well, well, you can learn. Maybe you're not as dumb as everyone says."

Sister Lupita led María to a nearby room that had a sewing machine on one desk and a typewriter and transistor radio on another. A number of framed photographs lined the windowsill above a magazine rack.

In the center of the room a short, frail nun stood next to an empty chair. She held a pair of metal scissors in her hand.

"Sit in the chair, 46," Sister Lupita instructed.

María went to the chair and sat. She liked haircuts. The hairdresser her mother took her to always gave her a lollipop when the cut was finished.

The short nun lifted a handful of María's long black hair and snipped it close to the roots.

María was horrorstruck. "My hair!" She tried to leap off the chair, but Sister Lupita seized her shoulders and pinned her in the seat. She twisted and thrashed.

The short nun produced a hairbrush from her pocket and rapped María on the head sharply with its wooden backside.

"Ow!" she cried, tears springing to her eyes.

"Sit still," Sister Lupita said.

Her skull throbbing, María obeyed, and the short nun went back to work.

Snip, snip, snip.

All around her, clumps of hair fell to the floor.

After the horrible haircut—her hair was now shorter than most of the boys' hair had been in her old school—Sister Lupita marched María down a hallway, stopping when they came to a staircase. There, she used a key on her keychain in an angled door built into the side of the stairs. She opened it to reveal a pitch-black space and said, "This is where little girls who don't know how to behave go to think about their sins and pray for forgiveness."

María didn't know how long she was in the cupboard, if that was indeed what it was. She guessed maybe she'd been there a day, maybe longer. She couldn't see her hands if she held them directly before her face, and there was a strong toilet smell. The long stretches of silence were occasionally punctuated by footsteps treading the steps above her head. She wanted to yell out, ask for help, but she didn't, fearing it might be Sister Lupita or another nun.

Mostly María closed her eyes and tried to banish her sadness and loneliness and fear with sleep, but she always ended up thinking about her mom and dad. Where were they right then? What were they doing? Why did they bring her to this awful place? Didn't they want her anymore? Didn't they love her? What had she done to make them hate her so much? And perhaps the most immediate question: Was she going to be living here forever, or would she be allowed to go home again at some point?

She was dreaming about her old school, walking into class with no hair while all her classmates pointed and laughed at her, when she heard the key in the cupboard lock. A moment later the angled door opened.

Squinting against light that seemed as bright as if she were staring at the sun, María nevertheless recognized the pudgy, blushed face of Sister Lupita peering in at her.

"Good morning, 46," she said.

Morning? So she really had been in the cupboard for nearly a full day.

"Good morning," she replied, trying to sound pleasant.

"Have you repented your sins?"

"Yes."

"Yes, *Sister.*"

"Yes, Sister."

"Then climb out of there. Hurry, I don't have all day."

María scrambled out of the cupboard and stood before Sister Lupita, avoiding eye contact.

"You didn't soil yourself?" the nun said, and it sounded as though she were surprised.

"No, Sister," María said, though now that the woman mentioned it, she realized she did have to go pee very badly.

"I suppose it's off to breakfast for you then. This way."

Sister Lupita led her through a series of echoing hallways to a large dining hall. There were a dozen tables in neat rows of fours. Six or seven children sat on long benches at each, eating in silence. Two nuns patrolled the room.

"Go on," Sister Lupita said, ushering her forward. "Go get your food."

María went to a small window that opened to the kitchen. A grubby-looking man smoking a cigarette scowled through it at her before dumping a bowl of beans and a crusty piece of bread onto a tray and pushing it toward her. As an afterthought he added a glass of milk.

María picked up the tray and turned to face the room. Sister Lupita was gone. The only sound was the clack of spoons on bowls.

María carried the tray to the nearest table and sat at the end of the bench. She looked at the beans before her. They were covered in a gunky sauce and didn't resemble the beans her mother made her. Ignoring them, she said to the girl next to her: "Hi."

The girl didn't reply.

"I said, 'Hi,'" she said again.

"You're not allowed to talk," a skinny girl hissed from across the table.

María frowned. Not allowed to talk? She returned her attention to her beans. Despite not eating since yesterday morning, she wasn't hungry. She was too upset, and she still needed to go pee. She glanced about for a bathroom and discovered one of the nuns looming behind her.

"What's your name, child?" the woman said. She was younger than Sister Lupita and had a mole on her chin.

"María," she said.

The nun rapped the handle of a feather duster across her head.

"Ow!" she cried

"What's your name?"

"Ma—" She remembered. "46!"

The nun lowered the feather duster. "What's wrong with your food, 46?" she asked.

"I'm not hungry."

"The Lord has provided you with nourishment, and you shun His generosity?"

"I'm not hungry."

The nun gripped María by the hair and jerked her head back. She scooped beans onto the spoon and tried to force-feed her as if she were a bird.

María pressed her lips together.

"Open your mouth, 46."

María kept her lips pressed together in a lipless line.

The nun released her hair and pinched her nose closed.

Pressure built in María's lungs until she had no choice but to open her mouth. The nun shoveled beans straight to the back of her mouth, forcing her to swallow them. She shoveled in another spoonful, then another, feeding María faster than she could swallow.

María gagged, then coughed, spitting beans at the skinny girl across the table. Then she lurched forward and vomited. Through teary eyes she watched in horror as the nun scooped up some of the sick with the spoon.

"Open up," she said.

Elizaveta

Elizaveta dashed through the rain and wind to the next hut. The interior was dark, shrouded in shadows, and inhabited with more ominous dolls, no two of which were alike. Jack sat next to Rosa on the floor, and it appeared they were playing an English nursery rhyme that involved clapping each other's hands.

"What are you playing?" she asked them, rubbing her wet arms to generate warmth.

"Jack's teaching me 'Pat-a-cake, pat-a-cake, baker's man! Rosa said. "He promised to teach me 'Little Miss Muffet' next."

"Jack is a man of many talents," she said.

"They tell you everything?" he asked her.

Elizaveta nodded. "I can't believe—" She looked at Rosa, closed her mouth.

"Rosa," Jack said, "can you go play over there with one of those dolls for a bit? I need to talk to Elizaveta about some adult stuff."

"Which doll can I play with?"

"Whichever one you want."

"But they're all attached to the wall."

"Here." He took a Swiss Army knife from his pocket and popped the blade. "Choose one and cut the string. Be careful though."

"I will!"

She accepted the knife carefully and went to the dolls, where she began examining the ratty things with great deliberation.

"I can't believe someone...killed him like that," Elizaveta said softly, even though Rosa wouldn't be able to hear her over the rain and wind. "Nitro thinks it was a serial killer. Do you believe that too?"

Jack nodded. "Lucinda didn't take the eyes. Neither did kidnappers."

"Kidnappers?"

Jack explained Nitro's previous theory.

"You're right," she said. "There's no reason Lucinda or kidnappers would do something like that. Still, a *serial killer*...?"

"Think about all those movies and stuff when the serial killer pins pictures of victims to his wall, and they all have their eyes cut out."

"Those are movies, Jack."

"But they're probably based on fact," he said. "Besides, there's a name for it. Dehumanizing or something. The eyes are windows to the soul, right? Or to the personality or whatever. Serial killers cut them out to make their victims less human, to make them easier to kill."

Elizaveta considered that, then said, "You know what Pita thinks?"

"That the ghost did it?"

Elizaveta nodded. "She was...how you say...flipping out? She even quoted Jesus—of Nazareth. I knew she was religious, but I never knew so much."

"It's her upbringing. Her whole family is super religious. Jesus is named Jesus after all."

"But Jesus isn't religious."

"Apparently his mother's death changed him. You know the details?"

"Of her death?" Elizaveta nodded again. "After Jesus's and Pita's younger sister died, their parents tried to have another child. There were complications with pregnancy. Their mother died along with unborn child."

"That's only half of it," Jack said. "Her death wasn't sudden or unexpected. She had pulmonary hypertension. Doctors told her if she had an abortion, she would live; if she didn't, she would die. Their father, Marco, forbade it. Abortion went against his beliefs. So, yeah, their mother died along with the unborn child. But it didn't have to happen. That's why Jesus changed his tune toward religion."

"Pita told you this?"

"Marco did," he said. "We were pretty close. He eventually came to regret his decision not to save his wife."

"But Pita, she never changed?"

"Nope," Jack said. "She's still as zealous as they come. The way she talks about God sometimes, and faith, it's like she thinks He lives in the attic or something." He shrugged. "Look, I might not be religious, but I don't really have a problem with it. In fact, I think in moderation it might be a good thing. It teaches you values and all. My problem is when it's taken to extremes, when it makes you choose between knowledge and myth. You know, Pita still takes everything in the Bible as the literal word of God. She doesn't believe in evolution. She doesn't believe in the Big Bang. The first time she mentioned the world was made in seven days, I thought she was joking. She was dead serious. I couldn't get my head around it, and she couldn't get her head around the fact I didn't believe this too. We argued, but you can't get through to her. Even when the proof is right in front of her she refuses to see it. I mean, if humans and other living things existed in their present state since the beginning of time, how do you explain the variety of dogs and horses and other animals we've created through selective breeding?" He shrugged. "The neurons that fire together wire together."

"What do you mean?"

"The more you believe in something, the more that something becomes your reality. It's probably why Pita's so into ghosts. Part of it stems from her spirituality. But more, I think, stems from seeing her sister's ghost, or thinking she did, at such a young age. She's believed this for so long, that ghosts exist, she can't change her beliefs. When her Yorkshire terrier died, she buried it in a pet cemetery in Vegas and packed its coffin with all sorts of things that it could use in its afterlife. I felt like we were back two thousand years in Ancient Egypt. And when her father died, she lit one of those candles for him at the bedroom window for a couple of months, every night."

"That's not so strange," Elizaveta said. "Many people do that. Pay respect to dead."

"Yeah, but Pita would actually sit there in front of it some nights. She said she was praying, but I'm pretty sure she was waiting for her father's spirit to appear, like her sister's supposedly did. Anyway, just a heads up. Don't get sucked into a debate about the supernatural with her. You won't win. You can't."

"I guess that's why Jesus agreed so easy."

Jack frowned. "Agreed to what?"

"We're having séance, Jack."

They returned to the hut with the shrine to find everyone in a sober mood. Jesus and Pepper and Pita sat on the floor. Jesus's face was impassive while Pita appeared both quietly angry and terrified. Pepper seemed to be dozing. Nitro stood by himself in a far corner, his back to everyone.

Pita looked at Elizaveta. "Did you tell him?"

She nodded.

"Well?" Pita said to Jack, and it was almost a challenge.

"We have all night and nothing to do." He shrugged. "You want to hold a séance, let's hold one. The question is, do you know how to?"

"Pepper does. He performed one before on his show. He'll be the medium."

Elizaveta had seen the episode of *Mexico's Scariest Places* to which Pita was referring. It had focused on a haunted vicarage in Todo Santos, a small coastal town at the foothills of the Sierra de la Laguana Mountains. According to the locals Pepper interviewed, supernatural events had been documented there since the nineteen twenties when the chaplain, who kept a journal of the goings-on, claimed an unseen force would tear his laundry off the line and toss him out of his favorite chair. In the following decades several different priests claimed to have seen the apparition of an old woman dressed in gray. In the eighties, the vicarage was turned into a café, which included a guesthouse. One guest that Pepper tracked down said she had been staying in the guestroom in 1987 and was awoken in the middle of the night to find three old women staring at her. She turned on the light and could still see them for a few moments, though they were blurry, before they disappeared.

Pepper and his crew held a séance in the guesthouse, which resulted in strange noises, automatic writing, and the table levitating. The Travel Network received close to one hundred complaints, mostly from religious groups that took offence to the show's pagan subject matter.

"Pepper?" Pita said. "Hey—are you sleeping? Wake up. You need to tell us what to do."

Pepper opened his eyes. Yes, he really didn't look well, Elizaveta thought. His complexion remained grim, and his bouncy energy was gone. In fact, he seemed downright lethargic. She wondered whether he was drained from the ordeal of discovering Miguel's body, or whether he had come down with something.

Pepper cleared his throat and said, "First we need to decide who's participating in the séance. The number must be divisible by three."

Pita counted everyone present. "Good, we have six!"

"No," Pepper said, shaking his head. "Rosa can't participate. Children can't participate."

"I'll sit it out with her," Jack said.

Pita frowned. "That leaves us with four."

"Count me out too," Nitro said.

"So it's just me, Pepper, and Jesus?" Pita shook her head. "No, the more participants the better. We can generate more psychic energy that way. Pepper, are you sure we can't let Rosa join?"

"Please?" Rosa said.

"Oh...well...okay," Pepper said, and he didn't seem to care one way or another. He was definitely not in top showmanship form. "Now," he went on, "spirits seek warmth and light. Candles would be best, but since we don't have any, we're going to have to improvise." Moving slowly, like an old man with aching joints, he opened his bag and withdrew an LED lamp that could either be mounted on his video camera or held via a handle. He turned it on and set it in the middle of the floor, so it shot a beam of white light to the ceiling, scattering the shadows nesting there.

Pita appeared dubious. "That doesn't look very séance-like."

"It going to have to do. Also, we need food."

"Food?" Jesus said.

"You don't have incense, do you?"

"No..."

"So we need food, something with a strong aroma."

"I didn't bring any food."

"I have vodka," Jack said.

Pita frowned at him. "Why do you have vodka?"

"I brought it."

"You can't go a day without alcohol?"

Jack ignored that. "Will vodka work, Peps?"

"Better than nothing."

Jack withdrew a bottle of vodka from his daypack, unscrewed the cap, and set the bottle next to the LED light.

"The ghost is only a little girl, Pepper," Pita said. "I don't think she drinks vodka."

"She's not going to drink it," he told her curtly. "But the smell can help attract her."

Next, Pepper instructed them to form a circle and hold hands. Elizaveta sat between Jack and Rosa, Jack's big hand in her left one, Rosa's little hand in her right one. Pita was to Jack's left, then Nitro, then Jesus, then Pepper.

"To summon a spirit..." Pepper began, then frowned, as if he'd just realized something. He cleared his throat. "There might be a problem, Pita. To summon a spirit, you need the spirit's name."

"But we don't know the girl's name," she said.

"We can't summon her without a name."

"Well, that was a quick séance," Jesus said, and started to stand.

"Sit down, Jesus!" Pita said. "We'll just make up a name. She's the only ghost on this island, right?"

Elizaveta was watching Pita, trying to figure out whether she was having a lark, or whether she truly believed they were about to summon the spirit of a little girl who died fifty years before.

What was it Jack had said?

The neurons that fire together wire together.

"Why don't we summon Solano instead?" Nitro offered as a solution to their dilemma. Elizaveta suspected he, like everyone else with the exception of Rosa, was playing along for Pita's benefit. "He died here too."

Pita seemed to contemplate that, then shook her head. "No, I want to summon the girl. We'll just call her...Candelaria. Is that okay, Pepper?"

"Sure, Pita, why not?" he said. "Candelaria's fine."

"You okay, Peps?" Jack asked him. "You're not looking all that great."

"I'm just tired. I might lie down after this. Okay—we're ready?"

"Ready," Pita said.

"Ready!" Rosa said earnestly.

Pepper offered a short prayer and a request for protection, told them to repeat after him, and said in a theatrical voice: "Spirit of the past, move among us."

They repeated: "Spirit of the past, move among us."

"Be guided by the light of this world and visit upon us."

"You couldn't miss that light," Jesus mumbled.

"Quiet, Jesus!" Pita said.

"People!" Pepper said. "Negative energy will dissuade the spirit. And try sounding a bit more respectful, like you're inviting someone into your home." He started from the beginning again: "Spirit of the past, move among us."

"Spirit of the past, move among us."

"Be guided by the light of this world and visit upon us."

"Be guided by the light of this world and visit upon us."

"Beloved Candelaria, be guided by the light of this world and visit upon us."

"Beloved Candelaria, be guided by the light of this world and visit upon us."

"Now close your eyes," Pepper instructed them softly. "And wait."

Elizaveta closed her eyes. She half expected someone to scream, to try to scare them, but no one did. One minute stretched into two, then three.

Finally she opened her eyes to peek at the others. Jesus and Nitro both had their eyes open as well. Jesus was screwing up his face, trying to make Nitro laugh.

"Did you feel that?" Pepper said suddenly.

"What? Pita breathed.

"I felt a presence."

"I think I did too!"

Elizaveta hadn't felt anything. She closed her eyes again.

"I think Candelaria's spirit is with us," Pepper said. He adopted the theatrical voice: "Our beloved Candelaria, thank you for joining us on this cold and wet evening. We are honored by your presence. We seek answers from the world you inhabit beyond the grave, and if you so choose to reply, please use one rap for 'yes' and two raps for 'no.'" He whispered: "Okay, Pita. Ask your questions, but keep them simple."

"What should I ask?" She sounded unsure of herself.

"How about next week's lottery numbers?"

"Jack!"

"People!" Pepper said.

"Our beloved Candelaria," Pita said loudly, mimicking Pepper's mannered intonation, "did you drown on this island fifty years ago?"

There was no response.

"Ask again," Pepper said.

Pita repeated the question.

They waited in silence until Pepper whispered, "Did you hear that?"

"Yes!" Pita said.

Elizaveta did too. A knock on the exterior of the hut. A chill iced her spine, but she quickly chided herself. It was nothing but a doll blowing in the wind, a limb striking the wall. She didn't know whether the dolls had been making these noises all along, though she suspected they had been; she simply hadn't been listening for them. Yet Pepper would have been. It was likely why he suggested this method for communication.

"Ask her another question," Pepper said. "She might not remain for long."

"Our beloved Candelaria, is your spirit trapped on this island?"

There was no response.

"Ask again," Pepper said.

"Beloved Candelaria, is your spirit—"

Knock.

Pita gasped.

Elizaveta opened her eyes. Everyone else had theirs closed now. Rosa's were not merely closed but squeezed shut, as if she was terrified. Jack appeared bored, while Nitro and Jesus seemed to be biting back smiles.

Pita's face was a mask of concentration.

Elizaveta closed her eyes.

"Beloved Candelaria," Pita went on, "are you responsible for the murder that occurred on this island?"

More knocks.

"Was that three?" Pita breathed.

"It was two," Elizaveta said.

"It was three!" Rosa said.

"Ask again," Pepper said.

"Beloved Candelaria, are you responsible for the murder that occurred on this island?"

Two raps on the wall.

"Beloved Candelaria, is the killer still on this island?"

Silence.

"Beloved Candelaria, is—"

A clap of thunder, the loudest yet, exploded above them.

At the same time a doll began to cackle.

Everyone, Jesus with his sprained ankle included, sprang to their feet. Although dusk had descended while they'd participated in the séance, claiming the last of the daylight, Pepper's LED lamp continued to illuminate the hut. Elizaveta was able to zero in on the laughing doll. "It's that one!" she said, pointing a finger at a doll clad in a blue dress with white polka dots. Its lips seemed to be smeared with red lipstick.

"Don't touch it!" Pita said, her voice jumping to a soprano level. She backed toward the hut's door. "It's possessed! She's in it! The girl's in it! Don't touch it!"

Ignoring her hysterics, Nitro went to the doll.

Jack grabbed Pita's wrist as she passed him. "Calm down!" he said.

"Don't touch it!" she wailed.

Nitro lifted the doll away from the wall and turned it over. He cried out and stepped back.

Everyone started shouting, asking what happened.

It was instant chaos.

Pita tore loose from Jack and disappeared outside.

Nitro was flapping his hands madly.

"What happened?" Jack demanded.

"It's covered with spiders!" he said.

Not understanding Nitro's Spanish, Jack reached for the doll.

"Jack, don't!" Elizaveta said, hurrying toward him. "There are spiders!"

He tugged his hand back. Together, they bent close to examine the doll. Dozens and dozens of tiny black spiders were scrambling out from beneath the dress.

The doll continued to laugh.

"Shut the fucking thing off!" Jesus said.

Jack produced his Swiss Army knife and lifted the doll's dress with the tip of the blade, revealing a cobweb that was as thick as cotton candy and crawling with more spiders.

"Move back," he told Elizaveta even as he cut the string from which the doll depended. It dropped to the floor. The impact sent spiders flying off it. Jack raised his foot and crushed the plastic torso where the electronics and battery would be located.

The laughing stopped.

In the stunned silence that followed Pepper blurted, "What the hell just happened?"

"It was the thunder," Jack said.

"What are you talking about?"

"The thunder set off the doll."

Spiders continued to pour out from beneath the doll's dress, searching for refuge between the floorboards. Elizaveta kicked the ghastly doll into the far corner.

"Thunder?" Jesus said. His back was pressed to the opposite wall, by a window. "It started laughing right after Eliza asked if the killer was still on the island!"

"At the same time as the thunder," Jack said.

"Thunder doesn't make—"

A scream cut him off.

Nitro burst out the door of the hut first, Elizaveta right behind him. Pita stood rooted to the ground, staring into the rain-thrashed jungle, still screaming.

Elizaveta saw the woman immediately. She was twenty meters away, leaning against a large tree, supporting herself with one arm. She was naked, her pale skin standing out in stark contrast to the gathered darkness.

All Elizaveta could think was: *It's the ghost, ghosts are real, I'm seeing the ghost, we summoned the ghost, oh my God ghosts are real!*

Then, from behind her, Rosa cried, "Lucinda!"

Lucinda! Elizaveta sagged with relief. *Of course it was, of course—*

Nitro rushed past Pita to help the woman. Elizaveta forced her legs to move and went to Pita. "It's okay," she told her, slipping her arm around her friend's waist and turning her back toward the hut. "It's Lucinda, the friend of Rosa's brother. It's okay."

Pita stopped screaming and started to mumble gibberish.

Elizaveta led her to the hut and eased her to the floor where she had previously been seated. Nitro came in a few moments later, carrying Lucinda, telling everyone to get out of the way. He set her down on the floor. Her head lolled to one side, limp. Long black hair, wet and tangled, spread away from it like a bed of snakes. Her face was ashen and muddied. Elizaveta's eyes flicked over the woman's body, almost guiltily: slender shoulders and large breasts with light brown nipples, the left one pierced; an hourglass waist and wide hips; a pierced bellybutton above her pubic hair; long, toned legs; fingernails and toenails painted plum.

Everyone was crowding around her. Rosa, clutching Jack's legs, said, "What's wrong with her?"

"She's hurt," Nitro said, and rolled her gently onto her chest.

An angry cut split open her right shoulder. It was filled with blood the color of puce that turned a brighter red where it leaked down her back. Elizaveta thought the wound resembled a slightly parted mouth smeared with raspberry jam.

Pita was saying something in a frantic, frightened voice. Rosa began crying. Jack scooped her into his arms and carried her away.

"Was she stabbed?" Jesus asked. "Was she stabbed too?"

Nitro nodded. "Looks similar to Miguel's wounds."

"What should we do?" Pepper asked. "She needs help. What should we do?"

Elizaveta grabbed Jack's bottle of vodka, knelt next to Lucinda, and dosed the gash.

Lucinda moaned softly.

Nitro asked the woman what happened, who did this to her. She didn't respond. Her eyes remained shut. He peeled off his tank top. Bare-chested, he folded it into a compress and pressed it against the wound.

Elizaveta felt the woman's forehead. "She has fever."

Pepper draped his purple blazer over her, covering her nakedness.

"She needs something warmer than that," Jesus said.

"Got anything handy, bro?" Nitro said.

"We should take her to Solano's cabin," Jack said. He stood separate from them in the corner, holding Rosa in his arms.

"There are clothes there?" Nitro asked.

"I didn't check. But there were two bedrooms, two dressers. At the very least there were sheets on the beds."

"How far is it?"

"Ten minutes."

Elizaveta glanced out the hut's door, at the dark and rain.

"I'm not going out there," Pita said. "No way. She's out there, she'll get us—"

"Enough, Pita," Jesus said severely.

"She's out there—"

"Enough!"

She bit her bottom lip and glared at him.

"We'll vote," Nitro said. "Everyone in favor of moving to the cabin, raise your hand."

Everyone except for Pita raised their hand.

The icy rain pelted Elizaveta's skin. The wind threw her hair in front of her face and threatened to knock her over. She planted her legs apart and held onto a tree for support. Everyone was struggling against the storm, especially little Rosa, who was holding onto Jack's leg with all her might.

Pita went down with a yelp. She lay on her back, unable to get back up. It was as though she were wrestling an invisible opponent who had close-lined her and now was sitting on her chest. Her wavy black hair seemed electrified, whipping this way and that. Pepper removed his arm from around Jesus's waist and helped Pita back to her feet.

"The storm's gotten too strong!" Jesus shouted, balancing on his good foot. Like Elizaveta, he held onto a tree for support.

Nitro, who was in the lead, turned to face them. He carried Lucinda in his arms. His biceps flexed powerfully. Raindrops pinged off his bare shoulders. "Don't stop!" he shouted as he continued on.

Heads down, blinking away rainwater, they followed. Progress was exhausting. They'd been in the storm for all of five minutes and already Elizaveta felt waterlogged, each step an effort.

She focused on the ground, where she stepped. In the dark everything was layered in shades of gray, browns, and blacks, and it was hard to see hazards such as fallen branches. The rain churned the dirt, making it thick and slippery.

She almost bumped into the back of Jack when he stopped to hike Rosa into his arms. The girl's face poked over his shoulder, her skin glistening wetly, her black eyes wide and haunted. Nevertheless, she smiled at Elizaveta. Elizaveta wanted to reach out, touch her, reassure her. The poor thing had just lost her brother. She'd been adopted by a band of strangers, and now she was slogging through what felt like the end of the world.

Elizaveta raised her hand, but Jack was moving again. Rosa squeezed her eyes shut and buried her face against his neck.

The odd couple. That's what came to Elizaveta's mind. Jack didn't like children. He often said as much, and when Elizaveta saw him around kids, he was stiff and awkward, and he usually did his best to ignore them altogether. So why had Rosa taken such a liking to him? Because he was the first person she had contact with after Miguel's death? Because he reminded her of her brother in some way?

A peal of thunder rumbled across the turbulent sky, drawing near. A particularly nasty gust of wind whooshed through the trees, icing her blood.

A loud crack sounded.

Elizaveta snapped her head up and saw a large branch strike the ground next to Nitro. He spun toward it, cursing. The branch was massive, the length of a car and sporting several smaller boughs sprouting spiraling needles. It hadn't missed him by much.

They all looked up. The branch had fallen ten or fifteen meters; Elizaveta could see the where it had broken away from the trunk. If it had struck Nitro, it likely would have killed him.

"We have to go back!" Pita shouted above the weather.

"How much farther is the cabin, chavo?" Nitro asked Jack, shielding his eyes from the lashing rain with his hand.

Jack bumped Rosa higher up his chest. "It's not far!"

"You better not be lost!"

"I'm not lost!"

"We have to go back!" Pita repeated. She was scanning the blowing canopy, as if expecting another branch to fall.

"Maybe we should..." Elizaveta said before the wind drowned out the rest of her words.

"It's not far!" Jack insisted, and marched on.

They reached Solano's cabin five long minutes later. It sat to the right of the path, little more than a tenebrous mass huddled amongst the trees, unwelcoming. It featured a crude open porch sheltering a drunkenly leaning door. No windows adorned the exterior, only dolls, all banging about animatedly in the wind.

Jack, still carrying Rosa, started toward it.

"Wait," Nitro hissed. He set Lucinda on a grassy patch of ground, gestured everyone closer so he didn't have to shout to be heard, and said, "We need to check it out first. Make sure it's all clear. I'll go."

"I'll come," Jack said.

"No, stay here and keep watch."

Without another word, Nitro approached the cabin. He stopped in front of the closed door, pressed his ear to it. He waited, a motionless silhouette. Then he pushed open the door and disappeared inside.

"I don't like this," Pita said.

"It'll be dry inside," Jesus said.

"It feels like a trap."

"What feels like a trap, Pita? It's just a—"

"Shhh!" Elizaveta said. Because she thought maybe Pita was right. The cabin appeared not only sinister but...wrong? This was a feeling, nothing more. Still, the sight of the ramshackle place gave her the creeps.

Thunder boomed overhead, though no one took their eyes from the gaping door and the blackness beyond it.

The seconds dragged. Elizaveta blinked water from her eyes and wondered what was taking Nitro so long. The cabin wasn't that big. He only had to poke his head in the different rooms. Had the killer been waiting inside for him then? Had he ambushed him, taken him out silently? Was he waiting for the rest of them to investigate?

Elizaveta looked at the others. Only Jack looked back at her. He seemed uneasy as well.

"I'll check," he said quietly. He set Rosa down.

"No," she said. "We should go together—"

Nitro shouted a curse.

Something small and black darted out the cabin's door and past Jack's legs. It brushed Elizaveta's right ankle before vanishing into nearby vegetation.

A cat, Elizaveta thought, her heart pounding. *Just a cat.*

"What the fuck?" Jack said. He had already stepped inside the cabin and was presumably speaking to Nitro.

Jesus and Pepper and Pita piled in behind him. Elizaveta glanced at Lucinda's inert body lying on the ground in the rain. But she couldn't move the woman by herself. Nitro or Jack would have to get her. She took Rosa's hand and entered the cabin as well.

It was nearly pitch black—nearly, because Elizaveta could make out what Jack was pointing at.

Nitro held a semiautomatic pistol in his hand.

He slipped off his backpack and dumped the weapon inside the main pocket.

"Why do you have a fucking gun?" Jack said.

"Why do you think?" he said. "For protection."

"Protection from what? Solano's nephew? Because he's the only other person we had any reason to believe might have been here—unless you knew something we didn't?"

"Fuck off, Jack Goff. You're pissing me off more than usual."

Jack said to Pita, "Did you know he carried a gun around?"

Pita seemed stunned. She shook her head.

"I didn't know either," Jesus said, frowning.

Nitro scowled. "What's the big deal?"

"What are you, a fucking gangster?" Jack said.

"I bought it legally."

Pita said, "I thought you could only have a gun for home protection?"

"That's what it's for," Nitro told her.

"So you don't have a permit to carry?" Jesus asked.

"A permit? Fuck, no."

"Bro, if you're caught with that gun, you're looking at up to thirty years in prison."

"There might be a fucking killer on this island! You should all be happy I have a gun—"

"Okay, okay," Elizaveta said. "Calm down. Maybe it's a good thing he has—"

"It's fucking weird," Jack said.

"Don't ask me to save your ass when you're getting your eyes ripped out—"

"Enough!" Elizaveta said. "Let's just..." Her gaze fell on a table behind Jesus and Pita. "Look, candles."

She went to the table, took her lighter from her pocket, and lit two red candles set in glass jars. The scent of burning wax fumes and the sight of the tiny flames buoyed her tremendously. The dark became a little less threatening.

"Light!" Pita said. "Thank God."

"There're more candles over there," Jesus said, pointing to what appeared to be a big pirate chest. "And there..."

Elizaveta went around the room, lighting six candles in total. The candlepower was modest, but at least they could now see each other clearly.

While she did this, Nitro collected Lucinda from outside and carried her to one of the two bedrooms.

"I don't trust that guy," Jack said under his breath to nobody in particular.

"Cool it, Jack," Jesus said.

Pepper cleared his throat. "Would anyone object if I lay down in the spare bed?" He stood a few feet away from everyone, his arms folded across his chest, huddled into himself. His cherub face drooped miserably. He appeared ten years older.

"Shit, Peps," Jack said, frowning. "You look... What's wrong?"

"Just tired. I know it's not fair I take the bed, but just for a bit..."

"Come on," Jack said, leading Pepper toward the vacant bedroom. Rosa followed dutifully.

Knowing they would need water at some point, Elizaveta went to an old enamelware bucket bristling with paintbrushes in one corner. She dumped the brushes onto the floor and looked inside it. Clean enough. She went to the door.

"What are you doing?" Pita asked, alarmed.

"Getting water. I'm not going far."

Outside Elizaveta set the bucket on the ground a meter from the cabin, then retreated to the rickety porch. She crossed her arms and studied the storming night. There was a feeling of foreboding and desolation to it, nothing moving yet everything moving.

There's a murderer out there somewhere.

The thought came easily, opening a pit in her stomach. She clenched her jaw and told herself she didn't know there was a murderer out there for sure, and even if there was, it didn't matter. There was only one of him and eight of them. And Nitro had a gun. That was protection enough for any threat. So, no, they didn't have anything to worry about, not really. Night would come and go. The storm would end. In the morning the boatman would arrive. If not, someone could take the canoe and get help. Either way, they would be dry and safe by noon at the latest.

A flash of lightning shocked the sky, turning patches of black a deep-sea blue. Rainwater began spilling over the lip of the bucket.

Elizaveta snatched it up and returned inside.

1957

The days at Saint Agatha's School for Lost Children were long and busy, and there was never any time for rest or play because, according to Sister Lupita, these were Satan's darling hours to tempt children to all manner of wickedness.

Each morning at five o'clock one of the nuns would enter the dormitory clapping her hands or banging a wooden spoon on the bottom of a metal pot. Once all sixty or so girls were up, the nun would supervise them getting changed. There was always a scramble to be the first to line up before the communal wardrobe. María sort of understood the others did this to select the best pieces of clothing for themselves. But then she sort of didn't understand either; she didn't understand why clothes needed to look good, which was why she often ended up in ill-fitting and mismatched outfits.

After everyone was dressed, the nun marched them in single file to the dining hall for breakfast. There, she would choose a girl to sing a hymn as well as say grace. María had been selected once before, and because she couldn't sing the hymn right, or remember the words to grace, she was made to sweep the hallways with a toothbrush.

For the rest of the morning the girls went to "work." Depending on what you were assigned each week, you might be sewing, knitting, peeling sacks of potatoes in the kitchen, cleaning, fetching water, or cutting wood. A lot of the girls complained in private about the jobs they were made to do, but this was María's favorite part of the day. It was all pretty straightforward, and she could do what was asked of her as well as anyone else without getting in trouble.

The same couldn't be said for school, which began after lunch. They had different nuns for each subject. María liked arithmetic the best, not because she was good at it but because Sister Francesca who taught it never punished her for getting the answers wrong. The other nuns were not so forgiving, especially Sister Vallín who taught scripture. She must have hit María on the head with her cane three or four times a class, and on the rare occasion she wasn't in a hitting mood, she would make María copy out pages from the Bible until her hand didn't work anymore.

Dinner was at six o'clock, followed by church at seven, during which the school's only priest, Father Pardavé, used his sermons to remind the girls they were unwanted and unloved, castaways, forgotten by the world, lower than a snake's belly, and they would never amount to anything. Some of the older girls called him Father Finger behind his back because of special examinations he did to them when they reached puberty. And sometimes at nighttime he would select one of them to accompany him to his cottage for "special lessons," though no one ever told María what these special lessons were about.

Finally at eight o'clock a nun supervised everyone as they changed into their nightgowns and knelt at their bedsides to pray for a half hour. María always prayed for her parents to come and take her away from the terrible school, and when she didn't find them downstairs waiting for her in the morning, she would pray a little harder and a little louder the next night, so God would hear her above all the other girls likely praying for the same thing.

Then it was lights out, and regardless of whether you were tired or not, you had to go to sleep. If you didn't, the nuns said the Sandman would come for you. He'd pluck out your eyes, put them in a bag, and carry them to his nest on the moon, where he would feed them to his beaked children, who loved nothing more than the eyeballs of naughty human children.

One Saturday morning María woke before dawn and found Laura sleeping next to her, sucking her thumb. She must have climbed into María's bed at some point during the night.

Laura was six years old, one of the youngest girls in the ward. As there were more girls assigned to the dormitory than there were beds, the younger ones often shared beds with the older ones. Laura, however, usually ended up sleeping on a pillow on the floor by herself because she was a bed-wetter and nobody allowed her in their bed—nobody except María.

María was about to go back to sleep when she realized her nightgown was wet. She peeled back the quilt, sat up, and swept her legs to the floor. There was a damp patch in the center of the mattress.

She shook Laura awake. The little girl looked at her tiredly.

"You wet the bed," María whispered.

Laura sat up slowly, rubbing her eyes.

María pointed to the damp patch.

"I didn't mean to!" Laura's chin began to tremble.

At that moment the door to the dormitory opened and Sister Vallín entered, rapping her cane against the wall loudly. She was a sturdy woman with beady eyes and a permanent scowl.

Almost immediately all the girls roused themselves, yawning and stretching and taking their places next to their beds. María and Laura did the same.

Sister Vallín moved down the line of beds, examining each mattress. She stopped at the foot of María's. Bright malice lit her beady eyes.

"Bed-wetter!" she crowed triumphantly.

An excited rustle passed through the other girls: anticipation at the entertainment in store for them.

Sister Vallín smirked at Laura. "You just can't help yourself, can you, 53? This is, what, your third bed-wetting so far this month? You are a filthy little girl, a filthy, disgusting little girl—"

"It was me," María said, not really knowing what she was doing. "I couldn't hold it in."

"You?" Sister Vallín said, surprised.

"I'm sorry."

Sister Vallín glared at her, and María was convinced the nun knew she was lying, could read her thoughts. But all she said was: "Bring me the sheet."

María peeled the sheet from the bed and handed it to her.

"Take your places, children," Sister Vallín instructed. "You know how we discipline bed-wetters."

The girls formed a big circle, each of them swallowing the smiles wanting to worm their way onto their faces. Sister Vallín draped the sheet over María's head. The smell of pee was strong. All she could see was white.

Then a sharp pain tore across her backside as Sister Vallín struck her with her cane. María yelped. She heard laughter erupt from the other girls. The nun struck her again and again, parading her around the circle, calling her everything from "child of the devil" and "enemy of God" to "unclean animal." This went on until María's behind hurt so badly she began to limp. Eventually she could no longer remain on her feet and collapsed to the floor, where she curled in a ball, sobbing in humiliation and pain.

Distantly she heard Sister Vallín speaking to the girls, heard them lining up before the wardrobe, heard them changing into their day clothes. Then they filtered out of the room, heading downstairs to the dining hall for breakfast.

A long time passed, and just as María was beginning to forget what she was doing on the floor, she heard the door to the dormitory open. Footsteps approached. The sheet was torn away.

Scowling down at her, Sister Vallín said, "The one thing God despises more than a filthy little girl is a filthy little liar." She raised her cane.

"Don't—"

The cane struck María on the side of her head. Stars exploded across her vision, and she was already spinning into unconsciousness as the nun struck her again and again and again.

María came around in a bed in a room she didn't recognize. Vivid light shone through the tall, arched windows, making her squint. Vaguely, she made out Sister Vallín and Father Pardavé. They were standing by some metal filing cabinets, speaking to each other. They seemed somehow very far away, and she could only catch snippets of their conversation:

379

"...becoming difficult...deceitful..."

"...mentally deficient..."

"...fits...dazed, unresponsive..."

"...God's mistake..."

"...no friends...Laura..."

"...equally unfortunate..."

"...her disobedience...aggression..."

"...American doctor...operation...very successful..."

María could no longer keep her eyelids open, they fluttered and shut, and then there was nothing but darkness once again.

Elizaveta

Lucinda's bedroom was furnished with a small, plain dresser and an iron-framed twin bed. A candle sat on the dresser, the stout yellow flame staving off the encroaching darkness. Nitro had hung Pepper's purple blazer from a hook on the wall to dry. Lucinda lay on the bed on her side, a ratty red sheet pulled to her chin.

"How is she doing?" Elizaveta asked, moving next to Nitro, who remained bare-chested, not an ounce of fat on him. She studied Lucinda. The woman's eyes were closed, her face gaunt and insipid. Her breathing had developed a burr, a phlegmy rasp, as though she had been a two-packs-a-day smoker for twenty years.

Nitro shrugged. "We need to keep her warm. But there're no covers, nothing, only these sheets."

Elizaveta looked at the dresser.

"Empty," he said, "except some socks and underwear."

"Where are Solano's clothes?"

"He was a hermit. He probably only had one outfit."

"What about the wound in her back?"

"Bleeding's stopped. Not much more we can do."

She raised the bucket. "Can she drink water?"

"Not while she's unconscious."

Elizaveta frowned, frustrated. She wanted to help, but there was nothing for her to do. She looked around the room for something warm, for something Nitro might have missed. Her eyes fell on his backpack. He'd taken it off and set it on the floor against the wall.

She recalled the way he had acted when Jack caught him with the pistol in his hand: surprised, guilty. How he'd quickly stuffed it away.

Why hadn't he told them he had it earlier? What was the big secret? It wasn't like they'd turn him in.

She felt Nitro watching her and said, "Will you stay here?"

"For a while," he replied. "Need to keep an eye on her. Make sure she doesn't stop breathing or go into shock."

"Shock?"

"From loss of blood."

"Oh..." Elizaveta hesitated, still wanting to help. "Is there anything I can do?"

He shook his head. "Go get some rest."

Jesus and Pita were seated in the two rattan chairs at the table, speaking softly to one another, Pita smoking a cigarette and appearing agitated. Elizaveta let them be and went to the far side of the room, where she found a spot against the wall to settle down. Her clothes and undergarments clung wetly and miserably to her skin. A hearth would have been wonderful right then, the heat of the fire and the musky smell of burning wood divine.

At least there were candles, she thought. It would have been horrible to have to sit there in midnight blackness, the only sound the violent wind and rain, not knowing where the others were, not knowing whether someone had slipped into the cabin with them.

Elizaveta cleared her throat and reigned in her imagination. She lit a Camel, noting she only had four left in the pack. She took a drag, held the smoke in her lungs, almost as if this action would warm her up, then exhaled slowly, reluctantly.

Unlike the Spartan bedroom, the main room was filled with Solano's personal belongings. Alongside the countless dolls, there were primitive-looking farming tools, miscellaneous items of the variety you might find in a homeless man's shopping cart, an incongruous car seat, and wood carvings of, unsurprisingly, miniature dolls. These were colorfully painted and reminded her of *matryoshka* dolls, a popular toy of Russian children for much of the last century.

Elizaveta hated *matryoshka* dolls. They reminded her of the orphanage and of a man named Yevgeny Popov. Yevgeny had been part of the staff at the orphanage. At first Elizaveta liked him. The other care-workers were indifferent and cruel to her. They were trained to be like this, products of a cold-hearted system, for orphans were as stigmatized as the disabled and the elderly and femininity in the Soviet Union: a problem to be dealt with in the shadows far from the public eye. Yevgeny, however, always smiled and waved at her. Sometimes he would sneak her a piece of chocolate when no one was looking. He also told her lots of haunted stories concerning the orphanage, strange things that had happened to him, such as lights mysteriously turning on in certain rooms and footsteps sounding behind him, even though when he turned around nobody was there. These tales gave her nightmares, but she eagerly awaited the next one. Life then was bleak and routine, and they relieved the doldrums.

One day Elizaveta had been in the girl's dormitory rec room. It had a vaulted ceiling with twelve windowed eves and had once served as the chapel before it moved to the administrative building. She was alone, cleaning; all the children had daily chores that rotated on a weekly basis. Yevgeny arrived, crouched before her, and told her he had a surprise for her. Smiling, showing his crooked and yellow cigarette-stained teeth, he presented her with a *matryoshka* doll. He told her it was her birthday present, even though her birthday wasn't for another month. Regardless, she had been thrilled. She had not had a toy of her own since her parents vanished and she was taken from her home.

Yevgeny told her to go ahead, play with the doll. Elizaveta sat on the floor and studied the outer layer. It depicted a woman dressed in a *sarafan*. She separated the top and bottom of the doll to reveal a smaller figure of the same sort inside. There were three more in total, each hidden inside the previous, the smallest being a baby turned from a single piece of wood and non-opening.

While she played with the dolls, Yevgeny began massaging her shoulders with his strong hands. She didn't like this, though she didn't know why.

It simply made her feel uncomfortable. Even so, she didn't say anything; she didn't want to hurt his feelings. He was her friend, one of her only friends in the orphanage, so she let him knead her shoulders all the while wishing for him to stop. Then his hands moved down the front of her chest. She was twelve then and had started to develop breasts. His hands moved around the small mounds, then over them, rubbing. She told him to stop. He didn't, saying he wasn't doing anything, they were just playing. His fingers pinched her nipples. Jumping to her feet, leaving the *matryoshka* doll behind, she hurried from the rec room. She thought Yevgeny would follow her, but he didn't. She went downstairs to the inner courtyard to be with the other children. She didn't tell anyone what Yevgeny did. She didn't think anyone would believe her. Plus, she still wasn't sure what actually happened, or if it was wrong. She just knew she didn't like the feeling of Yevgeny's hands on her.

After that day she hoped Yevgeny would go back to being the old Yevgeny. He didn't. He stopped smiling and waving at her...even though he rarely took his eyes off her. She became afraid of him, and afraid of being alone in the orphanage, yet sometimes the latter couldn't be helped. Twice, Yevgeny caught her on her own, exiting the bathroom. The first time she managed to dash past him to safety, but the second time he blocked her escape. He tried to give her the *matryoshka* doll again. She refused to accept it. He slapped her across the cheek, knocking her over. He slid his hand up her dress, between her legs. She screamed, which scared him off—but not before he threatened to kill her if she told anyone what happened.

Elizaveta didn't tell anyone. She believed his threat. Nevertheless, a few days later the headmistress, Irina Igorevna, summoned Elizaveta to her office and asked her why she hadn't been eating anything at mealtimes. Elizaveta broke down and confessed what occurred outside the bathroom. Irina Igorevna listened stoically, asked a few specific questions, then told Elizaveta a story she would never forget. It was about an Auschwitz survivor, a young Jewish woman who Elizaveta would many years later come to suspect had been Irina Igorevna herself. Although imprisoned under inhuman conditions, the young woman was the only one in her ward to wash her stockings each day, as she had done each day before the war. The other inmates shrugged their shoulders at her routine, having abandoned any attempt at hygiene to conserve energy. Yet when a typhoid epidemic struck the camp, the young woman was the only person to survive and to eventually find freedom at the hands of American soldiers.

"The world you enter after your time at the orphanage will be a very challenging place, Elizaveta," the headmistress concluded. "You will encounter others like Yevgeny Popov, men who would take advantage of you or worse. You can bow to their superior strength and hope they grow tired of you and leave you alone, or you can stand up for your core dignities, remain true to yourself, even if this means making difficult choices. You stood up for yourself today by confiding in me what happened, and it will be up to you whether you continue to stand up for yourself in the future, whether you choose to merely survive, or refuse to survive and live."

The next morning at breakfast the children learned that Yevgeny died in his sleep. No explanation was given, though over the following days rumors swirled he had taken his own life.

Elizaveta didn't believe this, but she never spoke of her suspicions to anyone.

Jack emerged from Pepper's bedroom, closing the door behind him. Despite the crazy stuff happening on this island, he stood tall and strong and confident. It might be selfish, but Elizaveta was very glad he was stuck here with her. She no longer trusted Nitro, not completely, Pita was a mess, and Jesus...well, he might control a boardroom, or a meeting with millionaire investors, but he was out of his element here. She knew him too well, could see past the brave front he put on. There was a sharpness to his eyes, a jerkiness to his movements, an uncharacteristic air of indecisiveness.

Elizaveta ashed out her cigarette, then went to Jack. "Where's Rosa?" she asked.

"I put her in bed next to Pepper," he said.

"She really likes you."

"Because I'm so handsome."

"Yes, you are handsome man." This came off sounding sincerer than she'd intended, and he gave her an inquiring look. She cleared her throat. "I joke, Jack. Please."

"Pepper says he's cold," he said...and was he trying not to smile? "He needs something warm, but there's nothing in the dresser."

"There was poncho in dresser there." Elizaveta indicated Lucinda's bedroom. "But Lucinda needs it."

"That was all?" Jack said. "One poncho?"

"And some socks and underwear."

"Where the hell are all Solano's clothes?"

"Nitro says hermits probably only own one outfit."

Jack grunted. "He has an answer for everything, doesn't he?"

Elizaveta wasn't sure whether he was being sarcastic, or whether he was implying something.

He lowered his voice. "What do you think...?"

She assumed he was asking what she thought about the fact Nitro had a pistol in his possession. "I don't know, but—"

"What are you guys whispering about?" Pita asked, standing up. She glared at them suspiciously.

"Pepper's cold," Jack said. "He needs something warm."

Jesus said, "What about the rug you're standing on? It's dry."

Jack and Elizaveta glanced at the rug beneath their feet. It was green with a beige pattern, natty, sullied. But Jesus was right. It was dry.

"Better than nothing," Jack told him. "Eliza, give me a hand."

They moved off the rug, took a corner each, and folded it back.

Elizaveta blinked in surprise. "*Yo-moyo!*" she said. "What is this?"

Jack and Elizaveta set the rug aside and knelt next to the trapdoor they'd uncovered. Jesus and Pita hurried over, Jesus limping because of his injured ankle, both of them clamoring loudly at the discovery. A moment later Nitro emerged from Lucinda's room, asking what all the fuss was about.

Elizaveta wasn't paying attention to them. She was focused on the trapdoor. It wasn't much larger than a manhole, square, and flush with the floor. A cord of rope nailed to the hatch opposite the hinges served as the handle.

Jack reached for it.

"Whoa, chavo," Nitro said. "Maybe you don't want to open that."

"Why?" Jack said, cocking an eye at him suspiciously. "You know what's down there?"

Nitro turned to Jesus. "What do you think?"

Jesus shrugged. "We should check it out."

Jack tugged the rope. The hatch had torqued a bit, and he had to tug a second time with both hands. This time the hatch lifted, revealing a dark hole and a crudely hewed wooden ladder. Cool, stale air wafted up.

Elizaveta couldn't see the bottom. She fetched a nearby candle, returned, and lowered the candle into the hole, careful not to move too quickly and extinguish the flame. "It's not so deep," she said, the bottom visible now. "Two meters maybe."

"And then what?" Jesus asked. He, Nitro, and Pita were looming over her. Jack held onto her shoulder so she didn't fall down the hole.

"I don't know," she said. "It's dark, but I think...maybe there is...how do you say...?"

"Crawlspace?" Jack said.

"Yes, crawlspace." She maneuvered herself back to her knees and set the candle next to her.

"Crawlspace?" Nitro said. "This shithole doesn't have pipes or nothing. Why would Solano need a crawlspace?"

"Maybe it's a tunnel?" Pita suggested.

Jesus said, "Why would he dig a tunnel?"

"An escape route?"

"Escape from who?"

"Could be a hurricane shelter," Jack said. "This house isn't too sturdy."

Pita said, "It's holding up to this storm."

"Fuck this dicking around," Nitro said. "I'll go down and have a look."

Elizaveta glanced at him. Was Jack right? Did he know what was down there? Would he do a perfunctory search and tell them there was nothing but dirt—all the while concealing...what?

Apparently Jack was thinking along the same lines and said, "I'm going to go."

"You?" Nitro said. "Why you?"

"Because I want to see what's down there."

"You're too big, chavo. You'll get stuck."

"I'll take my chances." Jack began positioning himself to climb down the ladder.

"We'll both go," Nitro said.

"I think you should stay here, Nitro," Elizaveta told him, not wanting Jack to be alone and out of sight with him. By way of explanation she added, "You have gun. Keep us safe." He was, she'd noticed, wearing his backpack again.

"That's why I should be the one to see what's down there," he said. "I can protect myself. All Jack Goff can do is scream like a girl."

"You want to put your shirt on again, Muscles?" Jack said. "You're giving my eyes a headache."

"I don't think you should go down by yourself, Jack," Pita said.

"There's nobody down there, Pita," he said.

"You don't know—"

"If someone went down there," he told her, "how could they pull the rug back over the trap door again?"

Pita folded her arms across her chest. "I was going to say, you don't know it's a some*body*."

Shaking his head, Jack attached himself to the ladder. Elizaveta, however, couldn't rid herself of the image that had popped into her mind: a handful of dolls huddled underground in the tomb-like blackness, knives or other deadly weapons clutched in their small hands, waiting.

"Maybe you shouldn't go," she told Jack, hating herself for letting Pita's superstitious hoopla get to her.

"We need to know what's down there."

"Why?"

"Pita was right when she said it could be a tunnel. Which means it's not just a way out, but a way in as well."

A drawn-out silence ensued.

"Fuck it," Nitro said. "Let Jack Goff go. Maybe he'll get stuck after all and we'll have some peace and quiet tonight."

Jack collected the candle and started down the ladder. After a moment's hesitation, Elizaveta latched on to the ladder as well.

Jesus seized her shoulder and said, "What do you think you're doing, cariño?"

"Jack shouldn't go by himself—"

"You're not—"

"I am, Jesus," she said, shrugging free.

The wood ladder leaned against the wall of the hole at a steep angle. The risers felt rough beneath Elizaveta's hands, and she hoped she didn't incur any slivers. Below her, Jack had stepped off the last rung and was now on his knees and elbows, bent sideways, as if he were peering beneath a sofa. "What do you see?" she asked him.

"You were right," he said. "Some sort of crawlspace. Dark."

"Be careful!" Pita called from above.

Jack army-crawled forward until his upper body disappeared, then his legs. Elizaveta continued down the ladder to the bottom of the hole. The ground was hard-packed earth. The crawlspace was barely half a meter in height and extended away from her in every direction; she couldn't be certain how far it went because everything was black. She started the way Jack had gone, the dirt cool beneath her hands and knees, the low ceiling scraping her back.

"Hey!" Jack said suddenly.

Elizaveta's heart leapt. "What?" she whispered. The claustrophobic space deadened her voice.

"There's a basket or something ahead."

Elizaveta scuttled to catch up. Jack pointed. The candlelight's reach didn't extend far, and she had to squint. At first she thought she was seeing a cardboard box, but it resolved into a wicker basket of the sort you might find on an apple orchard.

"Wonder what's in it?" he said, army-crawling forward again, pulling himself with his elbows.

Elizaveta reached the basket first. She tipped it to see inside, flinching in anticipation of the unexpected. She relaxed. "Potatoes!" she said.

Jack stuck his arm in the basket and retrieved a spud. He turned it over in his hand. The skin was yellowish-brown and covered with small sprouts.

"This is nothing but Solano's root cellar," he said, sticking the potato in the pocket of his shorts.

"You will eat that?" she said, surprised.

"Why not? Potatoes don't go bad."

"Everything goes bad."

"It's still firm. That means it still has its nutrients."

"You are some potato expert?"

"Are you?"

"Russians know potatoes."

"I'm hungry, I'm keeping it. And look, I think that's another basket over there."

They crawled through the deeper darkness and discovered two baskets placed side by side, one containing carrots, the other turnips.

"Nice," Jack said. "I love carrots." He grabbed three. They had lost their rigidity and flopped. The tip of one had turned black. Still, he tucked them in his pockets, adding a turnip as well. He had to roll to his side to do this, and when he rolled back his shoulder pressed against hers. It seemed accidental. In fact, he didn't even seem to notice.

"You're like chipmunk," she said, and blew out her cheeks to demonstrate what she meant.

"Some are for Rosa," he said.

She pointed. "There's another basket over there."

"This is like Easter," he said.

"What do you mean?"

"Don't you have Easter in Russia?"

"Of course," she said. "Easter is very important holiday." Some of Elizaveta's fondest memories of her pre-orphanage childhood were of saving yellow onion peels a month or two leading up to Easter day, which was always the first Sunday after the spring full moon. She and her mother would boil the peels with a half dozen eggs to turn the eggs a rich red.

Jack said, "What about the Easter bunny?"

She frowned. "What bunny?"

"The Easter bunny! On Easter morning it leaves a trail of chocolates all throughout your house, leading to a hidden Easter basket filled with a chocolate Easter bunny and chocolate eggs."

"Are you making this up?"

"Maybe it's an American thing..."

"It is definitely not a Russian thing." Elizaveta thought about the monthly stipend she'd received from the state to attend college. It was supposed to be enough to cover all her living expenses, yet it was barely enough to purchase two large chocolate bars. And Americans sprinkled their floors with chocolates and ate chocolate bunnies and eggs?

"You're supposed to follow your own trail so you can find your basket," Jack went on. "But my sister and I always picked up the chocolates as quickly as we could, erasing the trail, so sometimes it took hours to find where our baskets were hidden."

Elizaveta snorted. "What other stupid holiday traditions do you have?"

"Halloween was my favorite."

"Yes, I know Halloween. You dress up like ghost or witch."

"And go trick-or-treating."

"What's that?"

"You go around the neighborhood with a bag—I usually used a pillow-case—and knock on doors. Everyone gives you a chocolate bar or some other kind of candy. One year I think I filled up three pillowcases."

"Three pillowcases full of candy? And strangers, they just give you this?"

"If they have a jack-o-lantern on the front porch, yeah. If they don't, it means they probably don't want you knocking."

"You Americans are like cartoon character. You live in cartoon world."

"What are you talking about?"

Elizaveta was about to tell him if he walked down a street in Russia—the Russia she knew before she left four years before—with a pillowcase full of candy he wouldn't make it to the corner before he was robbed, if not killed. Instead she simply shook her head.

They continued their "Easter bunny hunt," moving in a general clockwise direction, discovering several more baskets filled with more vegetables.

The crawlspace turned out to be quite vast, and Elizaveta suspected it mirrored the floorplan of the cabin above. She wondered how long it had taken Solano to dig out. Even with a shovel and pickaxe it would have been long and laborious work. But what else did you do when you lived on an island by yourself with little to no human contact?

Elizaveta contemplated this. What *did* Solano do with all his time? He didn't have company, aside from the occasional local who swapped him dolls for produce. He didn't have electricity, which meant he couldn't watch TV or listen to the radio, even if he found either in a trash heap on one of his jaunts to Mexico City. Then again, people had managed without such modern conveniences for the vast majority of human history. They were hardly necessities for happiness. Solano had his freedom, his heath, a tropical climate, food and shelter. Maybe this was enough. Moreover, he created, didn't he? He built all the huts, and the cabin. He cleared the paths and constructed the bridges they had seen. And he hung up all the dolls, of course—and that was creating too, that was art.

Elizaveta recalled life in Saint Petersburg in the early- to mid-nineties. The brutal winters, the jostling for food and other basic supplies, the overcrowded buses, the cynicism and aggression, the robberies and racketeering, the misfortune and disdain etched on everyone's faces. Despite all this, her compatriots certainly had more than Solano—yet were their lives any better than his? Were they more fulfilled?

"There's another basket," Jack said.

"My knees and back hurt," she said.

"Okay, last one."

They adjusted their course slightly and stopped before the basket. Jack raised the candle to see inside it. "Whoa. Check this out," he said excitedly. He set the candle aside and withdrew from the basket a small, unadorned wooden box.

"What is that?" she asked.

"Beats me."

"Can you open it?"

"No, it's locked. Look, a keyhole."

"Can you break it?"

"Not down here." He glanced past her into the surrounding darkness. "Where the hell was the ladder?"

When they found the ladder, Elizaveta climbed it first. Nitro and Jesus and Pita were all bent over the trapdoor, looking down, talking to her, talking heads. She emerged from the hole into the candlelit room, which seemed bright in comparison to the dungeon-like crawlspace, then helped Jack out. His shorts bulged with vegetables, impossible not to notice.

"It's just a root cellar," he said in response to the barrage of questions. He emptied his pockets, setting the vegetables on the floor. "Help yourselves."

"They're dirty," Pita said.

"They're food," he said. "And we haven't eaten since midday." He took a crunchy bite of a carrot.

Nitro chomped into a turnip and shrugged.

"I'll pass," Jesus said.

"Ugh," Pita said.

"Oh," Elizaveta said, lifting her T-shirt, revealing the mystery box she'd stuffed down the front of her shorts. "We found this also."

"Let me see that." Nitro reached for it.

Elizaveta batted his hand away and unhoused the box from her shorts herself. "It's locked," she said, going to the wall on which hung the farming equipment. There was no shortage of tools to choose from. Large spanners, fencing pliers, an old fashioned saw. She selected a hammer, returned to the others, and set the box on the floor so the lock was facing upward. She gave it a solid whack with the hammer. Wood splintered but the lock held.

She whacked it again. This time the lid flipped open. A battered leather wallet tumbled out, along with several sepia-toned photographs.

"That's all there is?" Jesus said, unimpressed.

"Solano's wallet?" Nitro said.

"Who are those photos of?" Pita asked.

Jack picked them up. There were four in total: a handsome woman, two young girls, and a group shot.

"Solano's family?" he said, passing them to Elizaveta. She studied them before passing them to Pita.

"Open the wallet," Nitro said.

Elizaveta did. There was a single identity card printed on green paper issued to **Don Javier** Solano. In the money sleeve was an old article cut from a newspaper. Elizaveta unfolded it.

"What does it say?" Pita asked.

She read the Spanish out loud:

MEXICO CITY - At least 25 people were killed and 17 others severely injured when a firecracker factory exploded Sunday in a blast of flames and black smoke.

The factory was located on the ground floor of a 28-family apartment building. Officials searching the smoldering ruins said most of the victims sustained severe burns. Dozens of people were still unaccounted for, raising fears that the death toll could rise.

Police said the explosion took place at about 11:30 p.m. and could have been triggered by burning heating oil from an overturned stove in an adjoining apartment. They were not ruling out other potential causes, including the improper mixing of the raw materials used in firecrackers.

Dolores Elias, a twenty-year-old retail clerk who lived in the neighborhood, said the explosion sounded like the end of the world, and she saw people flying through the air "like flies."

Firecrackers are often produced in small, home-based factories that are unregulated and lack proper safety equipment. They are usually used in rural areas to celebrate weddings, circumcisions, and other festivities.

Last month, a spark set off boxes of fireworks in a market in Celaya, killing 55 people, injuring hundreds, and levelling parts of the downtown area. Most of those killed or injured were buying firecrackers for the celebration of the Day of the Virgin of Guadalupe.

While Jesus, Pita, and Nitro debated with alacrity why Solano would care enough about a firecracker explosion to keep a newspaper clipping in his wallet, Elizaveta summarized the story for Jack in English.

"Maybe Solano caused it?" Jack said.

Elizaveta frowned. "Set off explosion?"

"Could be why he ended up on this island. He was wanted by the cops and needed a place to hide out."

"For fifty years?"

Pita was listening to them and said, "What about the photographs?"

"What about them?" Elizaveta said.

"They're probably of his family. You think he'd just leave his family behind?"

"Maybe they died in explosion."

"But if he caused it," Jesus said, chiming in, "you really think he would stick around to search the rubble for family photos?"

"The photos are all the same size, wallet size," Jack said. "Good chance he always had them in his wallet. Anyway, whatever," he added. "It doesn't matter what happened. The question is: why would he hide the wallet and pictures in a basket in a root cellar?"

Jesus shrugged. "Painful memories?"

Pita nodded. "He wanted to forget them, forget his old life."

"Why bother even keeping the wallet and photos then? Why not—" Jack cut himself off, and when he spoke again his voice was low and edged with caution: "Eliza, don't move."

Elizaveta froze, her muscles in lockbolt, every nerve ending tingling with sudden alarm. "What?"

"There's something on your back," Jack said.

Pita and Jesus were crouched before her, while Jack and Nitro were to either side of her. They both had a view of her back.

"Oh, fuck," Nitro said, seeing whatever Jack had seen.

"What is it?" she blurted.

Pita and Jesus both scrambled around behind her so they had a view too. They gasped.

"*What is it?*" She couldn't feel anything on her back. Nevertheless, she wanted to tear off her top and toss it across the room. She didn't do this though. Whatever was freaking everyone out might bite her.

Jack was up and moving, looking for something.

"*What is it?*" Elizaveta said.

"Stay still," Nitro told her. Then to Jack: "Get the saw."

Saw? *Saw?* Did they need to cut it off? *What was it?*

She was going to ask what was on her again, but she didn't. She realized she didn't want to know until it was off her.

Jack returned with the saw. It was old, the hard-toothed blade rusted.

"Careful," Nitro told him. "Just slip it beneath it."

Elizaveta felt the saw blade press against her back, near her left shoulder.

"Slip it under."

"I'm trying!"

"Ow!" A white hot pain seared her back.

"It stung her!" Pita exclaimed.

"Get it!" Jesus said.

In a blind panic now, Elizaveta leapt to her feet, tearing her shirt off her back, tossing it away, so she stood there in nothing but her bra. Pita was yelling, but so was she.

"Is it off?" she cried. "Is it off?"

"Yeah, yeah," Jack said.

Jesus and Nitro hurried to her shirt. Nitro toed it, trying to startle whatever was hiding within it into the open.

"What is it?" Elizaveta said. "It bit me!"

"It didn't bite you," Jack said.

"I felt—"

"It stung you."

Stung her? Was it a wasp?

"There it is!" Jesus cried.

"Kill it!" Pita shrieked.

Elizaveta felt sick. On the floor, scurrying away from her shirt, was a great fat scorpion. It was black, its segmented tail carried over its body. Its pincers alone must have been a couple of inches long.

And it had been on her back.

It had stung her.

Nitro tried stomping it beneath his flip-flop, but it escaped under the table.

"Fuck!" he said.

"Get it!" Pita said.

Jack, still holding the saw, went to the table. He ducked down and swung the saw, using the flat of the blade to squash the awful thing.

"Did you get it?" Jesus asked.

"It's still moving."

Jack swung the saw again, then again. He stood a moment later, holding the saw before him. The scorpion rested on the blade, its pugnacious body twisted and broken.

"It's dead," he said.

"It stung me," Elizaveta said, folding her arms across her breasts. She didn't care she was half naked; she wasn't being modest. She was shaking with fright, her flesh covered in goosebumps. "Scorpions are venomous, and *it stung me.*"

"Most are harmless," Nitro said.

"Most? What about that?" She pointed to the big fat horror that still rested on the saw blade, which Jack had set down on the table.

"Turn around," Jesus said. "Let me see the sting."

Elizaveta turned.

"It's red," he said. "But it doesn't look too bad. How do you feel?"

"Are you a doctor? Have you been stung by scorpion before?" She was acting a bit hysterical, but she had every right to. Most scorpions might be harmless to humans, but some had venom that could be fatal. And that one—God, it was so *big*.

"How do you feel?" Jesus repeated.

"It hurts. Like bee sting."

"But you can still breathe fine, talk? That's good."

"Nitro's right, Eliza," Jack said. "Most scorpion stings are harmless. You usually only have to go to the hospital if you're a kid or elderly."

"In Las Vegas maybe, Jack," Pita said. "Not in Mexico. The scorpions here—"

"They're not that different," he said brusquely, silencing her with a look.

Elizaveta didn't miss this, and she knew he was trying to reassure her...which made her all the more alarmed.

Was she going to die?

"I can breathe now," she said. "But what of future? Maybe I will get worse. And there is no help here, no hospital, no anti-venom."

"Someone should suck it out," Pita offered.

"What?" Jesus said.

"Someone should suck out the venom. I saw it on TV once. A person was bit by a snake, and this man sucked the venom from the wound with his mouth."

"That doesn't work, Pita."

"You don't know, Jesus. We should at least try. Nitro—you do it."

He shook his head. "I'm not sucking out venom with my fucking mouth."

"I'll do it," Jack said.

"Nobody will suck my back!" Elizaveta snapped. "This is serious!"

"Look, Eliza," Jesus said reasonably. "You said you feel okay. If the scorpion was really poisonous, you would know by now. We're overreacting."

"You are just saying that—"

"No, I'm not, cariño," he said. "I promise, okay? You'll be fine."

Elizaveta retrieved her damp shirt and pulled it on, shivering as the cold material slid over her bare skin. Jack took the green and beige rug to Pepper's bedroom, to drape over Pepper, while Jesus and Pita and Nitro stood near the dead scorpion, speaking quietly to each other. Elizaveta began to pace back and forth. She couldn't relax. She couldn't stop thinking about the sting in her back. Originally she'd felt a sharp pain, followed by a burning sensation. Now, however, all she felt was a strange tingling. Still, she didn't believe Jesus when he said she would be fine. She had seen people stung by scorpions in movies. They always ended up foaming at the mouth, having heart attacks, and dying.

Jack returned from Pepper's bedroom. She went to him.

"How is Pepper?" she asked.

"Sleeping," he said.

"What can we do?"

"Nothing. He just needs rest. You do too."

"I'm not tired."

"Still, you should rest, relax."

"How can I relax? I have venom inside me. It's spreading—"

"Right, Eliza," he said, touching her arm. "And the more worked up you get, the faster your heartbeat, the faster the venom gets absorbed."

She considered this, nodded.

"Take a deep breath," he said.

She did.

"Another."

"I am not in labor, Jack."

He smiled. She did too.

"Thank you," she said softly.

"Why don't you go to Pepper's room, lie down?"

"What will you do?"

"Keep watch."

She blinked. "Watch? Oh, you mean..." She'd gotten so caught up with the discovery of the trapdoor and the subsequent scorpion sting she'd completely forgotten about the potential killer on the island. "You need partner," she added. "I will keep watch with you."

Jack shook his head. "Pita will."

Elizaveta frowned. "Why her?" she said, feeling a bump of irrational jealousy.

"Because if we let her go to sleep, she won't want to wake up again for a subsequent shift."

Elizaveta glanced at Pita. She stood by the table with Jesus and Nitro, the three of them still talking softly in Spanish. She couldn't hear what they were saying—and she sensed that was the point.

"I'll keep second watch then," she said.

Jack shook his head again. "I don't want you alone with Nitro."

"So I keep watch with Jesus."

"That leaves Nitro and me on the last watch, and I know he won't be cool with that."

"So who keeps second watch?"

"Nitro and Jesus. Then, if you're feeling up to it, you can join me on the last one. Two hours each. That should get us to dawn. Hopefully the storm will have died down, and we can head to the pier to wait for the boatman."

"And hopefully," she said solemnly, "I will not die a painful, poisonous death."

They went over to the others and explained to them the watch schedule.

"Does anyone have any problems with this?" Jack concluded.

"Do we get the gun?" Pita asked.

Everyone looked at Nitro.

"Fuck no," he said.

"But whoever's on watch should have the gun."

"She has a point, Muscles," Jack said.

"You'd just end up blowing your own balls off, chavo."

"I've fired a gun before," he said.

"There's no way in hell anyone's touching my piece, and that's that."

"If I'm sitting out there on the porch," Pita said, "I want a weapon."

"Help yourself," Nitro said, gesturing to the wall of farm equipment.

Resigned to the fact Nitro wasn't giving up his pistol, they scrounged through Solano's wall of farming instruments for something to defend themselves with. Pita selected a sickle, Jesus a hatchet with a broken half and rusty patina, Elizaveta a long-handled garden claw scabrous with corrosion. Jack considered an antique post-hole digger but apparently deemed it too unwieldly and instead settled on an eleven-inch iron hay hook.

Standing there examining their weapons of choice, they resembled a motley band of peasants about to march on Doctor Frankenstein's castle. Nevertheless, they were armed.

Jack opened the cabin's front door for Pita. Wet air blew inside, accompanied by a blast of angry wind.

"Scream if you see someone, Jack Goff," Nitro said.

Ignoring him, Jack followed Pita into the voracious night.

1957

The lobotomy was originally developed in 1936 by a Portuguese physician who would go on to win the Nobel Prize in Medicine. The procedure involved drilling two holes in either side of the patient's forehead to sever some of the nerve fibers in the frontal lobes of the brain. The hope was to treat intractable mental disorders by reducing the strength of certain emotional signals.

A few years later the procedure gained traction in the United States in a different incarnation called a trans-orbital lobotomy. It was not a precise surgery and simply involved hammering an icepick through the thin layer of skull in the corner of each eye socket and wiggling it about to scramble the white and gray matter located there. It took less than ten minutes to complete, and oftentimes no anesthesia was required (though patients were usually given electroshock treatment first so they were unaware of what was happening).

Around this time a neurologist and Harvard graduate named Dr. Jerome Asper was working as head of laboratories in a sprawling Boston mental institution that housed thousands of patients in abject Victorian conditions. Wanting to make a name for himself as a medical pioneer, he began performing hundreds of these trans-orbital lobotomies at the hospital. Despite his critics decrying that he was doing nothing more than turning his unwitting patients into vegetables, he had his share of successes, published his work in respected journals, and built a reputation for himself as one of the foremost experts in psychiatric science.

For much of the nineteen fifties, he became an evangelist for trans-orbital lobotomies, touring hospitals and asylums across the country, performing the procedure on thousands of individuals to treat a range of illnesses from schizophrenia to depression to compulsion disorders. It became so routine he started prescribing it for symptoms as mild as a headache, and he sometimes brazenly ice-picked both eye sockets simultaneously, one with each hand, to impress the media that usually gathered to cover his "miracle cures."

Nevertheless, by the end of the decade Asper's fortunes made an abrupt reversal due to two unforeseen developments. The first was the rise of antipsychotic drugs, which yielded the same pacifying results in the mentally ill as the lobotomy without the invasiveness of an icepick to the brain. The second was the widespread rumor that Joseph Stalin and the Chinese were using lobotomies to control their political enemies, fueling the Red Scare that vilified any activity related to Communism.

Consequently, Asper quickly fell out of favor with the mainstream medical establishment, and it wasn't long until no state hospital would touch him—not in the US at any rate. So in 1957 he relocated his sideshow to Mexico where he enjoyed revived success.

He had been performing the operation throughout Mexico City for several months when he received the call from Saint Agatha's School for Lost Children regarding a particularly troublesome ward.

Asper had never performed a lobotomy on someone so young before, but as one of the great men of medicine of the twentieth century, he was always up for a new challenge.

Dressed in a worsted suit and bowtie, Dr. Jerome Asper stood next to the school's resident priest, Father Pardavé, in a classroom turned makeshift operating theatre. His patient, a twelve-year-old girl named María Diaz, lay supine on the teacher's desk before them.

According to the priest, the girl had the IQ of a moron, participated in disruptive behavior, and was capable of violent outbursts. Moreover, she suffered several fits a week, during which time he believed the devil took control of her body and mind. Nonsense, of course. Religious gobbledygook.

These fits would be the physical manifestation of the illness epilepsy, not some occult affliction. Even so, in his opinion the surgery was necessary. It would not only calm her down but also make her happier.

Looking up at him with frightened yet trustful eyes, the girl asked him a question.

Asper had learned enough Spanish in his short time in Mexico to know she was inquiring whether the procedure was going to make her more like her housemates.

"Sí," he said, smiling as he slipped a mouth guard in her mouth and placed two paddles on her forehead. He gave Father Pardavé a brief nod. The priest held the girl down tightly by her shoulders. Asper adjusted the timer on the small ECT machine on the desk and flicked the main switch. The electrodes delivered an electrical stimulus of several hundred watts that caused the girl's body to convulse powerfully, her jaw to clamp shut, and the tendons in her neck to stand out. The current flowed for five seconds before shutting off. Her muscles immediately relaxed.

Now that she was suitably dazed, Asper selected his icepick and hammer from his medical case and went to work.

Jack

The storm had attained Armageddon proportions, yet it showed no signs of relenting. The rain fell in diagonal curtains with amazing force, chewing the ground and flooding shallow depressions. The wind, vicious and cold, threatened to strip leaves from their branches and uproot the smaller vegetation. Yellow bursts of lightning tortured the sky and lit the frenetic faces of the dozens of dolls dangling from nearby trees. Thunder boomed and crackled.

Pita and I sat side by side, our backs to the cabin's façade, sheltered by the porch roof. We both had pulled our knees to our chests, wrapping our arms around them, in an attempt to retain our body heat. I remained alert, my eyes scanning the devastated jungle, the shadows dancing beneath the wind-frenzied trees. Yet as the minutes ticked away, and there was no sign of anybody lurking in the night, my mind began to drift, and I found myself reflecting on the racing accident that had ended my career. I didn't like going there. It filled me with sadness and resentment and regret. Nevertheless, sometimes I couldn't avoid it.

It was the third race of the 2000 NASCAR Winston Cup Series, the Daytona 500 at Daytona International Speedway in Florida. I won the Pole, and with the help of my teammate I ended up leading the field for the first ninety laps. But a miscue from my pit crew and a couple of other mishaps saw me fall back as far as twelfth at one point. However, I made a late charge, and with two laps to go I was running second to Ed Melvin in the No. 93 car. On the inside of Turn 1 I attempted to pass him. We made light contact, both cars veering up to the wall, my Chevy leaning on his. As soon as I cleared him I pulled off a bump 'n' run to take the lead. By Turn 4 Melvin caught up and we were at a virtual dead heat. At the white flag he pulled a car length ahead. I stuck directly behind him through Turns 1 and 2. I tried an overtake during Turn 3 but couldn't get around him. My chance came in the final turn. I'd entered it low and Melvin high. I cut to the bottom groove, straddling the double yellow out of bounds line, and drew even with him as we exited the turn for the front stretch. As we sped for the checkered flag at two hundred miles an hour, we were so close our side panels traded paint, and then somehow his car caught mine in such a way air got under me. The next thing I knew I was looking at my roof for a long time—and then waking in the ICU with the immediate and uncanny memories of floating above my body while I'd been dead.

I mentioned what happened to the surgeon who'd operated on me, more in passing than anything else. He didn't agree with my neurons dying theory, as the observations occurred while the EEG was recording a flat line, and he wanted to bring in a specialist to see me. I declined. I wasn't going on record as a near-death-experience survivor and an out-of-body nutter.

Instead, I put all my energy into my physiotherapy, hoping to jump back into the Winston Cup Series in March...not knowing then that my racing days were gone and over.

"What are you thinking about?" It was Pita. She was staring into the storm.

I blinked, coming back to the present, the cold and the rain and the wind. I considered making up something to tell her, because whenever the accident came up, we fought. Nevertheless, deceiving her seemed like too much effort, and I said, "Florida."

She didn't say anything, and I thought that was the end of the conversation, when she added belatedly, "It happened, Jack. You can't change it. Get over it."

Get over it?

Thunder rumbled. It sounded distant, as if the storm might be retreating.

This illusion was shattered a second later by another blast directly above us.

Still, I barely registered it.

Get over it.

"I'm sorry," Pita said quietly, knowing she'd struck a nerve. "I didn't mean that...I'm...I'm just scared..."

The antagonism building inside me evaporated. I reached out my hand, squeezed her knee, and said, "Me too."

She looked at me. "I didn't think you got scared."

I chuffed and released her knee. "Why did you think that?"

"Because I've never seen you scared before."

"I used to get scared before every race."

"I don't mean like that. I mean... I don't know." She seemed to be reflecting. "Those were fun times."

"The races?"

She nodded, then laughed to herself.

"What?" I asked.

"Remember when we got locked out of our room in Kansas City?"

I nodded. I'd finished first at the Kansas Speedway that day, and we'd been out all evening celebrating.

She said, "We were staying at that old hotel that didn't have twenty-four-hour reception. We ended up in the laundry room."

I smiled. At some point I'd lost the keycard to the room. We searched the hotel for a game room or library or somewhere we could crash until morning. The only place that offered privacy was a launderette with six coin-operated washers and dryers. We ended up fooling around instead of sleeping—which we did a lot back then—and when things heated up Pita told me she wanted to have sex on top of one of the machines. She even made me put money in it so it would vibrate.

She said, "Who the heck does their laundry at one in the morning?" She was referring to the woman who entered the launderette with a basket of clothes just as Pita was climaxing and biting my neck to suppress a cry.

I said, "She had a good look at my bare ass."

"She probably loved it."

"Probably scarred her for life."

"Fun times..." Pita said this with a healthy dose of nostalgia, and although likely unintentional, her tone communicated more than her words did: they weren't fun times anymore.

"I'm sorry," I told her quietly enough I wasn't sure she heard me over the storm.

But she did, because she said, "For what?"

"I've changed."

"We've both changed, Jack. Everyone changes."

"I'm not the same person I was."

"Because you can't race." It sounded less like a statement and more like an accusation.

I didn't answer.

"Dammit, Jack," she said. "I know. Okay? I get it. Racing was a big part of your life. You can't do it anymore. Okay. But...stop looking back. You had a good career—"

"Four years."

"And you did more in those four years than most professional racers do in ten."

"I could have been great."

"You *were* great!"

"I mean the records—"

"Screw the records, Jack! You're lucky you didn't die."

"I actually did."

"Well, you didn't stay dead. That's a pretty impressive accomplishment. So you should be thankful for that, for being alive. Why can't you just accept what happened and move on?"

"You don't understand..."

"No, I don't!"

"Didn't you hear what I told you, Pita? *I'm not the same fucking person.* If I'm not a race car driver, who am I? What do you propose I do with the rest of my life?"

"The rest of your life? You only had another five years of racing anyway."

"Ten, minimum. More like fifteen, even twenty."

"Why don't you at least consider broadcasting? Your agent—"

"I'm not going to sit in a booth and watch other people race."

"It's better than doing nothing, Jack. And that's what you're doing now. Nothing. You're miserable, and that's made me miserable. Don't you see that?"

"Yeah, I do."

"So do something about it other than drinking yourself silly every night."

"Fuck off."

"You don't think you have a problem?"

"I've never said that."

"You're an alcoholic, Jack."

I stiffened. I didn't like that word. It brought to mind images of bums sitting on the street, begging for change. But I suppose I was an alcoholic—just one with money.

"What?" Pita said when I didn't respond. "You're going to ignore me now? You know, lately, if I didn't start a conversation, we would never talk."

"You want to talk about why I drink?" I snapped.

"I know why you drink," she said.

I shook my head. "It's not just that I can't race..." I hesitated, wondering if I should tell her what was on the tip of my tongue, and decided why the hell not. "It's...being here," I finished.

Pita frowned. "Being here? This island? We just came today—"

"Mexico," I told her.

Silence.

"We were supposed to come here for a month or two," I added, "to get away from the media. We've been here for almost a year now."

"We spent four years in the US," she said defensively.

"That's different. You liked it there. I'm bored out of my fucking mind here."

"So why don't you go back to the Las Vegas, Jack?" she said coldly.

"Nobody's forcing you to stay here in this terrible country. Go. Then you can sit around your house all day there and drink."

I clenched my jaw but didn't take the bait.

A sky-wide burst of lightning shattered the night. Ancillary thunder followed.

Rain fell. Wind gusted.

More lightning, more thunder.

"Are we...okay?" Pita asked me eventually.

"Okay?" I said, though I knew what she meant.

"Us. Are we okay?"

I was going to tell her yes, we were fine, we were just going through a rough patch. But what was the point? We both knew the truth.

"No," I said. "I don't think we are."

We didn't say anything more after that.

I didn't want to think about racing, or Pita, or the fact we had just broken up—which I was pretty sure was what just happened—so I spent the next hour or so considering Miguel's murder, the mystery killer, the theories we'd come up with thus far. The more I dwelled on this, the more I felt as though we were missing something, overlooking some vital piece of the puzzle.

Miguel's eyes were not taken by someone doing something stupid in the heat of the moment. Whoever mutilated him—hopefully after he was already dead—was sick and twisted. So the serial killer premise I could buy. What bothered me was the fact the murder occurred here, on this island. Because a murderous sociopath was more often than not the guy next door who had a nine-to-five job, was on a first-name basis with the staff at the local Starbucks, paid taxes, had a mortgage, and waved to you from his car while you walked your kids to school. I'd never heard of Ted Bundy or Jeffrey Dahmer living as recluses in the wilderness. Jason Voorhees maybe, but we weren't dealing with an undead dude in a hockey mask. Despite what Pita may believe, there was nothing metaphysical going on. Whoever killed Miguel and injured Lucinda was flesh and blood. They put their pants on one fucking leg at a time.

So what were they doing on this goddamn island?

This line of thinking ultimately brought me back to Solano. He lived out here on his own. He was a crazy bastard. He would have been the obvious suspect, except for the fact he was dead...

I frowned. Sat a bit straighter.

What if he wasn't dead?

I mean, how did we know he was dead? All I knew was what Pepper told me. All Pepper knew was what someone told him. And what had that been? That Solano was found drowned in the same spot where the girl supposedly drowned fifty years before? Well, the first glaring problem with this was the fact nobody would have known where Solano found the girl's body except Solano himself—if there had ever been a girl to begin with. Moreover, Pepper had said the police hadn't been able to determine Solano's cause of death because he had been in the water, undiscovered, for too long, eaten by salamanders and fish. Well, if he was this badly gone, perhaps little more than a clothed skeleton, it went to reason they couldn't positively identify him either.

So the body might not have been his. It could have belonged to anyone. But who?

Someone like Miguel who had trespassed on his island?

Holy shit! Was Solano the killer then? And if so, he surely knew of our presence on his island. Of course he knew. We were camping out in his fucking house!

I turned to Pita, to share this discovery.

Her eyes were closed, her lips parted slightly. She was asleep.

I stared ahead again, into the night, the rain.

Was Solano out there somewhere? Watching us? Plotting?

I was dozing off, my chin touching my chest, when a sound caused me to start. I jerked my head up, snapped open my eyes. But it was only Jesus and Nitro, coming outside to relieve us.

It was 2 a.m.

Inside the cabin the candles burned warmly, beacons in the tempest, though two had extinguished themselves. Elizaveta sat at the table by herself. She smiled diffidently at us. "You survived," she said.

"It's crazy out there," I said.

"I know, Jack. I can hear. The thunder, it's like earthquake."

I checked in on Lucinda. She lay on her back, the red sheet pulled to her chin. Her attractive face was hoary, sunken, almost cadaverous. I peeled back the sheet, then Solano's poncho, which made me think of Clint Eastwood in his Spaghetti Westerns. Trying not to look at Lucinda's bare breasts, I eased her onto her side. Her skin was hot and clammy. Nitro's tank top/compress was stiff with blood. However, it seemed to have worked, as the laceration had ceased bleeding. I eased Lucinda onto her back and once more covered her with the poncho and sheet. The pulse in her neck was difficult to palpate, but it was there, faint and slow. Her breathing sounded raspy.

"Lucinda?" I said softly, not expecting an answer.

I didn't get one.

I left the room and checked on Pepper next. He lay with Rosa beneath the green and beige rug, only their heads poking out. Two peas in a pod, I thought. But although Rosa seemed snug, perspiration sheened Pepper's face, and he appeared to be shivering.

I felt his forehead with the back of my fingers. He was burning up.

"Peps," I said quietly. "You awake?"

He opened his eyes, saw me, closed them.

"You got a bit of a chill in the rain, buddy."

He didn't say anything.

Best thing for him, I figured, would be a hot drink. We had rainwater, but Solano didn't have a stove or microwave to heat up the water, and I didn't think it would be wise to start an indoor fire.

Second best thing for him would be to get him up and moving.

"Hey, Peps," I said. "Can you sit up?"

He shook his head imperceptibly.

"Just for a bit. Get your circulation moving."

"Can't," he said.

"Can you try?"

He struggled to his elbows with great effort, then flopped back down. He shook his head.

"Okay," I said. "Just rest. Do you want some water?"

"No..."

"I'll be back."

I turned to leave and found Pita directly behind me.

"Trying to give me a heart attack?" I said.

"I'm going to sleep in here for a bit," she said.

"I don't think there's any more room in the bed."

"On the floor."

"Be my guest."

She moved past me and settled on the floor at the foot of the bed. Then she lay on her side and curled herself into a ball, using one arm as a pillow.

I waited for her to say something, maybe goodnight. She didn't. I exited the room and closed the door behind me.

I went to the table and sat next to Elizaveta. Tired of carrying the hay hook around, I set it on the tabletop.

"Lucinda seems stable," I said.

"She's lost much blood."

"Hopefully she can hang on until morning."

"And Pepper too."

"He's not that bad."

"I think he has...how do you say?" She shook herself and said, "*Brrrr...*"

"Hypothermia?" That had crossed my mind. "Maybe," I said. "But he has a fever. I'm pretty sure if you have hypothermia your skin would be cool to the touch, not hot."

"He is shivering."

"I think he just has a nasty bug."

Elizaveta seemed alarmed. "Bug?"

"No, not like that. Speaking of which, how's your sting?"

"It hurts."

"That's all?"

"I was a bit dizzy for a while."

I frowned in concern.

"It's okay," she said. "I'm okay now. I feel better."

"I hope so."

"I don't trick you, Jack. So what is this bug you say?"

"It's an expression for a really bad cold," I told her. "I had something similar once. I was a teenager. A bunch of friends and I went to Mardi Gras in New Orleans for a weekend. No one had a car, so we took a Greyhound—a bus. It was air-conditioned. A vent was right above my seat. I didn't know how to shut it off, and I fell asleep with freezing cold air blowing on me. When we got to New Orleans in the morning—it was an overnight bus—I had all Pepper's symptoms. Fever, shivering, no strength. When we got to the hotel, I dropped into bed and couldn't get out of it for twelve hours. I couldn't eat. Couldn't do anything."

"And then what?"

"It just went away. Literally within an hour I went from feeling dead to almost normal."

"So you think Pepper will magically get better too?" she asked.

I nodded. "I think he just needs rest."

On that note Elizaveta yawned. I did too.

"So what did I miss in here?" I asked.

"Miss?" she said.

"What did you guys do while Pita and I were outside?"

"Nothing amazing." She shrugged. "Jesus and Nitro had arm wrestle."

"Who won?"

"Take guess, Jack."

"Did they talk shit about me?"

"Shit? No. They said some bad things. But never shit."

"It's an expression."

She smiled. "I know."

"So?" I pressed.

"What?"

"What did they say?"

"Why do you care?"

"I don't... So what did they say?"

"I cannot tell you."

"Why not?"

"Because Jesus will be your brother-in-law. I don't want to make trouble."

"He's not going to be my brother-in-law."

"Yes, when you marry Pita, he will—"

I lowered my voice. "Pita and I broke up."

Elizaveta blinked in surprise. "When?"

"When you guys were inside here arm wrestling apparently."

She was reticent. She fiddled with the garden claw on the table before her, turning it over in her hands. "I'm sorry, Jack," she said finally. "Do you want to talk?"

"No."

She looked at me. I looked at her. She seemed as though she wanted to say something, but she didn't. Still, her eyes didn't leave mine.

"You'll be okay, Jack."

I nodded.

"You know what you need do?"

I waited.

"Move to Russia."

"Russia?"

"You are rich American man. Handsome American man. You can have every girl in Russia you want."

This comment surprised me, because although she wasn't in Russia, I couldn't help but feel she was speaking about herself too.

So was she hitting on me—all of five minutes after I'd broken up with Pita?

I glanced at the door to Pepper's room, glad I'd closed it. But was Pita on the other side, with her ear against it, listening?

No. We weren't speaking very loudly, and the rain drumming against the roof would make it difficult, if not impossible, for her to hear our voices.

Even so, I wanted to change the topic, though for some reason my mind was drawing blanks.

"Please, Jack," Elizaveta said, cupping my hand with hers. "I joke."

But was she joking? There was mischief in her eyes—because she was joking, or flirting?

This was bizarre, the turn of the conversation, bizarre. And what made it even more bizarre was the fact I was attracted to Elizaveta, I'd been attracted to her ever since Jesus introduced us, and I was hoping she *wasn't* joking.

I cleared my throat. She removed her hand from mine.

Thunder crashed above us, petering to a growl.

"This storm," Elizaveta said. "Oh my God."

The storm, the sanguinary killer out there—right. "I was thinking about everything that's happened on the island," I said, relieved to find the knot in my tongue had unraveled. "Do you want to hear a new theory about who might have killed Miguel?"

"Yes, of course," she said. "Tell me."

I explained.

"Solano murdered Miguel?" Elizaveta said, and I thought she was going to laugh, tell me this was outlandish. But what she added was: "I think you might be right, Jack. It all fits. Everything."

"It does, right?" I said. "He lives out here. He's a crazy hermit. He doesn't want people trespassing on his island."

"So he kills them."

"And dumps them in the canals. Pepper told me it was filled with skeletons anyway, from the revolution."

"I didn't know that."

"The army supposedly dumped thousands of bodies in them."

"But Solano didn't dump Miguel."

"No, but that's because he probably didn't have time. He would have wanted to find Lucinda and Rosa first. Make sure no one could leave and give up his secret."

"But why take his eyes?"

"Maybe that's just his thing. Serial killers do all sorts of weird shit like that."

"Look, Jack, I have goosebumps." She showed me her arms. "You have solved this mystery!"

"It doesn't mean we're safe," I said. "He's still out there."

"Yes, you are right. But I feel safer because Solano is not some Rambo. He is just old man."

"Which is probably why he hasn't tried anything."

"You mean attack us?"

I nodded. "He has to know we're here. We're staying in his house. But like you said. He's an old man. He might be able to sneak up on someone like Miguel and stab him in the back, but there's nothing he can do against so many of us."

"Oh, Jack I'm so relieved!" She leaned forward across the table and kissed me on the mouth. Her lips stayed pressed against mine for way too long to be a simple celebratory peck.

But I didn't mind. In fact, I felt electrified, like one of those bolts of lightning in the sky had just zapped me on the head.

Then her lips parted. Mine did too. Our tongues touched—

I pulled back, frazzled, guilt-ridden.

What the hell was going on?

Elizaveta was looking at me with her sparkling green eyes. Her face was slightly flushed. She clearly had no problem with that kiss.

And I realized I had to stop whatever had started. What we were doing wasn't right. It didn't feel right. People were going to get hurt. Pita would, Jesus would. I didn't care about Jesus actually. But I cared about Pita. And this was wrong. It was way too soon. Elizaveta was her friend.

"What are you thinking about, Jack?" Elizaveta asked.

It was the same question Pita had asked me two hours before, while we'd been sitting out on the porch together.

I felt worse than ever.

"We can't—" The rest of the words caught in my throat.

"What's wrong?" Elizaveta asked. She looked where I was looking, at the table. She stood quickly. "Another scorpion? *Where?*"

I shook my head, standing too. I pointed at the table. "Did you move the doll that was there?"

"What doll?"

I remembered it clearly. Black hair that smelled like citrus, painted lips, heavy eyeshadow, the dress that may or may not have been concealing a hole between its legs.

I said, "There was a doll on this table earlier."

"So what?"

"Where is it?"

Elizaveta looked around the room. "There are dolls everywhere, Jack."

"There was a doll right there. It was special."

"Why special?"

"It just was. It was all dressed up. Solano put makeup on it."

"What?"

I moved to the end of the table, opened the shoebox, and slid it to Elizaveta. "Makeup."

"I don't remember any doll on table, Jack."

"When I came here before, when I found Rosa, it was still daytime. It was the first thing I saw. A doll. Right there." I pointed again. "Did someone move it? Did Jesus or Nitro move it?"

"No," Elizaveta said. "Nobody did. There was no doll, Jack. I remember. I lit that candle when we first arrived." She indicated the half-melted candle on the table. "There was no doll."

"What doll?" It was Pita. She stood at the threshold to Pepper's bedroom. We'd raised our voices, woken her—if she'd ever been sleeping and not eavesdropping on us.

"Do you remember seeing a doll on the table?" I asked her.

"No..." She shook her head more decisively. "No."

"There was one there earlier, and now it's gone—

The front door to the cabin burst open, and Nitro staggered inside, spraying blood everywhere.

I'd never witnessed anything like the spectacle that unfolded before us, and I found myself rooted to the spot in horror.

Nitro's eyes blazed with blustery panic. His mouth was cranked open in a silent scream. His hands clamped his throat, trying to stem the freshet of blood gushing from it.

He came straight toward me, and for a moment I thought he was going to attack me.

He released his throat and seized my tank top with blood-soaked hands, pulling me forward. Powerful jets of blood shot from his jugular veins straight into my face, into my eyes, my mouth. I tasted it on my tongue, coppery, salty, sweet.

Nitro slumped to his knees, tugging me down with him. He was like a drowning person, flailing, dangerous.

I tried to pry his hands from my top, but he wouldn't let go.

Pita and Elizaveta were screaming. I wanted to tell them to shut up, but my mouth was full of blood.

Nitro was surely screaming too, though he could no longer make any sound. His throat had been slit from ear to ear, his vocal cords severed at the same time as the rest of his plumbing. I could see straight into his gaping windpipe.

Dismayed, disgusted, I shoved him away from me, hard. He released my top and fell onto his back, his arms and legs flopping akimbo. He suffered a paroxysm of agony, as if he were being kicked by an invisible boot. Then his body relaxed, went still. The fountain of blood spurting from his throat shut off.

His heart had stopped beating.

He was dead.

My paralysis broke. I dropped to my knees next to Nitro and attempted CPR. Nevertheless, I knew this was futile. His head was only half attached to his neck.

Someone was behind me, talking to me, pulling me away. It was Jesus.

He'd returned inside. I stared at him blankly, watching his lips move, wondering what he was saying. Elizaveta and Pita were nearby, hugging each other and crying. I couldn't hear them either. I couldn't hear anything except for a plaintive drone in my ears.

I lumbered to my feet and went to a corner, away from them. My balance was skewed. I leaned against the wall, spitting blood from my mouth, waiting to be sick.

What the hell happened?

Nitro was dead...

Solano!

I whirled toward the cabin's front door, seeing Solano charging inside, bloody knife swinging, slashing.

He wasn't there.

It was my imagination.

I returned to Nitro's body. I rolled it over, which proved oddly difficult, for it was slick with blood and had become a dead weight. I cringed at the feel of the warm flesh beneath my hands.

Pita was asking me what I was doing in a semi-hysterical voice.

I unzipped Nitro's backpack and searched the pocket for the pistol.

It was missing.

I panicked before seeing the outline of the gun's handle poking out the top of his board shorts. I retrieved it and stood, leaving him facedown.

Better that way. Nobody wanted to look at his sightless eyes or smiling throat.

I checked the pistol's magazine. Still several cartridges locked and loaded.

Flicking off the safety, I went outside.

I scanned the night, searching for movement—but everything was moving in the near hurricane winds: trees, branches, shrubs, dolls, grass.

Pistol held close to my chest, muzzle pointed skyward, I followed the trail of blood. It went right along the porch, all the way to the bannister.

What had Nitro being doing down here? Pita and I had remained huddled near the door our entire watch. Had he heard a noise and come to investigate?

Then what? When his back was turned, Solano emerged from the night and slit his throat?

I poked my head over the bannister, looked down the length of the cabin. Nobody there. No footprints. Nothing.

Whoever had killed Nitro, it seemed, had vanished into thin air.

1957

Patricia Diaz was putting Salma, her six-month-old newborn, to bed in her crib when there was a knock at the front door. She tucked Salma's blanket beneath her chubby chin, then left the bedroom. In the foyer she opened the front door and was surprised to find a policeman standing on the little stoop. He had a moon face and a large belly testing the buttons of his uniform. He was holding the hand of a feral looking girl dressed in a ratty nightgown, her hair chopped short—

"María!" she exclaimed.

"Mommy?"

"Baby? Oh my God...*Oh my God!*" She enfolded her daughter in a great hug. "Oh baby! What's happened to you?"

"Officer Rodriguez, ma'am," the policeman said. "I picked her up earlier not far from here. She was loitering in the park. Actually, she appeared to be living there."

"Living?" Patricia released her daughter and frowned at her. "Why were you in the park, sweetheart? Why weren't you at Saint Agatha's?"

"I didn't like it," she said simply.

"The school?"

"I just left."

"You left?"

"I just left," she repeated. And she sounded angry. Her voice was shrill, her eyes hard.

"Why don't you go inside, honey. You can lie down in my bed. Okay? I'd like to speak with the policeman in private for a moment."

When María disappeared inside the house, Patricia looked at the policeman and swallowed tightly. "This is very strange," she said, feeling suddenly nervous even though she had done nothing wrong. "You see, María has a certain condition. She doesn't learn well like others her age. Two years ago her school psychologist recommended she enroll in a special boarding school."

"Saint Agatha's?" the policeman said.

"Saint Agatha's School for Lost Children. Some of the children, their parents have died, or they're alcoholics, or...there are many reasons why they are placed there. But some are like María. They are mentally deficient in some way."

"How long has your daughter been at this school?"

"Eighteen months or thereabouts."

"When was the last time you saw her?"

"Well, when we placed here there." She added quickly, "We tried to visit her early on, but the nuns wouldn't let us see her. There was always some excuse or another. But they assured us she was doing fine. And then, well, I became pregnant, and that sort of took over my life, and then Salma was born..." Patricia took a deep breath, realizing the hot poker inside her wasn't nervousness; it was guilt. "Anyway, my husband and I decided if María was happy, perhaps it would be best if we kept our distance. It would be easier for her this way." She glanced over her shoulder the way María had gone, then returned her attention to the policeman. "What have they done to her? She seemed so..." The word that came to mind was "cold," but she only shook her head. "How did you know where to bring her, Officer? I didn't think she knew her address. She could never remember information like that."

"She didn't," the policeman said. "When I asked her where she lived, she said the park. It took a while until I got her to tell me the name of her school—her old elementary school. I took her there. The principal recognized her. He had your address on file." He shrugged. "But if she belongs in this school—Saint Agatha's—I'll take her back there."

"No," Patricia said. "I mean, no thank you. Not until I know why she left.

Something must have happened to her for her to just leave like that, for her to prefer to live in a park, for God's sake. And surely the nuns would know she was missing. So why haven't they contacted me?" She shook her head. "I need to talk to María. I need to talk to my husband. But thank you, Officer Rodriguez, thank you for bringing my daughter home."

Patricia went to her bedroom, but María wasn't there, sleeping or otherwise.

"María?" she called.

No response.

Patricia ducked her head into the kitchen, then the dining room. She was on her way to the back door, to check the backyard, when she passed the playroom-turned-nursery. María stood next to the crib, holding Salma in her arms, rocking her gently.

"María?" Patricia said, alarmed. "What are you doing?"

"I found Angela."

"That's not Angela, sweetheart. Her name's Salma. You have to be very, very careful with her." She started forward, holding out her arms. "Please give her to me."

"No."

Patricia froze. "What do you mean *no*?"

"She's mine."

"She's your baby sister, yes, but—"

"She's mine!"

"María, pass me your sister." She steeled her voice. "Right now."

María glowered at her, and for a terrifying moment Patricia feared she might throw Salma across the room. But then she held the infant out at arm's length, gripping her by the wrist as if she were nothing but a doll.

Salma woke and began to cry.

Patricia snatched the baby quickly and cradled her tightly against her chest, staring over her head at María with frightened eyes.

Patricia didn't know what those nuns did to María, but the eight-year-old girl who had been living in her home for the last three days was not her daughter—or at least not the daughter she had once been. She was a stranger. A violent, angry stranger. Patricia felt she was walking on eggshells whenever she was in the same room with her, worried about saying something or doing something that would set her off. María had already had several temper tantrums. The worst occurred earlier that morning when Patricia found her in the kitchen, carving up a heel of cheese. Afterward she placed the dirty knife back in the knife block. Patricia explained she had to wash the knife otherwise someone could get sick. María responded by throwing the knife block against the floor and going around the house shouting and slamming doors. Patricia had been so terrified—for both herself and Salma—she quickly collected the baby and went down the street to her girlfriends', remaining there until her husband Diego returned from work. By then María had calmed down and was curled up in her bed (they had left her bedroom untouched in her absence), staring at the wall.

Presently Patricia sat in the living room, rocking Salma in her arms. Diego sat in a chair across from her, still in his construction clothes, a beer in his hand.

"Saint Agatha's was supposed to help her," she said softly.

"It didn't help her," Diego grumbled. He sipped his beer and wiped foam from his mustache with the back of his hand.

"At least before she would listen. Now...now nothing gets through to her."

"She doesn't listen," he agreed.

"When she threw the knives, all I could think was..."

"What if Salma was in the kitchen, playing on the floor?"

Patricia nodded. "I'm scared, Diego," she admitted. "When María was younger, when she had her temper tantrums, they were almost cute. But they're not cute anymore. And what of when she's older? When she's fifteen, or twenty, or thirty? Will she still be having temper tantrums? What will people think? They won't understand."

"That's a long way away, dear."

"But it's inevitable. She's not going to get better. She's not. I know that now. Not even a little bit." Patricia adjusted Salma and wiped a tear from her eye. "She's never going to fall in love. Never get married. Never have children of her own. Never..." More tears leaked from her eyes. "And I should be there for her. I'm her mother. I should be there for her. But I don't think I can be, Diego. I don't think I can. I'm...I'm scared of her. I'm scared of my own daughter."

He hushed her, getting off his chair, kneeling beside her, stroking her back.

"We never should have given her away," she went on. "She was our daughter. We should have loved her. We should have taken care of her. Now look what's happened to her. Look what's happened to our daughter."

"We'll take her back. I'll take her back. Tomorrow—"

"To Saint Agatha's?" she said, shocked. "Look what's happened to her there!"

"We'll be better this time. We'll visit her. We'll make sure they treat her right."

"No, Diego." She was shaking her head. "She can't go back there."

His face hardened. "She can't stay here, dear. Not with Salma. I won't allow it."

"No, she can't stay here," she agreed.

"I'll start looking for another school then—"

"Who's to say another school will be any more kind to her? And what of when she's too old for school? She will have to go to one of those institutions. Do you know what those places are like? And she's pretty, Diego. She's still so pretty. That's the worst part. She will be a victim, taken advantage of. I don't think I could live with myself knowing she was locked away in one of those places, getting beaten and raped and—" She took a deep breath and held her husband's eyes. "I know this is a terrible thing to say. I pray for my soul. God, I pray for my soul. But this world wasn't meant for her. There is nothing in it for her except suffering and pain."

"What are you getting at, dear?"

"I'm saying…" But she found she couldn't form the words. She couldn't bear to hear them coming from her lips. Yet in the end it didn't matter. She didn't have to say anything.

Diego understood.

Jack

I returned inside the cabin. Pita and Elizaveta still embraced, their heads buried in each other's shoulders. Jesus hovered next to them, speaking softly. And...aw shit. Rosa stood at the threshold to the bedroom, her eyes sullen, her hands clamped over her mouth. She seemed to be staring at everything and nothing.

Sticking the pistol into the waistband of my shorts against the small of my back, I went to her, knelt so we were the same height. She tried to hug me. I held her at bay; I was covered with blood. In fact, my face must have been painted red.

"It's okay, Rosa," I said absurdly, the empty reassurance something only a child would find comforting. "It's okay."

Tears shimmered in her eyes, yet she didn't say anything.

"Go back in the bedroom. You'll be safe there."

She opened her mouth but no sound came out.

I stood, turning her around, nudging her into the room. She went obediently.

Pepper was propped on his elbows, staring at us with dusty eyes.

"Hop back in bed," I told her.

Instead of climbing back into the bed, however, she crawled beneath it, her hiding spot where I'd found her earlier.

"What happened...?" Pepper asked me. He couldn't see out the door from his position, but he certainly heard all the shouting.

"Nitro was attacked."

"Who...?"

"Solano."

"Solano?"

I explained my theory to him.

"We need to leave," he said, lying back down.

"We will. In the morning."

"Keep watch..." He closed his eyes.

He didn't say anything more, and I figured he'd sunk back into sleep. I left the room, closing the door behind me.

I confronted Jesus. "What the hell happened?" I was tingling everywhere—arms, thighs, balls, the nape of my neck—but I kept my voice controlled.

"I—I don't know." He shook his head.

"Don't know? You were out there with him, man!"

"I was sleeping."

"Fuck, Jesus..."

"He *said* I could sleep. He said he would keep watch. All I saw, when I woke up, all I saw was him pushing open the door and disappearing inside. I didn't even know he was injured—until you guys started screaming." He almost seemed like he might cry. "*What the hell's happening, Jack?*"

So I was right. Solano must have made a noise, lured Nitro to the end of the porch. Then when his back was turned...

I hadn't given the old hermit enough credit. It seemed he wasn't deterred by our superiority of numbers after all.

"You have to get rid of him," Pita said, looking at me over Elizaveta's shoulder. Her cheeks were streaked with tears and mascara. Her nose leaked snot. She wiped at it with the back of her hand.

She meant Nitro. And she was right. We couldn't leave him in the middle of the room, pretending he wasn't there, ignoring him.

"Jesus, help me," I said.

"Where are we going to move him?"

"The porch."

I pushed open the cabin's front door, then went to Nitro's legs. Jesus went to his arms. On the count of three we lifted Nitro and carried his heavy weight outside, stepping through the small lake of blood that had pooled around his body. We set him on the floorboards a few feet to the left. I folded his hands atop his bare chest in an attempt at dignity, but I couldn't bring myself to slide closed his eyelids. I recalled attempting that with the Pepper-doll earlier in the day—or yesterday now, for that matter—and the eyelids springing open again. If this happened with Nitro...I don't know, but I already had my fill of ghastly images from this island, and I didn't need another.

Back inside, I closed the cabin's door, then dragged the table in front of it. The rudimentary barricade would not stop a persistent assault. That was not the intent. It was meant to prevent Solano from sneaking up on anybody again.

"That's not going to stop her," Pita said.

"Not now, Pita," I said.

"Not now? *Not now?*"

"I don't want to hear anything about ghosts."

"Why are you so blind?"

"There's no ghost on this island."

"We contacted her—"

"It was a hoax—"

"I felt her—"

"Ghosts don't fucking exist!"

"Jack..." Elizaveta said.

"Solano snuck up on Nitro. That's it."

"Solano?" Pita said. "Solano's *dead.*"

"Solano?" Jesus said, frowning.

I explained my theory again. Jesus seemed thoughtful. Pita, of course, wouldn't have any of it.

"I *felt* her, Jack," Pita repeated. "She's here and she's angry and—"

"It's okay," Elizaveta said. "We are safe."

"Safe?" Pita said. "*Safe?* Look what happened to Nitro!"

To Jesus I said, "Can you calm her down?"

He went to her, speaking reassuringly. She lashed back. Their argument escalated until she threw up her hands and went to Pepper's bedroom, slamming the door behind her.

I could hear her crying from the other side of it.

Later. I wasn't sure how much later. I'd fallen asleep and had just woken up.

It was quiet—too quiet—and I realized the storm had stopped.

No wind, no rain.

Silence.

The cabin was dark. A few candles still burned.

I was alone.

Elizaveta and Jesus must have gone to the bedrooms.

I should probably get up, stick my head outside, make sure the storm was indeed over, but I found I didn't want to move.

The table was no longer in front of the door.

Where was it?

Who'd moved it?

Jesus?

Probably. He'd probably gone outside just as I'd planned to go outside.

Too quiet.

Was I alone? *Alone* alone? Had Jesus and Pita and Elizaveta left me? Were they down at the pier, waiting for the boatman?

That's what it felt like, that the cabin wasn't empty, that it was deserted.

A noise—from Lucinda's room, like the shuffle of cards.

"Hello?" I said.

The door swung inward. The hinges protested, issuing a prolonged *weeeeeeeek.* I squinted, trying to see into the room. I couldn't make out anything but darkness.

"Hello?"

A giggle.

I stiffened.

Rosa? I wanted to believe it was Rosa. But it wasn't her. The giggle was more a cackle, malevolent, threatening.

Lucinda? Had she recovered? Was she sitting on the bed, naked and giggling in the dark?

Time to get the hell out of there, I thought.

I stood—but didn't leave. The person was cackling in the bedroom again. I knew I should ignore whoever it was, leave the cabin, run, but instead I found myself moving toward the witchy sound.

I stopped inside the door. I still couldn't see anything in the room. It was cauldron black.

"Hello?"

"Jack..."

The voice was female, young, raspy.

Something moved very quickly. I heard the frantic patter of small footsteps. Then a snick, a whoosh. A tiny flame appeared to my right.

A doll stood on its tiptoes, a burning match in its hand. It was attempting to light the candle on the dresser. The wick caught and light bloomed. The doll extinguished the match with a quick flick of its wrist.

Its head twisted ninety degrees, owl-like, to look at me.

"Jack..." it rasped.

"Who are you?"

"Jack... It's *me*..."

The doll was female. It had dark wavy hair that fell halfway down its back, thick-lashed brown eyes, a tiny nose, playful lips—

"Pita?" I said.

"Jack..." Her lips weren't moving, and I realized she was communicating to me how she claimed to have communicated with her sister Susana, telepathically.

"What happened to you?"

"Solano..."

"What about him?"

"He caught me..."

"Caught you? But what did he do? You're a doll, Pita."

"That's what he does... He catches people... He turns them into dolls... He hangs them up everywhere... But we're still alive... We're alive inside them..."

"Where's Eliza?" I asked, alarmed. "Where's Rosa?"

"Dolls..."

"No!"

She began to cackle once more.

I came awake with a start and found myself in candlelit darkness. It was late, the time when graveyards yawned and decent folks slept snugly in their beds. Not me though. I sat cross-legged on the hard floor in the middle of the cabin's main room, groggy and exhausted.

I raised my head from my chest, blinking. I remembered sitting there, closing my eyes, not to fall asleep, to think...and maybe to forget. Yes, I'd wanted to forget I was covered in Nitro's blood, forget his lifeless body was lying on the porch, his eyes staring at eternity, forget we were trapped on the island, stalked by a killer.

My stomach, I realized, felt bloated and bilious. At first I thought this was due to hunger. But it wasn't hunger. It was fear.

I glanced at the barricaded door, then at Elizaveta, who sat in front of me, hands held together on her lap, head bowed. She could have been meditating had her posture not been slumped. "Hey?" I said quietly.

Her eyes blinked open. "What happened?" she whispered.

"You were sleeping."

Her shoulders sagged. Her fingers massaged her face, making small circles.

"And you snore," I said.

"I do not."

"How would you know if you were sleeping?"

She grimaced. I glanced at my watch. It was 3:41 a.m.

I'd only been asleep for twenty minutes or so. Still, that was twenty minutes too long. Solano could have sneaked into the cabin during that time, slit my throat, slit all our throats...

Dismayed by my lack of vigilance, I sat straighter. "Where's Jesus?" I asked.

Elizaveta gestured to Pepper's bedroom. "He said smell bothered him."

I sniffed. The room reeked of blood, cloying and sickly sweet. It made me think of a cookie factory my parents had taken me to while we'd been RVing around the country, a visit that turned me off cookies for the rest of my life. The smell of molasses and dough and butter hadn't necessarily been bad; it had simply been too omnipresent, too overpowering. I'd ended up disgorging the contents of my stomach on the floor in front of everyone.

"I brought you this," Elizaveta said, indicating an enamelware bucket next to her which was filled with rainwater. She slid it to me.

I dunked my hands into the cold water and scrubbed them. The water turned red.

"Let me help." Elizaveta picked up a rag she'd fetched. She dampened it in the water and proceeded to clean my face. Her touch was delicate yet firm at the same time, maternal. "There," she said when she finished.

I looked around for my daypack. It was by the junk heap that included the car seat. I stood and stretched, retrieved the bottle of vodka from the pack, then sat back down. I twisted off the cap and offered the bottle to Elizaveta. She took an impressive sip and passed it back. I took an even bigger sip, swishing the vodka around inside my mouth to kill the lingering taste of blood. I didn't have anywhere to spit it out, so I swallowed.

Elizaveta produced her cigarettes, offered the pack to me.

"You only have four left," I said.

"I'm trying to cut down. You have one, you help me."

Shrugging, I accepted a cigarette. She held forth a lighter and pushed the button that ignited the flame. I lit up. She slid a cigarette between her lips and lit up too. I didn't smoke. Well, I did, but not regularly. I wasn't addicted. During one of my binge nights out, I could burn through a pack by myself just for the hell of it. But I wouldn't crave a cigarette the next day. In fact, I could go a week, or several weeks, until the fancy for one took me again.

Funny why that was, given I was addicted to almost every other vice.

I took a drag and turned my head to the left, so I didn't blow the smoke in Elizaveta's face. I couldn't help but see the blood-smeared floor, the crimson splatter leading to the front door. My mind hit me with an image of Nitro, the way he looked at me when he'd stumbled into the room, scared, pleading, expressions so alien to him.

"I didn't like him," Elizaveta said, as if reading my thoughts.

"Nitro?"

"I didn't like how he always teased you."

"He was a prick," I said. Then laughed. "But he was sort of funny."

"Funny?"

"If we weren't arch enemies I probably would have liked him."

"That makes no sense, Jack."

I took another drag. "You know what he told Pepper earlier, when we were looking for Rosa's canoe? He told him to switch weather channels because the weather girl on his channel had a major hot front."

"Yes, that was his humor. He was always telling Jesus sexist jokes except when—" She stopped abruptly.

"Except when what?"

Elizaveta shrugged, contemplated her cigarette. "Except when Pita was around."

"Pita?"

"Yes. But anyway..."

I frowned. Did Elizaveta know something I didn't?

Avoiding eye contact, she picked up the bottle of vodka and took a sip.

I said, "What's up, Eliza?"

"Nothing is up, Jack." She still wouldn't look at me.

"Were Nitro and Pita..." I didn't know how to articulate the question. "Was something going on between them?"

"I don't know, Jack. I don't know anything."

She was lying. That was clear as day...and that meant...what? What did she know? Had Nitro and Pita fooled around? Had they fucked? Had they been fucking on an ongoing basis?

The girl I'm pounding right now, she's vaginamite.

My heart sickened, and I felt suddenly nauseous, as if I'd inadvertently stepped on a baby bird. I was also angry—furious—though this almost immediately burned itself out. If Nitro were alive, I would have beat the living shit out of him. But he wasn't. He was dead, and no matter what he did, I couldn't be mad at a dead guy.

Pita though—she was a different story. I had half a mind to go wake her up, confront her. But what would that accomplish? She wasn't coping well. A confrontation like that might push her over the edge.

Are we okay? she'd asked me earlier on the porch.

Yeah, except for the fact you're fucking Nitro behind my back.

"Jack?" It was Elizaveta. She was looking at me with concern.

She'd known. Jesus had likely known too. How many other people had known?

"I'm sorry," she added.

"Whatever," I said. It wasn't her responsibility to tell me Pita was cheating on me. She was dating Jesus. Her loyalty was to him, to his family, not me—

Elizaveta rocked forward onto her knees. She stubbed out her cigarette on the floorboards, plucked mine from my fingers, and put it out as well. Then she placed her hands on my chest. For a moment I thought she was going to try to hug me, console me. She didn't. Instead she pressed me backward. I resisted. I didn't know what was going on.

"Lie back," she whispered, still pressing.

And then I was lying back. My baseball cap slipped off my head.

"Eliza..." I said.

She lifted her pink top, exposing her midriff, then her violet bra, lifting the top over her head. She moved forward so she straddled me, her groin against mine. She took my hands in hers and pressed them against her breasts.

This was reckless, I thought. Madness. Nitro's corpse was outside, no more than two dozen feet away. His blood stained the floor. Pita and Jesus were in the next room.

But a switch had flicked inside me, and none of that mattered.

My hands were working on their own, exploring the firmness of her breasts, the weight of them, the hardness of her nipples.

I undid the clasp of her bra. The spaghetti straps slipped down her arms. The cups released her breasts, which were perfect in the dim candlelight, full and round.

Setting the bra aside, she leaned forward, placing a hand to either side of my head. Her lips tickled my neck, my ear, her breath warm, erotic. She leaned farther forward, so her breasts brushed my face. I could smell her sweat pushing through her perfume, but it wasn't unpleasant.

My tongue probed, trying to catch her moving nipples. She moaned quietly. I fumbled open the button on her shorts, tugged the zipper down. But that was all I could manage with her straddling me. She understood this and eased back, then stood, gracefully, like a cat.

Her emerald eyes never left mine. They were intense, beautiful. She was beautiful.

She skimmed her shorts down her legs. They dropped around her ankles. She fit her fingers into the elastic waistband of her panties, which were violet like her bra, and skimpy. She pushed one side down, then the other, revealing a trimmed strip of pubic hair—then pulled them back up.

Teasing.

Finally she slid them down her thighs to her ankles. She stepped out of them, and her shorts. I kicked off my board shorts and boxers.

She settled on top of me, warm, tight, rocking, gripping, gliding.

Soundless.

Afterward, clothed again, we sat on the floor as we had before, almost as if nothing had happened. And I couldn't believe something had happened. It had been so unexpected, spontaneous, surreal.

I felt lightheaded, amazed not only at what we'd done, but that we'd gotten away with it.

I also felt like total shit.

Pita cheated on me, I told myself.

We broke up.

I've done nothing wrong.

Only it felt wrong. Very wrong.

But right too.

"Can I ask you a question, Jack?" Elizaveta said.

"What?" I said.

"Why did you stop racing?"

"Oh," I said, relieved. This wasn't my favorite topic of discussion, but it was better than talking about what just happened between us, what it meant. "You don't know?"

"I know about crash. Jesus told me. But that was one year ago. You are better, da? Why not race again?"

"Because I can't."

"But why?"

"I'm not better."

"You look better."

It was true. My body was fine and functioning. I'd bruised my ribs in the accident, fractured my wrist, and whacked my tailbone so hard I couldn't sit comfortably for days. Even so, I was back in my Chevrolet within two weeks...yet I wasn't the same. I was getting daily headaches that affected my racing, distracted me. At the CarsDirect.com 400 I hit an embankment with the driver's side of my car. Halfway through the Cracker Barrel Old Country Store 500 I smacked the wall in Turn 2 and spun out. Then, a few days before the next race at Darlington Raceway, I was scheduled to do a media tour. However, I bowed out halfway through the day due to the worst headache yet.

My sponsors became worried. My PR guy wanted me to stay off the track. I stubbornly refused. The next race was the Food City 500 at Bristol Motor Speedway. Around lap 340 I developed another headache, this one so severe my crew chief threw in the towel at the next pit stop.

I ended up seeing three different doctors. None could answer for certain what was wrong with me. They simply advised me to slow down, get some rest, I'd feel better soon.

"I get headaches," I told Elizaveta now. "Sometimes when they get bad, my vision gets blurry."

She frowned. "That is problem?"

"Maybe not so much if you're a banker. But if you're a race car driver, running at three thousand feet a second, yeah, it's a problem, a big problem."

"Can you take medicine?"

"Nothing that's worked." I shrugged. "Well, except this, sort of." I picked up the vodka and took a belt.

"I didn't know this."

"You never asked."

"So what do you do now? I know, I see you at parties sometimes. But you don't race, don't work. What do you do every day?"

"Drink."

"I'm serious."

"I am too."

"Well, what do you do when you drink then?"

"Do you really care?"

"I'm curious, Jack."

"I have a car I'm working on rebuilding."

"That sounds fun."

"It's more work than fun, but it fills in the time. I'm also working on a board game."

She frowned. "A bored game? Why?"

"Huh? No—board." I pantomimed a square. "Like Monopoly."

"I know Monopoly."

"Do you know IQ 2000?"

"IQ 2000?"

"It's a board game too."

"You forget where I come from, Jack. We did not have Coca Cola or Pepsi when I was child in Soviet Union. You think we had this IQ 2000?"

Sometimes I did forget Elizaveta grew up in the Soviet Union. It might have only collapsed a decade ago, but to me it seemed as relegated to the past as Nazi Germany. "Well, the game I'm working on is like IQ 2000, trivia. But the questions and categories relate to NASCAR."

"That sounds fantastic. I will buy it."

"It's never going to be published. It's just a hobby." I shrugged. "What about you?" I asked, wanting to switch topics. "What do you do every day?"

"I work," she said. "I am governess, you know."

"But what about your free time?"

"Ha. Free time? I have zero free time, Jack."

"You're that busy?"

"I am like mother to these twins. It is exhausting."

"But rewarding, I imagine."

"Maybe if the children were...normal."

"They're not?"

"Their father is a Russian oligarch, Jack. They get anything they want. At last birthday party, they had pony rides, wild pigs, piñata, a cake bigger than me. They are..." She pinned her nose up with her thumb.

"Piggish?"

"Yes, but not that word. Snotty? Yes, they are snotty monsters."

"Can't you quit?"

"And do what? Go back to Russia?"

"Is it still that bad?"

Elizaveta nodded. "We have a president who says he will help poor, but he won't. He only helps himself. He is corrupt. Everybody is corrupt there. Da, it is still bad."

"Do you like Mexico?"

"Better than Russia."

"Then just get another job. There are some good international schools around."

"You don't understand, Jack. You are American. You can work anywhere. Mexico, Europe, anywhere. Your government has agreements with other governments. Russian government has agreement with nobody. No country wants Russian worker. No country gives visa. I was very lucky. The family I work for is very powerful. Only they can get me visa. I can't quit."

I chewed on this because I'd never given it much thought before; I'd never had any reason to. I said, "When does your visa expire?"

"Next spring. So I still have time."

"Time for what?"

"To convince Jesus to marry me."

Her words slapped me. I felt hurt, bitter. However, I immediately swept these emotions aside. She and Jesus were still a couple. Of course they were. What happened between us, the sex, it was just that: sex. A diversion, an escape, albeit temporary, from Nitro's death, this island of horrors.

Still, I found myself asking: "You want to marry him?"

"I would be a permanent resident. I would not be forced back to Russia. I could quit job as governess." She offered a playful smile. "Then I could build cars and make board games too."

I wasn't amused; I was jealous. It was stupid. Nothing more was going to happen between Elizaveta and I.

Still...

"So you're just with him for the visa?" I asked.

Elizaveta's smiled vanished. "I like him, Jack."

"Because he has money? Because he can get you a permanent visa?"

Her eyes flared. "Do not judge me, Jack," she said dangerously. "Not everyone has easy life like you."

"I've had an easy life?" I said, genuinely surprised. "I worked like a dog to get to where I was—"

"But you *could* get there," she said. "How many Russian race car drivers do you know? Well?"

"None," I admitted.

"Because they cannot drive race car? Nyet. Most cannot buy shee-it car. You think they can buy *race* car? You take much for granted, Jack." Before I could say anything, she added: "Let me tell you, okay? I lived in building with six other families. I woke up before light every morning just to avoid line for bath. In winter my floor, the fourth, was always very cold, but the third floor was always very humid with steam. Go figure. My school was also always very cold. You needed jacket, hat, scarf. Sometimes the ink in pens would freeze. The children I taught—you know what they all wanted?"

I shrugged. "To become astronauts?"

"To move to United States." She shook her head, reflectively. "Life in the Soviet Union was not so bad. You did not have to think about having food, paying bills. You had zero concerns really—as long as you didn't...how do you say...stand out of crowd. And most people didn't. They didn't know better, what they were lacking. But after Gorbachev, everything changed, everything. For first time you could see beyond iron curtain. You could watch CNN or BBC. People realized how shee-it their lives were compared to Western countries, especially the US."

I stared at her, digesting what she was saying.

"Let me tell you about one day," she went on. She was getting worked up, and I didn't want to interrupt her. "I was walking back from the school where I taught. I was carrying bags. You know, I carried bags everywhere I went—everyone did. This was no fashion statement, Jack. We didn't know when basic commodities would be available. So better to be prepared, right? I passed a grocery store near my building. There was line, forty people maybe, waiting in cold. I didn't know what they were waiting for, but I didn't want to miss out on getting something—anything was better than nothing—so I joined line too. I waited maybe one hour. Snow started to fall. My fingers and toes were frozen. My face and lips and nose, frozen. I remember a car pulled over on the road. The driver took the windshield wipers from trunk and attached them to car. They go automatically, there is no off switch, so you have to take them off in dry weather or they fall apart. I watched him from the line, him and his old car, thinking he was very lucky, because he *had* car. I got angry. Because why did he have car? Why couldn't I have car too? Why did I have to stand in line? Standing in lines was for grandmothers. That was their purpose in life. They wait and wait and wait for whatever might be at the end. But I was no babushka. I was about to go to front of line...bud in...when another woman tried this first. A man yelled at her. She yelled back, saying she had kids to feed. The man, he seemed drunk, he punched her. She fell to the ground, bleeding in snow. No one helped her. They didn't want to lose spot in line."

I was shocked. "You didn't help her?"

"Of course I did. I couldn't let her lie there in snow. I let her go in front of me in line. Others were not happy. They yelled at me too."

"Did you ever reach the front of it?"

"Yes. All that was left was bread. Crumbs, more like it. The shop owner, Yury, sometimes had items from black market, but that day I had nothing to trade him."

"What did you usually trade him?"

"My rations of vodka usually. Sometimes US dollars."

"Where did you get US dollars?"

She shrugged. "From trading something with someone else. That was how it worked. Once, I found fur hat on street. It was like finding gold. I ate very well that month."

"Someone traded you their rations for a hat?"

"A *fur* hat."

"Yeah, but if they were starving...?"

"You don't understand, Jack. It was because people had nothing that they wanted something. How do I explain? It is not wealth that makes you happy. It is simply having more than your neighbor. If you are poor, but have more than your poor neighbor, you are rich. It makes you feel good. Human nature, I suppose.

"Anyway, my point, the system was broken. Nothing worked. Then the war in Chechnya happened and everything got worse. Violence everywhere. People planting explosives in apartment buildings. Murders, robberies. So, no, Jack, my students didn't want to become astronauts. They wanted what they saw on TV, what they saw in America. Because you work hard in America, you can do anything, right? American dream, right? They just want fair chance in life." She paused for a long moment. "So you ask me if I am with Jesus for money and visa? Da, maybe. Do I love him? Do you want truth, Jack? I don't know love. I don't know what this is. But I do know surviving, and I don't want to survive always, I want to live. Can you understand that now?"

"Yeah, Eliza," I said, believing her last statement to be an apt aphorism.

"I think I can."

"I hope so."

"I can."

"Good."

We were quiet after that, during which time Elizaveta smoked her last two cigarettes and I finished off the vodka. Elizaveta's revelations had caught me off guard. I'd had no idea how tough she had it growing up in the Soviet Union and the subsequent Russia that emerged from its ashes. All I'd really known of that part of the world was what I'd seen in movies, and this was more *James Bond* than *Gorky Park*: frozen tundra, international spies, Machiavellian women, and cold-hearted assassins. And what was that bit about Elizaveta not knowing what love was? What about her family, her friends? She made it sound as though she'd grown up in an icy hell.

With these thoughts in my head, I got up to give Elizaveta some space and to check in on Lucinda. Her condition hadn't changed. She was alive but corpse-like, pallid, unresponsive, fading inward. Even her hair seemed flat, lifeless. Her rapid deterioration bothered me all the more because I was helpless to prevent it. I could not provide her the medicine or assistance she needed. I could do nothing but hope she pulled through until morning, or whenever the storm moved on. Frustrated, I was about to leave when her eyes fluttered open.

I knelt next to her. "Lucinda?" I said softly, quickly.

She stared at me.

"Lucinda?"

"...*muñeca*..."

"What?"

Her eyes closed.

"Lucinda?"

She didn't reply.

When I returned to the main room Elizaveta was exactly as she'd been, sitting cross-legged, staring at the floor. The candlelight cast a gentle chiaroscuro pattern across her features, making her appear statuesque, ageless. When I sat down, she came out of whatever trance she'd been under and looked at me.

"Lucinda opened her eyes," I said.

"*Yo-moyo!*" Elizaveta swiveled her head toward Lucinda's room. "And?"

"It was only for a couple of seconds. She's unconscious again."

"Did she speak?"

I nodded. "She said, 'Monica,' I think. Something like that. She mumbled it. But that's what it sounded like."

Elizaveta frowned. "Monica, like person?"

"I don't know. Maybe it was 'munica?'"

"Munica..." She sat straighter. "*Muñeca?*"

"Yeah, maybe," I said. "What does that mean?"

"Doll," she said.

"Are you shitting me?" I said.

Elizaveta shook her head. "*Muñeca* is Spanish for 'doll.' This island, it is called, *Isle de las Muñecas.*"

"Ah, right," I said. I pondered this, examining the possibilities, the implications, then added, "I wonder if she thinks she's in a hospital or something. She wanted to tell us where she was attacked."

"Hmmm."

"What?"

"Maybe she thinks doll attacked her."

I chuffed. "Come on, Eliza."

"I said she *thinks*. She is injured. She is dying. Maybe she is... What is word? Sees make-believe? Del...?"

"Delirious?"

"Yes, that."

I nodded. "She might not have been fully conscious. Could have been speaking from a dream."

"Should we try to wake her again?"

"How?"

"Shake her. Or pour water on her."

"On her face? I don't think that's a good idea, Eliza."

"But she could tell us what happened."

"Or go into cardiac arrest."

Elizaveta frowned. Thunder resounded. "Earlier," she said, "before Nitro...before what happened to him...you mentioned a doll. It disappeared. Do you think Solano took it?"

I nodded. "I think he's been watching us ever since we arrived at the island. I had a feeling, after I had that fight with Nitro and left you guys, I had a feeling of being watched. I thought it was the dolls...having their eyes on me. But now I think it was probably Solano. It makes sense he would follow me, doesn't it? He didn't want me stumbling across Miguel's body, or Lucinda and Rosa."

"But you found Rosa."

"And he realized he could no longer just wait and hide and hope we left. We knew something happened, we would call the police. So he went in the cabin after Rosa and I left to get more weapons or whatever he needed. That's when he must have taken the doll. I don't know why he would. Maybe it was special to him. His favorite. Actually, I think it was—the way he put makeup on it, bathed it. Anyway, he's crazy. It doesn't matter why he took it. He just did."

"He never attacked us though. When we split up, it was just Jesus, Pita, and me. Why not attack us then?"

"That's still three against one, and he's an old man. Besides, he would have known by then the storm was coming. He would have known we were staying on the island overnight. Probably figured he'd try to knock us off one by one."

"He didn't attack you or Pita. You had first watch. Why not attack you? Why wait for Jesus and Nitro?"

"Maybe he hadn't worked up the nerve yet. Or maybe he was waiting for us to all go to sleep. But when Nitro and Jesus went out, he realized we were keeping watches, and he had to act."

Elizaveta considered this. "These are many 'maybes,' Jack."

"It's speculation, yeah," I said. "But, hey, if you got something better, something that doesn't involve ghosts or animated dolls, please tell me, I'm all ears."

1957

María sat in the front of the *trajinera*, watching the trees and colorful flowers float pass on the banks of the canal. Angela was seated next to her, watching the scenery too. She wasn't the real Angela that Sister Lupita stole. She was a new one that her father had purchased for her the day before.

"What's that, Angela?" she said. "You want to go swimming?"

"Can we?" she asked.

"Do you know how to swim?"

"Not really. But I can learn."

"I guess I can learn too."

María turned to look at her mother, and her father behind her, pushing the boat with a long pole. They returned her look, puzzled. They couldn't hear her speaking to Angela. María and Angela were using their special voices that only each of them could hear.

She said out loud: "I want to go swimming."

"We're going to have a picnic first," her mother replied.

"I said I want to go swimming!"

"After we eat, sweetheart. Then you can go swimming. Is that okay?"

María faced forward again. She heard her parents talking behind her, but she ignored them. She said to Angela, "We can go swimming after we eat."

"Okay."

A short time later María's father steered the *trajinera* through weedy water until it bumped against the bank of an island. He got out and held the gondola steady as María climbed onto land first, then her mother. They went a short way inland until they found a patch of soft ground beneath a big tree. María's mother set down a *serape* for them to sit on. It was woven in shades of gray and black and had fringes at the ends. Her mother owned all sorts of these blanket-like shawls, and she used them for everything: bedspreads, sofa covers, car seat covers. There was even one hanging on the wall in the living room, next to the picture of the Virgin Mary. Before María went to Saint Agatha's School for Lost Children, she had loved all of them. They made her feel safe and special when she was curled up in one. Now, however, the *serape* on the ground meant nothing to her. In fact, if anything, it angered her. Everything seemed to anger her recently.

Except Angela.

"You're my best friend, Angela," she said in her silent voice.

"You're my best friend too."

"I'm never going to let someone take you again."

María's father and mother began unpacking the picnic basket they'd brought, setting the food on the ground: watermelon slices, tortas, nachos with avocado salsa, pickled potatoes, white-powdered cookies, candied pecans, and a big bottle of lemonade. María was hungry and stuffed herself until her belly ached. Afterward her mother asked María if she could brush her hair. María always used to like when her mother brushed her hair—when it had been long and thick—so she said yes. While brushing it, her mother began to sing a lullaby under her breath. It was one she had often sung to María when she was younger.

María closed her eyes, enjoying the warm sun on her face and the brush's bristles tickling her scalp and her mother singing in her soft, beautiful voice, and although she wasn't aware of it, she was smiling for the first time in a long, long while.

The water felt cold on María's bare feet and ankles, even though it was summer. Nevertheless, she waded farther into the canal, gripping Angela in her hand. The water rose to her knees. The rocks beneath her feet turned smooth and slimy, and she had to be careful not to slip.

She wasn't wearing a bathing suit, because she wasn't really going swimming. She was just splashing around, and that was okay with her. The hem of her dress was already wet and clinging to her thighs. That was okay too. It would dry when she got out.

She kept her eyes fixed on the water. It was very clear. She could see all the way to the bottom and the small little fish darting away from her feet.

"This is fun," she told Angela.

"Don't go too deep."

"I know that."

"Don't slip."

"I know, Angela! I'm not a baby."

On the rippling surface of the canal, she saw her reflection grinning up at her. And then she saw her father's reflection looming next to hers. His shadow fell over her.

"Turn around," Angela said quickly.

María was already turning when the rock her father was swinging struck her in the side of the head and sent her crashing into the cold water.

Jack

Close to an hour later, pushing four in the morning, the storm finally seemed to show signs of moving on. The rain still fell in relentless droves against the corrugated iron roof, but the wind and thunder had eased off, and it no longer felt as though the cabin might be torn from its foundation and tossed to Kansas.

Elizaveta and I sat in silence, trying not to fall asleep. I was lost in half-lucid thoughts of Nitro, of his blusterous personality, his machismo, how I despised yet respected him, respected not only his ability to remain cool under pressure, to lead rather than be led, but also his discipline, the work he obviously put into keeping fit, which, oddly, made his death even more tragic. In my half-lucidity I drew a comparison between a neglected yard shriveling up in a drought to a lovingly tended garden suffering the same fate. Because all those years spent lifting weights and watching what he ate...for what? He would never lift weights or eat anything again. All his hard work ceased to mean anything in the second or two it took a maniac to slit his throat open. It all seemed so senseless.

At some point I realized I didn't want to reflect on Nitro anymore, on his meaningless death, I didn't want to be sad or feel despair, and I ended up thinking about my sister, Camille. She was a year younger than me and still living in Vegas, a dancer in a show playing in the Broadway Theater at the Stratosphere Hotel and Casino. I saw the show once. It was a matinee, filled with dancing, music, and comedy. The dancing was great, the comedy not so much, with most of it being raunchy. I remember the singer though. She was pretty and a capable performer. I met her backstage. I'd been chatting with Camille when the singer—I think her name was Joan—came down the corridor carrying a bouquet of flowers, presumably given to her by an adoring member of the audience. Camille introduced us, saying, "Joan, this is my brother, Jack. He's a NASCAR driver." It always embarrassed me when she introduced me with not only my name but profession. After all, you didn't say, "This is Steve, he's a waiter over at The Olive Garden," or, "This is Joe, he's a dentist." Anyway, Camille was proud of me, I guess, and I was proud of her (and come to think of it, I do believe I've introduced her, saying, "This is Camille, she's a performer in a Vegas show").

I missed Camille. The last we saw each other was in Florida. She and my parents flew there to visit me in the hospital after the accident. They remained for a few days, leaving only when I assured them I was one hundred percent okay.

In hindsight, I wish I'd made more effort to see them over the years.

I'll be seeing them all shortly, I told myself. Once I'm back in Polanco, I'll arrange movers to transport my stuff, pay off whatever remained on the house lease, pack what I need into the Porsche, and drive north for the border. It was about a thirty-hour drive from Mexico City to Vegas. I'd split it up over a few days. I liked long road trips. Pulling over whenever you pleased, wherever you pleased, checking into random motels, trying local food, starting out again first thing in the morning with a hot coffee and some tunes on the radio. All this reminded me of the first two or three years I'd been with Pita, when we would cruise the interstates from race to race together, free as birds, our biggest concern the distance to the next rest stop when we were busting to use the toilet.

And then I saw Elizaveta in the car with me instead of Pita. The image caught me off guard, yet it excited me too. I imagined the two of us heading north through the desert, stopping at small towns for a day or a week, we had no schedule to keep, making love whenever the urge took us, only with a bed beneath us, perhaps some music, clean and showered, no fear of waking anyone else up...

Nevertheless, this was a fantasy, nothing more. Even if she wanted to run away with me, she didn't have an American visa. She wouldn't get across the border.

We could always stay in Mexico. Go south instead of north, go to *Cancún*. Live in tropical paradise—until her visa expired and she had to go home.

I could marry her.

Right. It wasn't that easy. It took time to get a greencard, there was a lot of paperwork involved, a lot of hassles.

Besides, why would I want to marry her? I barely knew her. Plus, she'd only be marrying me for the same reason she wanted to marry Jesus: money and a visa.

I glanced at Elizaveta now. She was looking at me, and I couldn't shake the feeling she knew somehow what I was thinking about.

"You look tired," she said.

"I'm okay."

"You can rest. I will keep watch—"

The door to Pepper's bedroom creaked open.

Rosa appeared. She looked guilty, as though she were up past her bedtime and knew it

I said, "What's wrong, Rosa?"

"I can't sleep," she said.

"Do you want to hang out with us?"

She nodded.

I got up and went to her, closing the door quietly behind her and leading her back to where I'd been sitting. She settled between Elizaveta and I.

"What are you guys doing?" she asked.

"Waiting," I said.

"For what?"

"For morning."

"Then we'll leave?"

"That's right."

"Good. I don't like it here."

"I don't either."

She studied the floor, and I could guess her next question.

"What happened to Muscles?" she asked.

"He was...hurt."

"Is he dead like Miguel?"

I couldn't see how lying would help any. I nodded.

"Did the ghost get him too?"

Elizaveta said, "We don't know anything for sure."

Rosa looked at her. "Why do you talk funny?"

Elizaveta blinked. "I don't talk funny."

"Yeah, you do."

"How funny?"

"Like the bad guys in movies."

Elizaveta snorted. "*American* movies."

"She's from Russia," I said. "That's how Russians speak English."

"Are there Russian movies too?" Rosa asked.

"Of course," Elizaveta said.

"I haven't seen any."

"There are, don't you worry," Elizaveta said, somewhat indignant.

"There are," I agreed. "But they're so bad nobody outside of Russia watches them."

Elizaveta made a *pfft* sound.

We fell silent and listened to the machine gun patter of rain on the roof.

Rosa said, "You promised to teach me 'Little Miss Muffet,' Jack. Can you still do that?"

"Sure," I told her. "It's really easy. It's only six lines."

"I'm ready."

I recited the nursery rhyme, explaining along the way to both Rosa and Elizaveta the words "tuffet" and "curds" and "whey."

"What a stupid song," Elizaveta said at the conclusion. "Girl sits on tuffet? Runs away from spider?"

"Have you ever heard the Russian version?"

"There is Russian version?"

I nodded and said, "Little Miss Beautymark, crawled in the dark, searching for carrots and potatoes; along came a scorpion, who made her scream like an orphan, and frightened Miss Beautymark away."

"Wait!" Rosa protested. "Eliza doesn't have a beauty mark."

"I needed something that rhymed."

"Well, 'potatoes' and 'away' don't rhyme."

"Sorry, Rosa. I was sort of making it up on the spot."

"You can be real jerk, Jack," Elizaveta said, and her eyes were daggers.

I looked at her, surprised. "It was just a joke, Eliza."

"You think being orphan is joke? You think it's funny?"

"It rhymed with scorpion, that's all."

"You didn't know I was an orphan?"

"What? No! You were an orphan?"

"Pita didn't tell you?"

"No. Eliza, I swear. Shit... If I knew..."

"You don't have any parents?" Rosa asked her.

"No," Elizaveta said, still glaring at me. But then the edge left her. She shook her head and said to Rosa softly, "They were taken away."

"Where did they go?"

"I don't know."

"Did they do something bad?"

"No. They were good people."

"So why were they taken away?"

"It is complicated," she said. "But very simply, when I was growing up, the leaders in my country had great power. They were like... Do you know puppet-master? They were like that. They controlled everything. Media, economy, political opponents, free speech. They were so afraid of losing power they used surveillance to watch everybody, and terror to keep everybody obedient. They were especially afraid of people like my parents, people who told truth. So one day they just took them away."

I was watching Elizaveta closely. I could see the pain these memories brought her.

What was it she'd told me earlier?

Not everyone has easy life like you.

I really did feel like a jackass now.

Rosa said, "I don't think I ever want too much power."

Elizaveta smiled sadly and rubbed the girl's hair.

"Why don't you try to get some sleep, Rosa?" I said.

"I'm still not tired."

"Morning will come faster if you're asleep."

"Can you sing me a lullaby?"

"Me?" I said. "No. I don't sing."

She looked at Elizaveta. "Can you?"

"I don't know lullaby."

"I can teach you one. But I only know the Spanish. Is that okay?"

"Yes, I can understand Spanish—if you don't think I will sound too funny?"

Rosa missed the sarcasm and said, "Great! It's called 'A la roro niño.' It begins like this: *A la roro niño, a lo roro ya, duérmete mi niño, duérmete mi amor.*" There were six verses in total. Rosa would sing one verse, Elizaveta would repeat it, then they would move on to the next. They were melodic, repetitive, and soothing, with long pauses and alternating harmonies. Rosa sang with a slightly higher pitch than Elizaveta, though both conveyed the emotions of love and affection.

When they finished I said, "You guys are awesome."

Rosa beamed. Elizaveta blushed.

"I know more," Rosa said. "Can we sing another? Please?"

So over the next ten or fifteen minutes Rosa and Elizaveta sang several more lullabies. Some were mournful and haunting, like a lament. Others were hypnotic and moving. All were therapeutic, lifting some of the heaviness that had settled over my heart.

While Rosa sang the latest verse, Elizaveta smiled over the girl's head at me. I smiled back. Then her eyes focused on something behind me. Uncertainty and confusion flickered in them a moment before her face drained of color.

When I was a kid, traveling the country with my parents in the RV, we'd spent much of one summer in a caravan park in Montana near the Little Belt Mountains. I'd really enjoyed it. There were the remains of railways and mines to explore, cold streams to splash in, rugged trails to follow, and a lot of neat wildlife. I made friends with a raccoon that loved toffee, a particularly brave chipmunk that would hop right onto my outstretched hand for a few nuts, and a girl from Canada named Sally who was into catching insects. Sally carried around her insect of the day in a Tic Tac container, which she liked to show off. Her prepubescent interest in entomology rubbed off on me, and soon I had my own collection of ants, beetles, butterflies, crickets, so forth. Every now and then we'd have a beetle death match. A cereal box with the back cut away served as the gladiatorial ring. Usually the chosen beetles would try to escape rather than fight each other, but they were still fun to watch and egg on. One evening, however, I left the gladiatorial ring outside during a light rainfall, and the cardboard became soggy and warped. The cereal boxes in my RV were still mostly full, so I couldn't make a new ring. I knew Sally would blame me and maybe beat me up—she was two years older and a bit of a bully—so I went to the edge of the campground to search the line of garbage bins for a cereal box. I tipped the first bin over as quietly as I could and prodded through the trash. That's when I heard a deep chuff. I turned, scanning the dark, and spotted a huge black bear no more than ten feet from me. It stood on all fours, a plastic bag hanging from its snout, just standing there and watching me. In fact, it must have been standing there and watching me for a good minute.

This had always held the title of the scariest moment of my life—until now—when I turned around and saw the eye peering through a hole in the wall, watching us.

The hole was an excised knot in a plank of wood maybe three feet from the ground. It was the size of a golf ball. The iris of the eye peering through it appeared brownish-red, surrounded with white. It gleamed wetly in the candlelight.

Then it blinked.

Elizaveta and Rosa leapt to their feet but remained oddly silent, as if they'd lost their voices. I was on my feet too, my blood icy sludge in my veins. I snagged the pistol from the waistband of my shorts. I raised it toward the devilish eye and squeezed the trigger.

Click.

The safety!

I found it, flicked it off, aimed at the eye again.

It was gone.

Nevertheless, I squeezed off two shots. The rounds blew two new holes through the wall.

The reports were earsplitting and toneless. Blue smoked trailed up from the end of the barrel. Cordite filled my nostrils.

Jesus and Pita emerged from the bedroom, demanding to know what was going on.

"Solano's outside!" I said, shoving the table aside and throwing open the door. I expected an ambush, a blade to arc through the air.

Nothing.

I swung the pistol to the left, to the right.

Nobody on the porch.

I scanned the dark forest.

Nobody fleeing.

Nobody anywhere.

From behind me Jesus swore softly.

He was looking at Nitro's body. It was exactly where we'd left it. I was about to ask him what was wrong when I noticed Nitro's eyes—or lack of eyes.

Like Miguel's, they were missing.

1957

She sank below the surface of the canal in a cloud of red until she came to rest on the rock-covered bottom. Unconscious, she wasn't holding her breath. Instead water gushed down her airway, filling her lungs, preventing the transfer of oxygen to her blood. There would be a feeling of tearing and burning inside her chest, though she wasn't aware of this. She was blissfully ignorant of any physical sensation.

Then her breathing stopped altogether, and she was in respiratory arrest.

Somewhere deep inside of her, however, in the womb of her mind where all thoughts were born and most dwelled without being spoken out loud or acted upon, she was wondering why this was happening to her, and this bewilderment was mixed with surprise that she was drowning, that she was dying.

And then the strangest thing happened. She experienced a kind of hiccup, and the part of her responsible for these thoughts was outside of her body. It was floating back up through the water, through the surface, and she could see her little body lying at the bottom of the canal, convulsing violently now, in the final stages of death, and she could see her father and mother already in the gondola, moving quickly away, her father's face a steely mask as he pushed the boat with the pole, her mother sobbing into her hands.

And as she watched them leaving her for a second time, abandoning her to her cruel fate, a hatred of frustration and despair roared through her, consuming her entirely, a banshee-like madness driven by a single purpose.

Revenge.

Elizaveta

Jesus blundered into the cabin, his face manic with fear, shouting in Spanish that Nitro's eyes were missing. Pita moaned miserably. Elizaveta felt sick. Whoever was out there—*Solano, it was only Solano, an old man*—took Nitro's eyes too? But why?

She clutched Rosa against her, covering her ears with her hands.

Jack returned next, pistol in hand. He seemed agitated.

"Did you hit him, Jack?" Elizaveta asked.

He shook his head. "He got away."

"What did you see?" Jesus demanded. "What did you shoot at?"

Elizaveta pointed at the knothole. "Solano was watching us through that."

"Watching you? Christ! For how long?"

"I don't know. Maybe five minutes? Maybe all night?"

Jesus whirled on Jack. "And you let him get away? How did he get away? You had a *gun*."

"The safety was on. I wasn't ready."

"Fuck, Jack!" Jesus exclaimed. "You could have killed him!"

"Whatever, he didn't do anything. Everybody's okay—"

"He took Nitro's eyes!"

"Did you see him, Jack?" Pita asked. Her hair was tousled and frizzy from the wind and rain, while mascara and dried tears streaked her cheeks, making her look zombie-like. "Solano? Did you actually see Solano?"

"I saw his eye watching us."

"But did you see *him*?"

461

"I know what you're going to say—"

"*Did you see him?*"

"He ran away when I fucking shot at him, Pita. Since when do ghosts run away from bullets? Wouldn't bullets go straight through them?"

She clamped her mouth shut.

Jesus said, "Maybe you should give the gun to me, Jack."

"Fuck no," he said.

"You blew your chance. Give me the gun."

"Blew my chance?"

"You weren't prepared! You let him get away!"

"And you've been super vigilant sleeping in the fucking bedroom—"

Jesus punched Jack, striking him directly in the nose. There was a sound like knuckles cracking. Jack spun away, dropping the pistol and cupping his nose. He examined his hands, which were bright red with blood. Jesus stood on the balls of his feet, holding his ground, ready to run. Jack charged him. Jesus made for Lucinda's room. Jack, however, caught him before he could barricade himself inside the room, hefting him off his feet and slamming him to the ground.

Pita leapt on Jack's back, wrapping her arms around his neck.

"Go to the bedroom!" Elizaveta told Rosa, shooing the girl away.

Rosa fled.

Elizaveta ran into the fray, wrapping her own arms around Pita's neck and pulling the smaller woman free. Pita shrieked and cursed. Elizaveta tripped and fell, dragging Pita with her.

"Bitch!" Pita yelled, flipping onto her front.

"Calm down!"

Pita didn't. She was possessed. She snagged fistfuls of Elizaveta's hair and yanked so hard Elizaveta rocked forward. She clawed blindly at Pita. She grabbed something soft—a breast? She squeezed. Pita screeched, then yanked Elizaveta's hair harder.

Scalp on fire, Elizaveta got hold of the throat of Pita's chambray shirt. She tugged with all her strength. Buttons popped. Pita screeched. Her left hand released Elizaveta's hair and went after her pink top, hooking her fingers around the collar and pulling. Fabric tore with a zipper-like sound.

Elizaveta shouted, more in frustration than anger or embarrassment. They were having a stupid catfight while Solano was outside somewhere. He might return, burst into the cabin wielding his knife while they were all distracted.

Elizaveta brought her knees to her chest and tried using her feet to push Pita away. Pita clutched Elizaveta's hair with both hands again, shaking as though she were trying to dislodge stubborn weeds from the ground.

Elizaveta kicked. Her foot struck Pita in the gut. Pita's grip loosened.

Elizaveta kicked again. This time her foot winged Pita's face.

The bitch finally released her.

Elizaveta tumbled away, the roots of her hair raw with pain. Pita lay on her side, panting, her bottom lip bleeding.

"Jesus!" Elizaveta said, pushing herself to her feet.

Somehow Jesus had gotten the better of Jack, and he now knelt on top of him, his hands around Jack's throat, strangling him.

He didn't show any signs of hearing her—or letting up.

The pistol lay on the floor a meter from her. She retrieved it, surprised by its cold, heavy weight. She aimed the barrel at the ceiling and squeezed the trigger.

The report boomed.

Jesus turned his head to look at her. His face was so twisted with hatred she barely recognized him.

"Get off him!" she said.

"Put that down!"

"Get off him!"

"Put—"

Jack bucked Jesus off him and rolled away, wheezing.

Jesus seemed ready to go for him again, while Pita was on all fours, spider-like, ready to come after her.

She fired a second round.

"Stop!" she shouted. "Everybody stop!"

Jack crab-scuttled farther away from Jesus. Blood smeared his chin. More blood soaked his tank top on the left side of his abdomen.

Had one of her bullets ricocheted off the ceiling and struck him there?

Elizaveta hurried to him, giving Pita a wide birth.

"Give me that," he said, holding a hand out for the pistol.

She hesitated only a moment before pressing the gun's grip into his palm.

He immediately swung the weapon at Jesus, who was bending over, picking up something.

A knife, she realized. A blood-drenched knife.

Had he stabbed Jack?

"Put it down," Jack told him.

"Put the gun down," Jesus retorted. The bangs of his usually slicked back hair hung in front of his face. His left shirt tail dangled from his pants. At some point he'd lost a penny loafer; one foot was bare.

"I don't think so, Jesus."

"What are you going to do, Jack? Shoot me?"

"I'm pretty tempted right now."

"Dammit, Jesus," Elizaveta said. "You *stabbed* him? Are you crazy?"

"Jesus...?" Pita said, appearing confused. She stood up. Her chambray shirt hung open to her sternum, revealing her breasts in a lacy bra a size too small so it acted like a corset, ballooning her cleavage.

"He attacked me," Jesus protested. "He was going insane."

"Where'd you get that knife, Jesus?" Jack asked. He pushed himself to his knees and grimaced, his free hand going to his bleeding abdomen.

Elizaveta helped him the rest of the way to his feet.

"Are you okay?" she asked, worried.

Ignoring her, he said to Jesus: "Where?"

He shrugged. "The kitchen. When you and Pita were outside, on watch."

"Where in the kitchen?"

"On the counter."

"Jack, stop pointing that gun," Pita said. "You're scaring me."

Jack ignored her too. "On the counter, huh?"

"So what?" Jesus said.

"Eliza, go see if there's a knife on the counter."

Elizaveta crossed the main room, wondering what was going on. Why did it matter where the knife was from? She poked her head in the kitchen, wrinkling her nose at the smell of something rotten. It was dark, no candles lit. Yet her eyes had long ago adjusted to the dim environment, and she could see well enough. A couple of bowls and plates rested on the counter. Next to them was a single fork. No knife.

She returned to the others. "No knife."

"See?" Jesus said. "Now stop pointing that fucking gun at me, Jack."

"I saw that knife earlier," Jack said. "When I was here by myself, when I first found Rosa."

"So what? I told you—"

"There wasn't any blood on it."

"Well, you shouldn't have attacked me, Jack. It was self-defense."

"There was blood on it before you stabbed me, Jesus."

A deep silenced ensured.

"What are you talking about, Jack?" Pita demanded.

Elizaveta frowned, trying to make sense of this. Where did the blood come from if it wasn't Jack's—

Her breath hitched in her throat.

"Nitro?" she said so quietly she wasn't sure she'd spoken out loud.

"Nitro?" Pita repeated, apparently hearing her. "Would someone please tell me what's going on?"

"Why'd you kill him?" Jack asked Jesus.

"Killed *who*?" Pita said. "*Nitro?*"

Jesus chuckled, shaking his head. "Are you listening to yourself, Jack?"

"What's he talking about, Jesus?" Pita asked him.

"Nothing. He doesn't know anything. This is bullshit."

"Why'd you kill him?" Jack repeated.

"Stop it, Jack!" Pita said. "Why are you saying this? Why would Jesus ever want to kill Nitro?" She glanced around the room, as if for answers. Her eyes paused on the empty vodka bottle on the floor, next to Elizaveta's forgotten garden claw and Jack's hay hook. "You've been drinking, Jack.

Are you drunk?"

"He's not drunk," Elizaveta said.

Pita whirled on her, temper flaring. "Shut up, bitch! Jesus is your *boyfriend*. You should be on his side. Why are you listening to Jack?"

"Where's your jacket?" Jack asked Jesus.

He shrugged. "I took it off."

"Where is it?"

"In the other hut. I didn't bring it."

Elizaveta thought back. She couldn't remember whether he'd worn his tweed jacket to the cabin or not. She'd had much more on her mind this night than trivialities such as clothing.

"Unroll your sleeves," Jack said.

Jesus had rolled the sleeves of his white button-down shirt to his elbows. "Fuck you, Jack," he said. "I've had enough of this."

"Me too, Jack," Pita said, going to Jesus's side. "You're acting like a lunatic."

"Eliza," Jack said, "check the bedrooms for his blazer."

"Jack..." Jesus said, taking a step forward.

Jack raised the pistol from Jesus's chest to his head.

Jesus stopped.

"Eliza, go."

Elizaveta checked Lucinda's room first, opening the dresser drawers, peeking beneath the bed. There was no jacket.

She was halfway to Pepper's room when the door opened. Rosa stood at the threshold, half in shadows, Jesus's tweed blazer balled against her chest. She had obviously been listening through the door.

"It was in the corner," she said.

"Give that to me," Jesus snapped, reaching for her.

She dodged his hand, then dashed across the room.

"Good girl," Jack said, taking the blazer. He shook it out, then held it up by the collar so everyone could see it.

Blood stained the left sleeve, from cuff to elbow.

Elizaveta felt hot and cold at the same time.

Could this be true?

Could Jesus have murdered Nitro?

No—there had to be a more mundane explanation for the blood.

"Let me guess," Jack said. "You're left-handed, Jesus?"

Jesus was shaking his head again, looking at the floor. He appeared to be smiling.

"Da," Elizaveta said. "He is."

Pita's saucer eyes bounced back and forth between Jesus and Jack. Finally they settled on Jack. "Why are you doing this, Jack?" she asked him. "You know Jesus wouldn't kill Nitro. So why are you doing this?"

"He has the murder weapon in his hand, Pita. Nitro's blood is on his jacket's sleeve. Maybe I'm wrong. I hope I am. But we're going to have to let the police figure that out. Jesus—put down the knife."

Jesus didn't.

Jack aimed the pistol at his legs. "You have three seconds."

"Jack!" Pita said.

"One..."

"Jack..." Elizaveta said.

"Two—"

"Okay!" Jesus set the knife on the floor.

"Kick it toward me."

Jesus hesitated, then kicked the knife. It clattered across the wooden planks, stopping several feet short of Jack. Rosa scooted from behind Jack's legs, retrieved the weapon, and returned to her refuge behind his legs.

"Tell me this isn't true, Jesus," Pita said.

"It's not. Of course it's not. It's bullshit."

"Then what about the blood...?"

"Jack's set me up."

"Oh, fuck off," Jack said.

"Nitro was my best friend, Pita," Jesus said. "We were like brothers. I loved the guy. Jack's the one who hated him."

"You were outside with him when he was killed!" Jack said. "I was inside.

With Eliza and Rosa."

"It's true!" Rosa said.

It was true, Elizaveta thought, though her mind was spinning. She was suddenly more confused than ever.

"I'm not saying Jack actually slit Nitro's throat. But he organized it." Jesus paused. "He's working with whoever's out there in the storm."

Everyone looked at Jack, Elizaveta included. She didn't believe Jack put a hit on Nitro. It was absurd.

Wasn't it?

"Give me a fucking break, Jesus," Jack said.

"You had the chance to shoot him," Jesus said. "Whoever was outside watching you guys through that hole. You had a chance to shoot him but you didn't."

"And I suppose I murdered Miguel too, huh?"

"I don't know. Did you? I certainly didn't."

"I'm not listening to this shit." He wiggled the pistol at Jesus. "Get on your knees."

"Jack," Pita said. "I think you need to put down the gun."

"Get to your knees!"

"Jack, stop it!" Pita said.

"You hated Nitro!" Jesus shouted. "You set this up! You killed him!"

"I didn't even know he was coming until this fucking morning!"

"Give me the gun, Jack."

"Get to your knees!"

"Jack!" Pita screeched.

"Eliza," Jack said. "Go get me Pepper's belt."

"His belt? Why?" she asked. The air was thick with confusion. She didn't know what was going on, who to believe.

"I'm going to tie Jesus up."

"Eliza," Jesus said. "Don't listen to him."

She glanced from Jack to Jesus, frozen with indecision.

Rosa bolted to the bedroom, returning a moment later with Pepper's purple belt.

"Pita," Jack said, "move away from your brother."

"You can't tell me what to do."

"Move, or I swear to God I'll put a bullet in his knee."

Glowering, she moved away a few steps.

"Get down," Jack told Jesus, approaching him cautiously.

"You won't get away with this," he said.

"Get down!"

Jesus lowered himself to his knees.

"Put your arms out, wrists together."

"Fuck you."

Jack pistol-whipped him on the temple, though not very hard.

"Ow!" Jesus said.

"Jack!" Pita said.

"Do it!"

Jesus put his arms out.

"Rosa, you're going to need to—"

"No," Elizaveta said, getting hold of herself. She had to pick a side, and she knew in her heart Jack didn't have anything to do with Nitro's murder. "I will."

She took the belt from Rosa, then went to Jesus and bound his wrists together. She could feel Pita's eyes into her.

"Is it tight?" Jack asked.

"Yes."

Jack pressed his foot against Jesus's chest and pushed him, so he toppled backward onto his butt. "Stay," he said.

Jack

Rosa and Elizaveta and I sat against one wall inside the cabin, Jesus and Pita against another. I set the pistol on the floor next to me and peeled off my tank top. The knife wound was far to the left of my navel, deeper than it was wide. I could barely see the laceration beneath the fresh-flowing blood, but I could feel my heartbeat in it, steady and slow, an unwelcomed reminder of my mortality.

The stabbing played over again in my head, step by step. I'd prevented Jesus from escaping to one of the bedrooms and tossed him to the floor. Pita leapt on my back. Elizaveta pried her away. I hiked Jesus up by the collar of his shirt and slammed him into the wall. I slammed him a second time and heard Pita and Elizaveta scuffling behind me. I turned to check on them. That's when Jesus withdrew the knife from beneath his shirt and slid it into my side. I didn't feel any pain; I was too keyed up on adrenaline. But my first thoughts were: *He stabbed me. The fucker stabbed me.* I looked down, saw the blood, and stepped away from him. I figured the fight was over, but Jesus came at me, throwing his weight into me and knocking me down, knocking the pistol from my grip. Then he was on top of me, his hands around my throat, squeezing. My vision blurred, spun—then the gunshot. Jesus released my throat, and I bucked him off me to find Pita on her side with a bloody lip and Elizaveta standing a few yards away, holding the gun in her shaking hands.

"This is not good, Jack," Elizaveta said. She was kneeling next to me, examining the wound. Rosa stood by her, a serious expression on her face.

"Nice bedside manner," I said.

"What does that mean?"

I shook my head. "It's not as bad as it looks."

"It looks bad."

"It doesn't even hurt very much."

"Maybe you're in shock."

"I'm not in shock."

"Maybe you are bleeding inside."

"Seriously, Eliza, knock it off."

"I'm trying to help."

"It doesn't look very bad, Jack," Rosa said.

"Thank you, Rosa."

"It really doesn't," she added. "I cut my knee once, and it bled almost as much. But I didn't even have to go to the doctor's office. My mom just rinsed it with water, put some stuff on it that stung, and then a bandage."

"Do you have any vital organs in your knee?" Elizaveta asked her.

"What's a vital organ?"

I folded my tank top into a square and pressed it against the cut. I hissed with pain and closed my eyes. I could feel the shirt turn spongy with blood. When I opened my eyes, I was looking across the room. Pita was in front of Jesus, trying to free his hands. I snatched the pistol from the floor and pointed it at them.

"Get away from him!" I said.

Elizaveta and Rosa spun to look.

Pita and Jesus stiffened, both appearing very suspect.

"Move away from him, Pita."

"Why?" she said. "We were just talking."

"You were removing the belt."

"I was not."

"I saw you! Now move away from him."

"Or what, Jack?" Jesus said. "You going to call your accomplice? Have us killed too?"

"He'll beat you up!" Rosa said.

"Getting seven year olds to fight your fights, are you now, Jack?"

"I'm eight," Rosa said defiantly.

"Pita, last warning," I said. "Move away from him."

Her expression hovered somewhere between vexed and sulky. But after several long seconds of pointed insolence she moved away.

"We know why you killed him," she stated.

I was growing sick of this accusation, but since I had not killed Nitro, I was curious to hear what she might have to say. "Enlighten me," I said.

"You knew Nitro and I were having an affair."

It wasn't so much what she said—I'd known about the affair for the last couple of hours now—that pissed me off; it was the way she said it. She seemed proud of the fact she'd cheated on me.

"I've been meaning to talk to you about that," I said.

"So you *did* know!"

"I told him tonight," Elizaveta said.

"How did *you* know?"

"I saw you and Nitro on beach."

"You were spying on us?"

"I went for a walk. You were there."

"I can't believe you're taking Jack's side in all this, cariño," Jesus said. "You know me. You know I'd never murder anyone."

"I know you stabbed Jack."

"He *attacked* me."

"You *stabbed* him."

"Eliza, you're my partner. I care for you. Come over here, join Pita and me. I'll forget all this nonsense."

"I can't do that, Jesus."

"Yes you can. Get up and come over here. Now."

"No, Jesus."

"Don't say no to me."

"No."

"*You don't say no to me!*" Jesus roared. Then, collecting himself: "You know what you're doing, don't you? You're putting yourself on a one-way plane back to Russia."

Elizaveta clamped her jaw. I did too.

Jesus was back to his usual ways, playing cheap.

"A couple of calls," he went on. "That's all it will take. They'll revoke your visa and you'll be on a plane. Is that what you want? To be a schoolteacher making piss all in Russia for the rest of your life? I can offer you so much more."

I wanted to say something, to tell Jesus to shut his trap, to tell him he was full of it, but this wasn't my fight. It was Elizaveta's. She had to see through his ploy on her own.

"Offer me what?" she asked.

"Everything!" Jesus said. "As my wife, you'll have whatever you want."

"You'll never marry me."

"Of course I will. I love you."

"He does," Pita insisted.

"Don't you see how ridiculous this is?" Jesus said. "You sitting over there with Jack Goff? He's a loser. A has-been. He's an alcoholic and a murderer—"

"Quiet."

"Eliza—"

"Quiet!"

My head ached, my neck and shoulders ached, the wound in my side ached. My entire body, in fact, ached. I swallowed dryly. My throat felt mummified. But I was too buggered to get up and refill Elizaveta's bucket with rainwater. I glanced at my wristwatch through a film of gritty fatigue. It was 4:10 a.m., which meant another hour or so until dawn. Everyone had settled down, and for the last half hour they were either sleeping or pretending to sleep. I yawned silently and fought the urge to close my eyes myself, even for a moment, knowing I would be out as quickly as a man on an anesthesia drip. Whenever my eyelids began to droop, I pressed the tank top harder against the wound in my abdomen. The resulting pain functioned like an electric shock, zapping me awake.

I was getting worried about the gash. Aside from aching all over, I felt lightheaded and dizzy. I tried to recall what I'd learned about the human anatomy in high school biology, but back then filling my friends' pencil cases with fish eyes or frog legs during dissection classes had been more important than listening to the teacher or studying the textbook. Nevertheless, I was pretty sure my liver was on my right side, which meant it was safe. Kidneys were on both sides, which scared me a bit. I had no idea where my pancreas was, but I believed my spleen was on my left side too. So had the knife blade punctured a kidney? My pancreas, my spleen? Maybe it nicked an important vein or artery. Like Elizaveta said, I could be bleeding internally. This could explain the lightheadedness...

My eyelids were drooping. I applied pressure to the wound.

I inhaled sharply—but the pain was good. It kept me alert.

I glanced again at my wristwatch. 4:16.

Christ, the minutes were slugging by.

Another hour—an hour and a half, tops.

Yeah, until first light maybe. But what about the boatman? When was he going to show up?

This was something I'd spent a fair bit of time thinking about. Not if the boatman would return. I was sure he would. He knew we were out here, stranded. He also knew we had money. I wasn't sure whether Jesus paid him the full fee up front, but I didn't think so. That would have been stupid, and Jesus wasn't stupid. Which meant the guy would be back. So the question wasn't if the boatman would return, but when.

The worst of the storm had definitely moved on. I could still hear the rain falling against the corrugated iron roof, but it was no longer a full-on assault; more a steady drizzle. Come dawn I was hoping it would have ceased altogether, but even if it didn't, the canals should be navigable. And this was where it would boil down to the boatman's character. Was he the type of guy who would wake up bright and early to come get us? Or would he sleep in, go about his morning chores, fill his belly, and come get us when the moment suited him? I wanted to believe the former option, of course, but if I was being honest with myself, which I was, the latter option seemed more plausible. After all, he didn't know us, he didn't owe us. He warned us about going to the island. He might think leaving us stranded here for a while was a suitable punishment, a lesson learned.

A lesson learned.

Right. And what was that lesson?

Don't go snooping around creepy islands?

Don't trespass on private property?

This got me thinking about our reception when we returned to Xochimilco. One thing people couldn't get enough of was seeing the high and mighty fall, and Mexicans were no different. Jesus might not be a famous politician, or athlete, or movie star. But he ran one of the country's premiere breweries. He was a bigshot in his own right. Moreover, he was young and handsome, key ingredients for juicy scandal. Throw into the pot an island infested with dolls and supposedly haunted by the ghost of a little girl and you had nationwide headlines.

Would Jesus be convicted?

I wasn't sure. I knew he was guilty, but would a judge reach the same conclusion? After all, Jesus would surround himself with the best lawyers. He would have numerous connections to lean on. Not to mention the crime scene was a mess. We'd tramped through Nitro's blood, moved his body, handled the murder weapon.

And you're forgetting about Miguel and Lucinda and Mr. Peeping Tom. How did they all fit into this? Did I still believe the Peeping Tom was Solano? But if not him, who?

Nationwide headlines? This was going to be the story of the fucking year. And to my chagrin I was going to be right in the center of all it.

4:24 a.m.

Nitro's missing eyes. Black, empty orbits in his bloodied face. I couldn't rid myself of the macabre image. Almost as bad was the thought of Solano sitting out there, nothing but a wall separating him from us, bent over Nitro's face, cutting, sawing, pulling.

4:35 a.m.

Elizaveta rotated her right shoulder, as if it were stiff. Then she reached her left arm beneath her right armpit and prodded the spot where the scorpion had stung her back with her fingers. She kept her eyes closed. I didn't think she was doing this in her sleep. She was awake, or at least semi-awake. Even so, I didn't say anything. I didn't ask her what was wrong, or how she was feeling. What was the point? She would either tell me she was fine, which would likely be a lie, or she would tell me she couldn't feel her shoulder, or something equally frightening. And there was nothing I could do about that. There was nothing any of us could do.

Except wait.

4:41a.m.

Lucinda. Was she confused when she mentioned a doll? Delirious? Speaking through a dream? The doll on the table, gone, misappropriated somehow. Did Solano take it? But why? Because he was crazy? Wanted company? A grown man?

What was I missing?

4:50 a.m.

The ghost of the little girl. I hated myself for even contemplating this possibility. I felt like a kid at a sleepover being dared to look in the bathroom mirror at midnight to see Bloody Mary's reflection, sans scalp, which was said to have been torn away when she got her hair trapped in the doors of an elevator cab. Nonsense, of course. No grown adult could take it seriously. Just as no grown adult could—or at least should—take seriously the legend of a girl haunting an island in the middle of nowhere.

So why was I contemplating it?

I wasn't.

I couldn't help it if silly thoughts popped in my head.

Ghosts didn't exist.

Because if they did?

Well, if they did, I'd be more compelled to believe that my out of body experience hadn't been dead neurons firing, that I had indeed been crossing over to some other plane of existence, that the white light existed, along with whatever evil dwelled within it—

That was a dream.

But was it?

A dream—or a memory?

Fuck, Jack. Stop it. You're going to drive yourself batshit crazy.

Ghosts didn't exist.

Devils didn't exist.

Eternal suffering didn't exist.

End of story.

5:01a.m.

A humming had started in my skull, from fear or hunger or fatigue, I wasn't sure. My legs had gone numb from sitting in the same position for so long. I stretched the left one out in front of me, then the right, careful not to disturb Rosa, whose head was resting on it. Her eyes were closed, her mouth parted slightly. Her breathing was deep and regular.

Looking at her, a warmth bloomed in my chest. She was so small and innocent and beautiful. And brave. What other kid her age would cope with all the shit going on as well as she had? I certainly wouldn't have at her age. I wasn't really doing such a good job now at twenty-eight.

Her strength made her inexplicable affection for me all the more endearing. She'd even stood up for me, telling Jesus, "He'll beat you up!" I smiled to myself, but it was a smile of sadness. She shouldn't be here, going through this. She should be at home, in her bed, waking to her family and a warm breakfast, perhaps attending Sunday church, and later, playing jump rope and other games with her neighborhood friends.

Stroking her head affectionately with the back of my fingers, I vowed right then not to let her down, not to let any harm come to her. I would get her home safe and sound.

Even as I told myself this, however, I wondered whether it was true.

After all, how could I make such a promise when I didn't know for certain who or what was out there stalking us, hunting us, plotting our demise?

Who, Jack. Not what—who. No crazy Pita thinking, okay?

Okay.

Rosa's eyelids fluttered, then opened. Her brown eyes looked up at me. "Is it morning?"

"Not yet," I said.

She began to sit up.

"Go back to sleep," I told her.

"I can't. The floor's too hard."

"Come," Elizaveta said. As I'd suspected, she wasn't sleeping. Her eyes were open now, alert, and she held out her hand. "I'll take you to bed."

"I don't want to leave Jack."

"He'll be okay."

"He's hurt."

"I'm fine," I told her. "Go with Eliza."

Elizaveta and Rosa stood and crossed the room quietly, wraithlike in the candlelight and layered shadows.

Jesus, I noticed, raised his head and watched them until they disappeared into Pepper's room. Pita remained motionless on her side, sleeping.

"How does it feel, Jack?" Jesus asked me, speaking for the first time in a while.

"How does what feel?" I said, suspecting I was rising to some bait.

"Knowing Pita was fucking Nitro behind your back?"

I almost told him *not so bad after I fucked Elizaveta behind his back.* Instead I said, "How does it feel knowing you're going to be fucked six ways from Sunday in prison?"

"I'm not going to prison."

"I'm not so sure about that."

"I'm not. You know that. I know that."

"We'll see."

"Jack, Jack, Jack."

"Jesus, Jesus, Jesus."

"I don't like you, Jack. I never have. I think maybe it's time I make that perfectly clear."

"Oh, it's been clear for a while."

"I don't know what my father ever saw in you. But he was grossly mistaken."

"Not just your father, Jesus. Your sister too. Seems to me like your entire family was a Jack Goff fan. You're the odd one out."

"Seems to *me* like you didn't know how to satisfy a woman, otherwise Pita wouldn't have gone looking elsewhere for a real man."

"A real man? You've been reading too much *Cosmo*, pal."

"You know why I pulled support for you and your team?"

"Bad business sense?"

"Funny, Jack."

"No joke, Jesus. Your father built that brewery from nothing. He knew what he was doing. He knew the importance of breaking into the US market. He knew the returns would come. If he were alive today, the company would be worth five times its current value."

"You're dumber than you look, Jack."

"I'm not the only one who thinks this."

"What are you talking about?"

"I've followed the company, Jesus. And the pundits seem to agree with me. Pulling out of the US was a massive mistake, and nothing much has been going right for you since."

"Where do you get your news?" he snapped. "The *Gringo Gazette?*"

"Must be a pretty shitty feeling to know your entire board of directors is thinking about voting to oust you from your own company, huh?"

"You know nothing. *Nothing.* Dumping you was absolutely the right decision. Because you're a fuckup, Jack, a cocky, reckless, impulsive fuckup. I knew that from the moment I met you—"

"You let your personal feelings cloud your business judgment—"

"—before you crashed and ruined your career," he went on, speaking over me, "before you started drinking yourself to the gutter. I knew that, and I was right. *I was right.* Because look at you now. You're no longer just a fuckup. You've managed to become a drunk as well." He smiled mirthlessly. "You're a fucking joke, Jack. So congratulations—you've finally lived up to your name."

Elizaveta

Elizaveta helped Rosa into bed next to Pepper, who remained fast asleep, then pulled the sheet and rug up to her chin.

"What if I can't fall asleep?" Rosa asked.

"Huh?" Elizaveta said. Jesus and Jack were speaking to each other, and she was trying to hear what they were saying.

"What if I can't fall asleep?"

"Then you count sheep."

"That never works."

"Then imagine ice melting."

"What?"

"That is what children in Russia do. Trust me, it works."

"I don't know..."

"I will come back and wake you soon."

"Eliza?" she asked.

"Yes?"

"Will I see you and Jack again?"

"What do you mean?"

"After today?"

"Da, if you want to. If your mother lets you."

"Well, I'll probably be grounded for a month. But after that, maybe I can visit you and Jack? Maybe we can have a sleepover. Not like tonight. A fun one, with movies and stuff. I'm allowed sleepovers sometimes."

"Oooh. I don't know about that."

"Why not?"

"Jack and I don't live together."

"You don't?"

Elizaveta shook her head. "Jack lives with Pita."

"Who do you live with then?"

"I live by myself."

"That's great then! Jack and I can sleepover at your house."

Elizaveta smiled. "Go to sleep, Rosa."

Jack and Jesus had fallen silent. Elizaveta returned to her previous spot against the wall and sat down. She wanted to ask Jack what they were talking about—fighting about, more like it—and for a moment she wondered if it could have been her. Had Jack told Jesus what happened earlier? Instead of experiencing guilt over her infidelity and fear of Jesus's reaction, she felt strangely invigorated. *Had Jack been fighting over her?* No. This was a fantasy, her ego running away with itself. They'd had sex, that was all. And they'd only had sex because she'd instigated it. There was nothing more to it than carnal pleasure, a temporary escape. Why would there be? He was rich and famous and could have any woman in the world he wanted. She was just some displaced and disillusioned Russian schoolteacher with a closetful of skeletons and a headful of issues.

Jesus chose me.

But that was because he wanted a trophy girlfriend, something exotic to show off to his buddies. And that was all she ever was to him, wasn't it? Yes, it was. In their twelve months together he never told her he loved her. He never spoke of children. Marriage? The first she'd heard of it was earlier tonight, or this morning, and he'd only mentioned it to manipulate her like a pawn on a chessboard, to make her rebuke Jack and join his side. Ironically his efforts made her see the truth. He was simply using her to fulfill his needs and wants, to boost his self-esteem. Their relationship was a farce. It never stood a chance. She supposed, deep down, she always understood this, but she'd been so desperate for security and stability she'd refused to see what was right in front of her face. That was the double edge of hope: it made you weak, blind, foolish.

Elizaveta wondered whether Jesus would go through with his threat of getting her visa revoked. She knew he had the means to if he so pleased. If you had money in Mexico, and you were well-connected, you could do whatever you wanted, regardless of the law. Case in point, one night she and Jesus went to a trendy restaurant without a reservation and the owner refused to seat them. Furious and embarrassed, Jesus called a friend who ran the government's consumer protection agency, and the next day inspectors shut down the restaurant.

So if he wanted to get her visa revoked, he could do it. Not that she really cared. Her visa expired soon enough anyway. The bottom line was that she'd wasted her opportunity in Mexico, wasted it pursuing Jesus, pursuing a life that could never be, and now, whether it was sooner or later, she would inevitably be getting on a plane back to Russia.

Elizaveta was nodding off and tugged her head up. She was very lethargic. Keeping her eyes open took all her concentration. She wasn't sure whether this was a consequence of remaining awake all night, or whether it was a symptom of the scorpion's venom. She rotated her shoulder for the countless time. It had been stiff for a while now, the area around the puncture wound tingly and tender, almost as if a low-voltage current was running beneath her skin.

At least she hadn't suffered an allergic reaction. She wasn't drooling or twitching. She could still breathe and speak normally, which hopefully meant she wasn't going to drop dead from respiratory failure. Yet the scorpion sting still concerned her. She'd seen a picture of a young boy in a magazine once who'd been bitten on the ankle by a snake, and his entire lower leg had turned black and rotten, like something that belonged to an unwrapped mummy. And maybe, if she didn't receive anti-venom soon, that would happen to her shoulder. Her flesh would necrotize, spreading out from the puncture, consuming her shoulder, her arm, destroying cells and tissue, rendering her limb dead and useless, so the only medical option available (if they ever got off this island) would be amputation.

Jack reached over and took her hand in his, suddenly, unexpectedly. He

483

shifted so he was facing her, then leaned toward her. His lips pressed against hers. Their mouths parted, their tongues explored.

Elizaveta's heart raced. In the back of her mind she wondered whether Jesus was watching them—and realized she didn't care.

Jack liked her after all!

His hands moved off her waist, down her back, slipping beneath her shirt. They were soft and warm on her bare skin. They moved up. His fingers unclipped her bra. Then his hands were moving down again, beneath the waistband at the back of her shorts, beneath the elastic band of her panties.

He kissed the side of her neck, gently, affectionately, his lips like butterfly wings. He nibbled her earlobe. Tremors of pleasure tickled down her spine.

"Jack..."

Then his lips were on hers again, silencing her. Her breasts, loose in her bra, pressed against his chest. Her groin pressed against. He was aroused.

His hands sank deeper down her shorts. They clutched the cleft of her rear, strong now, rough, pulling her tighter against him. One curled around the inside of her thigh, moving higher, brushing her—

A noise startled them apart.

Elizaveta opened her eyes. The room was cauldron-black. Someone had extinguished the candles while she'd had her eyes closed.

Jesus?

Where was he?

Her heart continued to race, though no longer from pleasure but fear.

She heard the noise again.

Rusty hinges?

"What was that?" she whispered.

"Trapdoor," Jack said.

Why would someone be going down into the crawlspace?

Or were they coming out?

"Jack—"

"Shhh."

A heavy crash. The hatch slapping the floor. Then scuffling.

Someone climbing the ladder?

Elizaveta jammed a hand into the pocket of her shorts and produced her lighter. She clicked the button frantically. Metal struck the flint three times before a spark ignited the butane and a small flame whooshed into existence.

Holding the lighter high and in front of her, she gasped.

Two dolls stood before the trapdoor. They stared at her with their glass eyes and their furtive smiles. One wore a diaphanous tutu and nothing else, and its head seemed to have been transplanted onto its body from another doll, as it was much too large and a different skin tone. The other wore a dirty white infant bodysuit, its face and limbs charred black in a number of places.

They started toward her, their movement jerky, like clay animation.

Their brows furrowed in anger. Their smiles turned to snarls.

"Shoot them!" she said, but no sound escaped her mouth.

The topless one with the transplanted head seized Jack by the hair and dragged him back toward the trap door. It disappeared down the hole, dragging Jack after it like prey into its lair.

The remaining doll cocked its head, studying her.

Its bodysuit, she noticed, was undulating. Something was beneath it. No, many things were beneath it, moving, squiggling.

A black scorpion scuttled out of the neck hole, up the doll's face, into its hair. Another one followed. More emerged, dozens, hundreds, spilling out from the short sleeves and where the Velcro extension closed over the crotch.

The plagued doll opened its arms for a hug.

Elizaveta jerked awake, momentarily disorientated, unbalanced, the tatters of the nightmare raw and disconcerting.

"You okay?" It was Jack. He spoke quietly.

She looked around the room. The candles still burned. Jesus and Pita appeared to be sleeping against the opposite wall. The trapdoor was shut.

She nodded. "Bad dream." She rubbed her forehead with her fingers. This made her aware of the stiffness in her shoulder. She rotated it

485

experimentally.

"Still hurts?" Jack asked.

"A little," she said.

"It will be okay. If nothing bad happens in the first couple of hours after a sting, nothing will."

"So you are potato *and* scorpion expert?"

He imitated her voice. "Las Vegans know scorpions."

"Are you making fun of me?"

"Sort of."

"You can't do Russian accent."

"Da. It ees easy."

"No—you have to tighten throat. Seriously. And speak from bottom of mouth."

"I eem Boris. I vill conquer Yevrazia."

"Yevrazia?"

"Eurasia."

"Maybe you better keep practicing." She noticed him still holding his folded tank top against the wound in his side. She frowned. "Has it stopped bleeding?"

"Think so."

"Think?"

Grimacing, he peeled the shirt back. She leaned closer for a better look. The gash was lipless and filled with blackish-red blood, though it no longer seemed to be bleeding.

"It's fine," he said. He applied the shirt to it again.

"If we didn't drink all the vodka, we could disinfect it."

"It's fine."

"I can get some water, try to clean—"

"You said you had a bad dream," he said, changing topics. "What was it about?"

Elizaveta hesitated. She didn't like being dismissed. She was worried about him. But he clearly didn't want her fussing over the wound, and maybe that was for the best.

"Dolls," she said. "Two came out of trapdoor. One took you."

"Took me?"

"Down the hole, to crawlspace."

"Why?"

"I don't know, Jack. It was dream. Strange things happen in dreams."

"Didn't you go down to get me?"

"It was your fault. You didn't fight. You just let it drag you down."

He shook his head. "I would have fought it."

"You didn't," she said. "Anyway, I had my own problems. The other doll was covered in scorpions. It tried to hug me."

"Did *you* fight it?"

"Why are you so upset?"

"I'm not. I just wouldn't have gone down that hole without a fight."

"It was my dream, okay? In your dream, you can fight doll. You can fight one hundred dolls if it makes you feel like man."

"I actually did have a dream about a doll earlier," he said. "I heard a noise in Lucinda's room. I went in. There was a doll lighting a candle." He glanced across the room at Jesus and Pita. He lowered his voice further. "It was Pita."

"The doll?"

"She said Solano caught her and turned her into a doll."

"Da, that is something she would say."

"She said Solano caught you and Rosa too."

"And turned us into dolls?"

"Yeah."

Elizaveta thought about that. "Was I a cute doll?" she asked.

"I didn't see you. I woke up first."

"Oh." She smiled.

"What?" he said.

"You dreamed about me."

"I guess. Indirectly. You weren't actually in the dream."

"Do you dream about me often?"

He chuckled. "You dreamed about me too."

487

She almost told Jack what happened in her dream before the dolls arrived, but she didn't. Having a dream about someone was one thing; having an x-rated make-out session with them in the dream was something else entirely. She said, "Rosa asked me earlier if we would see her again."

"When we get off the island?"

She nodded.

"What did you tell her?"

"Maybe."

Jack shrugged. "Maybe we will."

"She wants to have a sleepover."

"A sleepover?"

"You, me, and her."

He didn't reply, and she couldn't read his face.

Then he said, "Where?"

"At my house."

"I heard you had a nice setup."

"It's a guesthouse."

"Are you allowed guests?"

"Of course."

"Maybe I can check it out sometime?"

Elizaveta's chest tightened. Her mouth went dry.

Was Jack asking her out?

"If you want," she said nonchalantly.

"Hey," he said, "there's something I've been thinking about."

She held his eyes. "Yes?"

"I'm wondering what you might think..."

"Yes?" she repeated.

"That newspaper clipping—the one about the firecracker explosion."

"Oh." She didn't let her disappointment show.

"We figured Solano caused it, killed all those people, came here to hide out and ended up staying. Well, what if his family didn't die in the explosion. What if he didn't leave them behind either? What if he brought them here, to the island with him?"

"Swiss Family Solano?"

"I'm serious, Eliza. It's possible."

"And nobody ever saw them?"

"If the cops were looking for Solano and his family, then it makes sense he would keep them out of sight. A single guy living as a recluse on an island is a lot less strange than an entire family living there."

"But keeping them hidden for fifty years?"

"This island's not exactly Times Square. Pepper said nobody even knew about it until the city council discovered it ten years ago. How hard would it be to keep his wife and daughters hidden from the occasional local who came by to trade dolls for produce?"

"So you're saying it's not just Solano after us? It's his entire family?"

"No, I'm saying maybe I was wrong. Maybe Solano really is dead. But his wife and kids are still here, or maybe his wife is dead too and just his kids are here."

"Why would they kill Miguel? Nitro?"

"Imagine you've lived most of your life in hiding. Then your father dies, the person who has protected you all that time. Then strangers begin showing up on your island. How would you react?"

She considered this in silence. Then she nodded. "You know, Jack, maybe you have solved the mystery a second time—"

Rosa screamed.

Bedlam ensued. Rosa continued screaming. Jesus and Pita were awake and on their feet and demanding to know what was happening. Jack was pointing the pistol at them, ordering them to stay put while telling Elizaveta to go check on Rosa.

She dashed into Pepper's room. Pepper remained fast asleep on the bed. Rosa sat bolt upright next to him, staring at the window.

She crouched next to the bed. "What is it, honey? What's wrong?"

Rosa turned her head. Her eyes were huge. "I saw it," she said.

"Saw what?" she asked.

"It was looking in the window."

WORLD'S SCARIEST PLACES: VOLUME 2

"What was, honey?"

"A doll," she said.

Elizaveta refused to accept this. For starters, the window was far too high off the ground for a doll to look through. Perhaps if five or six of them stood on each other's shoulders, the top one could peek in. Nevertheless, a troupe of acrobatic dolls was simply too farfetched to believe. Which meant Rosa had either seen someone or something else, or, more likely, she had imagined it. "What did it look like, honey?" she asked.

"A doll," she said.

"But...what else?"

"It had long hair."

"So it was female doll?"

"I don't know. Maybe."

"Did it say anything?"

"It waved at me."

"Waved?"

Rosa demonstrated using a princess wave, her little hand tilting left and right at the wrist.

"Then what happened?"

"You came in."

"And it went away?"

"Yes."

Elizaveta considered this, then said, "Maybe you were having night-mare?"

"No, I wasn't! I saw it."

"Maybe you thought you did. But sometimes when you dream, and you wake up, part of the dream comes with you. It can confuse you."

Rosa obviously wasn't happy with this explanation. She squared her jaw and stared at her lap. Elizaveta almost told her to go back to sleep, but what was the point? She likely wouldn't be able to. Plus, it was almost dawn. "Do you want to come with me to other room?" she asked.

Rosa's disposition immediately brightened, and she nodded.

Elizaveta offered the girl her hand, and they returned to the main room. Jack was still pointing the gun at Jesus and Pita. They were arguing but stopped when Elizaveta and Rosa appeared.

"She was having a bad dream," Elizaveta told them.

Pita's mouth turned down in a bow of disagreement. "She wasn't screaming like that because of a dream."

"She thought she saw something at her window."

"What!"

"A doll."

"A *doll*?"

"She was dreaming—"

"We have to go!" Pita snapped, everything about her changing in an instant, animated by fear: her posture, her expression, the sound of her voice. "This is too much. We have to go. We need to go. Right now. The storm's passed. We'll take the canoe. We can go right now—"

Jack shook his head. "We can't all fit in the canoe."

"Yes, we can, the four of us, we can fit—"

"What about Pepper and Lucinda? And Rosa?"

"Rosa can fit too. We'll send the police back for Pepper and Lucinda."

"We're not leaving them behind—"

"Nitro's *dead*, Jack!" Pita exclaimed. "Something got him! It got Miguel too! And now it's come for us. Whatever it is. Okay? Maybe it's a ghost, maybe it's not. I don't know anymore. But whatever's out there, whatever Rosa saw, it's *hunting* us. Don't you get that?"

"And you think you'll be safer out there in the dark than in here?"

"It's getting lighter."

"Stop trying to be a hero, Jack," Jesus said. "Think of the greater good—"

"No," Elizaveta said, shaking her head. As much as she wanted to leave the island too, she knew Jack was right. They couldn't leave anyone behind. "We can't go."

"Then stay," Pita said contemptuously. "Stay here and die. Jesus and I are taking the canoe." She turned to Rosa. "Do you want to come with us?"

"Well...I guess if Jack wants to wait...I guess I should wait."

"Do you want whatever was at your window to get you? Do you want to end up like Nitro? Do you want to end up dead?"

"Enough, Pita," Jack said.

"Because that's what's going to happen," she went on, her voice turning harsh. "You're going to end up dead, and whatever's out there is going to pull out your eyes. Is that what you want? *Is that what you—?*"

Elizaveta slapped Pita across the cheek. The sound was loud and flat, like a clap.

Jesus said, "Bitch!" and moved toward Elizaveta, as if to ram her with his shoulder. Jack stepped forward and cracked him across the temple with the butt of the pistol. His eyes rolled up in his head, so for a moment there was nothing showing but the whites, then he dropped to the floor like a felled tree.

Pita's right hand went to her cheek, which had already flushed red. Her bottom lip trembled. But instead of crying, she spat. A gob of saliva splattered against Elizaveta's chin.

While Elizaveta was wiping this away, Pita swung an overhead punch at Jack. It was easily telegraphed, and he batted it away.

"Stop it, Pita," he told her softly. "Stop this."

"Why are you doing this?" she said, and now she was crying.

"I'm trying to help us."

"You're not! You're getting us killed."

"It's still dark out there. It's dangerous. Wait twenty minutes, and we'll all go to the pier together."

"And do what? Sit there in the open?"

"In the light, on the pier, nobody can sneak up on us. The boatman will come. We'll all go back together."

Whether she believed what Jack was saying, or whether she realized he wasn't changing his mind, she gave up her arguing. She crouched next to Jesus, who was bleeding from the temple, and helped him into a sitting position.

Rosa went to Jack. Given he didn't have any free hands—one was holding his shirt to his wound, the other the pistol—she wrapped her arms around his legs and pressed her head into his stomach.

Elizaveta touched him on the shoulder reassuringly, and she was about to say something when there was as knock at the door.

1957

The fire cracked and popped and danced, an orange entity in an otherwise black and quiet night. Don Javier Solano sat on the hard-packed ground before it, the flames warm on his face, the photographs of his family held in his hands. The top one showed his wife, Paola, next to his two daughters, Carolina and Fátima. He and Paola married without either of their parents' permission when they were both nineteen years old. They eloped from Veracruz to Mexico City the following year and opened a tamale stand. It didn't make them rich, but it paid the bills and put food on the table, and they were happy. Solano knew he would have been happy even had they been dirt broke. Paola had that effect on him. She was pure and good, the kindest person he'd ever known—the last person in the world that deserved to be buried to death in the bed where she slept.

Carolina, his eldest, had inherited her mother's beauty, though she never had the chance to grow fully into it. She was fourteen when she too died in the bed where she slept. This was not only unfair, it was tragic. She had so much to live for, so much to give back to the world, so much joy to spread. She wanted to be a schoolteacher and eventually a principal. "But not like the mean principal at my school," she always added. "I would be a nice one. I would actually *listen* when students had a problem." She had a fantasy of living "down the block" so Javier and Paola could visit often, owning a dog and a cat and a rabbit, with a large kitchen so she could cook massive dinners for everyone.

She had been a great role model for her younger sister. In fact, Fátima had worshiped her, often imitating Carolina's hair styles and mannerisms and fashion. Fátima...always giggling, forever into mischief, innocent, angelic. The tears Solano had been fighting sprung to his eyes. She would be ten years old now. Ten years old and a triplegic, bed-ridden, nothing working but a head and an arm. Sometimes he thought it would have been better had she died with her mother and sister in the firecracker explosion. She would have been at peace.

The explosion occurred in the dead of night. There was a sound like thunder, and then the walls and ceiling were falling down all around him...then there was shouting and flashlights, firefighters lifting chunks of concrete off him, escorting him through the rubble of what had once been his bedroom, telling him not to look back. Barely conscious he did just that, looked back, and saw Paola—or what had become of his wife, for all that was visible beneath a slab of concrete was a blood-slicked arm and leg.

Solano must have blacked out, because the next thing he remembered was waking in a hospital bed, a doctor telling him Paola and Carolina were dead, but Fátima was alive, in critical condition. She was in a room on her own, hooked up to a machine, tubes going in and out of her. She didn't respond to his voice, but she was breathing on her own. He remained by her beside, praying for her throughout the night. In the morning she regained consciousness—and doctors were able to determine the extent of her injuries.

Finally Solano grieved, quietly and privately at first, but then his silent tears became racking sobs, and his sobs became howls of anguish, so loud and tortured two nurses escorted him from the building.

Solano spent the night in a bar drinking himself into an unthinking stupor. He woke in the morning on the street. He supposed the bar staff had carried him out there when they closed and realized he didn't have identification or money.

He knew he should return to the hospital. Fátima was alive. She needed him. But he couldn't bear to see her so fragile and helpless. He couldn't bear to tell her she would never walk again, never run, never ride her bicycle, never do anything on her own. Besides, what could he do for her? He couldn't give her back her legs, or her arm. All he could do was pity her. He wouldn't be able to help it. And she didn't need that. She would be better off without him.

He went to his apartment building. The police had cordoned it off, but an officer let him inside what remained of his unit to collect his wallet and pack some clothes into a bag. He tried not to look at the bloodstains shouting at him, but they were everywhere, and if he had a pistol right then, he might well have blown his brains out.

He spent the rest of the day wandering aimlessly around the city...and he kept right on wandering for the next year, sleeping in parks or alleyways, scrounging trashcans for food, panhandling for change to buy cheap tequila.

Eventually he ended up in Xochimilco. By then he'd pulled himself together enough to hold down a job as a dishwasher in a restaurant, and a few months after this, a job taking families through the old canals on a beat-up gondola. The gardens and greenery had a calming effect on him, the smog and noise and bustle of the city seemed a world away, and he began spending his free time exploring the waterways on his own. Sometimes he would disappear for days on end.

And then one day he never came back at all.

Solano had been living on the island on Teshuilo Lake for eight months when the family showed up. Until then he had not seen another soul so deep in the canal system. Frightened of being discovered, he kept hidden in the jungle, watching them in secret as they picnicked and went swimming. Then to Solano's horror the father struck the little girl with a rock and left her to drown in the shallow water.

As soon as the man and woman returned to the gondola and turned a bank out of sight, Solano collected the girl and brought her to shore, where he attempted to resuscitate her. Miraculously his efforts worked. She coughed and sputtered and opened her eyes. Then she looked at him and said, "My name's María."

"My name's Don Javier Solano."

"Where are my parents?"

"You don't remember what happened?"

She stared at him vacantly.

"Your parents left you here."

"They left me here."

"But it's okay. I'm going to take care of you."

"You're going to take care of me."

"Is that okay?"

She seemed to think about it. "Okay."

Solano slipped the photographs of his family back into the sleeve of his wallet, then he considered the wallet. It was time to move on, he knew. He had to put his old family, his old life, behind him. María was his everything now. God had sent her to him. She was his redemption, his second chance to do right for someone in need, to make up for the wrong he had done to his own daughter.

He looked at the fire. No—he couldn't bring himself to burn the wallet. Perhaps he could bury it somewhere? That seemed more appropriate.

He got up and went to the hut he had been spending his days building. María lay on a straw mattress, sleeping soundly, the doll she called Angela, which he'd also rescued from the canal, clutched tightly in her hand. He knelt next to her and pulled the quilt to her chin.

Tomorrow he was going into the city to trade produce for matches and rice and sugar and other supplies. It would be the first time he left María alone, and he was terrified of something happening to her. But she told him she would be okay, and he believed she would be. Despite her mental shortcomings, she was resilient and capable of taking care of herself.

Smiling down at her, he decided he would get her something from the markets. She really liked that doll.

Maybe he could find her another one?

Elizaveta

Elizaveta watched as Jack opened the front door to the cabin cautiously. She didn't know who to expect—a hulking axe-wielding maniac?—but the woman in a poncho and torn jeans standing on the threshold definitely wasn't anything she had imagined. She was petite, perhaps Pita's height, but skinny as opposed to curvy. Her hair, like Pita's, was long and wavy, though it was not only wet and knotted from the storm but festooned with dead leaves and twigs. She wore some sort of mask, what appeared to be the face cut from a doll. It was strapped to her own face with twine. Where the doll's eye would have been were two holes through which a pair of very real eyes, brownish-red and intense, peered out.

In one hand the woman gripped a doll by its hair, and in the other, a long knife.

"Who the fuck are you?" Jesus blurted.

"My name's María," she replied in a shrill, clear voice, eerily mechanical. Elizaveta couldn't see her mouth moving behind the doll face, and she almost believed the voice to be a recording.

"She has a knife!" Pita said. "She killed Nitro! Shoot her!"

Jack, who had already taken a couple of steps backward, aimed the gun at the woman. She stared directly into the bore but showed no fear.

"Tell her to put down the knife," he said in English.

Elizaveta stepped beside him. Holding out her hand, she said, "Can you give me the knife, María?"

"It's my knife," she said.

"Yes, I know. But can you give it to me for now?"

"It's my knife!" she snapped viciously.

Elizaveta raised her hands, palms outward. "Okay, okay."

There was a brief lull. Then the woman—María—said, "I'm hungry." She sounded perfectly pleasant again.

"Jack, she's hungry," Elizaveta said, translating for him. "Give her some of your vegetables."

He dug a carrot from his pocket and held it out for her. "Last one."

She simply stared at it.

"Don't you want it?" Elizaveta asked her.

"Where should I put my doll?"

"Why don't you give her to me?"

"She's my doll!" That viciousness again.

Hands up, palms outward. "Okay, okay!" Elizaveta considered. "Why don't you put her on table then?"

María looked at the table. "I'll put her on the table." She went to it, moving in a flat-footed staggerstep, her back stooped, and set her doll in a chair. Then she returned, took the carrot from Jack, and stared at it for a long moment.

"Are you going to eat it?" Elizaveta asked.

María pushed the doll face up her forehead.

The woman was not horribly burned or mutilated. She did not suffer from a disfiguring illness. She was in fact quite beautiful. The years had not been kind certainly—she must have been at least fifty, her leathery skin wind-burned and sun-creased—but her bone structure would be the envy of many women. The vertical marionette lines alongside her mouth were carved especially deep, giving her the hinged-jaw look of a ventriloquist's dummy.

She took a bite from the carrot, revealing a missing incisor. Then she chewed, staring myopically into space, apparently not bothered in the least that five strangers were staring at her with equal parts incredulity and confusion.

Elizaveta looked at the others. Pita and Jesus remained by the far wall, speaking quietly to one another. Rosa stood behind Jack, peeking around his legs.

"I don't think she's all there," Jack said softly.

"Shhh," Elizaveta whispered. "She can hear you."

"You think they have an English school out here on this island?"

Elizaveta watched María, but the woman showed no signs of understanding what they were saying. "Who do you think she is? Solano's daughter?"

Jack shrugged. "Must be."

"What about the other two in the photo then?"

"Ask her."

"She's dangerous," Pita hissed. "We have to at least tie her up."

Jack said, "You think she'll talk if you do that?"

"She has a knife!"

"I have a gun." Then, to Elizaveta: "Ask her."

Elizaveta cleared her throat. The woman looked at her.

"Hi, María," she said.

"Hi," she replied in her peculiar voice.

"I'm Eliza."

"My name's María."

"I know that, María. Do you live on this island?"

"Yeah," she said.

"Are you alone?"

She hesitated.

"Are you alone?"

"I don't know."

"You don't know?"

"I said I don't know!"

Elizaveta glanced at Jack. He was frowning, apparently having followed the gist of the questioning.

"She talks funny," Rosa said.

"I talk funny," the woman parroted.

Rosa giggled.

The woman smiled.

"I'm Rosa," she said.

"I'm María. My dad let me out of my room today."

"Your dad?" Elizaveta said.

She held out her hand, which gripped the partly eaten carrot. "I painted my nails today." Her fingernails were indeed a bright orange, though the paint was chipped. They clearly weren't done today; perhaps a week or so ago.

Rosa asked, "Did you paint them?"

"Yeah." She was still smiling.

"They're pretty."

"I have a spare finger."

Elizaveta didn't understand. She was wondering if María meant she had a mutated extra digit when she noticed that only three of the woman's four fingernails were painted orange. The index fingernail was untouched.

She said, "Is your father on the island, María?"

"He's gone to the city."

"When?"

"Yesterday."

Elizaveta was dubious. "Are you sure?"

"I said yesterday!"

"Okay—yesterday. What's his name?"

"He's gone to the city."

"But what's his name?"

"He's my father."

"Do you have a last name?"

"My name's María."

Elizaveta swallowed her frustration.

"She's got no bloody concept of time," Jesus said in English.

"Ask her a time question," Pita said.

"You ask her," Elizaveta said.

"She likes you."

"I'm not getting through to her."

Pita licked her lips.

"Go on, try," Jesus said.

She grinned at María a bit foolishly and said, "Hi, María. I'm Pita. Are you happy today?" She was trying to sound disarming but came across as more frightened than anything.

"My name's María."

"How old are you, María?"

"I'm ten years old."

"No you're not!" Rosa said.

"I'm ten years old."

"I think you're a bit older than that, María," Pita said.

María stared at her—*glared* at her, that switch inside her flipped to angry once again. Then she returned her attention to the carrot. After looking at it for a long moment, she took a bite.

"She's a fucking lunatic," Jesus whispered in English.

"Don't provoke her!" Pita said.

"She's clearly not making any sense. She thinks she's fucking ten years old! Jack, will you tie her up now so we can get the hell out of here."

"You want to leave her tied up here by herself?" he said.

"She killed Miguel and Nitro, man! Tie her up! We'll send the police back to get her."

Jack ignored him and said, "What's she been saying?"

Elizaveta shrugged. "Just...stuff. Jesus is right. She's not making any sense. She said her father went to the city yesterday, and she's ten years old. I don't think she's going to be much help—what?"

Jack was frowning at María. "What's she doing?"

Elizaveta looked at the woman. Her eyes were fixed on Jack, intense, unblinking.

"María?" Elizaveta said.

She didn't reply.

"María?"

No answer.

"Why's she just staring at me?" Jack asked.

Jesus smirked. "She's got the hots for you, Jack-o."

Jack tweaked the pistol back and forth.

María didn't react.

"María?" Elizaveta said.

Nothing.

"Maybe she's sleeping?" Rosa said.

"Her eyes are open," Jack said.

"*María?*" Elizaveta said.

She blinked. "My mom and dad had a baby."

"What did she say?" Jack asked.

"That her mom and dad had baby," Elizaveta said. "I think she just had seizure."

"What the hell do you know about seizures?" Jesus said.

"I've seen seizures before," she said, referring to the epileptic children she knew in the orphanage in which she'd grown up.

"Don't you shake and stuff?" Jack said.

"There are many different kinds of seizures."

"My mom and dad had a baby," María said again. "And her name is Salma."

Jack said, "Ask her about Miguel. Ask her if she knows what happened to him. Rosa," he added, "can you go into the bedroom with Pepper for a bit?"

She pouted. "But I want to stay with you."

"We're going to be talking about some adult stuff. It's best if you go in the bedroom. I'll call you when we're done."

She kicked at an imaginary object, scuffing the sole of her shoe on the floorboards. But she obediently went to the room.

"Close the door!" Jack said.

She closed it behind her.

He gave Elizaveta a nod to begin.

"María?" she said.

"Yeah?"

"Who's that?" She pointed to the doll she was holding.

"That's my doll."

"Does she have a name?"

"Her name's Angela. She's my doll."

"Can I ask you a different question, María?"

"Yeah?"

"Did you see anyone on the island yesterday?"

She stared blankly.

"A man and a woman?" Elizaveta pressed. "Did you see a man and woman?"

"Yeah."

"You saw them?"

"Yeah."

"And the little girl who was just here. Did you see her too?"

"She was singing a song."

"A lullaby."

"Yeah."

"Were you watching her through that hole in the wall earlier?"

"She was singing a song. My mom sings me songs."

"She was singing the song today," Elizaveta agreed. "But did you see her yesterday—the little girl, Rosa?"

"Yeah."

"She's simply agreeing with you," Pita said in English.

"No, I think she understands," Jesus said.

"She said she saw Miguel and Lucinda?" Jack asked.

Elizaveta nodded. "But she just keeps saying *si, si, si.*"

"Avoid yes/no questions then," Jack said.

"María," she said. "The man and woman you saw, what did they look like?"

"They were fighting."

"Why were they fighting?"

"I don't know what happened. They were fighting. The boy was hurting the girl. I stopped him."

"How did you stop him?"

Her eyes hardened. "I just stopped him."

"With that?" She pointed at the knife.

"Yeah."

"You stabbed him?"

"I stopped him."

"What happened to the woman?"

María stared blankly.

"María?"

"I stopped him with the knife."

"Did you stop the woman too?"

"I'm going to the city."

"María, the woman, she's hurt. She's in that room there." She motioned toward Lucinda's bedroom.

"That's my dad's room," she said.

"What about that one?" She indicated Pepper's bedroom.

"That's my room."

"Where's your dad, María?"

"He went to the city. He's going to bring me back a doll. He always brings me a doll."

"What's his name, María?"

"He's my dad."

Elizaveta gave up and explained to Jack: "She said Miguel was hurting Lucinda so she attacked him. I think. She won't say what happened to Lucinda. It's—I don't know."

"Can we agree this is a massive waste of time and go now?" Jesus said. "She's a fucking retard and a spaz. She stabbed Miguel and Lucinda, and she slit Nitro's throat. There's nothing more to it than that."

"You're not getting out of this so easily, Jesus," Jack said.

"What the hell are you talking about?"

"Maybe she killed Miguel, and maybe she stabbed Lucinda, but Nitro's blood was on your jacket. You had a bloody knife hidden on you."

"Give it a fucking rest, Jack—"

"You're telling me this woman sneaked up on Nitro without him any the wiser and slit his throat?"

"Ask her about Miguel's eyes," Jesus said. "Do it!"

Elizaveta said, "María, the man you 'stopped' yesterday, he's missing his eyes." She pointed to her own eyes for emphasis. "Eyes. Do you know what happened to them?"

"Yeah."

"What?"

"I took them."

Elizaveta swallowed. Jesus crowed triumphantly.

"You took them?"

"I took them," she said. "My dad showed me how."

"Your dad showed you how?"

"With fish. He showed me how to eat them."

"Oh my God," Pita moaned.

"See!" Jesus said. "She killed Miguel and Nitro for their eyes! She just admitted it. Now would you fucking untie me, please?"

"What did she admit?" Jack demanded.

Before Elizaveta could explain, María dropped the half-eaten carrot on the floor and reached into the pocket of her jeans. She pulled her hand out. It was balled into a fist. She uncurled her fingers.

Resting in the center of her palm was a white eyeball, the iris and pupil gazing sightlessly at the ceiling.

Elizaveta gagged. Her stomach slid up her throat, and she dry heaved twice before uploading a mess of watery yellow gunk. She rode a hot wave of relief before her stomach revolted a second time and more gunk splashed to the floor.

"Hey," Jack said, kneeling beside her. He pulled back her hair so she didn't get sick on it. "You okay?"

She wasn't sure. She waited, her eyes tearing, her throat stinging.

Several seconds passed. Jack stroked her back. She started feeling better and raised her head, pushing her hair from her face—and saw Jesus sneaking up behind Jack. He held the post-hole digger with his bound hands like a baseball bat.

"Jack—!"

That's all she got out before Jesus swung the makeshift weapon. Jack turned, tried to duck. The long tube of iron caught him on the side of his head. He dropped to the floor. The pistol clattered out of his hand.

Elizaveta stared at it. She knew she should grab it, but she couldn't think clearly, couldn't move.

Then Jesus tossed the post-hole digger away and snatched up the pistol. He stepped backward and started using his teeth to free the belt securing his wrists.

Elizaveta snapped out of whatever had gripped her. She scooted next to Jack. She bent over him, examining his head. A massive, bleeding bump had already formed on the side of his skull. "Jack?" she said. "Jack?"

He didn't respond.

She checked the pulse in his neck. It was beating.

She whirled on Jesus, eyes raging. The belt lay next to his feet, coiled liked a snake. He was now aiming the pistol at Jack's limp body.

Pita was yelling at him: "Put the gun down, Jesus!"

"You don't understand!" he said.

"Put the gun down!"

"Shut up, Pita!"

"You can't shoot him!"

"There's no choice!"

"*What are you talking about?*"

"Eliza," Jesus said. "Get out of the way." His face was feverish. The pistol trembled in his grip.

"Stop this, Jesus!" she said. "What are you doing?"

"Eliza, move!"

"Jesus!" Pita shouted.

"He's going to rat me to the police!" Jesus snapped, glaring at her.

"So what! You didn't do anything. You didn't kill—" She bit off the rest of the sentence.

"You killed him," Elizaveta stated. "You really did kill him."

"Nitro?" Pita said.

"You don't understand." Jesus ran the back of his hand across his lips. He took aim at Jack again. "He was a cop."

"Nitro was a cop?" Elizaveta said, dumbstruck.

"Nitro was not a cop, Jesus," Pita said.

Jesus flourished the pistol in a declamatory way. "This gun! It's a Beretta 92. Marco has the same one. He told me it's his service gun from when he was a cop. They let him keep it."

Marco was one of Jesus's bodyguards: big, overweight, greased hair and a goatee.

Pita said, "That doesn't mean—"

"No, it doesn't, Pita," Jesus said. "But it got me thinking. What does Nitro actually do?"

She frowned. "He has his father's money—"

"His father who builds highways in Spain. Right. Convenient he's across the ocean. No way to run into someone in the Mexican construction industry who might know, or not know, of him. And did you ever see Nitro spend much of this money he supposedly had? He gets around on a fucking Honda motorcycle. Does he even have a car? Have you ever seen his car? And what about his place? Where does he live? Napoles? Conveniently across the city from me. Did you ever go to his place? All that time you were fucking him, did he ever invite you over?"

Pita glanced at Jack. He remained out cold. "No..." she said quietly.

Jesus shook his head. "It was a lie. Everything, a lie, so he would fit in with our crowd. Think about it, Pita—when did Nitro and I meet?"

"At Ana's birthday party," Elizaveta said.

"Ana's birthday, correct. Nitro came up to me. Said he was a friend of a friend. I figured he wanted something and brushed him off. He tried a few more times—and then that whole screen door episode with Jack. Everyone knows Jack and I don't get along. So what does Nitro do to get my attention?"

"Picks a fight with Jack..." Elizaveta said.

"And it worked," Jesus continued. "After you took him home, Pita, Nitro and I spent the rest of the night laughing about Jack. We hit it off because of our mutual dislike for Jack. I gave him my number, told him to ring me some time."

Elizaveta's mind was spinning in overdrive. She remembered perfectly well the next time Nitro called Jesus. It had been the following Saturday morning. He had tickets to a bullfight in the Plaza México and invited Jesus and Elizaveta to join him. Jesus, a huge bullfighting fan (this was no secret to anybody that knew him), promptly accepted the offer. "But *why?*" she said. "What was the big act for? What did he want?"

Jesus hesitated. Then: "He was investigating the company."

"What!" Pita said.

Jesus shrugged. "Some stuff's been going on—"

"What 'stuff,' Jesus? That bribery probe? Is that still going on? You said—"

"It doesn't matter, Pita. Everything's fine. Everything's taken care of. It will all work itself out—"

"So you killed him? You killed Nitro because he was *investigating* you? Oh my God, Jesus! Oh my God—"

Jesus's face transformed. "He used me!"

"You killed him!"

"He was a piece of shit, Pita! He used you too! Yeah, he did. Come on, why do you think he put the moves on you? He was undercover. He was going to start something up with the sister of the guy he's investigating because he's in love with her?"

Pita blinked, as if she had been slapped.

Elizaveta felt dizzy, surreal. The scope of the deception! And she'd never suspected a thing. "Okay, Jesus," she said quickly. "Maybe you are right. But we can work this out. We'll figure this out."

"There's nothing to figure out. Jack's going to tell the cops I killed Nitro. Proof or not, if they suspect me, they'll put it together."

"Shooting him won't make situation better."

"Of course it will," he snapped. "There's a bona fide killer on this island." He glanced over his shoulder at María, who stood statute still, watching them in silence. "She killed Miguel. She killed Nitro. She killed Jack—"

"I'll tell them, Jesus," Elizaveta said defiantly. "I'll tell the police everything."

"No you won't, cariño," he said. "Because she's going to kill you too."

The words flattened Elizaveta like a truck. She had been dating Jesus for twelve months. She had loved him—or thought she had. And he was not only a killer, he was a cold-blooded sociopath.

"Move away from him," Jesus told her. "Unless you want to die first."

"Jesus, please..."

"Move!"

"You can't do this, Jesus!" Pita said. "It's insane. You can't kill everybody—"

"It's either them or me, Pita."

"And Pepper, and Lucinda?"

"They don't know what's happened. They'll believe what I tell them."

Pita began wandering in a circle, mumbling, a hand to her head as if she might faint.

"Pita!" Jesus barked. "You have to be in this with me."

"I..." She shook her head. Her eyes were filled with questioning fear. "Jesus, you can't do this."

"There's no other way. If I go to prison, I can't fix what's happened at the company. It will all come out. We'll lose everything. You'll have nothing. You'll be *poor*."

"I'm not feeling very well."

"Pita, I need to hear you're in this with me."

"I can't—"

"Pita!"

"Fine," she said so softly it was barely audible.

"Fine what?"

"Fine! Just do it! Hurry up!"

Jesus returned his attention to Elizaveta. He did not smile or revel in his victory; he displayed no emotion at all, which terrified Elizaveta all the more. Her heart slammed inside her chest, and she found it difficult to breathe. It seemed impossible she was about to die. She had to teach the twins on Monday. She had a hair appointment Tuesday evening—

"Last warning, cariño," Jesus said. "Move away from Jack."

She almost asked him why he wanted her to move, but she knew the answer. He didn't want her and Jack's deaths to look like summary executions.

"Screw you, Jesus," she said.

Now his face filled with cold malevolence. With a brutish grunt, he stormed over and grabbed Elizaveta by the hair, yanking her away from Jack. She yelped, clawing and kicking him. He drove his knee into her face, stunning her. Light flowered across her vision. She tasted the calcified bits of a cracked tooth on her tongue.

Then he was hitting her over and over and over.

Jack

A commotion was happening around me, a sonic orgy of shouting and struggling, a million miles away. Pain flared in my head, and I remembered Jesus swinging the post-hole digger. Wondering whether a chunk of my skull and brain were missing—that's what it felt like—I raised my hand, touched the fiery spot above my ear. It was numb, pins and needles. But everything seemed intact.

Groaning, I sat up. The room focused though remained soaked in an underwater slow-motion quality. Jesus stood several feet away, bending over Elizaveta. For a moment I thought he was speaking to her, but in fact he was striking her with short, straight jabs.

And then, behind him, María was raising the knife she gripped in her hand. Her eyes flamed, her lips curled back to reveal her gums and teeth. She brought the blade down into his back.

Jesus went rigid, his arms shooting out to his sides, as if he had been electrocuted. He issued an unholy noise, more roar than shriek.

María plucked the knife free and stabbed him again.

Turning, Jesus swung the pistol toward her.

Juiced with adrenaline, I found my feet and sprang at him, slamming into his midsection, sending us both careening through the air.

Elizaveta

When Jack and Jesus crashed to the floor, Jesus released the pistol, which skidded across the floorboards. Although Elizaveta felt nauseous with pain from the whooping Jesus had delivered to her, this time she didn't hesitate. She scrambled toward the gun.

Her head snapped backward.

Pita had her hair!

The bitch shook Elizaveta's head from side to side, and Elizaveta felt **déjà** vu from their earlier fight. "Let go!" she said, kicking out blindly behind her.

The kick made contact. Pita, however, was too close for it to have much effect.

Elizaveta flipped onto her back. She raked her fingernails down Pita's furious face. Three parallel lines of blood appeared.

Pita yowled but didn't release her hair. Elizaveta grabbed Pita's right breast through her open shirt and squeezed as hard as she could. The yowl jumped an octave and she finally let go.

Still turtled on her back, Elizaveta brought her knee to her chest and kicked. Her foot sailed past Pita, who dodged left. Then Pita was on her feet, standing above Elizaveta. She produced the sickle, which had been tucked into the waistband of her jean shorts.

The curved blade grinned wickedly.

Jack

I landed on top of Jesus. He went for my throat, strangling me, inadvertently tilting my chin so I was looking at the ceiling. I shoved my right hand against his face, pressing it into the floor. My palm covered his nose and mouth. His lips were wet with saliva. Then a sharp bite.

The fucker bit me!

One of my legs was between his. I drove my knee into his groin. His teeth released their pinch. He bellowed. I kneed him again.

The pistol was a few feet away. I twisted off Jesus and grabbed it just as Elizaveta cried out. I'd been peripherally aware of Pita and Elizaveta fighting, but I'd been so focused in my struggle with Jesus I hadn't paid any attention.

Now I saw Pita standing above Elizaveta, the sickle raised.

"Pita!" I shouted, leveling the pistol at her. "Don't!"

She swung the curved blade.

I squeezed the trigger.

The shot struck Pita in the center of her chest, stopping her mid-swing. Her eyes widened, confused. They met mine. Then her legs gave out and she collapsed to the floor.

For a long moment I couldn't move. There was dead silence, but at the same time my ears rang with the gunshot. All I was thinking was: *I shot Pita I shot Pita I shot Pita...*

Elizaveta elbowed backward, away from Pita's body.

"Pita!" I said, scrambling forward. I tried not to look at the wound in her chest but couldn't help it. A small hole marked her skin directly between her breasts, an inch above the center gore of her bra. It was gushing blood.

Her eyes stared at me, accusing.

"Pita...?" I said, hearing my voice in stereo, the thickness of it. Time seemed to have slowed down, as if by some quirk of relativity.

"You shot me..." she said, a rill of blood trickling down her chin.

"Pita!" It was Jesus, rolling onto his knees. He crawled frantically toward her, shoving past me to take my place. He lowered his forehead to his sister's. He mumbled something in Spanish, his lips inches from hers.

I backed away. Elizaveta cupped her hand on my shoulder. I was aware of her doing this. I was aware of María standing against the wall, staring at the bloody knife in her hand. I was aware of Rosa peeking out of the bedroom.

I was aware of all this but none of it. I was trying to comprehend what I did, waiting for myself to react to the horror of it.

Then Jesus's shoulders began to shake as he sobbed. A moment later he reeled on me, wiping tears from his eyes, a clenched expression on his face. "She's dead, Jack! You killed her! You fucking killed her!"

This isn't happening, I thought. *It's wrong. It can't be happening. But it's done. It's been done.*

I opened my mouth but had nothing to say. The right words weren't there.

"She was going to kill me," Elizaveta said.

"Bullshit!" Jesus snarled.

"She was!" Rosa cried. "I saw her!"

"You did this," Jesus wailed at me. "*You killed her.*"

"You did!" I said, directing my anger and anguish at him. "You were going to shoot us! *You fucking caused all this.*"

"You bastard!" He grabbed the sickle.

I pointed the pistol at him. "Calm down."

"Calm down? You shot my sister!"

"Calm down!"

Jesus got to his feet. I did too.

"Get back down, Jesus," I said.

"Fuck you."

"Get down!"

He started backing toward the front door.

"Stop!"

"Shoot me, Jack. Shoot me like you shot Pita, you fucking piece of shit."

I took up the slack in the trigger.

"Jack..." Elizaveta said.

And I knew I couldn't do it. I couldn't shoot him.

I lowered the pistol.

Jesus opened the door and disappeared into the breaking dawn.

Elizaveta

It took some time, but they eventually woke Pepper, coaxed him out of bed, and told him to drink water until he had enough strength to stand. Then they moved Nitro's body inside so the animals on the island wouldn't get to it. They set it next to Pita's body, covering both with the sheet from Pepper's bed. Finally they went to Lucinda's room, to attempt to rouse her as well. A sour, yeasty smell permeated the air. The woman's skin was dire, her face possessed with an unnatural stillness, and Elizaveta feared the worst before Jack confirmed it a moment later.

"She's dead," he said.

They collected their packs—Jack carried Pepper's camera bag also—and they made their way to the pier. The sky was overcast, smudged with anvil-headed clouds. The air held that trapped-breath quality that often follows storms. A gloomy stillness hung over everything like a funeral shroud. Numerous plants were uprooted or broken, while severed branches littered the ground. Amazingly, however, most of the dolls remained dangling from the dripping trees just as they'd been the day before, only now rinsed clean of some of their grime and spider webs, their ragtag clothes soggy.

When they passed the hut with the shrine, Jack led María inside to the portrait of the Mexican man with the mustache and poncho hanging on the wall. "Do you know him?" he asked.

Her eyes shone. "That's my dad. He went to the market to get me a doll."

Unsurprisingly the canoe was gone. Jesus had taken it; he would likely

517

be halfway back to Xochimilco by now. So they settled down on the pier and waited for the boatman to come.

At one point María wandered off into the woods without a word. They let her go. She'd survived on her own until now. The police could find her later.

Jack

The sky remained dreary for much of the morning, but gradually the sun burned away the depressing clouds. The cawing and screeching of birds greeted the new day. Then the flies and mosquitos returned, buzzing and biting, followed by the drone of the cicadas. I began to have my doubts that the boatman would come after all, but we had no option but to continue to wait and hope. For much of this time my mind was like a wheel caught in a muddy rut. It spun relentlessly on everything Pita, replaying the happy times we'd shared together. Nevertheless, this didn't lift my mood. Instead, it made me incredibly sad. Part of this was due to nostalgia, the sense that what was would never be again. But the other part, the big part, was because my thoughts kept coming back to her lying on the cabin floor, a bullet hole in her chest, dead.

I wanted to weep for her, to experience some sort of catharsis, but I couldn't. My eyes remained stone dry. I chalked this up to shock. When it abated, the floodgates would open, and the grief and darkness would come in torrents. But not now.

Occasionally I glanced at the dolls hanging from the surrounding trees, the dolls that had miraculously remained fixed in place during what had no doubt been hurricane-force winds and rain. Their eyes stared knowingly at me, their smiles as enigmatic as ever.

Watching and laughing, I thought. And then: *If it were up to me, I would burn the fucking island to the ground.*

I wondered about María. I had so many questions. Was she born with her intellectual disability? Or had her mind deteriorated over the years while she was held prisoner on the island? Had Solano treated her well, or had he abused her? She obviously harbored a strong affection toward him, but that was textbook Stockholm syndrome, wasn't it? And after he passed away, how had she survived on her own? She seemed capable physically. The vegetables in the root cellar came from a garden somewhere on the island. So had she simply lived off the land? And how had she avoided whoever discovered Solano's body, and the police who would have come to investigate? Had she hidden from them when they searched the island? Or had they not even bothered to do that? Had they known Solano lived alone, collected his body, and called it a day? And why had she "stopped" Miguel from hurting Lucinda? Given Miguel was naked, and Lucinda was too, my suspicion was that Miguel was not hurting Lucinda at all; more than likely they were having sex. María saw them, misinterpreted what was happening, and stabbed Miguel in the back. As for Lucinda, she was stabbed herself when she tried to stop María and fled in fear.

It seemed to fit. But then again, who knew?

"What's going to happen to her?" Elizaveta asked abruptly.

"Huh?" I said, blinking.

"María." Elizaveta sat with her knees pulled to her chest, her arms wrapped around them. Her makeup was cracked, her eyeliner curdled. Her hair stuck up all over the place, as if someone had taken a leaf blower to it. She'd stopped rolling her shoulder, so I assumed the sting wasn't bothering her anymore.

I wished I could say that about the stab wound in my side. It still hurt like a son-of-a-bitch, and I had the sense I'd incurred some serious internal damage. Even so, I was alive. I wasn't going to complain about that.

"María?" I said, and shrugged.

"From everything you've told me," Pepper said, "I don't think she'll be going to prison."

"I hope not," Rosa said. "She was sort of nice."

As opposed to Elizaveta—and no doubt myself—Pepper and Rosa appeared none the worse for wear. Pepper wore his purple blazer draped over his shoulders again, and now that his bug was marching a hasty retreat, he almost seemed refreshed. He complained of being weak and tired, but you couldn't tell this by looking at him. And Rosa was, well, Rosa. She had the glow and resilience of youth. Her brother was dead, and she'd just survived a night of hell, but she seemed as though she could spring up and run a marathon, or bake a cake, at a moment's notice.

"I hope not too," Elizaveta said. "But she killed two people."

"She won't go to prison," I said, thinking even if it turned out she had indeed committed a double murder, forensic mental health professionals would almost certainly deem her mentally unfit to stand trial. "They'll make her plead guilty but insane," I added. "She'll end up in an asylum somewhere."

"I don't think those exist anymore," Elizaveta said.

"In Mexico they do," Pepper said. "I researched them for one of my shows—"

"You guys are as dumb as that retard bitch."

We all turned as one to see Jesus standing some ten feet away.

He gripped the pistol in his hand, which I'd left on the bank on top of our bags, and he was aiming it directly at me.

We stood very quickly. Jesus was bare-chested and scowling and watchful. He'd sliced up his white button-down shirt and used the material to bandage up his shoulder. His hair was greasy and messy, his once-fashionable stubble now slovenly beard shadow. He looked like a refugee that had escaped some third-world disaster.

"You didn't leave the island," I said.

"And leave behind witnesses to contradict my version of events?"

"Where's the canoe?" Elizaveta asked.

"In the reeds. Sunk in shallow water."

"You pull that trigger, Jesus," I said, "it's murder."

"You murdered Pita!"

"She was going to kill Eliza."

He shook his head. "I'm not here to talk, Jack. I'm here to kill you."

"You're not God!" Rosa said. "You're the devil!"

"The devil doesn't exist, cariño," he said. "Haven't you learned anything?" He returned his attention to me. "I'd tell you to say hi to Nitro for me, Jack. But fortunately for you, I don't think hell exists either."

He squeezed the trigger.

The pistol clicked. Jesus's eyes widened. He squeezed the trigger again and again.

I stuck my hand in the pocket of my shorts and produced the cartridges I'd removed from the pistol's magazine earlier. I tossed them into the canal.

"Figured there was a chance you might have stuck around, Jesus," I said. "You know, to clean up your mess. And what better lure than a gun left serendipitously in the open."

His surprise metastasized into hatred. "You motherfucker!"

Elizaveta passed me the string she'd scavenged from some of the hanging dolls, and I walked toward Jesus. "We can do this the easy way or the hard way," I told him, "and I'm sort of hoping you choose the hard way."

2010

Seated in a Starbucks on Central Avenue in Los Angeles, I was sipping an espresso macchiato and reading the sports section of the *LA Times*.

It was early December, pleasantly cool. The forecast predicated light showers later in the afternoon. Elizaveta and I were staying at the Sheraton a couple of blocks away. We came to LA to see of all things a twenty-two-foot fiberglass sculpture called Chicken Boy. Elizaveta became obsessed with these so-called Muffler Men after I took her on a road trip along Route 66 a while back. I don't know what her fascination with them is, but we've traveled all over the country so she can snap pictures of herself with them. Some of her favorites so far include Paul Bunyan in Phoenix, The Casino Dude in Montana, The Gemini Giant in Illinois, and The Friendly Green Giant in Minnesota.

Elizaveta entered the United States on a fiancé visa almost ten years ago now. Two days after crossing the border we married in an Elvis-themed wedding chapel in Vegas, and she subsequently applied for a green card. Five years later she was granted citizenship, and all I can say is since then she's taken to the US with gusto. She asked me to install an American flag atop a pole in the front of our Tucson home, for instance. She knows every storyline and every devious subplot of every soap on daytime television. She's become the Phoenix Suns number one fan (we have tickets to a Suns-Clippers game at the Staples Center tomorrow evening). And perhaps most telling of all: the bumper sticker on her Audi reads "God Bless America." Sometimes her enthusiasm for her adopted country was a bit much, but I was happy she was happy.

So, yeah, things were pretty great between us. We rarely spoke about the night we spent on the Island of the Dolls. It was an experience both of us would like to forget, a horror story largely of our own creation in which we allowed our imaginations and fear of the unknown to overwhelm our better reason. Even so, although we might not speak about what happened, I still reflected on it every now and then, and when I did it seemed as though it all occurred only yesterday, and I suspect that's how it will always be.

The police had been waiting for us at the docks of Cuemanco. We'd called them in advance when our phones regained reception. Pepper, Elizaveta, and Rosa were taken to the local police station, while Jesus and I were taken to a hospital. As soon as the doctor fixed up the stab wound in my side, detectives were in and out of my room to question me. None were very friendly. They kept trying to get me to confess to an alternate version of reality—Jesus's version of reality—which led me to believe they were taking orders from someone deep in Jesus's pocket. The scenario went like this: when I discovered Pita was cheating on me with Nitro, I flew into a jealous rage, slit Nitro's throat, and shot Pita. The detectives told me Elizaveta and Rosa and Pepper had all confessed as much. I knew this was bullshit and pretty much told them to go fuck themselves. To be honest, though, for a day or two I had been worried they were somehow going to make the apocryphal accusations stick. But then the media caught wind of the story, and it became a national talking point that couldn't be contained or manipulated regardless of Jesus's money or connections. Consequently, he was arrested while still in his hospital bed and charged with the first-degree murder of Nitro, while I was allowed to walk free because Pita's death was ultimately considered a justifiable homicide as it prevented greater harm to innocents, namely Elizaveta.

I didn't attend Pita's funeral. I wanted to, but I couldn't. Her extended family and network of friends would have torn me apart. According to the rants they embarked on whenever a reporter put a microphone in front of them, I was the anti-Christ, a lying gringo, a spited lover hell bent on ruining Pita's reputation and framing Jesus for a crime he didn't commit.

I did, however, visit Pita's gravesite a few days after she was interred.

That's when the floodgates opened and I finally grieved, crying until it hurt. I had loved Pita. We had a pretty amazing run until the last few months or so. She wasn't evil. I didn't blame her for the eleventh-hour betrayal. Jesus had manipulated her, just as he'd attempted to manipulate all of us.

Although I never saw Pepper or Rosa again, Elizaveta and I started spending a lot of time together. She was promptly fired from her position of governess — "No respectable family can continue to employ someone of your newfound notoriety," the Russian oligarch had explained to her — so I invited her to move into my place...and the intimacy that had developed between us that night on the island grew into something real and sustainable. At first I felt guilty courting her. But I told myself I wasn't doing anything wrong. Pita might have been Elizaveta's friend, but Pita was dead now. I couldn't change that. There was no reason her memory should stand between our happiness.

And the other side of the coin, the fact Elizaveta was Jesus's ex? Well, fuck that. I couldn't have cared less about his feelings. The guy would have happily put a bullet between my eyes if he had his way. He could rot in prison — which, incidentally, was exactly what he was doing. His trial had lasted one week. Given our testimony, along with the forensic evidence the police gathered from the cabin and Jesus's clothing, the eventual verdict of guilty had never really been in question. The judge fined him $300,000 and sentenced him to life in Altiplano, a maximum-security federal prison that housed some of the most infamous drug lords and murderers in Mexico.

For my part, after Elizaveta and I were married, and we bought the place in Tucson, I cut back on drinking. I didn't go cold turkey. I didn't think I could do that, or wanted to do that. But I became what I guess you would call a moderate drinker, preferring wine over spirits, eventually garnering a taste for some of the older nutty vintages. Moreover, during that first year back in the States, my migraines cleared up, I got back out on the track, and it wasn't long before I returned to top form.

Jump to the present, and I'd just capped the 2010 season with my fifth Cup series championship, and my overall numbers now stood at 68 wins, 301 Top 10s, and 25 pole positions.

Not too shabby for a guy whose career was supposed to be over before it really got started.

And this was why I didn't feel too bad about calling it quits at the end of next season. This wasn't a result of age or lassitude. I didn't think I would ever grow tired of racing. But I wanted to spend more time with my seven-year-old daughter, Alexa. She wasn't my biological child. Elizaveta and I tried to conceive for a while but eventually discovered we were infertile. That's when Elizaveta suggested adopting a foreign-born child, specifically one from Russia. This was not for nationalistic reasons. She simply knew what the conditions were like in Russian orphanages, and she wanted to give a Russian child the life and opportunities that had never been afforded to her.

So we went through the long adoption process, visited Moscow twice, and finally brought home Alexa two years ago—and she was proving to be everything we could have asked for and more.

I finished the *LA Times* story I was reading about the Clippers owner heckling his own player from his courtside seats, then looked away from the newspaper to give my eyes a break. The Starbucks had emptied out a little in the hour or so I'd been there. Across the café an attractive woman dressed in a pastel sweater, metallic mini skirt, and sneakers was seated at a round table, staring at me. I lowered my eyes to the paper again. I wasn't Nic Cage or anything. A race car driver was like the drummer in a rock 'n' roll band: people might know your name, but not your face, and you could walk down the street in complete anonymity. Having said that, every so often someone recognized you. It's happened to me on several occasions off the track, or away from the typical driver hangouts, and I always loathed it. Not that I minded signing an autograph. But when other people saw me doing this, they came over too. They'd ask me what movie I was in or something along those lines, I'd tell them I raced cars, and more often than not they'd be suitably unimpressed and wander off, cracking a joke or mumbling a derogatory remark to their friend.

I scanned the NBA and NHL standings, but couldn't concentrate. I had a feeling the woman was still staring at me, so I looked up, and sure enough she was, only now her lips had curled into a playful smirk.

I was wondering if I should continue to ignore her, or get up and leave, when the front door opened and Elizaveta strolled inside. She would be turning forty in February, but she looked ten years younger. She saw me and waved. I waved back. She came over and sat down, setting her leather jacket and shopping bags on the chair next to her.

"What did you buy?" I asked her.

"Christmas presents," she said, pushing her sunglasses up her forehead.

"For who?" I tilted open one of the bags.

She slapped my hand. "For you. So do not peek."

"What did you get me?"

"Why do you always want to ruin surprise?"

"Did you get Alexa something too?"

"Of course. One of those new iPads."

"Like she doesn't spend enough time on her iPhone already." I glanced past Elizaveta to the woman in the sweater and skirt. She was still staring at me.

"What?" Elizaveta asked, turning in her seat.

"Don't," I said quietly.

She turned back. "Don't what? Are you checking out that girl?"

"She has the hots for me."

"Has the hots for you?" Elizaveta laughed. "She's about half your age, Jack."

"I guess she's a fan or something. She's still staring at me."

"You're encouraging her. You keep looking at her."

"Not on purpose."

"You can't control your eyes?"

"It's weird having someone stare at you."

"She's very pretty, Jack. Perhaps I better go see what she wants."

"What are you talking about?"

"Maybe I better have a word with her." She stood.

"Eliza!"

She ignored me and crossed the room. She spoke with the woman

527

briefly, then gestured to the spare chair at the table and sat down. She said something else, then pointed at me.

The woman smiled and waved.

Mortified, furious, I focused on the newspaper and waited for Elizaveta to return. What was she talking to the woman about? Was she telling her how I thought she had the hots for me? Probably. Elizaveta didn't have Pita's proclivity for jealously when it came to pit lizards and female fans, but that wasn't to say she didn't get jealous. She did. And she would sometimes do silly things like this to prove to me she wasn't jealous, which of course only underscored the fact that she was.

Abruptly Elizaveta stood. She pointed at me again. The woman nodded and stood also.

Then they were both coming over.

I set the paper aside and smiled pleasantly.

"Jack, I'd like you to meet my lovely friend," Elizaveta said. "You were right. She really is a big fan of yours."

I felt my cheeks redden. "I didn't say that."

"It's true though," the woman said. "I'm a huge fan of yours. I've been following your career for years."

"Please," Elizaveta said to her. "Have a seat."

"Actually," I said, "we probably should get going."

"Nonsense, Jack," Elizaveta said.

She and the woman sat. They exchanged amused glances, and I realized I was the butt of a joke I didn't understand.

"I didn't get your name," I said to the woman.

"Rosa," she said, holding out a delicate hand.

I shook. "You have an accent—" The words died on my lips. "*Rosa?*" I said. And it was. She looked completely different than she had when she was eight years old, but somehow she looked the same too.

"Hi, Jack," she said, appearing self-conscious for the first time.

"Surprise!" Elizaveta said.

"My God, Rosa, what are you doing here? In LA, I mean? Do you live here now?"

"Rosa has just started her freshman year at UCLA," Elizaveta explained. "I thought it would be the perfect opportunity to catch up."

"Catch up?" I said. "So you organized this? Today...the whole setup?"

"It wasn't a setup, Jack."

"Actually," Rosa said, "I was early. We weren't supposed to meet for another half hour. But I was too excited to see you, Jack. I didn't mean to go all *Fatal Attraction* on you. I just thought you might recognize me."

I looked at her more closely. Big almond eyes, nutmeg skin, svelte cheeks and chin. She wasn't attractive; she was beautiful—beautiful and, to be honest, sexy. I didn't want to think this. She was still eight years old in my mind. But I couldn't deny it.

She was, as Nitro might have said, a ten.

"Wow," I said. "This is blowing my mind. You used to be so small, Rosa."

"That was a long time ago, Jack."

"Yeah, I know..." I looked at Elizaveta. "How did you guys get in touch?"

"Facebook, Jack. Ever hear of it? Maybe you should get an account."

"You never told me you and Rosa were Facebook friends."

"We weren't. Not until recently anyway."

"When I found out I was accepted to UCLA," Rosa explained, "I looked you up on Facebook, Jack. You know there are actually a bunch of other Jack Goffs in the world? I thought it was a one-off name. Anyway, there was a Jack Goff plumber, a Jack Goff accountant, a Jack Goff blogger. But no Jack Goff race car driver."

"Jack is too famous for Facebook," Elizaveta said. "He would have too many girls with the hots for him tracking him down."

"I've never said that," I said truthfully.

"You should see all the pit snakes that try to talk to him at races."

"Pit lizards."

"I went to your webpage, Jack," Rosa said. "But the only contact was for your publicist. She wouldn't give me your email address, so I searched for Eliza on Facebook. I didn't know her surname, but Pepper told me—"

"Pepper!" I said. "You still talk to him?"

"All the time. He's still doing *Mexico's Scariest Places*. It's really popular, and he's actually thinking of doing some episodes set in the US. There's this mansion in California with over a hundred rooms he was talking about. It was built by the widow of the guy who invented the Winchester rifle, and it's supposedly haunted by a bunch of ghosts. He wanted me to ask you if you would be in his show."

"No way in hell."

She laughed. "He said you would say that. But, yeah, he told me Eliza's last name. I did a search, and imagine my surprise when Elizaveta Grechko-Goff turned up!"

"Yeah, well..." I shrugged. "She was going to be sent back to Russia to work in a pre-World War Two ammunitions factory, so I decided to help her out with a green card."

Elizaveta glowered. "Funny, Jack."

"Anyway, she and I got in touch," Rosa said. "And I decided instead of her telling you I was moving to the States, maybe I would keep it a surprise. After all, it's been almost ten years. What's another few months?" She smiled. "So here I am."

"Here indeed," I said. "So how have you been? I mean, after Xochimilco, you just sort of disappeared. I asked about you. I asked the cops and stuff. But they wouldn't tell me anything."

"My mom didn't want me involved in the media circus that followed. She was really upset about my brother. We moved to France to be with my father, and we stayed there until I was fifteen."

I said, "I'm sorry about Miguel, Rosa."

She nodded. "Thank you, Jack. It's strange, you know. I was so young. I barely knew him. Sometimes now I can't even remember what he looks like. But at the same time, he's still such an important part of me. I think about him all the time. I just wish, you know, that I actually *did* know him, or could get the chance to..." She shook her head. "Anyway, I'm not here to talk about Miguel. I'm here to see you guys. And to...I never told you this...but I wanted to say thank you. That night on the island...it was pretty fucked up, pardon the language. I still remember you finding me under the bed, Jack. I was so scared. I thought you were a ghost at first."

"You seemed pretty brave."

"Because I was too young to know better. But if it weren't for you guys, both of you, I probably wouldn't be here right now. I mean, I don't think María would have done anything to me. But I was eight. I just don't think...I'm not sure I would have...coped for long." She wiped a tear that had sprung to her eye. "God, that was harder than I thought it would be!"

Elizaveta gave her an awkward hug.

I didn't want to offer up some platitude, so I said, "Speaking of María, did you ever hear what happened to her?"

Rosa nodded. "I've seen her a few times."

"You've *seen* her?"

"Yeah, she's in an institution. To tell you the truth, it's pretty damn depressing. Just the condition of the place, how the staff treat the patients. Some of them don't have shoes. And there was this one old woman I saw tied up in her wheelchair."

"Did she recognize you?"

"María?" Rosa shook her head. "I told her who I was, but she was completely out of it, all drugged up. She was just sitting in the common room with her doll—that same one she had on the island. I feel really bad for her. She doesn't have any family, no one to visit her."

"Poor woman," Elizaveta said. "I mean, what a terrible life. You know, I used to think my life in Russia was bad, but I guess there's always someone who has it worse off than you do."

"What about the island?" I asked. "You haven't by chance gone back to it?"

"Are you kidding?" Rosa said. "It's a freaking tourist trap now."

"What!"

"Don't you ever go on the internet, Jack?"

"Sure, but I've never...wanted to...I don't really google 'Island of the Dolls.'"

"Well, you should, you'll see what I mean. It's a tourist trap. Especially with foreigners. The legend is still the same: it's haunted by a ghost of a girl who died there fifty years ago. The locals want to keep it that way. A ghost brings more tourist bucks than a disabled woman wearing a doll face. By the way, you know it was Solano who made up the entire legend? Yeah, to keep people away from the island, and to explain María's presence if she was ever spotted." She glanced at her silver wristwatch. "Anyway, I don't want to keep you guys. I just wanted to say hi—and thank you for saving my life and everything. But we should definitely stay in touch. Next time you race in California, Jack, I'm going to be there, cheering you on."

"Let me know which race. I'll leave you tickets."

"For my girlfriends too? They think you're super sexy."

I raised my eyebrows at Elizaveta as she rolled her eyes.

We all stood, and I said, "Where are you heading, Rosa?"

"Back to my dorm on The Hill—the northwest edge of campus."

"We'll give you a lift."

"You sure—?"

"Positive. All we have planned for today is a big fiberglass chicken."

"Huh?"

"Never mind."

We left the Starbucks together and walked the half block to where my midnight-black '79 Monte Carlo was parked alongside the curb.

"Wow!" Rosa said, running her hand along the hood. "That's a pretty mean looking car, Jack."

"Don't tell him that," Elizaveta said. "It's older than me. I hate it."

"Can I give it a spin?" Rosa asked.

"Do you even have a license?"

"Come on, Jack."

"It's a manual transmission."

"So what?"

"That means it has three pedals."

She held out her hand for the keys.

Shrugging, I tossed them to her.

We got in, Rosa behind the wheel, me in shotgun (somewhat nervous), and Elizaveta in the backseat. Rosa turned the key in the ignition, and the engine gurgled to life.

I said, "Careful not to stall—"

Rosa clutch-shifted to first, rev-matched, and engaged the accelerator, swerving aggressively out of the parking spot onto the street. She upped to second gear, blipping the throttle to match the engine speed to the wheel speed, keeping the engine in the sweet spot of its powerband.

"Not bad," I said, impressed.

"Like I keep telling you, Jack." She glanced sidelong at me. "I'm not a little girl anymore."

"No," I said, slipping on my Wayfarers to cut the glare of the morning winter light. The sky was streaked with brushstrokes of pink and gray. "I guess you're not."

About the Author

USA TODAY and #1 AMAZON bestselling author Jeremy Bates has published more than twenty novels and novellas, which have been translated into several languages, optioned for film and TV, and downloaded more than one million times. Midwest Book Review compares his work to "Stephen King, Joe Lansdale, and other masters of the art." He has won both an Australian Shadows Award and a Canadian Arthur Ellis Award. He was also a finalist in the Goodreads Choice Awards, the only major book awards decided by readers. The novels in the *World's Scariest Places* series are set in real locations and include Suicide Forest in Japan, The Catacombs in Paris, Helltown in Ohio, Island of the Dolls in Mexico, and Mountain of the Dead in Russia. The novels in the *World's Scariest Legends* series are based on real legends and include *Mosquito Man* and *The Sleep Experiment*.

You can connect with me on:

🌐 https://www.jeremybatesbooks.com

Subscribe to my newsletter:

✉ https://www.jeremybatesbooks.com/free-books

CPSIA information can be obtained
at www.ICGtesting.com
Printed in the USA
BVHW080841130220
572181BV00004BA/122